Lesbians on the Loose
Crime Writers on the Lam

Edited By

Lori L. Lake
&
Jessie Chandler

Launch Point Press
Portland, Oregon

LAUNCH**POINT**
PRESS

A Launch Point Press Trade Paperback Original

ISBN 978-1-63304-030-4

FIRST EDITION
First Printing, 2015

Editing: Lori L. Lake and Jessie Chandler
Proofreading: Carol Poynor, Pat Cronin,
Luca Hart, Patty Hansen, Judy Kerr
Book formatting/typeset: Patty Schramm
Cover design: Ann McMan, TreeHouse Studio

TreeHouseStudio

Published by:
Launch Point Press
Portland, Oregon
www.LaunchPointPress.com

LAUNCHPOINT
PRESS

Printed in the United States of America

This anthology is dedicated with great affection to trailblazing mystery author **Katherine V. Forrest** upon whose shoulders we stand

ACKNOWLEDGMENTS

We'd first like to thank the thirteen criminally talented authors – Elizabeth, Carsen, Susan, Andi, Linda, VK, Kate, Lynn, Sandra, Jen, Sue, JM, and Katherine – who agreed to go on the loose with us for this anthology. All of you have made this labor of love a lot more fun than we ever expected, and we greatly enjoyed reading all of your clever, kick-ass tales of mystery, suspense, humor, greed, rage, and revenge.

We couldn't have done it without the hillbilly brains of Patty Schramm, master typesetter and formatter, and the artful creativity of Ann McMan, cover artist extraordinaire. Thanks to Carol Poynor, Patty Hansen, Judy Kerr, and Luca Hart for the eagle eye proofreading.

Jessie says: To Betty Ann, who patiently waits for me to return to reality when I'm knee-deep in the crazy world of fiction. All my love.

Lori says: To Luca, with thanks for all your advice and good humor and love. I'll try to return the favors.

From both of us: Much appreciation to all the crime fiction readers out there who give us so much support and encouragement. We hope you'll go on the lam with us more often.

Lori L. Lake and Jessie Chandler
May 2015

CONTENTS

INTRODUCTION

In this day and age, with the multitude of crime fiction being published by lesbian authors, it's hard to believe that it's only a recent phenomenon. *Angel Dance*, published in 1977 by M. F. Beal, was the first novel of its kind. Featuring a one-of-a-kind Latina PI named Kat Guerrera, the complex, militant character was caught up in a case that questioned societal dictates about gender, sexual orientation, race, and class. Before 1977, there were no open lesbian characters published in crime fiction.

Unlike male authors who, in the early 1960s, began creating gay detectives and exploring homosexual themes in print, lesbian mystery writers didn't get published much until the mid-80s. There have been various explanations for this, including the ridiculous statement that women's "consciousness" was slower to be raised, but the fact of the matter is that we'll never know how many novels with lesbian characters were submitted to mainstream publishing houses and summarily rejected because of their lesbian content.

So the first lesbian detective novels were published by small lesbian presses which originally sprang up in the 1970s. The author who gets credit for kick-starting the genre is Katherine V. Forrest, who cracked things open with her first novel, Amateur City (1984). The novel showcased the first lesbian professional detective ever in print, Kate Delafield, a former Marine and an LAPD homicide detective. Her appearance as a new kind of female hard-boiled detective is pre-dated by only three other writers' straight characters: Marcia Muller's Sharon McCone (1977), Sue Grafton's Kinsey Millhone (1982), and Sara Paretsky's V.I. Warshawski (1982).

After 1984, a number of talented lesbian authors came on the scene including Sandra Scoppettone, Barbara Wilson, Val (VH) McDermid, Ellen Hart, Mary Wings, Sarah Dreher, and Claire McNab. All of them, except Scoppettone, were first published in the 1980s by small lesbian presses such as Naiad and Seal. Scoppettone's lesbian mysteries were the first (and some of the few) ever to be published by a mainstream house, Little, Brown & Co. in hardcover (1991), and Ballantine in paperback.

Romance novels and stories consistently dominated lesbian small press publishing well into the new millennium. While a couple dozen lesbian crime novels came out each year, lesbian short form mysteries rarely found a place for publication. Not until the advent of desktop publishing and ebook production did the path open up significantly for lesbian crime fiction writers, both in novel and shorter forms.

Today, a growing number of talented authors are finding ways to share their tales of mystery, intrigue, suspense, thrills and chills, and action/adventure. Still, while we are seeing many *novels* published, opportunities for the publication of short stories with lesbian themes and characters are few. This anthology is an attempt to rectify that.

From the offering by debut writer Linda M. Vogt to the Kate Delafield story by Katherine V. Forrest, this anthology covers authors who've been putting out crime fiction from one year to over three decades. There is great variety in topic, voice, and tone in these stories, but the one thing every author has in common is the desire to provide stories that entertain and show that lesbians have a place in the world of words, as well as the world in general.

Jessie and I hope you enjoy this collection. Please see the Contributor Biographies at the end where we've also listed each author's crime-related novels, all of which we highly recommend.

Lori L. Lake
Portland, Oregon
May 2015

UNTOLD RICHES

By Elizabeth Sims

I COULDN'T BELIEVE THEY used real money in class. I'd expected play money—not the kind for children but adult play money, near-real money with basic markings that's regulation-size. Phony coins I expected, too.

But there we were, a dozen brand-new teller trainees, up to our elbows in the real thing, ten thousand dollars of it. The trainer, a bored veteran of Human Resources, had counted it out before our eyes. This was the job for me, finally. I believe that was the bank's first mistake.

Moreover, though, I thought I'd forgotten how to flirt. Lord, it'd been years, my prime sliding away from me like a wad of bacon grease across a hot skillet. But I hadn't forgotten. No, I sure hadn't.

I'd been unable to take my eyes off of Giselle Brigsby from the minute she set her sleek little butt in the chair kitty-corner from mine. Unlike the rest of the class, women who were dressed as if for hooker tryouts, Giselle wore black slacks that just missed the category of "jean styling" (forbidden), a black turtleneck against the prairie chill, and a spring-green leather belt that slithered around her hips like a friendly python. The shoes? Well-worn Doc Martens, black of course.

She was a dewy little baby dyke whose attempts at looking and acting tough made the tips of my toes ache. And on top of it all, her parents had had the miraculous sense to name her Giselle. Alva Johnson, the trainer, butchered it: "Jizzayel? Brigsby?"

"President," answered Giselle, little smart-mouth.

At break I staggered to the washroom and sat whispering, "Giselle. Giselle." On leaving, I avoided my eyes in the mirror, my accusing eyes that, had I met them, would have asked, "Who in God's name do you think you are? You've got fifteen years on her at least. Your breasts sag and your bangs are cut crooked."

Yeah, but I had a new job, one I wasn't going to blow, a job that could lead to something. My self-esteem was at a high level.

So next break, lunchtime, Giselle happened to be right ahead of me going into the cafeteria, holding the door open, and I happened to place my warm, loving hand over hers for an instant. My lips are full and sensuous, and I sort of swirled a smile right into her fresh, startled face.

From then on I noticed her noticing me. She brought her tray to my table, where I and three other trainees got to know her a little bit, mostly because I asked her questions about herself. The other trainees would just as soon have discussed their hair and "Beach Wives of Bumfuck, Nebraska" or whatever stupid show. Giselle had gone to community college for one and a half semesters, then dropped out. She lived with her mother, who worked as salad lady at Sven's Family Place but was angling for hostess because her hands were starting to react to the lettuce. They rented an apartment in The Pines, a downtrodden place next to the railroad switching yard where the price was right but the incessant ringing of the crossing gates tended to turn brother against brother. Giselle's mom was thinking of going on disability if she didn't score hostess.

I felt sorry that Giselle hadn't had more advantages in life, but deep down I exulted: the more leverage for me.

"I would so love to get out of that craphole," Giselle told our table.

Then she did an astonishing thing. She went over to the vending machine, bought a package of Famous Amoses, opened it, and placed it in the middle of the table for everyone to share. "These basically suck," she said, "but oh well." A generous girl, she was. A girl who wanted to be liked, all the while pretending otherwise.

I knew what it was to want to be liked while pretending not to. That was pretty much my life. I'd pretended not to want to be liked so expertly for so long that most people took me literally and simply didn't like me.

They had a whole fake training branch set up in Main Office. It had counters and teller windows and panic buttons and everything, plus a small lecture-seating area. In the morning we'd learned to handle cash, to double-count and stack and band, and we'd learned to align the presidents' heads with the right-hand edge of the cash slots, plus so much more. Riffling through wads of the bank's cash felt both luxurious and surreal. All this jack right in your hands: a down payment for a new Mustang, a winter in Orlando, a complete Surround Sound system. The means to all of it right in your hands, only it's not quite yours.

After lunch we practiced basic transactions like cash deposits and check cashing. Not until tomorrow would we be taught the complexities of third-party checks, inter-account transfers, and utility payments.

I saw it; I saw her do it.

Giselle and I were working at adjacent windows, and Alva

Johnson had just told us to turn in our drawers for the day when I saw Giselle's hand slip from her drawer to her front pocket. She stuffed a bill in. She licked her lips. Just as she glanced toward me I looked away. A thrill ran through me. The kid's got guts.

Who knew that the day's routine would end with Alva Johnson consolidating all our cash drawers and counting the money again while we watched? She counted it once, looked up, pressed her lips together, then counted it again.

She sighed heavily and said, "A twenty-dollar bill is missin'."

No one spoke.

"Everyone remain seated, please." She pulled her chair from behind her table to sit facing us square. "Whoever has the twenty, bring it to me."

Silence. From my side-view seat I watched Giselle run her tongue over her teeth, trying to decide whether to be amused or scared.

"Class, this is disappointin'," said Alva. "We all have to wait here until whoever has the twenty comes forward."

My classmates, except Giselle, shifted and groaned. We sat in silence for six years, then I had a sudden thought. My wallet was in my coat pocket, which was hanging on the back of my chair. I made a loud, real-sounding sneeze, then fumbled in my coat pocket as if for a Kleenex. A minute later I bent down to look under my chair. "Oh, what's this!" I cried, holding up a twenty. "What the heck!"

Giselle's head snapped around, and she gazed at me in total awe.

Alva, narrow-eyed, took the twenty. "Everybody waits until I check the serial number."

Shit.

We resumed our vigil. Eventually the people spoke out.

"I have now missed three buses."

"My baby-sitter leaves at 5:30, and I mean 5:30."

"Come on! Which idiot took the money!"

Alva shouted, "Don't shout!"

"You don't have the right to keep us here!"

"I most certainly do!"

After ten more years of silence, Giselle rose from her seat. She stretched her shoulders in their sockets, then casually walked over to Alva. All eyes followed.

She plucked the bill from her pocket and held it up for all to see. The class as one heaved a sigh. Alva said, "Put it on the table."

"I won't do it again," said Giselle.

"You're damn right you won't," said Alva. "We'll do your termination paperwork now. Everybody else, you can go."

I couldn't believe they fired her. What if she'd had a good reason? Alva didn't even ask.

I passed the training and went to work in branch oh-five, at Elm and Third. It was an old branch, designed in pre-computer days, with cramped teller stations and a massive vault from the pages of Marvel Comics. Also an endless tunnel of safe-deposit boxes. Banks are getting out of the safe-deposit business, I was told by the branch manager, Joe Cool Boss. His name was Joseph Kulbosi, but he tried to get his underlings to call him Joe Cool Boss. I couldn't do it, and started using "Mr. K," which he decided was all right.

"Safe-deposit is labor-intensive," he said. I understood: I'd been trained to escort a customer to the boxes, do the horseshit with my key and the customer's key, then escort the customer and their box to the privacy cubicle. If I were a customer, I wouldn't be happy with the cubicle; the walls were barely chest-high. If you wanted real privacy, you'd have to pitch a tent inside it.

I got to know the other tellers, a sensible bunch of women plus one guy, who hosted a monthly potluck at his apartment. His name was Clarence, and by night he was a drag queen, a pretty good one, I guess. He and the head teller, Penny, were best friends, forever trading eyeliner secrets and low-fat recipes.

I quickly got to know and despise the regular customers. The women who would come in to make cash deposits, drawing crumpled bills from their cleavages, the money damp and hot. The crabby old-timers who distrusted ATMs or who just liked to visit their money every week.

The most morbidly fascinating of them was Nasty Patsy, a crone with BO who would slap down an endorsed check with two hands and say, looking down her nose, "You owe me. You owe me 173 dollars." As if we'd been withholding money that was rightfully hers and only now had she deigned to jump through the hoop we had so hatefully imposed on her. She'd stand there with her arms folded, stern and angry, until you finished counting out the money. If you went too fast, she'd yelp, "I can't follow you! Start over slow this time."

Nasty Patsy had a checking account, but she only kept the minimum in it so as to have the privilege of renting a safe-deposit box. It was a large one, and according to Penny and Clarence, who had both peeked into the privacy cubicle while Patsy and her box were occupying it, that was where she kept her bundles of cash as well as an eye-boggling stash of jewelry. She came in every Monday morning to visit her money and jewels. Penny and Clarence said that every month or so she changed small bills for a hundred and added that in.

To help the tellers deal with difficult customers, Penny and Clarence had worked up an official-looking sheet with important information on it. Each piece of information was numbered. When you were dealing with a real asshole, you'd say, "Excuse me for just a second," and leave your window. You'd go over to the next window—where the teller was well aware of what you were going through—and ask for, say, Form Sixteen. That teller would pull out the information sheet and silently read number sixteen, which said, "This customer got blown out of Hitler's ass after he ate a bean burrito."

That teller would have to keep from laughing and say, "No, I don't have Form Sixteen."

And there would be this moment of relief and solidarity, and you would gather enough strength to return to your window and finish the transaction.

Exciting though my new job was, it wasn't enough to make me forget Giselle. There was only one Brigsby in the phone listings. Giselle sounded flattered to hear from me. "So you made it through the training," she said. "Amazing."

I told her about my job at branch oh-five.

"And just think," she said, "that could be me, working over there at branch oh-five."

"Well, I just wanted to say, you were screwed."

I don't know why she laughed just then.

"Everybody in the whole class thought so," I insisted.

"Well," Giselle said, "the beat goes on." I could hear her trying to hide her hurt.

"Well," I said, "what are you doing now?"

"Watching *Lucy* on TV Land."

"Yeah? Well, I thought maybe we could get a cup of coffee or something."

"Okay."

I picked her up from her and her mom's apartment and took her over to The Clock.

"Are you hungry?" I asked as we settled into our booth.

That got a smile. "I'm always hungry." Dear girl.

Watching her put away a bacon cheeseburger, a whole order of fries, and a Coke, I fell more solidly in love with her than ever. The girl could eat. "Aren't you having anything?" she asked.

I was too thrilled to eat. "Coffee's fine for me."

We fell to talking about the main thing we had in common, our one day of teller training.

"So did you plan it from the beginning or what?" I wanted to know.

Giselle, it turned out, had been thinking all the same things I had about all that money we were handling. "You know," she said, "you're standing there with this tiny pack of twenties and it's a thousand dollars."

"What would you do with a thousand dollars?"

"Oh," with a crooked little smile, "I can think of lots of things."

We expressed anger at the bank.

"The sons of bitches," I said, "with all that money. Paying us shit. Firing somebody for a lousy twenty bucks."

"And I didn't even do it." Giselle wiped up ketchup with a fry.

"What do you mean?"

"Well, I mean, I didn't leave the building with it, did I? I never took that money off the premises."

My God, she was right. "You never even stole that money and yet they fire you. I could just take Alva Johnson by the neck and make her eat dog shit. I'd like to do that, I would."

Giselle sipped her Coke. She gathered up her hair, a crazy cloud of chestnut locks, then let it fall. "Well, you know, she's just a puppet."

"Huh?"

"She's as innocent as you and I. What choice does she have if she wants to put shoes on her kids' feet?"

"You mean—"

"I mean, there are forces out there that are beyond you and me and fucking Alva Johnson. I mean, we're all a bunch of dupes. All that money in the bank? Where do you think that money goes? To the people who need it? Right. Take a look around you. Take a look at America, Red!"

My name, since I haven't mentioned it, is Red. My hair on my head is red. On my arms it's blond.

Giselle went on, "How long do you think it's gonna last before it all comes crashing down of its own weight?"

I'd fallen in love with a prophet.

I said, "I have some marijuana at my place."

And that was the beginning. You're wondering: How does Red do it? How does she get this gorgeous young prophet into her bed not once, but repeatedly over the course of the next two months?

I'll let Giselle speak to that in her own words:

Unh...ayah, ayah, ayah, don't stop, oh please don't stop, please-dontstop pleasedontstop pleasedontstop, ayah, ayah, iiiiiiiiiiii!

When she asked how I did it, I played coy. The answer was: with a lot of careful prep. I circumvented the arthritis in my neck by using a special three-inch foam mat under her bottom and another under my chest. That way there was hardly any strain on my neck and I had all the staying power I needed. More, in fact. Giselle was so full of hormones, I could taste them. The flavor? I'd describe it as halfway between a Chessmen cookie and a good grade of malt liquor. Plus, orally speaking, I'm very nimble. I'd say my chief talent is pressure control. I begin very softly, and build gradually to a sustained crescendo.

And...? You're wondering. Well, I don't ask for much. "Oh, I am so okay," I'd say. "Later, my sweet. Later. You rest now, I'll order us a pizza."

Thus did Giselle become my own. I felt fifteen years younger and acted it.

We talked up a storm. "My mom is such a wage slave," Giselle said. "She thinks her job at Sven's Family is the real deal. She says, Well, I'm paying our rent, and what have you done today? When she's dead I'm going to have them carve on her tombstone SHE PAID THE RENT."

I said, "That ought to make her happy."

"Yeah." Giselle tossed a pizza crust and said, "My ex-girlfriend used to take forever."

"Oh, yeah?"

"She was very dependent on me."

"Yeah?"

"Plus she never had any money. The thing about you, Red, is you're fun and you're not a tightwad and you don't act like you think you're so great all the time."

That was true. I let Giselle talk. Over time I kept gently leading her to bed and I kept buying pizza, beer, and dope.

It was so good to not be lonely.

When I looked into the future, though, things looked slightly grim. I probably could convince my goddess to move in with me, but the thing was, my second Visa was approaching max-out from all the cash advances I was taking to keep us in Pakistani Thunderfuck and Canadian psilocybin.

She kept talking to me about big business running our country and American corporate-military hegemony ruining the world. I started to get into it. The more I thought about it, the more I realized how little I'd thought about that stuff before. To think that I'd actually wanted my job at the bank. I'd competed for that job, taking my binder home and testing my memory at night. Giselle helped me understand that the reality of my life was that my job had been shoved down my throat. Every job I'd ever had had been shoved down my throat and I hadn't known it.

One night after yet more great sex, if I say so myself, Giselle rose up on an elbow and said, "Red, it occurs to me that we should teach the bank a lesson."

"Well," I said, "I'm a trusted financial professional now. I'm on the inside." I'd learned in teller training that most stickups don't yield much money. You've got your exploding dye packs, you've got your panic buttons. Plus, computers have helped banks trim the amount of ready cash at tellers' windows.

I thought about Nasty Patsy. "Her jewelry is fabulous," Clarence told me one night at potluck. "Have you seen it yet?"

By then I had.

He went on, "Pearls the size of grapes, those pearl earrings? It's all vintage Tiffany and Cartier."

"Really?"

"Tons of diamonds."

"How do you know it's real?"

"The settings. I used to work for a jeweler who did estate appraisals. I don't know where Patsy got that stuff, but there's probably half a mil in diamonds alone in that box. Art deco settings. Platinum. Eighteen-carat yellow gold. Rose gold, green gold. Piles of stones."

Penny said, "And yet she looks like such shit." Patsy wore appliquéd sweatshirts and stretch clam-diggers with a pair of loafers, topped off with an acrylic tam o' shanter. And no jewelry.

"Yes," said Clarence, "she does have issues with presentation."

Nasty Patsy trusted no one, but her problem was that she was trustworthy. You could trust her to come in every Monday between ten and eleven o'clock, request access to her box, then hang with her treasure for about fifteen minutes.

I studied the flawless complexion of Giselle's belly. "Do you have a firearm?" I asked.

"Um-hmm."

"Is it big? I mean, does it look big and threatening?"

"Not really. Maybe I should get another one."

"Can you work on that?"

"Yeah. I might need some money."

"All right."

Giselle and I cooked up a simple plan. The Sunday night before we carried it out, we did no dope at all.

Patsy betrayed herself on schedule, coming in a few minutes after ten. As soon as she was alone in the privacy cubicle, I stepped over to the drive-thru window and pretended to swat a fly.

Half a minute later a masked gunperson dressed all in black stormed in, shouting for everybody to lie down. I obeyed with the rest. I heard nothing from the privacy cubicle.

"You, get up!" Giselle kicked my foot. "Put the money in this bag, and don't give me any marked stuff. I'll kill you if you do."

It was thrilling to be ordered around by Giselle. She used a growly, tough voice that I believe she intended to sound guylike.

"Faster!" she commanded. I scurried through all the teller drawers and picked out the good cash, bypassing the dye packs. She stuffed it into her pillowcase, then turned toward the privacy cubicle.

"No!" I cried. "No!"

Giselle easily boosted herself over the wall and dropped down on Nasty Patsy. I fumbled with my key, knowing that Patsy wouldn't give up her shit without a fight. My role was to prevent Patsy from beating the hell out of Giselle, who didn't want to shoot anybody. Giselle and I were pacifist people on a mission to get corporate America to take a look at itself, not rid the world of miserly old women.

Patsy yelled, "No, you son of a bitch!" and flung herself on top of her box.

"Ma'am!" I screamed. "Get back!" I grabbed her shoulder and pushed her into the corner away from the door.

"Let go of me!" she shrieked. "Goddamn you! Help!" She shoved me with all her might but, outweighing her, I stood firm.

I hollered into her face, "You'll get killed, it's not worth it!"

Giselle was gone. We'd planned it for speed, and it was done. Somebody had hit their button while we were in the enclosure. The cops surged in, but the gunperson in black had been away for about four minutes, I guessed. She would now be walking casually up Elm Street, a young imp with fluffy hair wearing a bright orange poncho, swinging a D&D Grocery bag.

What a high. The cops questioned the hell out of me, but I played dumb.

Joe Cool Boss and everybody else was awestruck by my selfless protecting of Nasty Patsy. Not that she was ever going to thank me. She shrieked at the cops, Joe Cool Boss, and me for like an hour.

My whole world had changed, from dull puppetry to meaningful action.

That night Giselle and I met up in a room at the Super 8 next to the expressway. We kissed. We laughed at our audacity. We did it. Nobody got hurt. We got the money. We did it.

Giselle upended the contents of the pillowcase onto the bed. The bundles of money were there, but instead of the jewelry there was a freezer-weight Ziploc bag filled with sparkly stones.

I asked, "Where's the jewelry?"

"That's it." Giselle lit a Marlboro Light and rubbed the back of her neck. "I spent all afternoon prying the gems out of the metal."

I was shocked. "Why'd you do that?"

"Because we're not going to take it to Antiques Roadshow. Because the bare gems, outside of their settings, they could come from anywhere. Belong to anybody. Be sold to any jeweler."

My crotch had been damp all day, but now it positively dripped.

Giselle said, "I threw the settings away, and if you don't know where, that's better for you."

"I love you."

"Now look. I'm getting nervous. Let's divide this stuff."

"Divide it? Okay."

The cash came to 12,450 dollars. We sorted the stones into piles and divided them one by one. Even the murky light of the motel room couldn't make those stones look dull. There were sixty-six pearls, including the two grape-size ones. There were a hundred and nine diamonds, twenty-one emeralds, and six rubies. I insisted that Giselle take the odd diamond and emerald.

"All right," she said. "We better get out."

I rose. "Where to?"

She looked at me. "Well. I don't think we ought to tell each other."

"What?"

"Safer for both of us."

"I don't understand."

"I'm going."

"You mean, we're going."

"No. Red, come on. This is it. We have to separate."

"The fuck!" My knees more or less gave out and I plopped down on the bed. I stared at her, and after a minute I began to understand. I said, "I thought...this was just the beginning, you know? I thought we were going to pull more of these, and more and more, and finance operations against more corporations, that would get the people to wake up. Or at least begin to question their shallow lives."

"If we were together and got picked up, they'd use one against the other."

"But we wouldn't—"

"Bullshit. I can't believe you didn't get this from the beginning. This was a one-shot deal, Red. The stars lined up for us here. Now it's over." Lifting her arms, she gathered up her rich hair, then let it fall. The gesture made my eyes sting. "Look," she went on, "You can do whatever you want. Buy those speakers you want. Sponsor a kid in Honduras. Join PETA."

"You mean you never thought we'd...you know...be...together?"

She was getting unnerved by my intensity. She edged away from me. "Red, it's been fun. I needed a fling. But—"

"A fling! I love you!"

"You do not. All right—I can see why you say that. A drowning person loves the life ring that falls in front of them. You only love me because I went to bed with you and made you think about something more than the view off the end of your own nose."

Crying now. "It's a start, isn't it?"

"You thought I was a kid you could manipulate with dope and your tongue. Well, lady, there's plenty more tongues out there waiting for the likes of me. And I can buy my own dope now."

"You're just trying to act tough. Come here."

"Get away from me!"

I sobbed, "Why are you so mad at me?"

"Because you're stupid. You think two dykes can convince anybody of anything? Bullshit! When the world gets changed, people change it for themselves. I've changed my world as of today."

She tucked her baggie of cash and gems under her arm and walked out.

She was right, of course. I loved her exactly for the reasons she said. She went to bed with me, and she opened my eyes to how the world really works. But she had no idea that she loved me. I repeat: She showed me the way the world really works. That isn't love? You tell me.

COLT .45

By Carsen Taite

THE LETTER SAID I was a hero, but I knew it wasn't true. Heroes rush in and save people. Heroes aren't quitters.

I'd rushed in, but my partner had died because of it. At least that's what some folks were saying. And as for quitting, I was on my way to do that right now. I glanced one more time at the official-looking stationery declaring my presence was requested for a medal ceremony a week from today, and then I pulled the Hefty bag over my shoulder and pushed through the big glass doors of the Jack Evans building. The uniform working security put his hand on his gun and looked me over, his eyes fixed on the big, black bag like he thought I'd brought a dead body to the police station and was ready to confess. I paused at the trashcan just inside the door and released the letter for the litter it was before walking over to the guard.

"It's okay," I said, reaching for the badge in the pocket of my jeans. I handed it to him.

"Name?"

"Luca Bennett."

Suspicion morphed into recognition even though I'd never met this guy. "Oh, you're the one who saved that family. Thought you took a bullet. What are you doing back at work?"

I didn't bother answering the question. "I need to see Captain Pierce. Can you call up and let him know I'm here?"

"Go on through." He motioned to the area to the side of the metal detector.

No way was I going all the way in. I shook my head. "I'm supposed to be off-duty. I'll wait here."

He nodded, like I was the consummate rule follower and he admired me for it. "Sure. Hang on a sec."

I set the bag down and glanced around while he made the call. Dallas Police Headquarters was an impressive place, if you didn't know better. Bronze statutes of helpful cops graced the entrance, and everything was nice and bright shiny new. I probably wouldn't be the last young recruit who'd be fooled into thinking her life would be better after walking through these doors.

"Hey, Bennett. Captain's out. You want me to call someone else?"

I looked down at the bag on the floor. It had taken all my energy to lug it here and I didn't want to make another trip back downtown. "You have a pen and a piece of paper?"

He ponied up both quickly, obviously anxious to please. I walked over to the counter where folks were filling out requests for police reports so they could sue whoever had done them wrong or defend their innocent clients. I let the pen hover over the yellow-lined legal paper for a minute while I decided what to say. The minute I resolved to keep it simple, the words started to flow.

Captain Pierce,
All my gear is in this bag. I quit.
Luca Bennett

I folded the paper into quarters and walked it back over to the duty cop. A few minutes later when the outside breeze hit my face, I was finally free.

LATER THAT EVENING, I turned the key in my Ford Bronco and stared at the gas gauge. The Bronco was a thirsty girl and I didn't have enough gas to make it very far, a valid concern since I didn't have a clue when I'd ever have another paycheck. I looked across the parking lot of my apartment complex at the ragtag building a couple of blocks down. The sign out front said "Bar." It wasn't the first time I'd seen the place. Hell, I have a magnetic pull toward dives, but I also had rules like don't drink in your own neighborhood. Bad things could happen, like chicks could follow you home and start stalking you, but I was a thirsty girl, too, and today was all about thumbing my nose at rules. I quickly calculated how far my coffee can's worth of savings might go if I could trudge fifty yards for a drink. I climbed out of the car and walked the short distance to quench my thirst.

The place was packed and it wasn't nearly as dingy inside as the shabby exterior signaled. I bypassed the booths and tables and walked directly to the bar that lined the far wall. I didn't see a bartender on duty, but I figured with this much business, one would appear at any moment, so I settled onto a bar stool and bided my time. A few seconds later, a tiny woman with flaming red hair and arms waving wildly burst through the doors of the kitchen.

She looked straight at me and narrowed her eyes. "You're new."

It wasn't a question and I wondered if I was supposed to know some secret password to get a drink. I didn't respond, instead taking a moment to assess my confronter. I don't know shit about fashion, but I was pretty sure that her bright yellow dress and purple scarf were at war with the fiery red mane. I didn't care though 'cause all I wanted was a drink. "Can new folks get a beer?"

"Draft or bottle? Draft's cheaper."

I'd waited a lifetime for a woman who could read my mind, and here she was just steps from my apartment. "Draft. Whatever's coldest."

I watched while she tapped a perfect pour and then slid it over to me. "Three dollars."

I pulled out my wallet and started to count out bills, but a hand on my arm stopped me.

"Maggie, I got this."

I looked at my benefactor. Big guy dressed in faded Wranglers, dusty boots, shirt with snaps, and an ancient John Deere cap. Every aspect of his attire signaled genuine Texan, not a wannabe westerner. Genuine or not, he wasn't my type. "Thanks, but I can buy my own."

He ignored me and slid a five across the bar and told Maggie to keep the change. She shrugged at me and sauntered off, leaving me to fight off this guy who apparently didn't know a dyke when he saw one.

I raised the mug, said "thanks," and started to walk toward to the other end of the bar, but he followed. "Your name's Bennett right? Luca Bennett?"

Not cool. I turned and squinted, trying to figure out where I knew him from but came up empty. He stuck out a hand. "Hardin Jones. Read about you in the paper. Heard you quit the force today. Can we talk?"

I'm not a big fan of people knowing more about me than I know about them and I almost said as much, but this guy's access to the most recent intel about me caused curiosity to win out over walking away. I had to make one thing clear first though. "I like chicks, so if you bought me a beer with the hopes of getting some, you're in for a big disappointment."

His laugh was hearty and infectious, and a minute later I was laughing, too. An hour later, I was four beers in and well on my way to finding levity in pretty much everything. Except for the part where I slurred through the story of what happened my last night on active duty. The domestic violence call, my training partner getting shot, my refusal to wait for backup, the gunshot that left me in a hospital bed, and the threats from another cop who said she'd ruin my career for letting her partner die. None of that was laugh-out-loud kind of stuff.

"Thought you were getting a medal. Paper said so."

"I'm not a medal kind of person. Besides, I'm not cut out for the job. Too many rules, too much black and white. Life isn't like that. Not for folks like me anyway."

He nodded and it was sincere. He signaled Maggie back over, pulled a diamond-crusted money clip in the shape of Texas from his pocket and settled his tab, throwing an extra fifty on the counter with a nod my way. "Whatever else she wants." He stood up while Maggie swept up the money and shook her head.

"Leaving already?" I said.

"I've got a job waiting."

"J-O-B. That sucks." My wisdom was boundless.

"It's not so bad when you work for yourself." He reached into his pocket and pulled out a business card and pressed it into my hand. "You can work for yourself too. Call me and I'll set you up."

I DON'T REMEMBER WHAT time I staggered home, but I was only sober enough to give thanks that I'd chosen a bar close to home and one with a generous benefactor inside. I fumbled to fit the key in the door and wrestled with it for a while before I heard a voice say, "Maybe you should just leave the door unlocked next time to you want to get wasted."

I didn't turn around. Didn't need to. I'd know Jessica Chance's voice anywhere. Since the first day at the academy, we'd locked on to something. Friendship. Fuckship. We were as different as two people could be. She paid her bills on time, kept her uniform spiffy, respected authority. Couldn't say any of those things about me. I should've known she'd show up to give me a hard time. Or maybe she'd shown up to *show* me a hard time. I grinned at the thought and levity gave me the strength to turn around and face her.

"Don't you have to work tomorrow?" I asked.

"Most people do."

"I'm not most people."

Her turn to grin. "Pretty sure I've known that from the start. You want to talk about it?"

"Nope. I just want you to figure out how to fit the key in my door and then..."

She shook her head and took the key, sliding it into the lock like a pro. A minute later we were inside. I fell onto the couch while Jess looked around.

"Guess you weren't expecting company."

"In case you don't remember, I've been recovering. If I'd known I was going to get shot, I wouldn't have left a mess. Besides, life's too short for only the expected."

"What the hell does that even mean?"

I let my head roll onto my chest in an attempt to keep the room from spinning while I pretended to think. I'm not sure how long I sat that way before I gave up. "I dunno."

Jess held out a hand and pulled me up off the couch. "Come on, let's get you to bed. Tomorrow, we can go see the captain together and get you your job back."

I heard the sound of her talking, but the words "bed" and "job" were the only ones I could focus on. I was up for one, but not the other and told her so.

"Really, Romeo?" She laughed. "In your condition, you'd pass out before you got past first base." She leaned in close and I felt her breath against my neck. "I like my women to be awake enough to come."

I held on to the back of the couch to keep from staggering and resisted saying that I'd been drunker. I had been, but not with her. I wasn't sure why it mattered and I wasn't in any condition to process the thought. Didn't have time anyway, because she started talking again.

"Get a good night's sleep. I'll pick you up in the morning."

I almost asked why, but then I knew it was something she'd just told me and I was a little embarrassed to admit I'd already forgotten. Didn't matter anyway. She was gone before I could form the words.

MY COUCH USED TO belong to my parents. I had taken it when I moved out. Dad didn't need it since he spent all his time in a La-Z-Boy recliner and Mom probably had a fancy new couch at her new husband's place. This non-fancy hunk of furniture reminded me of the one in that house on Santa Maria where I'd gone on my last call as a cop. I'd aimed for the couch when I crashed through the balcony, but like everything else that night I'd missed my mark. I'd taken down the drunk husband and saved his family from a life of abuse, but while I was blundering through the house, rescuing strangers, I'd let my partner bleed out. All because I'd been too stubborn to wait for back-up. The memory made my stomach roil, and I made a mental note to ditch this ugly sofa as soon as possible. Besides, it made a lousy bed. I rolled out of it to meet the day way earlier than I had planned. So much for a leisurely first day back at home with no place to be.

I scrounged through the fridge, but beyond a few beers, a half dozen ketchup packets, and a mystery substance wrapped in foil, I came up short on breakfast options. The kitchen counter didn't net anything in the way of food but I did find a note.

Luca, I'll be by to pick you up at 8:30.
Jess

A rush of drunk memories came flooding back. Now I had two goals: get food and get out of the house before Jess showed up. No way was I going in with her to see the captain. My Hefty bag farewell had said it all. I was done. A better person would stick around and tell her why I couldn't, wouldn't go back, but it wasn't just last night's alcohol that clouded my brain. I didn't want to process everything that had happened, and why should I when it was easier to just move on? I rubbed my head. Now I had a third goal—aspirin.

I took the Bronco because I wanted real food, not the crap that stayed warmed under lights at the Stop 'n Shop on the corner. Autopilot took me down to Industrial Boulevard. I made my way to Market Diner where a fleet of gum-smacking waitresses with beehive hairdos would pour me as many cups of coffee as I could drink. I was blocks from the courthouse, the jail, and police headquarters, but the law was the last thing on my mind.

A few minutes after I'd shoved the last bit of pancakes in my mouth, I opened my wallet and fished out the card Hardin Jones had shoved my way before I started losing brain cells from all the free beer. I hadn't given it a second glance last night, but in the light of day I was curious. Hardin Jones Bail Bond Agency. The address was less than a mile away. Figures. Bonding agencies thrived on being in clear view of the jail. My only stint on that side of the law had been a couple of minor in possession charges from my skip-high-school-to-find-something-worthwhile-to-do days—nothing serious enough to dis-qualify me from the police academy.

"More coffee?"

I looked up at the waitress holding the full pot of steaming brew. She'd been sweet to me all morning, 'sugar' this and 'darlin' that, but I could tell by the tap of her foot that she was ready to turn this table and it was time for me to go. Ah, the plight of those who needed to earn a living. I tossed my money on the table and headed out.

I drove by Hardin's place twice before I finally pulled in. The building looked exactly like an old gas station, complete with three bays to the left with pull down doors. The big sign out front stated its current business: *Get Out of Jail Fast. Open 24/7.*

I didn't know what to expect. I didn't know much about the business of bonding agencies other than hearing my field training officer tell the few folks we arrested that they could contact a bondsman as soon as they'd seen the judge for arraignment. The perp or the perp's friend or relative gave the bondsman some cash and promised to make sure their loved one showed up for court or they would lose their money. Why Hardin would think I'd want anything to do with that, I have no idea.

The door squeaked as I pulled it open, and I looked up and into inquiring eyes from the woman behind the counter. "Can I help you?" she asked.

"Luca Bennett. I'm here to see Hardin."

She gave me the once over, brow furrowed, and hollered, "Hardin. Got one for you. Asked for you personally." She shoved a clipboard my way and told me to fill out all the highlighted sections. I looked down at the paper. Wow. I must not be wearing my hangover very well because she thought I was here for their services and not the other way around. I started to say something, but a deep voice from behind me spoke up first.

"Well, you must be hard up."

I turned around. Hardin stood behind me, a broad smile on his face. "What makes you say that?"

"If you drank as much after I left as you did before, you should be snoring off a helluva hangover right now."

"I can hold my liquor." I straightened my shoulders. "I'm not a deadbeat."

He cocked his head. "If I'd thought that, I wouldn't have given you my card." He pointed at a door across from the counter. "Wanna talk?"

I shrugged. "Sure." Wouldn't do to play too easy to get. I shot the woman at the counter a childish smirk before I followed Hardin into his office.

His digs were like him, plain and solid. I slid into one of the heavy wood chairs in front of his desk and waited to hear what he had to say.

"I guess you know what I do for a living now. Thought about what you want to do?"

I hadn't, but it had only been a day, officially anyway, that I'd been unemployed. I supposed getting sloshed wasn't a lucrative occupation. I liked to gamble, but that required a stake and I didn't have a dime saved. I'd gotten a stipend while in training with the Dallas PD, but it wasn't enough to cover even my meager bills and I'd spent my first few real paychecks playing catch-up. "I know what I don't want to do."

"Really? What's that?"

"I don't want to wear a uniform. I don't want to have a chain of command. I don't want to write six-page reports about traffic accidents or sort out who hit who, or who stole what and why."

"Makes sense. I need some help. If someone I bond out doesn't show up for court, I risk losing the bond money."

"Don't you just collect that from whoever posted the bond?"

"Like blood from a turnip. It's better if we bring the jumper in ourselves."

"Jumper?"

"You weren't a cop very long, were you?"

"Long enough." I leaned back in the chair, curious about where his prelude was going. "So, you catch these fugitives yourself and save a bundle."

"Well, that's the catch. I," he pointed at his chest, "don't catch 'em. I hire a bounty hunter to do it."

I had no idea what that involved, but I nodded. "That so?"

"He brings the jumper in and gets a cut of what I would've lost if the jumper had gotten away. Problem is, my regular guy is out of commission."

"And you need a new regular guy."

"I'm too old to be out running down bad guys."

"Why me? I mean besides my obvious youth?"

He gave me a long, serious once over. I could only imagine his thoughts at my faded jeans, scuffed boots, and plain black T-shirt. I didn't have to imagine long before he finally answered. "I need someone who's hungry. Figured you might fit the bill."

IN MY SHORT CAREER as a cop, I'd never had the pleasure of doing a stakeout. In the movies, the detective parked across the street from the subject's house and spied in the window with a high-powered lens.

I wasn't a detective and I didn't have a high-powered lens. What I did have was a powerful urge to pee and a powerful aversion to having an accident in my Bronco, no matter how ancient she might be. I'd been parked across the street from Nicky Smith's townhouse for the last hour and I already sucked at this. Next time, I wouldn't drink a large black coffee while on the job.

Next time. Like there was going to be a next time. If I didn't catch this guy, Hardin was never going to give me another case to work. I opened the file and reviewed it again for the tenth time.

Nicky Smith was a thirty-year-old repeat visitor to the Dallas county jail. Two months ago he'd been arrested for the third time, charged with using his girlfriend as a punching bag. The third arrest made it a felony. A felony made his bond higher, which meant more money for me if I brought him in. He obviously didn't care about the money because he'd blown off his last court date and there was an outstanding warrant for his arrest. Cops were busy with new cases and they didn't have time to track down and arrest people a second time for the same crime, so I was the only thing that stood between Nicky and fugitive freedom.

I looked back at his front door and the windows with the blinds pulled tight. This wait-and-see routine was bullshit. Hell, I didn't even know for sure if he was home. For all I knew, he might have left before I'd gotten here this morning. If I was going to catch this guy, I needed to stir up some shit, flush him out of his hidey-hole, wherever that may be. I climbed out of the car and tried to not to flinch from the pain of sitting too long in one place. My injuries were technically healed, but I was so out of shape from lying around that every little exertion felt like I was being forced to run a marathon with cement blocks tied to my feet.

The townhouse barely had a backyard. Big enough to hold a grill and not much else, but it had an eight-foot fence protecting the tiny patch of turf. Luckily, the gate wasn't locked because there was no way I was climbing the fence. The back door was locked, but jimmying open the sliding glass door was cake. I paused as I crossed the threshold, waiting for the sound of an alarm. Two minutes later, I decided it was safe and wandered in. At first glance, it didn't look like anyone was home, which was probably best, since I hadn't thought this through. An observation that would likely be etched on my tombstone. Fact was, I'd grown accustomed to the uniform, badge, and gun doing all the hard work. The last time I'd tried to lay someone out with muscle alone, I'd taken a bullet. Not the best track record, but I was in here and I may as well take advantage. I decided to go through Nicky's stuff and see if I could get a lead on where he might be hiding out.

The bedroom was my first stop. Bed was unmade, which didn't mean much. My bed was always unmade. But the bathroom was another story. His toothbrush was wet and a still soft-looking trail of toothpaste lined the sink. I knew from personal experience that it took a good eight to ten hours for toothpaste to turn into cement once it was released from the tube. He'd been here, not long ago. I looked in the closet. Two suitcases on the shelf. I moved to the other room, hot on the trail. I dug through his desk. Lots of bills, lots of receipts, and there it was—a passport. At least he hadn't skipped the country, but that narrowed the field only slightly. I was still digging when I heard a door open. I froze. Seconds later, the door shut and I heard the click of the deadbolt. My hand was still in the drawer and I moved it very slowly to keep from making any noise. I needed to find a place to hide until I could get a jump on him.

As my hand slid out of the drawer, it bumped into something cold. I let my fingers trace the object, stroking the long, round metal barrel and the sleek, solid wood grip. I grasped it exactly the way I'd been taught and pulled it carefully from the drawer. I turned the gun on its side and checked the chambers, spinning the cylinder before snapping it back into place. A second later, Nicky Smith stood in the doorway.

"Nice piece," I said as I pointed the Colt in his direction. I meant it. I'd fired its cousin, the more compact Smith and Wesson, but I'd never handled this particular model. With its long barrel and substantial heft, the gun was unique.

"What are you doing in my house?" He puffed up his shoulders like he was some kind of bad-ass, but I could already tell his growl was the best thing he had going for him.

"The question is what are you doing in your house? You need to head down to another house." I tapped my head with my free hand, like I was trying to remember. "You know, the *court*house. Hardin Jones sent me."

Fear flashed in his eyes for just a second. Probably because I was nothing like the petite flowers he was used to kicking around. He gave me an intense looking over before he tried to mask his worry with an attempt at casual conversation. He pointed at the gun in my hand. "You like that? It's a Colt .45, a long Colt. Not a lot of folks carry them. It's not easy to conceal and not everyone can handle the kick." His smile was creepy. I wondered if he slept with it under his pillow.

"Well, I guess you won't be handling it anymore either. With your record, just having this in your place will get the charges bumped up." My turn to smile. This guy needed to do some serious time and me getting paid to turn him in was just a fraction of my satisfaction.

His attempt at casual turned whiny real quick. "It's not registered, so don't even think you can tie me to it. I'll just say you planted it. It's not like you're a cop or anything. Who's going to believe you?"

He was right about that. I pointed the gun at the wall just to the right of his head, and tested the feel of the grip, the weight comfortable in my big hands. This beauty was fully loaded. If I turned it in with him, it'd sit in an evidence locker for months, maybe years. I'd have to buy some more ammo for next time, but right now I had six shots worth of insurance to make sure that Nicky didn't get away. Once I got to the jail, I'd stow it in the Bronco while I turned him in. If I was going to work for myself, this was going to be my first piece of office equipment.

I leveled the gun at his head. "Let's go."

For the first time in months, I was excited about my work.

TOUGH TO CRACK

By S.Y. Thompson

I'M SUPPOSED TO BE one of the good guys. The line you don't cross is supposed to be clear, but for me, it isn't. How can it be when women are disappearing and one of them turned up dead days later? Worst of all, the first of those victims had once held my heart, or so I thought. We had dated for six months before things ended, but somehow managed to remain friends afterward.

I couldn't tell my partner or he'd tell our boss. Captain Kirth wouldn't hesitate to throw me off the case and that was one thing I could not allow to happen. I was a gumshoe working homicide, feeling like I was at the end of a three-week bender brought on by exhaustion.

"Harper, you okay?"

I glanced over my shoulder to see Roger Bennett standing behind my chair. He wasn't exactly silent and I was mystified at his sudden appearance. "Fine. How long you been standing there?"

"Long enough to wonder if you were in a trance."

I struggled not to roll my eyes. It wasn't his fault that my temper was short or that I was distracted.

"The funeral is tomorrow," he informed me in his gravelly voice. Roger shook out a cigarette, but refrained from lighting it inside the police station. "Everyone's going."

I took in his rumpled suit and loosened tie. Roger's hair looked like he'd just climbed out of bed and he appeared to have lost a little weight. While Roger wasn't exactly heavy, he did love a good cannoli.

"I'm not. We have a dead cop and two missing women. I'd like to solve this case before we have more bodies on our hands."

"I agree." Roger placed his coffee mug on my desk with a thump, shoved the cigarette behind his ear and settled into the spare chair.

I focused on running through the details. "Here's what we have so far. All of our victims are female, early thirties, Caucasian with red hair and green eyes. They all have shoulder length hair."

"Not to mention that they could be clones. They all have that same square jaw. Problem is, I can't see any connection between them other than appearance."

"True," I allowed. "Amy Sullivan was a homicide detective—"

"A damn good one."

I continued as though he hadn't interrupted, fighting to speak over the sudden constriction in my throat. "Jodi Davenport works at a dry cleaner and Carla McGill is a Pilates instructor. From what I can tell, they live in different parts of San Francisco and never crossed paths. This is just so frustrating." I deliberately spoke in the present tense because I refused to believe they were already dead.

I slammed my hand down on the desk, surprised by my own outburst. Apparently, Roger felt the same way. He jumped slightly and looked at me as if I'd grown a second head.

"Take it easy, Harper. We'll get this guy, but you're not doing anyone any good if you're burned out."

My eyes narrowed and I felt the heat of outrage rising up my throat. For a second, my jaw clenched as I chewed on words I knew I shouldn't speak. "What are you trying to say? That I'm not doing my job?"

"Hey," Roger raised his hands, his brow furrowing in confusion. "All I'm saying is that you should get some rest."

"I'm fine."

"So you said."

Roger leaned forward, resting his elbows on his knees to decrease the distance between us. Usually, he was so outspoken and brash. The change in tactics kept me riveted as I waited to see what would happen next.

"Look, your personal life is your business, but I want you to know that I'm not just your partner. I'm your friend."

"Meaning?" Fear made my heart pound against my ribs.

Voice low in a conspiratorial whisper, Roger said, "I know about you and Amy, that you were together for a while."

"Nonsense," I choked out. "It's against department policy to date a co-worker."

"Save it. We've worked homicide together for a while now, and I like to think I'm pretty good at my job. I won't tell anyone, but I want you to know that I'm here for you if you want to talk. Now about the funeral..."

I took a deep, cleansing breath, trying to push away the crippling sorrow. "I need to catch this guy, Roger. I'll never sleep again until I do."

Roger's large, callused hand gripped mine on the desktop, just a momentary touch of comfort. He pulled away almost immediately. He wasn't a touchy-feely kind of guy.

"I can understand that. Have we gotten anything back from the crime lab yet?"

I nodded briefly and moved the computer mouse to dismiss the screensaver. "I was just pulling up the report before you got here. This says there was no evidence left behind. Not so much as a fingerprint or DNA under the fingernails." It was difficult to recount such information in an impersonal tone, but habits died hard.

"That's an important detail in itself," Roger said, stating the obvious. "Amy was heavy into martial arts. Anyone who could do those things to her and not leave any trace is good."

"Either that or they surprised her. Regardless, they knew enough about forensics to clean up."

A gray haze clouded my vision as I kept my eyes pinned on the computer screen. Roger's casual reference to "things done" to Amy had set off a kaleidoscope of images in my mind. Blood everywhere, hair shorn with a dull knife and five gunshot wounds. So much rage poured out on Amy's innocent body.

I bolted from my desk, hearing Roger's worried query as I raced for the ladies' room. Just barely, I made it to the toilet before the meager remains of my breakfast made a return trip. Somewhere a toilet flushed, but it was all I could do to hold on to the bowl. When I finally finished, I was alone in the bathroom. At least I had some peace and quiet for a moment to splash water on my face and rinse out my mouth.

So much for the hardened homicide detective.

The cool water washed away the taste of bile, but did nothing for my watery, bloodshot eyes. I quietly inspected my appearance in the mirror. What was I doing here? I was waiting for pathology reports and for other people to do my job instead of tracking down leads, pounding the pavement. Unfortunately, I didn't feel I really had much choice. Roger was right when he said our victims had no connections. Until we discovered a link or stumbled onto something pointing to the killer, we had nothing.

I grabbed a paper towel from the dispenser and simultaneously tried to pull my shattered nerves together. My anger was at a simmering boil, burning steadily below the surface. I needed that silent rage. It kept me sharp, focused on seeking retribution for Amy's murder.

Centered, and back in control, I returned to my desk. Roger was gone and I didn't see him milling around the station anywhere. The occasional blue uniform passed by as patrol officers booked prostitutes and junkies, but most of the detective squad had left for the night. I assumed Roger had finally gone home to his wife to get some much needed sleep. Who could blame him? We'd both worked hours on end for the last week and were pretty much running on fumes.

Maybe he had a point. I logged out of the in-house system and shut down the computer. Perhaps a little fresh air and a change of scenery would help me see something in the crime scene photos that I had previously missed.

A quick glance at the wall clock told me it was late, even by San Francisco time. The fog would have set in, along with the chill. I grabbed my suit jacket from the back of my chair but before I could leave the bullpen, my telephone rang. San Francisco Police Department was still very much old school and so were the phones. I reached for the receiver and settled back into my chair, tethered by the cord attached to the handset.

"Homicide. Detective Harper speaking."

"Hello, Natalie."

The voice was unrecognizable, routed through a digital synthesizer. For all that, the tone remained strangely intimate. It wasn't the first time some whack job with a penchant for the latest in technology had called the precinct trying to make an impression. What caught my attention was the use of my first name.

"Do I know you?"

"Would you like to?"

This was getting us nowhere. "Who is this?"

"An admirer. Did you like the gift I left for you?"

A chill crawled down the nape of my neck and trickled down my spine. Now this guy was creeping me out. "What gift?"

"Amy, of course."

I looked around desperately for a techie to start a trace on the call. There wasn't anyone. The amusement in the caller's voice made my blood boil even hotter. I had the murdering bastard on the phone and there wasn't anything I could do but sit there and listen to him taunt me.

"You slaughtered her like an animal," I shouted. I gripped the receiver so hard I thought it should shatter in my fist. "Tell me where you are and I'll bring *you* a gift."

"No, I don't think so. We'll be seeing each other soon though, I can assure you of that."

"Why are you doing this? What have these women ever done to you?"

"Nothing," as though the answer was evident. "Maybe you should consider something else in your deliberations. Isn't that what you detective types do, think outside the box and all that?"

"I'm certainly open to suggestion. What is it I'm not seeing?" I finally pulled my head out of my ass and reached for a pen and pad. Scribbling furiously, I cradled the phone against my shoulder. "Where are the girls? Tell me what you want."

"To play a game, of course. You've ignored me long enough. Now you get to prove how superior you are. The girls live if you can find me."

"Great," I said. "Give me your address."

"It's not that easy. This time I call the shots."

That was the second reference to a personal relationship, even if only an incidental one.

Before I could ask anything further, I heard the click of a disconnected line. Excitement hammered through me where before I'd felt only frustration. I had gleaned several important facts from the brief conversation. The killer had chosen to contact me directly and intimated more conversations would ensue. Clearly, he was injecting himself into the investigation. That wasn't unusual. Thrill seekers and psychopaths often wanted police attention, to try and prove they were smarter. A cat and mouse game, with the victims being used as nothing more than pawns.

What I found disturbing was being singled out as the point of communication. The killer called me directly at my desk to say the "gift" was for me. That was a mistake. Whoever this was had inside information on when I would be at work and the direct number to my station. That wasn't something they could get from the phone company.

Suddenly suspicious, I turned my head to look around at my fellow protectors. Law enforcement officers mingled with civilian support staff. No one even glanced in my direction. It had to be someone who knew about Amy and me, otherwise there was no reason to mention her by name and not the others. A dreadful thought occurred to me and I felt my stomach lurch once again.

I hung up the phone as I considered the ramifications. Roger had left only moments before I received the strange call. *He* knew about Amy. I didn't want to think it was possible that a man I'd worked with for two years might be responsible for such a heinous act.

My heart denied the odds of that reality, but I'd learned the hard way in this job that logic didn't always fit into the picture. Even though he was supposedly happily married, Roger had hit on me when we first started working together. Of course that was before he met his wife. When he learned we played for different teams, things got tense for a while. I didn't want to think he'd nursed a grudge for so long, but found it damning that he admitted to knowing about my relationship with Amy just before I received the call.

Cops were people too and had just as many issues. Hell, we had more. Still, I didn't want to believe it. I shoved my body into my jacket to cover the shoulder holster and left the station. It was perfect weather for ducks. Rain poured down on me as I walked out onto the street. I was used to it and typically enjoyed it. The rain had a way of washing everything clean. Tonight, I just felt miserable.

The streets were flooded. Water covered the tops of my loafers and poured inside. I was soaked in seconds. The city was socked in tonight, a combination of the storm and the fog for which we were so famous. I couldn't see the moon, but I could see my breath every time I exhaled. At least the trolley stop wasn't far away, so I hoofed it with as much dignity as I could.

I thought about all the reasons I hadn't called Captain Kirth and informed him of this latest development. It was late and I didn't want to wake him. I'd tell him everything tomorrow. It was bad enough I might have a stalker, but that I suspected a fellow detective was even worse.

I took the trolley a couple of blocks and then walked the rest of the way to my favorite watering hole, The Velvet Fox. As I entered the club, I shook my head like a dog shedding water. A quick finger-comb was the best I could do to make myself presentable. Chelsea was on duty, collecting the cover charge and checking IDs.

The smell of stale alcohol and cigarettes hit me, welcoming me into a place that urged me to forget about my troubles. Just like every other bar in America these days, The Fox now banned smoking inside, but you couldn't eradicate history. It seeped into the walls.

"Hey, Nat. Where you been hiding out?" Friendly brown eyes sparkled in the artificial glow. Chelsea was the only woman I knew who could sport an '80s style afro with dignity.

"They're keeping me busy at the precinct, Chelsea. The work never ends."

She waved away my money when I reached for my wallet. "Girl, don't you know work is a four letter word?"

"You can say that again. Anything interesting going on?"

"Nah, not now. You missed the floorshow."

"That's okay. Drag queens don't really do it for me."

"How about paramedics?" Chelsea gave me a knowing grin that I returned despite the weight in my gut. The Velvet Fox wasn't a cop bar, which was one of the reasons I liked it so much. The paramedics in my precinct pretty much shared that sentiment.

"I'll never say a word."

"Don't have to, honey. It's written all over your face. You should take that girl home."

"Maybe I will," I shot back, allowing my off-duty cocky attitude to settle over me like a cloak. The friendly banter with Chelsea was just what the doctor ordered. I left her to her duties and headed for the bar, keeping my eyes open for the subject of our discussion. It wasn't hard to spot her.

Vera Carlino sat at a pub table near the bar. Her sherry-colored hair shone like fire and I could hear her tinkling laugh through the din created by the other patrons. Her work partner, Michelle Logan, sat beside her. I assumed she was responsible for Vera's laugh. The two had been together romantically way back in the Stone Age, but somehow managed to stay friends. Just like Amy and me.

The sobering thought made me realize how similar Amy and Vera were. Both were around the same age and redheads with shoulder length hair. I had a type. I headed for the bar and waited my turn.

"Hey, Jackie," I said.

Arms covered in tattoos and sporting a jet-black brush cut, Jackie was a fixture at The Velvet Fox on most nights. She served up my usual without me saying a word. I had just tossed back the shot of Jack when I heard someone call my name.

"Hey, Nat!"

I recognized Vera's voice. "Hit me again," I told Jackie before I turned around.

Vera waved for me to join them and I took a moment to appreciate the view. She had an American mom and an Italian father who once ran numbers for the mob. Vera had a tough childhood in a rough neighborhood, so she was street smart. She was also a real looker with the proverbial heart of gold. I laid a ten on the bar and ignored Jackie's sour look as I carried my drink over to the table. I guessed Jackie didn't like the cheap tip. Too bad. I worked for the city.

I said, "Ladies, what trouble are you two getting into tonight?"

"I have no idea what you mean," Vera responded playfully.

"I'll tell all," Michelle offered. She held out her hands, wrists together. "Especially if you show me your handcuffs."

Michelle was gorgeous in an exotic Jennifer Beals kind of way. Most people would have wet themselves at the thought of being with her. I preferred redheads, but reminded myself to play nice. As a paramedic, Michelle was still one of the city's unsung heroes, risking her own health every day to save lives.

"I only play with the furry ones and I'm afraid I left them at home."

Michelle stuck out her full lower lip. The lights reflected off the heavy, red lipstick. "No fun."

The night improved significantly from there. I was glad to concentrate on something other than senseless death. Vera imbibed a little more than she should have, influencing me to do the same. The suggestive touches began not long after I arrived, and the heat in Vera's eyes promised more later. At one point, I noticed Michelle's eyes narrow when Vera's hand caressed the back of my neck. Eventually, she caught a clue and took a powder, for which I was duly grateful. Apparently Vera agreed.

"I'm glad Michelle gave us some space. Let's not waste it."

"What did you have in mind?" My body throbbed.

In response, Vera grabbed my hand and led me from the club. I was relieved to see that she actually owned a car. It was a dark little thing, though I couldn't be bothered to identify make and model through the haze of lust.

Minutes later, we pulled up in front of a darkened brownstone. Vera maneuvered to an angle at the curb, in too much of a hurry to properly park. We raced for the front door and I saw a single light burning inside through a small gap between the curtains. Something moved within, temporarily blocking the light.

"Do you have a cat?"

Vera pushed the door open and we stumbled across the threshold. "Huh?" she asked, but her lips were on mine a second later, preventing any type of response.

My brain promptly gave up the query and I reached down to fill my hands with the twin globes of her ass. Vaguely, I heard the door close and realized Vera had reached over my shoulder to shut it. Then I forgot everything as I concentrated on the taste of her tongue exploring my mouth and the heat of her breasts pressed against me. I wanted her clothes off, to chew on the hardened peaks of her nipples and to spread her legs for my intimate invasion.

I had just shifted a hand around to unfasten her jeans when something hard struck the back of my head. The blow was a real bell-ringer, not only ruining the mood, but also sending me to my knees like I'd been pole-axed. I heard Vera cry out, but couldn't understand her words. My vision swam. In the shadows I couldn't see much.

The only thing I was sure of was that someone else was in the house with us. A dark figure, heavily concealed in a thick coat and hood. I couldn't make out any more details. Black gloves covered the assailant's hands. With everything obscured, there was no way I could even determine the gender.

I struggled to get to my feet, motivated by Vera's screams and the struggle that ensued between her and the attacker. A booted foot caught me in the ribs for my trouble. The air shot out of my lungs. When my head hit the floor, the double impact was too much for my abused cranium and the lights went out.

I KNEW I WAS sleeping, yet a voice inside my head screamed for me to awaken, saying that if I didn't, I'd be taking a permanent dirt nap. The idea scared me enough to force my eyes open. In keeping with the sleep theme, I awakened to a nightmare.

Three hard-backed, and in poor repair, chairs sat in a semi-circle. All were occupied. I recognized the two missing women while I resided in the third. Our wrists were strapped to the chair arms by some nappy-looking twine. The other two women were awake and watching the scene with wide, frightened eyes. I took stock of the situation. No usable weapons nearby. No help forthcoming from the terrified faces to my right and left. My service weapon was nowhere in sight, but I felt the lump of my folding knife in my right front pocket. The trouble was, my hands were still tied to the arm of the chair and I felt so sick that the room was swimming.

A frantic voice competed with the bells clanging in my head. It was hard to concentrate on the words since my mouth was so dry it felt like I'd gargled with cotton balls. Still, I managed to identify Vera as the speaker.

"Please, just let them go. You don't have to do this."

"Are you kidding me? Do you know how long it took to set this up? For me to be able to show you how much I love you?"

"By killing innocent women?"

"They aren't innocent. No one is innocent. Especially *that* one."

Michelle's psychotic eyes swiveled in my direction. Only a few hours ago, I'd thought her beautiful. Now I saw the monster behind the mask. She held a gun at her side and I realized she'd relieved me of my Glock.

"Why, Michelle?" I asked in honest confusion, forcing the words through a pounding headache. "You have everything going for you. Why this?"

"You don't know anything!" Spittle flew as she railed at me. "I tried to tell you how I felt about Vera months ago, and you had to take her from me. Exactly like you did with Amy."

I winced, suddenly reminded that Michelle once confided her attraction for Amy. Everything she said was true, but I hadn't set out to take anyone from her. It wasn't my fault we happened to have the same taste in women.

Michelle refocused on Vera. Her voice became eerie, in a reassuring, loony kind of way. "It's okay, sweetheart. I'm going to show you I love you by getting rid of these three."

I couldn't imagine what a Pilates instructor and a dry cleaner had to do with affronting Michelle, but there wasn't time to worry about it. Michelle raised the gun and pointed it at me. I cringed in dreadful anticipation. Vera stood too far away to do anything about it, and I didn't know if she could take Michelle anyway.

"Wait," Vera wailed, tears coursing down her face. "I want to do it."

"What?" I think I was as shocked as Michelle.

Vera took a few hesitant steps forward and reached for the weapon. "I know you love me. Now I want to prove you can trust me. Let me do this and we can be together."

"Vera, what are you doing?" I heard the panic in my own voice.

Michelle released the gun and Vera backed away. My eyes fixated on the only point in the room that mattered, the gun. Vera aimed it at me. From this perspective, I felt as though I stared down the barrel of a cannon. Vera's hands shook. I worried she would shoot herself.

"I'm sorry," she said. "I'm so sorry."

Unexpectedly, Vera shifted the gun and fired. Hot lead grazed Michelle's shoulder, and she cried out. Things happened fast from there. I tensed beneath my bonds and noticed the slack around my right wrist. Vera dropped the gun and ran. I couldn't fathom why she didn't shoot Michelle again. The nut case hesitated long enough to scoop up the Glock before she chased after Vera. The pitch of their pounding steps changed, altering from the slap of tennis shoes on concrete to the hollow ring of metal steps that led upward to another level.

I knew I had only moments to act or we'd all die. Straining hard against the bindings, I bent and added my teeth to the task. Blood slicked the strands before I managed to wrench free. I made short work of the other tether.

I had no time to reassure the captives. I could feel every second tick by. I spun on my heel and raced after the women. Instantly, I realized where we were. Michelle had brought us to an abandoned warehouse. From the chill and damp, I knew we were somewhere close to Fisherman's Wharf. The only place for Vera to hide out from Michelle was on the second level where I spotted several darkened offices overlooking the warehouse floor. A hurricane lantern illuminated Michelle's killing field, but no lights burned overhead. The warehouse smelled like old fish and had a clammy feel to it that sent shivers down my spine.

The heavy tread on my work shoes made flying headlong up the steel staircase almost silent. Keeping my thundering breath quiet was more difficult. Doors lay open ahead of me, three offices to clear. I heard Michelle's frantic mutterings coming from the room at the end of the shortened hallway so I ducked into the first room.

"Vera," I whispered. "It's me, Nat."

I almost jumped out of my skin when she materialized out of the darkness like a wraith. Somehow, I didn't expect Vera to be in the first room I entered. I'd been ready to search the whole damned place, if necessary.

"She went right past me."

"Get downstairs."

I encouraged her with a hand on her back. Vera went ahead of me and started back down the stairs. If we could cut the others loose and get outside before Michelle realized what was going on, we might have a chance. We'd only taken a few steps before I heard Michelle's furious shout. A quick glance over my shoulder told me the game was up.

"Run!" I yelled just as Michelle plowed into me.

We hit the top rail and, fortunately, didn't fly over the side. Michelle pummeled me with her fists. I raised my arms to block the blows. I managed a lucky shot that caused Michelle to half spin away from me and spotted the gun tucked in the back of her waistband. I couldn't reach it without getting smashed in the face. Instead, I punched Michelle in her wounded shoulder. She flinched under the blow and ducked away in an instinctive move to protect herself.

I focused on her sore spot, hitting her repeatedly. Michelle's return blows slowed and she staggered backwards near the top of the steps. Then she seemed to remember the gun. She reached for it, but I didn't intend for her to have time to use it. Before she could get the Glock free from the small of her back, I planted my foot in her chest and kicked her down the stairs.

Michelle tumbled all the way to the bottom. I raced down behind her, hoping to relieve her of my service weapon. There was no guarantee that launching her down a single flight of steps would do any serious damage. When she finally hit bottom, Michelle lay still. The gun spun away and landed at Vera's feet. I jumped over Michelle and picked it up.

With Vera and the other hostages at my back and the gun in my hand, I was back in control. Fury rushed over me now that I could think about something other than surviving our shared ordeal. Amy's murder, the threats against the rest of us, and the indignation of a throbbing cranium were almost more than I could bear. I aimed the gun at Michelle. She rolled over and looked up at me.

My finger tightened on the trigger. In her eyes, I saw expectation. Michelle didn't react the way I figured most people would when anticipating a violent death. She didn't seem scared. Instead, she looked pissed.

"Do it," Michelle said. "Show her that you aren't the hero she thinks you are."

A slow, steady squeeze. It was all I needed to end this threat for good. My mind shouted that Michelle deserved to die for what she'd done. I believed without a doubt that if she were ever released from prison, she would do something like this again. Once a killer, always a killer. I could change all that with one shot.

Vera edged out from behind me. I felt her eyes upon me, watching and waiting to see what I would do. My hand trembled from my desire to waste Michelle, but my heart worried what Vera would think of me if I did. I felt the trigger reach the tipping point, that final spot at which the hammer would fall. At the last second, I managed to ease off.

"Michelle Logan, you are under arrest for the murder of Amy Sullivan."

I HAD NO IDEA where my cell phone had gone, so while I held the gun on Michelle, Vera managed to scoot down the street to one of the few remaining pay phones in San Francisco. In no time the cavalry arrived and took Michelle into custody. It turned out the Pilates instructor had once punched Vera in the face during a work call for hurting her dad. Of course Vera had been performing CPR on the old man at the time. As for the dry cleaner, apparently burning Vera's favorite shirt was enough motivation for Michelle to seek retribution. It just proved that I'd never understand how a psychopath's mind worked.

Roger Bennett walked toward me, shaking his head. My partner was on call, and I'd managed to force him out of bed.

"How you doing?" he asked.

I grimaced as a paramedic wrapped the rope burn around my wrist. Seemed like I'd been asked that question a lot lately. "I'm doing great. I caught the bad guy."

"True. At least now we can both make Amy's funeral today."

I felt guilty about my earlier suspicions and decided to come clean. "You know, Roger, for a while I thought you were the killer."

"Me? Why would you think that?"

"Well, I got a call last night from someone who knew an awful lot about my private life. I had the impression I'd snubbed whoever it was in the past somehow."

Roger's brow furrowed for a second. "Is this because I made a pass at you a few years ago? Geez, I was single then. Are you ever going to get over it?"

"I know, I'm sorry." I felt even worse for having my doubts.

Suddenly, Roger grinned and stuffed his notepad in his hip pocket. "Hell, Harper. Sheila would have my balls for breakfast if I even *thought* about another woman."

He walked away chuckling, and the paramedic finished working on me. Michelle was wheeled out on a stretcher, accompanied by her own personal police escort. Jodi Davenport and Carla McGill agreed to be checked out at the hospital, so the paramedics packed them into the bus and took off. I knew I'd be spending the next several hours at the police station, but for the moment I was alone again with Vera.

As the warehouse emptied, I felt her warm arms encircle my waist from behind. "Thank you for not killing her."

"I didn't do it just for you." I turned to face Vera and planted a gentle kiss on her cheek. "The line might get hazy from time to time, but at the end of the day I'm still a cop. I couldn't have lived with myself if I'd pulled the trigger when I didn't have to."

Vera's amazing green eyes smiled up at me. "Feel like coming back to the brownstone?"

I'd dreamed of her asking me that question for months and my heartbeat tripled in spite of my exhaustion. "Later, but only if I can sleep before you have your way with me."

"I might let you have an hour or two."

"Unfortunately, this isn't over yet. We'll still have to go to the station to give our statements and Roger won't let me be until I have my head examined at the hospital."

"Honestly, that's an excellent idea. I'd hate for you to keel over when it matters most."

"Not a chance."

Her kiss promised much more later, and it was enough for now.

THE FALCONE MALTESE
By Andi Marquette

"DID YOU HEAR? ONE of Mrs. Falcone's show dogs is missing." Fred lowered his voice to sound like he was all conspiratorial or something. "Big city problems come to a small town. Next thing you know, we'll be the center of a missing dog black market." He was currently going through a Duran Duran phase, as evidenced by his mass of messy hair streaked with blue, black Simon LeBon pants, as he called them, and modish black boots. He wore a deep red button-down shirt and a black skinny tie. The Union Jack took up the bottom half of the tie. His book bag also had a Union Jack on it, along with several pins of bands he liked.

"That's majorly bogus. Which dog?" Nattie took her biology book and notebook out of her locker. She feigned only passing interest but she thought immediately of Jo, Mrs. Falcone's daughter, and one of Nattie's classmates. And also her current crush. She glanced at the lockers next to her to make sure nobody was listening to their conversation. The locker to her right was open and the inside of the door was plastered with various sheets of paper that said "Seniors Kick Ass" and "Class of '85" in different colors though this was the juniors' hall. The locker's owner had a crush on a senior boy.

"Giorgio. But they call him Gigi. The paper said if you see him running around, try calling him with both names."

"How did it happen?" Nattie asked.

"Cops said somebody broke in."

Nattie closed the locker door with her foot. "So the dog was stolen."

"Way." He twirled his sunglasses in one hand.

Nattie shoved a pen into her back pocket next to her comb. "Who would steal a dog out of somebody's house?" And in this town, where everybody knew everybody else?

"Therein lies the mystery." He leaned in, like he was about to share a major secret. "You should totally take the case. Nattie Brew, Detective at Large."

She laughed. "Oh, right. Because I didn't get in enough trouble the last time."

"Since when has that ever stopped you?"

"Since I was totally grounded for a month."

"This is different. You probably wouldn't have to break into anything. Plus," he added with a smirk, "I'm sure you'll have Jo Falcone's un*dying* gratitude." He pretended to swoon.

Nattie's cheeks flared with heat. "Shut up."

"Un*dying* gratitude," he repeated, grinning.

"Fred—"

"Hey, fag. This hall is now for seniors. Not butt ugly faggy juniors."

Nattie's stomach clenched. Josh Jacobs was a major dickweed. And always with a few other dickweeds from the football team. Three, today, and they all guffawed at the insult.

Fred gave him an "oh, please" look. "Really? That's the best you can do?"

Josh's fake smile disappeared. "Flamer." He shoved Fred hard, knocking him into the locker next to Nattie's.

Several other students stopped to watch.

"Takes one to know one," Fred said.

The crowd uttered a collective "ohhh" in acknowledgement of a good comeback.

Josh reached for him. "Piece of—"

"Leave him alone," Nattie said. Her voice didn't sound as scared as she felt. Her knees were shaking.

Josh turned, puzzled, as if it never occurred to him that anybody would say anything. "What?"

"Leave him alone. Go waste somebody else's time." Her heart pounded in her ears and she forced herself not to run down the hall.

He glared, his hands clenched into fists. "You a fag, too?"

"Not likely, since 'fag' is an insult most often applied to guys. Or, in England, a term used for cigarettes."

Several students snickered. Josh shifted his glare to the small crowd. The giggles died immediately.

"Is there a problem here?"

Nattie's knees almost buckled in relief as Mr. Grafton approached from his classroom down the hall.

"No," Josh said.

Mr. Grafton looked at Nattie.

"Not anymore," she said.

Fred shook his head.

"All right," Mr. Grafton said. "Everybody get to class."

Josh gave Nattie a final glare before he walked away, his posse of teammates right behind him.

Nattie looked at Fred and they stared for a moment before bursting into nervous laughter.

"Major dickweed." Fred adjusted his bag and smoothed the front of his shirt.

"Are you okay?"

"Yeah. You're so big and strong," he teased. "Jo will totally appreciate it."

Nattie rolled her eyes. "Be careful, okay?"

"I'll just run and find you. Nobody messes with you 'cause of your dad." He batted his eyes.

"If that's what it takes." She gave his arm a gentle squeeze. Nattie rarely talked about her dad at school, but everybody knew he was with the sheriff's department. She never talked about her mom, either, who had died when she was a toddler.

"Gotta go," Fred said. "Catch you later."

She watched him, since Josh was right down the hall leaning against a locker. But he was busy hanging all over—Nattie stared a few more moments—Pam Howard? Pam was back with that jerkoff? Gag. She checked to make sure Fred had gotten past Josh then went to class.

"Hey, Nattie," Jo said as Nattie approached the door to the biology classroom. She was leaning against the wall, holding her books in front, flat against her chest. She wore her basic Jo uniform, as Nattie categorized it. Loose jeans pegged at the ankles above her black high-top Chucks and a light blue T-shirt rolled up at the sleeves. She also wore a men's black vest over her shirt, which added to her boyish look but in a good way. She'd started streaking her dark hair blonde in the front, which only made her cuter.

"Hi." Nattie hoped she sounded calm and cool.

"Got a sec?" Jo pushed off the wall.

"Yeah." Ohmigod.

Jo stepped away from the doorway and the students filing in. She moved closer and lowered her voice. "My mom's best show dog was stolen."

"I know. I heard. I'm really sorry."

"Um. So, do you think you could help find him? I mean, if you want to. I wouldn't want you to get in trouble or anything."

Nattie stared at her.

"I mean, after the last time you solved something, I wasn't sure I should ask, but you're really good at finding stuff, so—"

"Yes," she said, and immediately regretted it, but only a little. Her dad didn't have to know.

Jo grinned. "Really? Awesome. Could you come over after school today?"

"Uh—" Nattie had never been inside Jo's house and the thought made her nervous, but giddy, too.

"To see where it happened. The scene of the crime."

"Oh, yeah."

"Awesome. Meet me after school by the parking lot."

Nattie followed her in and took a seat on the opposite side of the room. Jo sat nearer the back, and Nattie wished the order was reversed so she could see her during class. She opened her notebook and started listing potential suspects in Giorgio's dognapping and possible motives. Jo would have some ideas, too. She shoved the other thoughts she had of Jo out of her mind. This was an investigation, after all.

NATTIE AND JO STOOD outside Jo's house and studied the trellis that ran up the side to the roof right next to the window of the second-floor room where the dogs had been crated. "Stately" fit as a descriptor for Jo's house, a modified white Tudor-style with brown peaked roof and accents on the front. Nattie liked architecture and geeked out over books on the topic. The trellis was practically a ladder because it had vertical and horizontal slats. The thief could have climbed up, gone in through the window, put Giorgio in a duffel bag or backpack, and made his way back down the trellis. She used the male pronoun, for ease of hypothesizing.

"Cops think he went in through that window," Jo said. "Maybe somebody knew Gigi, because he's weird around people he doesn't know. That's his nickname," she added. "He gets all wiggly and totally cute when you call him Gigi." She sounded sad.

"Where were the other two dogs?"

"They were in the house. But whoever took Gigi ignored them. And they were fine. My mom had the vet check them out."

The thief knew which dog to nab. "Was the window locked?" Nattie asked.

"Not when the police looked around. Normally, the windows upstairs are latched, but we don't check all that much, since they're, like, twenty feet up."

Nattie took a notepad and pen out of her shoulder bag. "What about other windows? Maybe whoever it was just came in from the first floor."

"No, the burglar alarm would've gone off."

"Okay, so if somebody went through that window, it had to be unlatched or maybe even open a bit." Nattie brushed a strand of hair out of her face, trying to concentrate on the case and not on how close Jo was standing. "Who was over in the last week who might've gone upstairs?"

Comprehension dawned in Jo's eyes. "You're thinking somebody might've, like, come up here and unlatched the window."

"Seems logical." She looked up at the trellis again. "Have you ever climbed up there?"

Jo laughed. "Lots of times. Not hard to do. Want to try?" She grinned, a mischievous glint in her eyes.

Nattie followed the vertical line of the trellis with her gaze, hoping the flush she felt on her neck wasn't showing.

"Hold on." Jo jogged to the front of the house. A few moments later the curtains over the window of the room where Giorgio had been stolen moved and Jo appeared. She unlatched the window but didn't open it, waving to Nattie before she retreated and came back outside.

"Okay. Here we go." Jo put her hands on a couple of the cross-slats of the trellis.

"Are you sure this is a good idea?"

"No prob." Jo easily climbed up and braced her foot on the trellis. She held on with one hand as she reached for the window. "Look," she called down. "If the window's closed but unlatched, I can open it from here." She demonstrated and then, keeping her foot on the trellis, grasped the sill for leverage to pull herself inside.

She poked her head back out the window. "Come on," Jo said, smiling down at her.

Fine. This was an investigation, after all, and she should reconstruct the crime. Nattie set her bag on the ground next to the trellis. She'd done stuff like this before. No prob, right? She wiped her palms on her pants. No big deal. She'd snuck out of her room plenty of times, too. Of course, her room was on the first floor. She started climbing, aware of the feel of the wood against her hands. It seemed sturdy enough, but she doubted it would hold anyone bigger than her or Jo. Once at the level of the window, she concentrated on imitating Jo's movements, glad she'd worn her Chucks. They were grippy.

"Okay, I'm right here," Jo said. "Reach for the sill. Keep your foot on the trellis. Yeah. You've got it. Okay, now just move your other hand. There you go. Good job."

Nattie pulled herself in. Jo hovered, hands poised for a rescue, but she didn't have to help. Once inside, Nattie exhaled in relief.

"Stellar," Jo said. She gave Nattie's shoulder a friendly squeeze. "Knew you could do it." She motioned at the window. "Come on, Magnum P.I. Let's go back down. See how long it takes."

Reversing her motions was a little trickier, even after watching Jo. Nattie was just able to reach the window from the trellis and pull it closed. The thief must've used a backpack for Giorgio, because he would've needed both hands. Or maybe an accomplice.

"Okay, so we proved it can be done," Nattie said after they were both on the ground. "Was anybody at home that night?"

"No. I was hanging out at Lisa Stone's watching a movie. My mom called at ten totally wigging out, and I got home quick. She was at a party and when she got home was when she found out."

Lisa Stone, Nattie catalogued. She was on the basketball team with Jo. "Where was your dad?"

"Out of town. Doctor conference."

Somebody had been watching them, or knew their schedules for that night. "Who do you think might have taken him?"

Jo sighed and for a moment looked like she was going to cry. She cleared her throat before Nattie could offer any comfort. "The person who would benefit the most is Mrs. Adkins. But she and my mom have been friends for years. They totally don't rag on each other at all. Mrs. Adkins was totally crying when she heard."

"Any other people who compete?"

"I guess Josh Jacobs' mom."

"Cindy shows dogs?"

"She just started showing Maltese, like, two years ago. Her most experienced dog took fourth in the last show."

Nattie had heard something about Cindy Jacobs and her dogs a few months earlier. She really didn't want to have to talk to her. Cindy was just as skanky as her son Josh.

"Is Mrs. Jacobs a friend of your mom's?" She hoped not.

"Not really. They see each other around."

"Was anybody else around in the few days before Giorgio got stolen? Especially anybody who went upstairs?"

"His groomer, Ruth Howard," Jo said. "She was over on Friday. And my mom's golfing partner, Theresa Landers, came by Saturday morning. But she never goes upstairs. She and my mom stay downstairs and drink coffee before they go to the course."

"Did Ruth go upstairs?"

"Yeah. My mom forgot to bring Gigi's favorite brush down—" she stopped, as if she realized that she might be implicating Ruth. "No way," she said after a few seconds. "Ruth would totally never do anything to hurt my mom. They've been friends for years. Plus, she doesn't show dogs, and she loves Gigi."

Nattie hoped Jo was right, because she liked Ruth. "Does Theresa show dogs?"

"No. She doesn't even really like them. She's more a cat person."

Not much of a motive for either Ruth or Theresa, but you never know. Some people carry weird grudges. "Could I see some recent pictures of Giorgio?"

"Sure. Come on in."

Nattie grabbed her bag and followed her inside and up the stairs. Way cute. She chewed her lip. Crushes sucked. Especially when you were a girl with one on another girl.

The house looked like it could've been on TV. Organized, clean, and it smelled of furniture polish. Not sure what else to do, Nattie waited in the room Giorgio had been dognapped from.

"Here you go." Jo returned, carrying a small photo album. "The last two pages are from two weeks ago."

Nattie took it just as the phone rang from a different room nearby.

"Be right back." Jo said.

Nattie focused on the pictures. Fairly typical show-dog Maltese, she decided. He'd been posed with his white fur all combed out and shiny. The hair above his eyes had been pulled up and fastened with a red bow. Poor guy, having to wear that. But he was pretty.

"Not a fan of the hairbows," Jo said when she returned, as if she'd read Nattie's mind. "I don't think the dogs are, either, but it's part of the whole pageant thing. Oh, I just remembered something weird. Gigi's vitamins are missing. They were up here, on that shelf." She pointed to a set of shelves that held dog shampoo, brushes, and dog treats.

"Does he have to take any other medicine?"

"No."

"If the thief took the vitamins, that means they're trying to take care of him. Which could be a good thing. Can I take one of these?" Nattie gestured at the photos.

"Yeah. There are doubles of each. My mom's a spaz that way." She took the album and peeled back one of the plastic covers and removed a photo. She was right. The same photo was underneath. She handed it to Nattie. "Do you think he's all right?" she asked, worry in her eyes and maybe tears.

"I hope so." And she hoped she sounded positive as she slid the photo into her bag. When she looked up, Jo was wiping her eyes with her sleeve. "Hey," Nattie said. "The police are working on it and I'll do what I can. We'll find him."

"You want a pop or anything?"

As enticing as that was, Nattie shook her head. "I have to get home. Thanks, though."

"Okay. I'll drive you."

Nattie's stomach flipped like it was on a trampoline. "You don't have to. It's not that far."

"I don't mind. Come on."

Nattie followed her down the stairs, trying not to look at Jo but totally failing.

A few minutes later, Jo pulled her Celica against the curb in front of Nattie's house.

"Thanks," Nattie said. She started to open the door.

"Can I call you?"

Her stomach did the flip thing again. Jo Falcone wanted her number. "Yeah." She wrote on a blank sheet of paper in her notepad and tore it off to hand to Jo. "Thanks again for the ride."

"No prob. I'll call you later, after I talk to my mom. See you tomorrow."

Nattie exhaled in relief once she was out of the car. Jo waited for her to unlock the side door before she pulled away. Did other detectives get crushes on a member of a victimized household? So unprofessional! She put her headphones on, flipped the tape over in the Walkman, and made a sandwich while she hummed along with Cyndi Lauper.

RUTH HOWARD. NATTIE TAPPED her pen against her notepad and frowned. Why would Giorgio's dog groomer want to steal him? She had opportunity, though. Jo said she'd been over to groom Giorgio this past Friday, but Nattie couldn't come up with a motive. Ruth didn't show dogs. Plus, it was in her best interests if Giorgio did well because Mrs. Falcone would tell everybody who groomed him.

Theresa Landers also had opportunity but nothing to do with dogs. She'd been over Saturday, the day after Ruth. Giorgio was taken on Monday. Nattie scratched her off her list of suspects. Did the thief just get lucky? Maybe someone had accidentally left the latch undone.

What about Cindy Jacobs? Nattie frowned. Motive, but no opportunity. She had never been to the Falcones' house. Which bumped everything back to Ruth. Bummer. Nattie liked Ruth. Too bad her daughter didn't have enough sense to date decent guys. Ick. Josh Jacobs. She looked up from her notebook and studied the front of Doggone Good Grooming. Fortunately, numerous benches circled the town square, which made it easy to pick a surveillance point.

A red and black Camaro pulled into one of the diagonal parking slots in front of Ruth's shop. Gag. Josh. He got out of the driver's side and Pam Howard emerged from the passenger's side. They went into the shop.

"Yo," Fred said as he approached, eating a candy bar, still doing his Duran Duran impression from his hair down to his boots. He could easily have been in one of the MTV videos with the band. The lyrics to "Hungry Like the Wolf" popped into Nattie's head.

"Doing a stakeout?" he asked. "You can be Cagney. I'll be Lacey." He plopped down next to her. "So how's Jo?" he added with extra innocence.

"I don't know. I haven't talked to her today." It came out sharper than she intended, but she didn't want to deal with his comments about her crush.

"Geez, chill. She's cute and nice and would probably be perfect for you—"

"I don't want to talk about that."

"Fine. Want a bite?" He offered a piece of his candy bar to her, a Whatchamacallit, and she took it.

"So who took Mrs. Falcone's dog?" Fred asked after he'd finished the candy bar.

"I don't know yet, and the show's day after tomorrow."

"But you think Ruth Howard's in on it."

"What makes you think that?"

"Elementary, Watson. You're sitting on the bench with the best view of her shop. Either that or you're crushed out on Pam Howard, too."

"Eew. Like, never. Anybody who goes with Josh Jacobs is warped."

"I'd do the nasty with him."

"Ohmigod." She looked at him in horror.

"Psych!" he said, laughing. "As if."

She smacked him on the arm.

"There he is," Fred said.

Josh headed to his car without looking toward the bench, got in and started the engine, and backed away.

"So he dropped Pam off," Fred said. "Aw, how sweet. Not."

Nattie stared at the shop. Josh dropped Pam off. Because she worked for her mom every day after school until Ruth closed up. "Pam really likes dogs," she said aloud. And Pam was dating Josh Jacobs, whose mom competed against Jo's mom.

"Duh," Fred said. "She'd have to."

She'd been working at the shop since forever, helping her mom groom them. Nattie jumped to her feet and grabbed her bag.

"Where are you going?"

"Library. Come if you want." She needed to see the newspaper articles from the last dog show where Cindy Jacobs' Maltese took fourth.

"Fine," he said with a groan. "I'll do some homework."

Twenty minutes later she had a stack of newspapers on one of the big, solid library tables. The last dog show in the county had been two months earlier, around Valentine's Day. She started at February 1 and found an article about the upcoming show—scheduled for February 17—in a newspaper from the week before the show. Nattie checked the February 18 edition, which included a big article. Cindy Jacobs' dog, Percy, had only been ten months old then. The photos were black-and-white, which didn't give her many clues about differences in appearances.

She needed better photos. She went to the main information desk, borrowed the phone, and dialed Jo's number.

"Hello?"

"Um, Jo?"

"Yeah. Hey, Nattie."

Ohmigod. Jo recognized her voice. She calmed herself. "Sorry to bug you, but do you have any pictures of the dog show in February?"

"Oh, totally. I told you Mom's a spaz about pictures. She likes to take pictures of the other dogs, too."

"Can I see them? Just the last show."

"Yeah. I'll bring them to school tomorrow. Do you have an idea about who took Gigi?" She sounded excited and hopeful and Nattie hated to disappoint her.

"Maybe. How's your mom doing?"

"She's really upset still. I keep telling her that we'll find him, and he'll be okay." She paused. "Anyway, I'll bring the pictures tomorrow. Can you come a half-hour early to school?"

"Yeah."

"Meet me by the west entrance at quarter 'til eight."

"Okay." God, could she sound any more inarticulate?

"Awesome. Thanks, Nattie. I'm really glad you're helping. See you tomorrow. Bye."

"Bye." Nattie went back to the table, where Fred was packing up his books.

"Solved it, Sherlock?"

"Not yet."

"Well, I have to get home."

"Hold up. I'll walk with you." Nattie gathered her things, slung her bag over her shoulder, and took the newspapers back to the circulation desk. A little jolt of anticipation raced down her spine. She always got that way when she had lots of pieces to a puzzle and she wasn't sure where they fit. But she knew they fit together somehow. She just had to find the right combination.

"THAT'S PERCY," JO SAID, pointing to the Maltese Cindy Jacobs was holding. "He wasn't quite a year old in this photo, and you can see he's got a tan splotch on his ear, there."

Yes, there it was. About the size of a silver dollar at the tip of his left ear. "I thought Maltese were all white."

"For the most part. It's not weird for puppies to have some tan on them, especially their ears. The coloring fades after they're about a year old."

They sat next to each other on a low concrete bench outside the school entrance. Jo's thigh bumped Nattie's when she moved to reach over and turn a page of the album, and Nattie gave herself a mental high five for not passing out. Jo wore jeans and Chucks again, but today she had on a dark blue button-down shirt that looked more like a guy's. Totally cute. And she had on some kind of perfume that smelled like Charlie.

"Would the tan count against him?" Nattie asked.

"It's not supposed to. He took fourth, and that's not bad for his first outing."

"Do you have a picture that shows both dogs?"

"Yeah. Here." Jo flipped to a photo that showed five dogs lined up with their handlers, preparing to go into the ring. "Gigi's here, and there's Percy, right behind him."

Nattie studied the photo. The dogs were roughly the same size.

"State is tomorrow," Jo said softly. "My mom refuses to take Gigi off the roster." She flipped the album's page. "Here's one of Pam with Gigi in the grooming area at the last show. She came with Ruth that time and he really likes her."

Nattie thought about that. Gigi really likes Pam. Pam really likes dogs. Pam works in a grooming shop. In the photo, Pam was petting Gigi while he was up on the grooming table as Ruth prepared him for his showing.

"Do you ever hang out with Pam?" Nattie asked without looking up from the photo. The pieces were clicking into place.

"Well, yeah. She's on the team with me."

Nattie raised her gaze to Jo's. "But do you hang out with her outside of that?"

"Yeah."

"So she comes over to your house."

"Sometimes. We're not besties or anything, but we do chill every once in a while. She was over on Sunday with some other girls from the team—" Jo stopped. "Wait. What are you saying?"

"Nothing yet."

"Are you seriously thinking Pam took Gigi?" Jo closed the album and held it on her lap.

"We have to consider all the angles, and I was only focused on adults. So who else was at your house on Sunday?"

Jo named off five other girls and Nattie wrote them down in her notebook, but she was pretty sure she wouldn't be following any of them after school. "Okay, I'll check these out and get back to you as soon as I can. Thanks for bringing the photos."

The first bell rang for class. They both stood. "Hey," Jo said as Nattie headed for the school entrance. "Think you could come over next week to study for biology?"

Nattie stopped and stared at her. Jo had never asked to study with her. Maybe she figured Nattie was smart, so why not use the smart girl to get a good grade? But Jo did well in biology, from what she could tell. "Um, okay."

"Awesome. C'mon. We're gonna be late." Jo caught up and grabbed her arm to pull her inside. Nattie practically floated down the jammed hallway. She didn't even care that it probably didn't mean anything to Jo, asking her over to study. But it was the best feeling anyway, and it stayed with her until the end of the school day.

That evening, she rode her bike to Pam's house. Ruth's car wasn't in the drive and neither was Pam's dad's. Ruth was probably still at the shop, which meant Pam was, too, so Nattie rode downtown and took up her seat on the bench. She'd brought her notebook along as well as her dad's Polaroid camera. She pretended to be reading through her notes when Josh arrived and went in. A few minutes later he came out with Pam, and they got into his car and drove away.

Nattie waited ten minutes, then went across the street. She leaned her bike against the outside window and went in the shop. Ruth looked up from the counter, wearing the pink hospital-style scrubs she favored at the shop. She was an older version of pretty blonde Pam, though a little heavier around the middle.

"Oh, hi, Nattie. What are you up to?"

"Hi, Ruth. I was hoping to catch Pam. Is she still around?"

"You just missed her."

Nattie pretended to be disappointed. "Do you know where she went?"

"Dinner at Josh's house. Do you need me to pass a message along?"

"No, I'll catch her at school tomorrow. It's not that important. I figured since I was down here anyway, I'd stop by. Thanks."

"Well, that was nice of you. Send my best to your father."

Nattie smiled and left before Ruth could ask her anything else. Outside, she checked her watch. Her dad would be home around nine tonight, so she had some time for another stakeout.

HOW LONG DID IT take to have dinner? Nattie checked her watch again in the growing gloom and adjusted her position behind the big oak tree in the back corner of the Jacobs' lawn, up against the high wooden fence that enclosed it. Fifteen feet away stood a tan wooden shed that looked well-maintained. If Cindy Jacobs was like Jo's mom, she might use the shed for dog stuff, now that she was all serious about showing.

Nattie adjusted her position again, not entirely sure what she was looking for, but willing to sneak into the Jacobs' backyard to see if she could figure it out.

The back door opened. Josh held it open for Pam with his foot.

Nattie pressed her front harder against the oak and peeked around it. Both Josh and Pam were carrying small white dogs. They descended the steps from the back deck and walked toward the shed. Nattie held her breath.

"How long will this take?" Josh asked.

"An hour, maybe. I have to get it right." She didn't sound too enthused about whatever she was doing.

He said something else but Nattie didn't catch it. They went into the shed. Light splashed out of the side and back windows. She waited a minute, then carefully peeled herself off the tree and worked her way along the back fence. She'd worn dark clothing, but it wasn't completely dark out yet, and she needed to get out of sight again. Fast.

She made it to the back of the shed where she crouched, avoiding the light beaming like a ray from the Death Star onto the lawn. She waited a few seconds for her heart rate to slow and heard Josh's voice again.

"That's too much. It's too dark."

"Chill," Pam said. "It'll dry lighter."

Nattie carefully stood. The window was barely a foot from her head. She inched along the wall—it felt like an hour—until another inch would have put her in the Death Star ray. She took a deep breath and peeked in.

The shed was clearly for dog stuff. She counted four plastic dog kennels on the counter and several leashes hanging on little hooks above the kennels. Pam's back was to Nattie, but she stood next to a grooming table like Ruth had in her shop. Nattie caught a glimpse of a little white dog butt.

"It's okay," Pam crooned. "Just a few more minutes."

Josh held another dog. He faced the back window but was focused on whatever Pam was doing. Nattie didn't breathe. He adjusted the dog's position and held the animal next to the other dog on the table, like he was comparing.

"That looks pretty good," he said, but Nattie couldn't tell what he was talking about.

"Almost." From the edge of the grooming table Pam picked up a bottle that Nattie hadn't noticed. She couldn't tell what that was, either. "This needs to set for a little bit, so I can tell what the color tone is."

"Way cool." He lowered the dog he was holding to the floor of the shed and, to Nattie's horror, opened the door. "Go take a pee, you little doofus."

Speaking of pee, Nattie realized that she could use a quick trip to the bathroom. Not going to happen any time soon, though.

The Maltese trotted outside, and Nattie drew back from the

window. Maybe the dog wouldn't come around the shed. Maybe it preferred to pee closer to the house.

No such luck. It walked toward the tree she'd hidden behind earlier and immediately got really busy sniffing it. Probably picked up her scent and would come looking for her next. The dog kept sniffing, its butt to her, and she ducked behind the side of the shed farthest from the tree but peeked out around it to keep an eye on the dog. He finished with the tree and trotted toward the back of the shed.

Way, way bogus. Nattie held her breath again and didn't move. The dog sniffed the back of the shed and made snuffling sounds in the grass. The noise stopped suddenly and so did the dog. The only reason Nattie could see what it was doing in the deepening shadows of night was because of its white coat. It started sniffing again, closer.

Did Maltese bark? Probably. Nattie studied the fence. Was she fast enough to climb it before Josh came running out to see why the dog was spazzing? Probably not. Josh played football. He was big and strong and fast.

So not cool.

The dog was inches from her shoes. She was so going to get so busted and so grounded.

"Percy," came Pam's voice from the other side of the shed.

The dog bounded away.

Nattie sagged against the wall. She listened to the shed door closing and then the back door to the house opened and closed. She waited a few minutes, not daring to move, which made her urge to pee even worse.

Finally, the light over the back door went out. Nattie returned to the shed's back window. She took the flashlight out of her back pocket and covered it with her hand before she turned it on. She aimed it through the back window before she took her hand away and shone it on the shed's interior.

Pam had left the plastic bottle she'd been using on the grooming table. It had a narrow applicator tip and it looked familiar, but the label was turned away. A white towel hung partially off the table, like it was too tired to pull itself all the way on. In the beam of the flashlight, Nattie saw smudges on it, like paint.

She checked her watch. Time to go. She moved along the back fence to the tree and used it for leverage to climb back over the fence into the alley. She landed next to the trash can she'd used to climb into the backyard earlier, a few feet from where she'd stashed her bike and bag. She was on her way home within seconds, and by the time she got there, she had figured out what the bottle on the grooming table was.

THE MALTESE JUDGING STARTED in ten minutes. Nattie raced across the county fairgrounds, backpack banging against her shoulders, camera inside smacking her hard enough to leave a bruise. She'd brought it just in case.

She hadn't counted on her dad getting called in to work. Stupid. She should have. Always have a Plan B. Jo had already left for the dog show when Nattie called at seven a.m., hoping for a ride. She had to ride her bike across town. And now she wasn't sure she was going to make it in time.

She practically threw her ticket at the man standing at the arena entrance. He looked at her disapprovingly.

"Sorry. Love the Maltese." Out of breath, she hurried to the stairs. Jo had said the dog area was downstairs, on the same level as the arena floor.

"Miss, you can't go down there," the man at the door called after her. She ignored him.

"Miss," he shouted. He was probably going to call security. Or he didn't need to, because of the cop standing at the entrance to the dog and handler area. She heard the rumble of the audience from the arena and barking from the dog area behind him.

"Hi," she said. "I'm late. I was supposed to meet Jo Falcone here. I'm working on a school project about dog shows."

"I'll need to see your pass."

Nattie made a show of going through her backpack. "Oh, no," she said, faking panic. "Great. I think I left it on the kitchen table."

"I'm sorry," he said, barring her way.

"Look, you can come with me. Just take me to the Falcone dogs. I'm a friend of Jo's from school."

"The Falcone dogs, huh?" he said with a "that's a likely story" tone.

Maybe she could outrun him.

He asked, "And why, exactly, did you pick the Falcone dogs for this so-called report?"

"I'm a friend of Jo's, and that made it easier."

"No pass, no access."

Nattie groaned. "Please?"

"Sorry."

"Nattie!" someone called out.

She turned and only just barely refrained from throwing herself at Jo to give her a huge hug. "I forgot my pass." She looked at Jo pointedly, then glanced at the cop.

"Oh, bummer. She's with me," Jo said. She held up a plastic card and lanyard that hung around her neck. "I promise I won't let her out of my sight."

"All right." To Nattie he said, "Next time, bring your pass."

"Yessir." She followed Jo into the dog area, which reminded Nattie of the gym locker room because of its dingy yellow cinderblock walls and fluorescent lights. The cramped space was filled with every shape and size of dog carrier, kennel, dog supplies, and all kinds of dogs in various stages of preparation. Some of them managed to nap while others, overcome with all the excitement, barked. People milled around, talking and laughing.

"They'll be starting the Maltese in a few minutes," Jo said.

"Where's Cindy Jacobs?"

"Out in the audience. It's mostly handlers that take care of dogs at shows."

"I need to talk to Cindy's dog handler."

"Barry Foster. Okay." Jo worked her way through the rows of grooming tables and dog kennels. "Right there," she said.

A pudgy man in a gray suit was busy brushing a Maltese on the grooming table. He finished and set the dog on the floor and gave it a treat with one hand while he held the dog's leash with the other. The dog tugged at the leash, like it wanted to be elsewhere.

"Wait here," Nattie told Jo. "Hey, Mr. Foster," she said as she approached him.

"Yes? Oh, hi, Nattie." The dog sniffed Nattie's sneakers, then started to tug again. "I don't know what's gotten into him," Barry said, pulling the dog back. "It's like he doesn't even know who I am. How's your father?"

"Good. Working. I was wondering...I'm doing a paper on dog shows for school. Could I talk to you about being a handler?"

"Certainly. I can't right now—"

"It's time now for the Maltese showing," said a deep male voice over the intercom. "Handlers, please proceed to the arena entrance for line-up."

"Time to go. Come by after this segment," Barry said. He looked down at his suit. "Oh, bother," he muttered. "Do you mind?" He handed the leash to Nattie and reached for a lint roller that he began running up and down the lapels of his jacket. Nattie crouched and petted the dog, who pulled away. A tan splotch marked the tip of his left ear.

Barry started rolling his pants, turning away momentarily to reach a spot on his hip.

Nattie slipped the collar off the dog. "Mr. Foster, I don't think his collar's on right."

The dog bolted like it was in a race.

"Percy!" Barry ran after him, still clutching the lint roller. His foot caught on one of the kennels. He went crashing to the floor, knocking over a neighboring grooming table. A woman shrieked and scooped a dog into her arms. The Maltese zig-zagged around her, looking like some kind of possessed mop.

Several people lunged for him, but the dog was too fast. Grooming tables went over like dominos, and barks and howls added to the general cacophony of crashing tables and shouting.

Jo grabbed Nattie's arm. "What the hell?" She pulled Nattie out of the way of a hefty man with a red face who was bellowing orders to a woman nearby holding on to a dog that looked like a Doberman.

"Come on," Nattie said. "That's not Percy."

"What? What are you talking about?"

"Come *on*." Nattie barreled after the Maltese, who had figured out where the entrance to the arena was. Barry clambered to his feet and huffed after him, yelling, "Percy!" at the top of his lungs.

People dodged out of the way as the strange procession raced up the slight incline into the arena. A hush fell over the crowd at their entrance, but only for an instant. People realized that a dog had spazzed, something that happened every once in a while. Security guards tried to grab the Maltese as he zoomed past, his bright blue hairbow bouncing with his movements.

Handlers already lined up for the showing quickly picked up their own Maltese as the one on the loose ran up and down the line, as if he was looking for something.

"Percy!" That was Cindy Jacobs, who had managed to join the fray, Josh and Pam right behind her.

"I'll get him," Josh said. He dove as the dog ran past the judging table. Nattie stopped to watch the action, which was like a slow-motion sports replay—except the Maltese didn't move like a loose football. Josh missed him and slid into the table leg. The table collapsed on top of him and two of the judges—both older men—went sprawling. The woman judge had just managed to get out of her chair and avoid being tackled.

"Oh, my God," Jo said.

And then the loose Maltese stopped. He glanced around, panting, a few feet from the judges' table. As Josh tried to extricate himself from the table and judges, Cindy Jacobs said, "Percy! You come here this instant."

The dog looked at her but didn't move. The bow in his hair had partially unraveled and hung along the side of his face.

"Percy," Cindy shouted, sounding desperate. The dog ignored her. The crowd seemed to still.

"Percy," Pam said, but not with much conviction.

"Call him," Nattie said to Jo.

"What—"

"That's Giorgio."

Jo stared at her.

"Call him," Nattie said again.

Jo took a step toward the Maltese. "Gigi."

The dog bounded toward her, yipping happily.

"No way," Jo said. She picked him up, laughing, and he wriggled in her arms, licking her face. "It is. It's Gigi."

"What's going on?" the female judge demanded.

Nattie said, "Cindy Jacobs had the Falcones' dog kidnapped so she could pass him off as hers to win the competition." Nattie gestured at Pam. "She dyed his ear to make him look more like Percy, the Jacobs' dog." To Pam she said, "I'm guessing you climbed the trellis, too. Since Giorgio knew you, he'd come when you called him."

Pam looked like she was going to cry.

"But you probably lowered him down to Josh," Nattie added. "Because it would've been hard to climb down with a live dog."

"This is appalling," the judge said. "Where are the police?"

"Right here," Mrs. Falcone said. She approached, tugging on the arm of the officer Nattie had encountered earlier. "Cindy," she said, her tone outraged, "how could you?"

"I'm not saying another word," Cindy snapped.

"Should I call Dad?" Josh asked, sounding nothing like his usual cocky jock self.

"Shut up." Cindy smacked the back of his head and he cringed.

"Pam, what were you thinking?" Ruth had arrived, a look of horror and disappointment on her face. "Oh, no."

Ruth turned toward Jo's mother. "I'm sorry," she said. Nattie actually felt bad for her.

Giorgio leapt from Jo's arms and Mrs. Falcone scooped him up, laughing and smiling. He licked her face, too, and then there were all kinds of people around, including several security guards. Nattie stepped back from the growing crowd around the broken judges' table, but she knew there was a long day ahead. And a possible grounding. At least her punishment wasn't even close to what Josh and Pam had to face. She sighed anyway.

"HEARD THE DOG SHOW turned out like a Hulk Hogan match with the A-Team," Fred said as he sat down next to her on the concrete bench outside the school. He was wearing pegged jeans and black and white Creepers today. He'd rolled the sleeves of his turquoise shirt up and several jelly bracelets encircled his wrists. She put her biology book aside.

"Are you in major trouble?" He sounded worried.

Nattie smiled. "No, because Jo's mom intervened with my dad."

"Lucky," he said, drawing out the "L" with a little smirk. She ignored it.

"And you would have totally loved the scene," Nattie said. "Lots of guys screaming like girls chasing this little dog."

"My kind of party. Did Josh really try to tackle Giorgio?"

"Yep. Totally missed. Hit the judge's table. It was insane to the max."

"Next time you decide to disrupt a dog show, call me." He watched a couple of guys walk by.

"Scammer," Nattie said.

"Duh." He put his sunglasses on. "What's going to happen to Josh and Pam?"

"I don't know. My dad said that since they're still juveniles under the influence of an adult, that'll probably help them. Right now, they can finish school, but they're under major supervision and I heard Cindy's under house arrest. I guess we'll find out more when the court cases start up."

"Bummer. I was hoping Josh would be carted off to a jail somewhere with a big, hairy, cellmate with really bad breath who only showers once a week. Oh, well. A boy can dream."

"Eww. That is way heinous."

"What? It'd serve him right. Though I'll bet in five years I see Josh at a gay bar in the city."

"God, Fred. Not everybody is gay."

"Sadly. Speaking of, has Jo shown you her un*dying* gratitude yet for saving the day?"

"Would you shut up with that?" She tried to keep her tone light, but her crush was a sore spot for her, especially since she had no reason to hang out with Jo, now that Giorgio was home.

Fred started digging in his pockets.

"What are you doing?"

"Looking for a chill pill to give you."

"As if. Just shut up."

"What? You're totally righteous. Girl detective and all. Bet she thinks you're cute."

"Fred, seriously. Shut up."

"Hey, guys."

"Hi, Jo," Fred said with extra emphasis. "We were just talking about you. Weren't we?" He held his shades up and stared at Nattie.

"Um," Nattie said, unable to form more words.

"And I was just going." Fred stood. "Glad your dog's back. Our little Nattie does it again." He gave her a half-hug. "So proud of her." He wiped his eye as if he was crying.

Jo smiled but Nattie tried not to glare at him.

"You kids don't be late to class, now," Fred said. "Catch you later."

Nattie would kill him. Later. "So how's Giorgio?"

"Awesome. And my mom's awesome, too. Everybody at my house is awesome." Jo sat on the bench where Fred had been and dropped her backpack on the ground between her feet. She'd used a red marker to draw a skull and crossbones on the right toe of her Chucks. She wore jeans, a black T-shirt, and a men's black blazer rolled up at the sleeves. Pins for Simple Minds, Depeche Mode, and Cyndi Lauper decorated the lapels of the blazer.

"Cool." Maybe, if she was lucky, Jo's thigh would bump hers.

"Hey, I wanted to thank you again. You went above and beyond. I can't believe what you did for us."

"Besides totally destroy the dog show?"

Jo laughed. "Okay, that was pretty hardcore. But it got rescheduled, and this time Gigi's ready to roll."

"I'm really glad your mom talked to my dad."

"Is he still pissed?"

"No. But I did get a lecture on *proper investigative procedure*," she said, mimicking her dad's tone. He didn't need to know about her backyard expedition. Maybe she'd tell Jo, some day.

Jo laughed again. Nattie really liked how it sounded.

"So I was talking to my mom and it would be way rad if you came to dinner." Jo looked at her expectantly. "Like, tonight. Or tomorrow, if you're doing stuff tonight."

"Tonight should be cool. I'll call my dad and let him know."

"Tell him that me or my mom will drive you home."

"Okay. When should I come over?"

"Just come with me after school. You can meet the other dogs and we'll chill."

Nattie's heart was pounding almost as hard as it had been at the arena when she set Giorgio loose.

"Cool." But she didn't feel cool. She wiped one of her palms on her jeans and tried to make it look like that wasn't what she was doing.

The bell sounded. "Ready?" Jo asked as she grabbed her backpack and stood. "Yay, biology," she added with exaggerated excitement. "And we need to study for the test this week. Think you can pencil me in around all your investigations?"

Nattie grinned. "I think so." As she rose, she wondered how she didn't float away.

"Awesome. And do you think maybe I could help you out if you do any more detective stuff?"

"Um..."

"Unless Fred's your sidekick," Jo said with a sly little smile.

Nattie laughed. "Sometimes. But he complains the whole time."

"Well, I don't complain. And you can teach me *proper investigative procedure*." She imitated the tone Nattie had used earlier.

"Most definitely. You're hired."

"Awesome." Jo smiled. "Anyway. Really glad you're coming over."

Nattie smiled back. "Thanks for asking."

"Definitely. It's been really fun, hanging out with you. If I'm going to be a decent sidekick, we'll have to do that more."

Nattie's stomach felt like it had taken the first big drop on a roller coaster then shot up the other side.

"C'mon," Jo said. "Biology awaits."

And Nattie followed her into the school, thinking that this latest development most definitely required further investigation.

ROAR

By Linda M. Vogt

"COME ON, MEG!"

"Whaaaaat?"

"It's getting late."

"Whaaaaat?"

The deafening sounds of Katy Perry's pop tune "Roar" filled the small dance floor of the bar's back room, and I knew my girlfriend couldn't hear me. I danced a little closer to her, trying to keep the weird rhythm and formulate a thought at the same time. Kind of a stretch, especially after four Coronas in the past two hours.

"It's almost one-thirty!" I yelled. A cute dyke dancing next to us looked annoyed, but I didn't care.

"Oh, come on, Joey!" Meg hollered back over the din. She always called me Joey, and I liked it. It suited me so much better than Josephine, the big name my parents had hung on me. Besides, much like the girl in Robert Frost's poem, "Wild Grapes," I had been a "little boyish girl my older brother could not always leave at home." I was still a boyish girl, even at 24, with a boyish name. Meg, not so boyish. She loved femmy clothes and bright red lipstick. Okay with me. On her, I liked it.

Meg kept moving to the music, then motioned for me to come closer. She pulled her iPhone out of her pocket. "Let's do a selfie!" she shouted. "To remember this song and this night." I snuggled in close to her. Meg held the phone up high and took several shots. I hoped we didn't look too goofy, but, really, who cares?

The music kept blasting, the dancers kept moving, and Meg didn't look like she wanted to leave anytime soon. Everybody was singing along with Katy's feminist anthem about having the eye of the tiger, dancing in fire, and being champions—culminating in a giant crescendo when they all sang "Roar!" I was singing, too, and the blur created by drinking beer helped me not care how I sounded.

"I never really listened to those lyrics!" I shouted, hoping Meg could hear me over the boom of the bass. "It's about courage, that song. Cool!"

Meg smiled and nodded, and we kept dancing. Gyrating bodies were everywhere, and the place smelled faintly of sweat and a lot like beer. The dance floor was crowded for a Sunday night, but since it was the only lesbian bar in Portland, we all called it home.

"I have to be at work at eight." I was still worried about the time, and trying to appeal to her sensibilities, assuming she still had any. She'd had four white wines.

Meg grabbed my hand and pulled me toward her as "Roar" wound down and a slow one started. I didn't recognize the song, but I didn't care. She smelled sweet, like peaches.

"We'll leave after this one, okay?" Her eyes were smiling. Fine with me.

A WHOOSH OF COLD air blew past us as we opened the bar's back door that led to the off-street parking lot. Meg zipped up her red Columbia parka. "Love my new jacket," she said. "I'm cozy and warm inside it."

"Warm is good," I said. "It is October, after all."

The parking lot was jammed with cars. We stepped onto a sidewalk that ran adjacent to it just as three young guys in green and white Portland State lettermen jackets passed us. I heard them stop behind us, and one of them made a remark we couldn't make out. The other two laughed.

"Hey, butch girls!" one shouted. "Why don't you come party with us and have some real fun?"

"Keep walking," I said under my breath. We neared the back corner of the parking lot where we'd left the car. "They're probably drunk."

"Well, that's a coincidence 'cause we are, too," Meg said as she grabbed my hand. "Come on. Let's get out of here." The lot wasn't well-lit, and I felt a little tipsy and a little anxious. I fished in my jeans pocket for my car keys.

"You girls all right?" The voice startled us both, and Meg jumped. A guy in a baseball cap emerged from behind the bar. Neither of us had seen him. He wore a dark blue windbreaker with a yellow patch that said "Neighborhood Watch."

"Yeah, I guess so," I said.

"Those PSU guys hassle you?"

"Nah," Meg said, "not so much. They're just being college kids."

"I've been keeping an eye on them and some other yokels who like to hang around back here," the man said. "Just want to make sure it's safe for the gals who come out of the bar."

I wasn't sure who this guy was, but he seemed nice enough and I relaxed.

"Name's Karl Jones." He extended his hand and Meg shook it. I nodded a hello, and we introduced ourselves—first names only. He seemed okay, but I still didn't think we should give him any extra information.

He said, "Thought I should let you gals know that the Portland police are patrolling this neighborhood pretty heavily tonight. I just saw another young woman get pulled over for driving under the influence. The cops know this bar and they seem to enjoy ticketing whoever comes out, gets in a car and drives away."

As if on cue, a patrol car drove slowly by.

"See what I mean? It's one of the reasons we're out here, to make sure folks don't get cited."

"We?" I asked. "Who's 'we'?"

"Oh, sorry. I should have explained." He pointed to the patch on his jacket. "Neighborhood Watch is a bunch of volunteers trying to make sure this area is safe. We keep an eye out for any yahoos who might be causing trouble, and we help people so they don't get in a car and drive if they've had too much to drink. Stuff like that."

I was thinking about my four Coronas on an empty stomach. I felt a little tipsy, and I sure didn't need a drunk driving arrest.

Meg said, "So you call a cab for the inebriated, or what?"

"Sometimes. But at times we also give folks a ride home. It's okay to leave vehicles here overnight, so some people opt for that. Whatever works, I say."

Meg looked at me and raised her eyebrows. I shrugged. I had no idea what to do.

"You okay to drive?" Karl asked me as I jingled my keys. "Or shall I try to get you a cab?"

"We don't live far from here. I can probably do okay for that short distance," I said, still unsure if that was true.

"Maybe, but you won't get far if that cop pulls you over. If you've had more than three drinks, you probably won't pass a sobriety test, depending on how long you were in the bar."

Geez. I was screwed. I looked at Meg.

"Maybe we should have you get us that cab," she said. "Joey, we can come back for the car in the morning." Meg had always been the practical and reasonable one, ever since we were in college.

I acquiesced. "Okay, Karl. Thanks. I guess we'll take you up on that."

Karl pulled a cell phone out of his jacket. "Calling right now. Hang on." He punched in some numbers, and we waited in the dim light of the street lamp.

"Yeah. Need one down at Northwest Fifth and Davis," he said. "Oh. Really? That long?" He held the phone away from his ear. "The guy says it will be 45 minutes to an hour. Not many cabs running after one a.m."

Crap. Now what? Meg was looking at me like I should know what to do. Usually, I do. I like to take charge, be strong, figure things out. "We really can't wait that long," I said. I was thinking about having to be at the FedEx store at eight a.m. for the day shift. That hour was coming soon. "Thanks, anyway."

Karl ended the call, put the phone back in his pocket and frowned at me. "So, you're going to risk getting arrested, after all?"

Meg shook her head. "No, we can't. Maybe we should take you up on your offer of a ride."

This made me really uncomfortable. We didn't know Karl. He seemed friendly enough, but—a ride? I summoned up my most butch, capable self and said, "Well, maybe. We are just two exits down I-5. And I don't mean any disrespect, Karl, but we need to see some ID."

Karl laughed and reached for his back pocket. "Of course! I'd have to wonder about you if you didn't ask me. Can't be too careful these days." He flipped open a wallet, and in the dim light I saw an official "Neighborhood Watch" ID card with his photo and full name.

"Thanks, Karl," I said. "Guess we're your next fare."

"My car's right over here. Follow me." Karl opened the front passenger door for Meg, and I got in behind her in the back seat of his Nissan Pathfinder. I glanced behind the seat and saw various camping items in the back: camp chair, sleeping bag, tent, hatchet, ropes, water jug. The guy looked prepared.

"Camp a lot?" I asked as he slid behind the wheel.

"I do. Love Oregon camping in September and October. Great weather, no people."

"For sure. We love it, too. Last weekend we were over at Nehalem Bay State Park. Ever been there?"

"Sure. Down by Lincoln City, right?"

Geez, the guy sure didn't know his Oregon geography. "No. Over near Manzanita."

"Oh, yeah. I knew that. Guess I was thinking of someplace else."

Meg adjusted her seatbelt. "Nice car. I want to get an SUV like this someday."

"Lets you go anywhere," Karl said. "Gotta love four-wheel drive. You buckled up back there?"

I was, and said so. We were off, cruising slowly down the deserted streets of Portland toward the freeway on-ramp. We didn't see the patrol car anywhere, so I figured they'd stopped trying to ticket drunk lesbians. I thought if we'd waited a little while, I could have driven us home. Too late for that now.

Interstate 5 was nearly deserted at two a.m. We'd gone a couple miles and passed the Lake Oswego exit. "Next one is ours," I said. "Then the apartment is only about a minute off the freeway. Sure appreciate this."

"Right," Karl said. "Got it. No problem. I'm happy to help."

The Terwilliger exit was next, and just before it, Karl put on the right turn signal. I was feeling tired, still a little drunk, and so ready to be home and in bed. Meg looked like she was about to nod off.

"That's it," I said. "Terwilliger."

But Karl didn't turn off.

Meg was the first to speak. I was watching Karl from the side, trying to see his face and read his expression. I didn't want to panic, but I had a funny feeling in my stomach.

"Hey, Karl," Meg said. "That was our exit. You missed it, but you can take the next one and double back." She seemed to think he had made a mistake, but I was beginning to think he hadn't.

Karl silenced the turn signal. He held the steering wheel with his left hand, reached inside his jacket with his right, and pulled out a revolver. He pointed it at Meg.

I gasped. She screamed.

"Shut up!" he yelled. "Just do what I say." He waved the gun. "It's only a twenty-two but very effective at close range."

My mind raced. What could I do, stuck in the back seat of an SUV speeding down I-5? Why had we been so stupid? Who the hell is this guy, and how could I get us out of this? Save the girl, Joey! I felt powerless, terrified and panicked. This was bad.

Karl looked at me in his rear view mirror. "Don't do anything stupid, like trying to use your cell phones. "Everything will be okay if you just stay calm and do what I tell you." The tone of his voice had changed to menacing. "Get out your cell phones and drop them on the front seat here next to me."

What else could we do? Meg and I fished out our phones and followed his instructions.

"That wasn't so hard now, was it?"

I kept quiet.

Meg turned to look at me. Her eyes were filled with terror.

What had we done?

As Karl kept driving south along Interstate 5, no one spoke. What was he planning? Where were we going? I was suddenly more sober than I ever had been in my life. How could I get him to stop the car so we'd have a chance of escaping? At least forty miles flew by and my feeling of dread deepened. We were almost to Salem. He took the Highway 22 exit, and we headed east, away from the freeway and the city, and toward the black, black night.

Karl fumbled with something in his jacket pocket and brought out a small plastic container. Still driving, he flipped off the cap with his thumb. He handed a water bottle to Meg, and dropped a pill into her hand. He pointed the gun at her. "Take that."

She looked horrified.

"I said take it and wash it down! Then hand the other pill and the bottle to your girlfriend back there."

I didn't know what the pill was, but I did know that he wanted to drug us, and I couldn't let that happen.

"Why would we do that?" I said, thinking that our best hope was to try to change his mind.

"Because if you don't, we'll pull over right here on this dark stretch of highway and neither of you will see tomorrow. I'm already wanted by the cops, so I have nothing to lose. Is that a good enough reason?"

I didn't answer. Meg took the pill, put it in her mouth, took a drink and swallowed. Oh, God. Meg handed the pill container back to me. He watched me in the mirror. I popped a pill into my mouth, took the water bottle from Meg, and drank.

I swallowed.

"There," I said. "We both took it, whatever it is."

"Perfect. Now the fun can begin."

The pill stayed under my tongue until he looked away, and then I covered my mouth to cough and let the pill fall into my hand.

Meg said, "Please let us go. Please. You don't want to do this."

"Shut up."

Karl kept driving through the darkness, and I could see that we were headed for the mountains east of Salem. Very few people live along that highway, and at almost three a.m., no one would be around.

I had to think of something. Anything. We had to get out of the car.

Twenty minutes passed. I watched Meg to see if she showed any signs of being affected by the drug. She kept nodding and looked too relaxed. If she'd swallowed the pill, she would be unable to fight back if we could somehow get him to stop. How could I signal her that we needed to do something now? Would she even respond?

We'd passed farms, one tiny town where no one seemed to be around, and the turnoff to a campground along the Santiam River. Wherever Karl was headed, it was obvious there would be no one nearby to help. We were on our own.

I decided to act.

"Hey, I have to pee," I said, trying to slur my words. "Now. Really. You need to stop."

"You'll have to hold it 'til we get there," he said, watching me. "It won't be long. I have a nice place in mind for the three of us." His voice sounded creepy.

"Well, I can't wait. I need to go now. I had four beers at the bar. Geez. Stop the fucking car!" I thought maybe swearing would drive the point home. Karl slowed down.

"Meg," I said. "You okay? Need to pee?"

I leaned forward. Meg had her eyes closed and I watched her carefully as she opened them. "Huh? What?"

She seemed barely able to speak. God. She was definitely drugged.

"Uh huh. I do," she said in a sing-songy voice.

I started singing the Katy Perry song—the part about the tiger and the roar. Maybe it would give her the same idea I had: we need to fight back! She started humming along.

"Shut the fuck up, you two." Karl didn't seem to like Katy Perry.

I tried to make my voice sound slow and spacey even though I was totally on edge. "I'm going to pee all over your back seat. I'm warning you."

"Okay. Okay. I'll pull over. You can get out to pee, one at a time." He waved the gun in the air again. "But don't forget this."

He slowed the car and pulled over at a wide place along the highway. It looked like the start of someone's long driveway. There was a mailbox. Maybe someone lived down the lane, but I couldn't see any lights.

Karl stopped the car and turned off the headlights. The night was pitch black and stayed that way, even after my eyes adjusted. He turned to Meg. "You first. Go right there, by the car."

Meg unbuckled her seatbelt and opened the door. Karl undid his, too, and stepped out of the car. He ducked back in and said, "You stay put." He reached down and scooped up something. In the overhead light, I saw he had our phones in his hand. He ducked back out and slammed the door, then pitched them, one at a time, as far as he could into the darkness.

My heart beat fast and I knew this was our only chance. He had camping gear. He knew where he wanted to take us. We had no way to call for help.

Now or never.

I heard Meg's footsteps on the gravel. Quietly I unbuckled my seatbelt. Karl lit a cigarette. I could see his face in the glow of it. He pulled the revolver out of his jacket, held it in his right hand, and leaned against the car. Slowly, slowly I reached behind me with my left hand, still keeping my eyes on him. I felt the sleeping bag, the camp chair and . . . the hatchet. I pulled it into the back seat, slid the hatchet head under my armpit and the handle against my side.

God. Could I really do this?

"Jesus. How long does it take?" Karl walked around the other side of the car where Meg was pulling up her jeans. "That's enough time. Get back in your seat." I could barely see him, but the end of his cigarette glowed fire red when he inhaled. Meg opened her door. He came toward mine, in the back on the passenger side.

"Your turn, bitch" He grabbed the door handle. My mind screaming, I braced myself and managed to stay quiet.

Karl pulled the door open, and all in one swift motion, I yanked the hatchet out. I slid my feet to the ground, leaned forward to stand, and slammed the hatchet's blade end into his knee.

"Run, Meg!" I yelled. Karl dropped to the gravel on his other knee and screamed in pain. The gun fell from his hand. I shoved the car door fully open and bent to get the gun. He grabbed my ankle and upended me. The gun skittered away in the dark.

Karl let go of me to reach for the hatchet, which had been kicked under the car in the scuffle. I scrambled to my feet and ran, my breath hot and fast.

Meg had disappeared. My heart pounded in my ears. I kept running and didn't look back.

"God damn dyke!" Karl screamed.

He kept shouting, but his voice trailed away. I ran through the darkness, stumbled over rocks in some sort of plowed field.

The sound of a gunshot came, exploding through the night. I fell to the damp earth, waited, wondered if I'd been hit. How does it feel, getting shot? I felt nothing, only the agony of bursting lungs and pounding heart.

What if he'd shot at Meg? If it was Karl who had retrieved the gun,

Meg and I were both still in grave danger.

Thank God for a moonless night, black clothes and adrenaline. I stood up, took a quick look behind me. I barely made out a dark shape, moving slowly, but not toward where I was. Was he looking for Meg? I couldn't know that. I could only try to keep going and pray that she had gotten away. Where was she? How would we find each other without him finding us?

I ran.

Another gunshot.

Please, God, let her be okay.

As if in answer to my fear-driven prayer, a glimmer of headlights fell across the long driveway adjacent to the field. A car turned in, its lights reflecting off the Pathfinder that was parked not twenty feet from the driveway. The vehicle made its way slowly along the gravel lane. I crouched behind some bushes, watching the car go by. I couldn't risk trying to get the driver's attention. Karl was still out there somewhere. Besides, I didn't know who the driver was. Too risky.

I kept low and made my way along the drive, where a line of scrubby bushes was my only cover. The car had gone on down the driveway—toward a house, maybe? The lane dipped just ahead, so even if it weren't so dark, I couldn't see what was at the end of it.

I stopped, listened, tried to see if Karl was moving. The dark night made it impossible. I didn't know where he was.

Then, a perplexing sight: Karl's headlights came on. Had he gone back to the car? I heard the engine start up and saw the Pathfinder peel out, the tires spitting gravel as he pulled onto the deserted highway. What the hell? Either he was badly injured, or the fact that someone had seen his car parked there spooked him. Or—I froze at this thought—did he have Meg with him? Were they both gone?

"Meg!" I hollered into the night. "Where are you?"

No answer.

The car that had passed by a minute earlier was slowly coming back up the drive, toward the highway. I decided I had to take a chance. I waved my arms and yelled "Please! Stop!"

The woman behind the wheel looked right at me, her pale face frightened, but she kept on driving. As she passed, I saw that the back seat of her station wagon was piled high with newspapers wrapped in plastic bags. She was delivering *The Oregonian*. Of course. That's why she was out at this ungodly hour. She sped up at the end of the lane, and I watched her taillights disappear in the same direction on the highway that Karl had gone.

Jesus. Now what? "Meg!"

No answer.

If Meg was hurt, or lying dead somewhere, there was no way I would find her in the black of the night. If Karl had found her and she was back in that car, would I ever see her again? I had to get to the house at the end of the driveway and hope someone would help.

I ran, hoping I didn't fall in the dark. The gravel crunched beneath my feet. I was alive, Karl was gone, but the dread of what had happened to Meg was all I could think about.

I picked up speed on the way down the sloping drive. A porch light glowed dim in the distance. Finally! I kept running toward what I hoped would be help. At the porch, I stopped. Would someone come to the door in the middle of the night? How would they react? I had no choice.

My knock made a loud, angry sound in the stillness.

A light came on inside.

"Who are you? What do you want?" a man's voice asked through the door.

"Please! I'm hurt. My friend and I were kidnapped. I need your help."

"I'm calling the police."

Well, I thought, that's a good idea. "Will you open the door?

"I will not." He sounded indignant. "Do you know what time it is?"

I had no freaking clue what time it was, but I decided he didn't really want an answer to that question. At least he was calling the police.

I waited under the porch light wondering how far it was to the nearest town? How long would it take?

I saw a curtain move and the silhouette of someone looking out. I waited some more. Suddenly, headlights appeared along the driveway along with the red and blue lights of a police car, which stopped in front of the house. A sheriff's deputy stepped out, his hand on his holster.

"Please stay where you are, Ma'am. We had a call from a motorist that there was a woman out here who might be injured or in trouble. I'm thinking it was you. Are you all right?"

For a moment, it crossed my mind to wonder if the cops were even safe. What if "Mr. Neighborhood Watch" had law enforcement accomplices?

I had to make a split-second decision. The cop *seemed* safe.

"I'm okay, but we were kidnapped," I blurted out. "And my friend's still out there somewhere and could be hurt. Or he may still have her. Or she could be dead. He shot at us." I realized I was babbling. I stopped.

"Who shot at you?"

"Karl. But maybe that's not his real name. The guy who kidnapped us in Portland. He's still out there."

"Where did he go?"

"He took off in a dark green Pathfinder." I pointed. "He went that way."

"East?"

"Whatever. And my friend could be with him. I hope not, but I don't know."

The deputy walked over, put his hand on my shoulder. "I'll call it in. We'll find him. I'm Deputy Collins. What's your name?"

I told him. The front door opened, and an elderly man stepped out onto the porch. "Everything okay, officer?" he asked, looking warily at me.

"It is, sir. You can go back inside."

"I called nine-one-one when she knocked on my door," the man said. "My wife's scared. What the blazes is going on?"

"You folks will be okay," the deputy said. "Just go back inside and keep your doors locked. I'll take this woman back to the station."

The old man retreated into his house. I heard him slide the deadbolt into place. The porch light went off.

"But we have to find Meg!" I said. I was beginning to panic.

"We will. Come on. Get in the car."

The deputy opened the back door of the patrol car, as though I was a prisoner. What the hell? "Can't I sit in the front?"

"Protocol, Ma'am," he said. "Let's look for your friend."

Deputy Collins turned the patrol car around, and we headed slowly up the long driveway. He flipped a switch, and a powerful spotlight mounted near his mirror shone into the darkness. He moved the light back and forth along the gravel lane as we made our way toward the highway.

"Where did you see her last—your friend?" he asked. "Did you see her get in the car with him?"

"I never saw her again after I hit him with the hatchet."

"You did what?"

"It was self-defense."

"Where did the hatchet come from?"

"He had it with some camping gear in the back of the car. I swung the hatchet into his knee, and Meg and I both ran." I said this matter-of-factly, as though I did these things all the time.

"That was pretty courageous of you. Especially if he had a gun. Seems like you're pretty lucky to have gotten away."

"It would have turned out badly if we'd stayed in that car. We had to get out of there. It was our only chance."

"So, he's injured? That should help us find him. He may need medical attention."

"I'm pretty sure he will. I think I hit bone."

The deputy glanced at me in the rear-view mirror but kept driving. I focused on scanning both sides of the long driveway.

Nothing. No sign of Meg. We were almost back to the highway.

"If she ran from the car, which way do you think she might have gone?" he asked. "Maybe along the main road?"

"I didn't see where she went. I only know she couldn't have been anywhere near me, because I called her name and she never answered." I didn't say what I was thinking: she *couldn't* answer, either because she'd been shot, or because Karl had found her first. I could only hope that the reason Meg didn't respond was that so drugged that she wasn't able to.

Collins said, "Let's try the highway back toward town."

A deep ditch filled with water ran alongside the highway. When the searchlight passed over the ditch, I saw color.

Red!

"Stop the car!"

He slammed on the brakes and redirected the searchlight.

"There she is!" I said. I tried to open my door, but couldn't get out.

"Hang on. I'm coming," the deputy said.

He'd barely disengaged the latch before I launched out, and we both scrambled down the embankment.

Meg lay face up in the ditch, her left leg submerged in dark, murky water. She was moaning.

"It's okay, Ma'am. I'm a sheriff's deputy. We're here. You're safe."

Meg mumbled something I couldn't hear, but the deputy must have because he said, "Yes, Ma'am, looks like you may be injured. Come on. I'll help you up."

In the bright glow of the searchlight, Meg looked drugged. Then she saw me and mustered a crooked grin.

"Are you all right?" I asked. I got an arm around her to help Collins bring her up the embankment.

"I think I can still roar."

The deputy looked confused.

I smiled back at Meg.

We had survived.

TWO DAYS LATER, BACK home in Portland, the phone rang.

"Josephine Barton?" a female voice asked.

"Yes. That's me."

Meg was on the couch, bandage on her left leg, her eyes closed. The gunshot wound was superficial, the doctor had said, but she needed to rest. We both did.

"This is Detective Morgan with Portland Police. We have identified your assailant from the photos on one of the cell phones the officers found at the crime scene. Karl Leroy Wilson is a known felon, served time for rape, and is wanted in four states. He's kidnapped young women before. We've put out an APB. It's just a matter of time."

I shuddered. We had come so close to disaster. "Thanks for letting us know."

"Of course. You two were a big help. When we apprehend him, I'll call you. Shouldn't take too long. We have his name, his vehicle description and a photo, all thanks to you. Nice work."

I felt odd, being complimented for what we'd done to survive the terrifying ordeal. Odd, but good.

"I'm glad we could help. I'll testify against him, if you need me to."

She thanked me again and hung up.

"What did she say?" Meg asked.

"They're going to catch the bastard because of the photo. Good thing you decided to take those selfies while we were dancing. There he was, in the background. I don't even remember seeing him in the bar, but he was watching us. And the police identified him from that picture. We did good."

"We did, indeed. I'm proud of us."

The Katy Perry song came floating back into my head. "Know what? We're champions!"

Meg just smiled. I love that smile.

AUTHOR'S NOTE: This fictional story is based on an actual event that happened in 2010 to someone I care about. Since the time I wrote the story in late 2014, human remains were found in the vicinity of where the two women escaped. The Oregon State Medical Examiner's Office has determined the remains to be from the man, a registered sex offender, who kidnapped these women outside a Portland nightclub/concert venue. We are all grateful for closure, and to know he can't harm anyone else.

JUST DESSERTS

By VK Powell

"In the matter of the State versus Milton Langley, has the jury reached a decision?"

The judge looked over the top of his wire-rimmed glasses, and I clenched my fists until my palms ached. I'd worked the investigation, and from a police perspective, it was airtight. The sick bastard was a pedophile, plain and simple, but juries were fickle.

The jury foreman mumbled, almost inaudibly, "We have, your honor."

Three victims' parents sat behind the prosecutor's table, their children waiting in another room, shielded from this predator. Langley's wife and teenaged stepdaughter sat two rows behind the defense table, the young girl hunched forward as if praying. She'd refused, or been forbidden, to talk to me during the investigation. But she didn't have to talk. The signs of abuse were obvious in her tentative walk, inability to make eye contact, and hypervigilance around strangers. If her stepfather didn't go to prison, there was no justice in the world.

"How do you find on three counts of statutory rape and indecent liberties with a minor?" the judge asked.

Visibly shaking, the foreman stared at the verdict form in his hand. He couldn't make eye contact with the judge, prosecutor, or the parents. I knew what he was going to say before his lips moved.

"We, the jury, find the defendant, Milton Langley, not guilty."

The parents' wails were muted as fury blanketed everything around me in a thick, red haze. The judge's gavel made no sound as it landed repeatedly and he tried to restore order. The case file—photographs, statements, timeline, and physical evidence—flashed through my mind like the hypothesized end-of-life movie. I was halfway to the front of the courtroom on automatic pilot when my partner, Jerry, grabbed my arm and pulled me toward the exit.

"Let's go, Syl. This isn't the time or place."

"Get off me. Seriously." The stare I gave him would've stopped most men in their tracks, but Jerry was braver than most. He had no idea how close he was to getting punched in the face. I'd never been so furious over a verdict, but this one was wrong on so many levels.

"I know it's not right, but you can't do anything about it now. You've done your best."

As he pulled me toward the door, I said, "I obviously haven't, but I'll correct that."

"Syl, don't say another word."

We walked to the top floor of the Greene Street parking deck and to the side railing. We came here often to brainstorm cases, pacing the open-air concrete slab, coffee cups in hand. The view over the city's western skyline usually comforted and inspired me, but today the gathering clouds suited my mood perfectly. "I can't believe that just happened, Jerry."

"I know. It sucks the big one."

"I've never been so certain of a suspect's guilt. Why couldn't the jury see it? We worked the case together from start to finish. Did we miss something? If we did, I'll never forgive myself. Those poor kids...and their parents. None of them will ever be the same. And that bastard gets to walk free? I don't think so. If he was here right now, I'd toss him over this railing and watch with pleasure as he flailed eight stories to the ground."

"I know how you feel, Syl, but you can't say stuff like that to anyone...but me. We did everything exactly right, by the book, but you know juries. They're unpredictable. Who knows what went on during deliberations."

"I won't be able to let this case go until I know what happened. If we made a mistake, I have to be damn sure we never make it again. How will we ever look those parents in the eyes again? I told them he would do time, lots of time. And his stepdaughter. Did you see the look on her face when the foreman read the verdict? I thought she was going to be sick."

Jerry put his bearlike hand on my shoulder. "You know I'm with you, right? Just don't do anything stupid. We'll talk to a couple of the jurors when things calm down. In the meantime, take a day off and clear your head. You're my partner and I'm not looking for another one. Maybe you and Lois could take a day trip somewhere."

Jerry's six-foot-five frame and bulky muscles gave him a formidable presence, but when he went into dad mode, it was almost humorous. "Are you trying to handle me? Does this not-so-subtle approach work with your teenagers?"

"Not usually. They see through me just like you do, but it's always worth a try before I get serious. Just promise you won't get into any trouble."

"Sure."

"No, I mean it, Syl. Promise me."

I raised my right hand and placed my left over where my badge would've been if I were in uniform. "I, Sylvia Cutter, do solemnly swear I won't do anything stupid, whatever that means, until I've had a chance to cool down." I lowered my hands and started toward the stairs. "Happy?"

"Nervous and worried. You ready to go home?"

"Yeah, but I think I'll walk."

His brow furrowed before he broke into a wide grin. "Ah, I know where you're going—Jacques'. Am I right?"

"You know me too well, partner. Nothing soothes this savage beast like chocolate. See you later."

When I stepped into Jacques Chocolates, I felt like I was in a European specialty shop. The space was narrow with small tables, centerpiece flowers, and soft Mediterranean music that made it feel intimate. Jacques specialized in fresh, handcrafted chocolates that I usually enjoyed while sipping a latte, and I always took Lois a freshly baked *pain au chocolat*. Today I'd need handfuls of chocolate.

"Sylvia, so nice to see you again." I loved the way his heavy French accent made my name sound exotic.

"Jacques, how are you?"

"*Tres bon*, but you not so much, I suspect. I heard the verdict. *C'est horrible.*"

"It is indeed, my friend. Could I have two dark chocolate bonbons, two milk chocolate covered gingers, and a milk chocolate-dipped praline—and a skinny latte."

"Of course." Jacques studied me as he gathered the order and brought it to my usual table in the back corner. He'd placed two small brownies on the plate as well. "Would you try these for me, please? I'm testing something for my gluten-free customers."

"I'll force myself."

He lingered at the table, wiping his hands on his apron and looking like a child with something to confess. "All the kids involved in your case come in with their parents. I've seen them change from carefree children to wounded victims. I feel so sorry for them. And Langley's poor stepdaughter comes in, for the same reason as you, I think—consolation. She seems very sad."

"Does *he* ever come in with her?" My first bite of chocolate ginger tasted slightly off, probably didn't mix well with the thought of *him*.

"Sometimes, yes, and she always seems terrified. She wants

chocolate pecan brownies, but he makes her get plain. Such a disagreeable man." He mumbled something in French and twisted his apron like a huge lump of dough.

"I don't know what you said, but I'd probably agree. He's a despicable individual who should be serving the rest of his life in prison, if not waiting to die on death row."

"Is there nothing you can do, Sylvia?"

"I'm still trying to figure that out. If people could be put down like rabid animals, he'd be first on my list."

"I'm sorry. I know you will do what you can, but the police are so restricted sometimes. It's not right, just not right. I'll let you enjoy your desserts." Jacques returned to the counter, shaking his head and occasionally muttering in French.

After he'd gone, I cleansed my palate with a couple of sips of latte and tried the two brownies. The only difference I could determine was the slightly denser texture of one. "What's with the brownies? They taste almost the same to me."

"That's good news. One is made with almond flour, so my gluten-free customers should be happy."

"I'll be your guinea pig any time, Jacques."

I'd just plopped another chocolate ginger in my mouth when one of the bailiffs from the courthouse walked in. His step faltered slightly when he saw me, but he continued to my table.

"I'm so sorry about the verdict, Cutter."

"Yeah, but it wasn't your fault. Do you have any idea what they were thinking inside that room? Did they consider the evidence at all?"

"I don't know, but I plan to find out. I just wish the jailers had been a bit slower last week. The problem might've solved itself."

"What do you mean?" I offered him a seat but he shook his head.

"Langley had a reaction to the food, and the jailers had to shoot him with an Epi-pen. He's apparently pretty allergic to nuts. If only..." His voice trailed off as he turned back toward the counter. "See you."

Sometimes being good at your job just didn't pay.

AFTER A RESTLESS NIGHT from caffeine and chocolate overload mingled with images of Milton Langley going free, I slid out of bed trying not to wake Lois. She reached for me, but I kissed her cheek and tucked the covers back around her. "It's still early. Go back to sleep."

"I love you, Sylvia Cutter. Never forget." Lois always knew exactly what to say even when talking in her sleep. I needed to hear those words this morning.

I pulled on sweats and a T-shirt and hit the button on the coffee maker on the way to get the morning paper. My first steaming cup of rejuvenation was halfway to my lips when I saw the headline: *Langley Freed and Died Same Day.* If I hadn't been so shocked, the dark liquid soaking into my T-shirt and through to my skin would probably have hurt much worse.

The article was short on details, just that Milton Langley had been found dead in his home late last night by his wife, cause of death as yet undetermined. The remainder of the half-page article recounted the rape charges against him, the trial, and subsequent verdict. I reached for my cell phone to call Jerry but it vibrated in my hand as he rang in.

"Yeah?"

"Tell me you didn't do this," Jerry said.

"Wish I could claim it, but no, I didn't. How did he die?"

"I talked to one of the homicide detectives handling the case and he wouldn't say. The captain has put a tight lid on it, and he wants to see both of us ASAP."

"Does he think we're involved?"

"I think he just wants to head off any outside speculation. Anybody who was looking could see how upset you were about the verdict. Tell me you have an alibi for last night."

"Does my lover count?"

"Probably not, but it's better than nothing. See you at the station in twenty."

When Jerry and I walked in, Captain Brady was tapping his number-two pencil on the desk and staring at us like we were suspects. "You know why you're here."

"I have no idea," I said. "I'm supposed to be off work today. Why don't you tell us what's going on. A sick pedophile dies and suddenly we're hauled in for questioning? Class act."

Brady shook his head. "Shut up, Cutter. You're not really suspects. The homicide guys aren't questioning you, are they? I just need to know where you both were last night. This case meant a lot to you and it didn't turn out the way you'd hoped."

"So I resorted to murder because I'm pissed? Thanks, Cap."

"Just tell me where you were and let's move on."

Jerry answered first. "I worked extra duty at the coliseum until after midnight. You can check the duty roster. Sergeant Miller was the on-scene supervisor."

Brady turned to me.

"I was at home having sex with my beautiful wife."

"Too much information," Brady said.

"You asked."

"Did you go out at all, talk to anyone on the phone, or have any visitors?"

"No, but we ordered pizza for dinner, if that helps."

Brady scribbled on his notepad. "It might, if it comes to that."

I stood and retrieved my weapon from the holster. "You want to check my weapon, test my hands for gunshot residue, what?"

"Put that away. And that's another reason why we need to clear both of you...and the parents. This wasn't simply a case of someone being pissed off and taking a shot or shoving a knife in the guy's gut. It was a sneak attack. Look at this."

He shoved a photo across his desk and I leaned forward without touching it. Milton Langley looked like he'd been underwater for days and started to bloat. The tip of his swollen tongue protruded slightly between bluish lips and his eyes were puffy slits. "What the hell?"

"Holy shit," Jerry said. "He didn't look anything like this in court. Was it drugs?"

Brady retrieved the photograph. "We're not sure yet. The medical examiner is conducting the autopsy this morning. She ruled out gunshot or knife wounds and manual asphyxiation because of the lack of petechial hemorrhaging and markings around the neck, but everything else is still being considered. Do either of you have any ideas or suggestions?"

"Yeah," I said, "I have a suggestion. Don't even think about questioning his victims' parents today. They've been through enough—their children brutally victimized, a drawn-out investigation, public humiliation in court topped off by an incredibly unjust verdict." Blood rushed to my face and the anger from yesterday rose again.

Brady shrugged, but his eyes were filled with regret. One of the down sides of investigating any serious crime was repeatedly gouging the emotional wounds of our victims in the name of justice.

"Please don't do it, Captain. Haven't they suffered enough?"

"You know I can't interfere with the investigation. They'll have to be questioned at some point."

Even if I'd ever considered killing Milton Langley, this was one of the reasons I'd have resisted the temptation. "Can't they give it a few days? Let them have time to grieve the outcome of the trial. Though

I'm sure they're ecstatic that Langley's dead, the injustice of that verdict has got to hurt. Can't we give them some time?"

"I'll recommend it to the homicide detectives, but I can't make any promises. So, *do* either of you have any idea how this happened?"

I couldn't resist. "If you're asking me, I'd say poetic justice. And if I knew who'd done it, I'd give him a medal. This guy deserved killing." I suppressed a grin. "Just saying."

"Thanks for that, Cutter," Brady said. "Get out of here and don't talk to the press about this *at all*. Am I clear?"

"Crystal," Jerry said, but I just nodded.

When we stepped outside the station, I pumped the air with my fist and shouted, "Thank you, God!"

"You're entirely too happy about this. Are you sure you—"

"Been there, covered that," I said.

Jerry was smiling, so I knew he wasn't serious.

"I did not have anything to do with his death, but I'm also not sorry he's gone. It couldn't have happened to a more deserving guy. Now, if you don't mind, I'm off, and I'm going to stop by Jacques' for a celebratory chocolate. Then, I'm going to take my wife a treat and maybe, if I'm lucky, she'll respond in kind."

JACQUES WAS CLEARING A table on the sidewalk in front of his place when I walked up. I snagged two cups to help out and followed him inside. "And a very good morning to you, Sylvia. Isn't it a beautiful day?"

"It is indeed, Jacques."

"Your usual?"

"I'll have one custard-filled and one chocolate-filled éclair with my latte. To go. And if your *pain au chocolat* is fresh, I'll have a couple of those for Lois."

While Jacques prepared my order, he slid a copy of the morning paper across the counter. "Sometimes the news is not all bad, no?"

"Yeah, sometimes."

"Last night I took that poor girl some chocolates on my way home. I thought she could probably use a treat. I couldn't face the father, so I left them on the doorstep and rang the doorbell."

"That was nice of you, Jacques." Then I remembered the bailiff's comment about Langley's allergy. "What kind of chocolates?"

"Her favorite with pecans...and some of my gluten-free brownies. You never know who is watching their wheat intake these days. Can't be too careful."

If Langley was deathly allergic to nuts, he'd surely be smart enough not to eat the pecan chocolates, but if he didn't know the brownies were made with almond flour...

I dropped the money for my desserts on the counter as I collected my order and ducked into the alley beside Jacques' shop.

My heart rate spiked as I considered the situation. Jacques, an upstanding businessman and compassionate human being, while trying to comfort a distraught child, had inadvertently poisoned and killed a sick, sadistic pedophile.

Or did he know about Langley's allergy?

Should I tell the homicide detectives? Would the medical examiner rule the death suspicious or accidental? The letter of the law made my decision clear, but the spirit of the law left room for interpretation.

I gripped the bag of chocolates in my fist and walked toward home. One more day wouldn't make Milton Langley any less dead or me any more culpable. And by tomorrow, I might even change my mind completely. Sometimes Lady Justice exacted her own revenge and it was much sweeter than any dessert.

SEASONS OF DECEPTION

By Kate McLachlan

BEATRICE PULLED INTO HER driveway and saw that Kenny Wingate had built a haunted house on his front porch. All month long the orange Halloween lights lining his eaves flashed through her windows on the other side of the cul-de-sac, keeping her awake at night. At Christmas time Kenny's yard was filled with giant inflatable reindeer and Santa Clauses. On the Fourth of July he lined his yard with tiny flags and shot off the loudest fireworks. Aside from Kenny, it was a quiet neighborhood, and residents kept to themselves. Kenny was the closest thing they had to a kid.

Kenny Wingate was seventy-four years old.

On this particular day, he had a new dog, which caused Beatrice to break from her usual habit of a casual wave and tiny smile. She got out of the car just as Kenny walked by, still wearing his usual uniform of Birkenstocks and many-pocketed shorts, his ropy legs tanned from near year-round exposure to the sun. Instead of closing the garage door, she stepped out to the sidewalk.

"You have a new dog," she said.

"Yes." He smiled and bent to pat the dog's head. It barely reached mid-calf, but he was limber despite his age. "This is Doro. She's a Shih Tzu."

Beatrice leaned down and let the dog lick her fingers. "Hi Doro. You're a cutie." She rose. "What happened to Nellie?"

"I had to put her down last week."

"I'm sorry."

"Yeah. She was sixteen, though, and the pain pills weren't working anymore. I couldn't let her suffer."

"I understand."

"I didn't see the point in waiting," Kenny said. "It's no good being alone, you know." Beatrice did not answer. "Besides, if I'd waited, I would have missed out on Doro here."

"Mm hmm."

"If this weather holds, maybe I can get you to come over for a barbecue."

"Sure." Beatrice knew the weather wouldn't hold. A hard frost was forecast for the end of the week. "See you around."

"Take care."

She entered the kitchen through the garage, hung her keys, and dropped her purse over a chair. "Honey, Kenny's got a new dog," she said. "Named Doro."

"Short for Dorothy, I bet," Leigh said. "He's so gay."

"He only put Nellie down last week. I don't see how he could replace her so soon."

"Some people are ready to move on sooner than others."

Beatrice said, "Well, I'm not ready."

"Too bad," Leigh said.

BEATRICE DIDN'T PAY MUCH attention to the strange absence of Christmas decorations at Kenny's house later that year. She left for work in the morning before the sun rose, and she returned after it set. She didn't have much holiday spirit anyway. Snow fell, it melted, fell and melted again. A glaze of ice coated the sidewalks and never really went away until March.

She would have seen Kenny on the weekends if he'd been out and about, but she didn't realize she hadn't until one Saturday when he went past in a strange car, a blue Toyota Prius. He was the passenger, and the driver was a woman. He didn't see Beatrice, though she waved. He stared straight ahead and looked small.

She grabbed three reusable grocery bags in each hand and hauled them into the kitchen, her knuckles cracking from the weight.

Leigh said, "You just can't stand to make more than one trip from the car, can you?"

"I hate wasting steps," Beatrice said. "Besides, I don't see you helping."

"I would if I could."

Beatrice instantly felt bad. "I'm sorry."

"It's okay. I know."

Beatrice reached into the first bag. "I saw Kenny in a car with a woman. She was driving. She looked young enough to be his daughter, or granddaughter even. He never had any kids, did he?"

"Not that I know of. I don't think he has any family at all."

"I didn't either. In fact," Beatrice paused with a pack of tofu in her hand, "I know he doesn't, now that I think of it. He told me once he was an only child and that his bloodline would die with him. I wonder who that woman was."

"A friend?"

"Maybe. I was surprised he wasn't driving his regular car. He loves that old Monte Carlo but he was in a Prius."

"Maybe he's getting too old."

"If he is, it happened fast. Besides, seventy-four isn't that old."

"Speaking of getting old, have you decided what to do about Christmas?"

Beatrice closed the refrigerator door with her butt and slumped against it. "I don't want to go anywhere. I just want to stay here with you."

"Your family will be disappointed."

Beatrice sighed. "I don't care. I'm just so tired of people telling me I have to move on."

BEATRICE DIDN'T SEE KENNY's dog again until spring. Doro was being walked by the same woman who had driven the Prius. She was short and wore dark glasses with thick round lenses.

Curiosity tugged. Beatrice donned a jacket and caught up with her on the sidewalk. "Hi," Beatrice said. "This is Kenny's dog, isn't it? Doro?"

"Yes." The woman tried to keep moving, but Doro had ideas of her own. She lunged for Beatrice, stretching the leash taut. Beatrice squatted and let the dog jump on her knees.

"I haven't seen Kenny around much. Is he all right?"

"He's fine." The woman gave a tight smile. "I'm taking care of him."

Beatrice blinked. "Does he need someone to take care of him?"

"Well, he's not getting any younger."

Beatrice let Doro down and stood. "He seemed great the last time I saw him."

"He's fine," the woman said again. "Just needs a little help, that's all. You know, remembering things."

"Huh." Beatrice used the same doubting tone she'd used with fractious witnesses when she was still a prosecutor. "Can't he even walk Doro?"

"It's easier if I do it. He's too slow."

"Slow? What happened?"

"Nothing happened. He's getting old, that's all."

"Really."

The woman's lips narrowed and she frowned at Doro, who circled a shrub for the third time. "Hurry up, dog. I haven't got all day." She reversed direction and headed back around the cul-de-sac toward Kenny's house. Doro scrambled at the end of the leash behind her.

Beatrice watched until they entered Kenny's house before returning to her own.

"I don't trust that woman," Beatrice said, throwing her jacket at a chair.

"Why not?" Leigh asked.

"She's not nice to that dog. Her little legs were spinning trying to keep up with her."

"At least she was walking her."

"For the first time in months."

"You don't know that," Leigh said. "You haven't been home to see if they walked by."

"Doro didn't like her. Besides, Kenny was fine last fall. How did he get too slow to walk Doro in this short period of time?"

"Maybe he had some medical issues since then. People that age do."

"Then why didn't she say so? She says he's fine, but she talks about him like he's not. He's so old he can't even walk that little dog anymore? Last year at this time he was skateboarding. People don't get that old overnight."

"Some do."

"Anyway, I think I can tell when people are telling the truth or not. That's my job, after all. I don't believe her."

"What exactly do you think she was lying about?"

"He's not fine. If he was fine, he would be walking Doro."

BEATRICE MISSED THE RED, white, and blue petunias Kenny planted every summer. This year, his flower boxes remained empty. She was on her knees on her front lawn wrestling with a sprinkler head when she heard the woman's voice.

"Get in the car!"

Beatrice looked up.

The Prius idled in front of Kenny's house. The woman sat in the driver's seat, her head barely visible above the steering wheel. Beatrice saw movement at the front porch.

Kenny descended the stairs. There were only three steps, but he took them gingerly, lowering his left foot and securing it before bringing his right down. He gripped the railing with one hand and cradled Doro in his other arm. Finally, he reached the bottom of the stairs and shuffled forward, his gait so unsteady she thought for a moment he was going to fall.

Beatrice leapt to her feet, but he steadied himself and moved forward.

The woman beeped the horn, stuck her head out the window, and shouted, "I said get in the goddamn car!"

Kenny moved more quickly and wobbled a bit. Beatrice dropped her spade and ran forward. She was too far away to help, but he didn't fall. By the time she reached him, he had opened the car door, dropped Doro inside, and was lowering himself to the seat.

"Kenny," Beatrice said.

He looked up and squinted, as if unsure how he knew her, but he couldn't stop his momentum. He fell back into the seat with a grunt. Doro scrambled onto his lap. He started to close the door, but Beatrice grabbed it and studied him.

The day was hot, but instead of the shorts and Birkenstocks she was accustomed to seeing him in during the summer, he wore long tan trousers stained in the front and a limp green sweater. He had always been a trim man, but he had lost at least twenty pounds and was gaunt as a skeleton. His face was pale.

"Kenny, what happened to you?"

He blinked and shook his head as if to say he didn't know. He put a hand out to her, fingers trembling.

"We're running late," the woman said. "No time to talk." She leaned over Kenny's lap and reached for the door handle. Before she could close the door, though, Kenny grabbed Doro and thrust her through the opening. Beatrice caught the dog, and the woman wrenched the door closed. She yanked the seat belt at Kenny's shoulder, pulled it across his chest to latch it, and quickly latched her own. She hit the gas and sped away from the curb.

Beatrice turned and sprinted home. "I'm calling Adult Protective Services," she told Leigh breathlessly. She put the dog on the kitchen floor. "That woman is horrible."

"What did she do?"

Beatrice explained what had happened while Doro hid behind a table leg and barked in Leigh's direction. "What's wrong with that dog?"

Leigh said, "I don't think she likes me."

"Anyway, the woman tore out of there practically burning rubber."

"In a Prius?"

"I know, can you believe it?" Beatrice grabbed her phone and Googled the number for Adult Protective Services.

"What are you going to tell them?" Leigh asked. "That she swore? That she drives like a teenager? She let him give you his dog? They'll think you're a crackpot."

"No, they won't. I'm a judge."

"That and five dollars will get you a latte, love."

"There's more going on than that," Beatrice said, but Leigh was right. Beatrice was familiar enough with Adult Protective Services to know that the immediate response to a report like hers would be a cursory investigation. An APS investigator knocking on Kenny's door would accomplish little and only tip the woman off.

She dropped the phone in her pocket, put some water in a bowl for Doro, and tried to think what to do. A rustling at the front door drew her attention and she saw the mail carrier stepping away from her porch. She had an idea.

"I'm going over there."

"What for?" Leigh asked.

"Maybe she's getting mail there. I'm going to find out who this mysterious woman is."

"Tampering with the mail is a federal offense, Bea."

"I'm not going to tamper with it. I'm just going to look at it."

"What about the dog? You can't leave her here with me. She doesn't like me."

Doro had her head on her paws. Low growling sounds rumbled in her throat.

"I'll only be gone a minute." Beatrice slipped out the door.

To make herself look like a legitimate visitor, she knocked on Kenny's front door. As expected, no one answered. The mailbox was mounted beside the door. She opened the lid and peeked in. The box was nearly full and didn't appear to have been emptied for days. She sorted through plenty of junk mail, some bills, an envelope from the state, and two from the bank, including one addressed to Melanie Wingate.

Beatrice was surprised at how strong the temptation was to take that letter. A standard lecture she gave when sentencing criminals was to urge them to exercise self-discipline and resist temptation. Aside from some petty shoplifting as a teen, for which she was never caught, Beatrice had never been tempted to commit a crime. Until now. She silently lectured herself and closed the lid of the mailbox.

She rounded the house and let herself through the back gate. She was trespassing, but that was only a misdemeanor. It was one thing to read someone's mail coming in, but it was something else to read it going out. No matter how many times people were warned to shred their discarded mail, hardly anyone ever did.

The brown garbage bin beside the back porch was piled high with trash, its lid flopped open. The blue recycling bin was on its side, also with the lid open, and it was empty. Based on the leaves and debris that had blown inside, it had been lying there for some time. Doro's tiny piles of poop littered the yard, an accumulation of weeks, if not months. Kenny's yard had always been immaculate.

Beatrice approached the garbage bin. The muck that filled it was not bagged. Cans and bottles, paper, and empty cartons were mixed in with the trash, which explained the empty recycling bin. Kenny had always been an avid recycler. Melanie, apparently, was not. Nor was she a vegetarian. Bones and skin and grease layered much of the trash and raised an overpowering stink. Beatrice hadn't eaten meat in years. The look and smell of the rotted flesh in Kenny's garbage bin was too much. There was no way she could stick her hands in it.

She debated whether she should get Kenny's hidden key and snoop inside, but that was going too far. Instead, she fled around to the front of the house, darted up the steps, and snatched the mail from the mailbox.

"OKAY, I TAMPERED." BEATRICE tossed the mail on the dining room table and sat. Doro leaped onto her lap and licked her face.

"Oh, Bea."

"I know. I couldn't help it. But it's okay. I know how to open it and reseal it just like new." She put the old teakettle on. "Her name is Melanie Wingate. Same last name as Kenny, so she must be a relative after all."

After holding the glue strip of each envelope over the arrow of steam coming from the kettle's spout, Beatrice was able to pry open each envelope. She spread them out on the table and took tally. "The state pension fund sent him a change of beneficiary form. Who's he going to name—Melanie? And the bills aren't getting paid, some of them anyway. The cable bill's up to date, and someone made a double payment on the utilities last month, but the mortgage hasn't been paid in four months. These medical bills are going to collection." She compared Kenny's bank statements to Melanie's. "Cash has been going out of Kenny's account every month, right after his pension goes in.

And look, she gets a deposit at the same time for the same amount. She's stealing from him, Leigh!"

"Maybe. Or maybe he's giving her the money. Maybe he's paying her to help him."

"Unlikely," Beatrice said, but she got Leigh's point. Quite often the most logical explanation was the truth, but it wasn't always. She set up the ironing board and turned on the iron. "This'll make the envelopes look like new again."

"How do you know all this?"

"You'd be surprised what I've learned from criminal trials. I could get away with murder."

"Good to know."

Beatrice snapped photos of the documents with her phone, ironed each page flat, and tucked them back into their envelopes. A quick swipe over the steam rejuvenated the glue, and she resealed the envelopes.

"I'm going to return these. Be right back."

Beatrice sprinted back. She dropped the mail into the box, turned, and the Prius wheeled into the driveway, its electric engine nearly silent. Beatrice tucked her hands into the pockets of her shorts, then realized she was the picture of false innocence. She forced her hands out to her sides and attempted a more genuine look.

The Prius stopped beside the house and Melanie stepped out. "What are you doing?"

"I was just checking to see if you were home," Beatrice said. "I wasn't sure how long Kenny wants me to keep Doro."

Melanie glanced at the mailbox, and Beatrice knew she'd been spotted with her hand on it. She hoped the glue had time to dry.

"Keep the dog," Melanie said. "Going to the doctor wears Kenny out. He'll sleep 'til morning. You can bring the dog back then."

Kenny remained in the passenger seat. He looked at Beatrice but seemed uninterested in why she was there. He did look tired.

"All right." Beatrice descended the stairs. "I'll bring her back tomorrow."

Melanie nodded, got back in the car, and pulled forward to the garage.

"BEATRICE, WAKE UP. WAKE up, honey. Bea, wake up!"

The words were part of her dream at first, but suddenly Beatrice sat up, fully awake, her heart pounding. "What is it?"

"Listen," Leigh said.

After a moment of silence she heard a voice calling from outside. "Nellie! Nellie, where are you?"

Beatrice leaped out of bed and stuck her feet in her slippers. "Nellie's Kenny's old dog." She threw on her robe and darted for the door. Doro tried to follow. "Stay here. I'll be right back."

"Be careful," Leigh said.

There were no overhead streetlights in the housing development, but in front of each house was an LED light on a five-foot pole. The light was not bright, but it was clear, and Beatrice had no difficulty seeing Kenny standing in the center of the cul-de-sac calling for his dead dog. He wore a T-shirt and the same stained trousers he'd worn to the doctor that day. He was barefoot.

"Nellie, come home," he called.

Beatrice approached. "Kenny, are you looking for your dog?"

He turned to her. Tears leaked from his eyes, but he was wide awake. "I can't find Nellie."

"Your dog's at my house. You loaned her to me today, remember?"

"You found my dog?"

"Yes. Come with me. I'll show you." She held out a hand. Kenny let her lead him to her house. Doro met them at the door.

"You found her! It's Doro," he said, instantly reverting to the correct name. The dog scrambled frantically at his legs. Kenny tried to touch her, but when he bent down he lost his balance and would have fallen if Beatrice hadn't grabbed and steadied him.

"Sit down, Kenny. Sit here." She ushered him into the kitchen and pulled out a chair. He sat, and Doro jumped onto his lap. They both smiled.

"Are you all right?" Beatrice asked. "Are you hungry? Can I get you a cup of tea?"

He didn't answer, so she popped an herbal tea K-cup into the Keurig and turned it on. From the remains of a peach pie in the fridge, she cut a slice for each of them and brought the pie and tea to the table.

"I love peach pie," Kenny said, sounding normal.

"I know," Beatrice said. "Kenny, what's going on over at your place? Who's Melanie?"

"She lives with me. She takes care of me."

"When did that start?"

Kenny fed Doro a crumb of crust and didn't answer.

"Did you get sick? Or have an accident?"

He looked down at his lap as if embarrassed. "I have accidents sometimes. I'm sorry."

"No, I don't mean that kind of accident. Don't be sorry." Beatrice took a bite of pie. She would have to be careful with her questioning. He was like a child, suddenly, and not in a skateboarding way. She knew dementia could have that effect on people, but she'd never heard of someone deteriorating so quickly. "How are you related to Melanie?"

His brow creased. "Related?"

"She's related to you, isn't she? Is she a niece or something? Or is it by marriage?"

"Yes," he said. "By marriage." He put his fork down, having eaten only two bites, and yawned heavily. "Let's go to bed, Doro."

Beatrice didn't want to let him go home. "Do you want to sleep on my couch?"

"Yes. Let's sleep on the couch, Doro."

Kenny lay down as soon as the sheets were spread, closed his eyes, and fell asleep.

Beatrice returned to the bedroom.

"You think she'll come looking for him?" Leigh asked.

"She can't have him. I'm keeping him."

"Are we talking about the dog? Or Kenny?"

"Both."

BUT IN THE MORNING, the front door was unlocked and both were gone. Beatrice assumed they'd returned home, but the uncertainty of it niggled at her. He could be roaming the city, barefoot and lost.

"I'm going over there," she said.

"Eat something first," Leigh advised. "And get dressed. You can't wander the neighborhood like that."

Beatrice looked at herself. She wore nothing but panties and a T-shirt, an old one of Leigh's, now worn threadbare. Leigh was right. So it was eight-thirty before she knocked at Kenny's. Melanie, wearing a long sleep shirt, opened the door.

"Is Kenny here?" Beatrice asked.

"Of course. He's sleeping."

"Are you sure? Because he was out walking last night, looking for his dog. I didn't know if he'd made it home."

"I'm sure." Melanie's eyes blinked behind her owl glasses. The lenses were thick, but there was no distortion of her eyes. "Give me a little credit."

Beatrice wasn't about to give her any credit, and she nearly asked to peek in Kenny's bedroom to make certain when she heard barking coming from inside. Kenny's voice followed, faint and muffled by distance, but it sounded like he was calling Doro 'Nellie' again.

"That's just great," Melanie snapped and moved onto the porch, forcing Beatrice to step back. She closed the door behind her. "Now the damned dog woke him up, just when I got him settled in to sleep, too. Please go now."

"But he's awake. Let me talk to him."

"No. I've been taking care of that old man for months now. I know what's best for him, you don't. If you'll just go, maybe the dog will shut up and Kenny can go back to sleep."

Beatrice slunk back home.

"Maybe I've got it all wrong," she told Leigh. "Maybe she's exactly what she seems."

"A rude sloppy meat-eater who doesn't like dogs?"

"A rude sloppy meat-eater who's volunteered to care for an old, sick relative."

Just then the mail arrived, nice and early. Their usual carrier was back from vacation. Beatrice met her at the door.

"Do you happen to know when that woman moved into Kenny Wingate's house?"

"Melanie?" the carrier asked. "She's not just a woman, she's his wife."

"His *wife?* No! Are you kidding me?"

"I wish I was. She moved in last winter some time. They got married in April, I think."

"But he's..." *gay,* Beatrice almost said, but she didn't know how out Kenny really was. He was a generation ahead of her, and that generation had a harder time stepping out of the closet than Beatrice's. "He's old enough to be her grandfather. And in April he wasn't even well enough to walk his dog. How could he get married?"

The carrier shrugged. "It happens. Old guys fall in love with their nurses all the time. There's no law against it, thank God. We're trying to get rid of laws that say who people can marry, remember?"

"That's true. Thanks." She took her mail and closed the door. "Leigh, did you hear that?"

"I heard."

"Kenny did *not* fall in love with Melanie."

"No, he's as queer as a three-dollar bill."

A thought occurred to Beatrice. "You know what? I don't think he did say 'Nellie.'"

"What do you mean?"

"When I stood at the door this morning, Doro barked, and I thought I heard Kenny say 'Nellie.' But now that I think about it, I'm pretty sure he was saying, '*help me*.'"

"Help me? Why? You think she locked him in?"

"Why wouldn't she let me see him? He was awake. There was no reason for her to—he was calling for help. I'm sure of it now. I'm going to talk to him. I'm going to sneak in the back way."

"You mean right now?"

"He needs help, Leigh."

"Maybe, but not from you. Call Adult Protective Services, like you said before. Call the police, if you're that sure he's in trouble."

Beatrice sighed. "That's the problem. I'm not sure. I'd hate to be one of those paranoid people who call in suspicious behavior when there isn't any. I'd look like a nutcase."

"Do you think it's suspicious?"

"Yes, but what if I'm wrong? What do you think?"

"You know better than that."

"Yeah. Well, I'm going. If I'm not back in an hour...no, that won't work."

"No."

"I'll leave a note on the table saying where I went and when and why. Not that anything's going to happen. Besides, I'll have my phone with me."

"I wish you wouldn't go," Leigh said, but Beatrice went.

SNEAKING IN WAS EASY. The gate to the backyard was unlocked, just like before, and the key to the back door was where Kenny had always left it. Beatrice retrieved it from the fake rock and let herself in.

The kitchen smelled greasy. The floors were sticky, the counter was covered with old spills, and the sink was piled with dirty dishes. The television in the living room played something with a laugh track. Beatrice crept through the kitchen to the hall where she could see more. Melanie sat on the couch in front of the TV with a laptop on her knees. Brightly colored candies slid and popped all over the screen. Beatrice slipped past the opening and moved further down the hall to Kenny's bedroom door.

She peeked inside. No one was there, but the room was obviously occupied. Women's clothes and shoes were strewn all over. Melanie had taken over the master bedroom.

Beatrice couldn't imagine that Melanie and Kenny were sharing a bed. He must be sleeping somewhere else. The layout of Kenny's house was identical to Beatrice's, so she slipped up the stairs to the guest room. The door was closed. A shiny new locking bolt was installed on it.

Nobody puts a bolt on a bedroom door, not on the outside anyway. Even if Melanie kept Kenny locked in for his own safety, it was illegal as hell. If there were a fire, he wouldn't be able to escape.

Beatrice slid the bolt and opened the door. She was careful to be silent, and even Doro didn't hear. The dog lay on the bed beside Kenny, and both appeared to be sound asleep. Beatrice closed the door behind her as quietly as she could, and this time the dog heard her. She sat up and barked.

Kenny's eyes flew open and met hers. Before either of them could speak, though, Melanie called from the living room.

"Shut that goddamn dog up or she's going back in the basement!"

Kenny's eyes widened, and he grabbed Doro to his chest. "Hush, Doro. Be a good girl. Stay with daddy."

Beatrice put her finger to her lips and moved close to the bed. "Kenny," she whispered, "what's going on here? Did you really marry that woman?"

Kenny's brow creased. "She showed me a certificate. I don't remember it. Why would I marry her?" he asked, as if he expected her to know the answer.

Beatrice shook her head. "Is she keeping you locked in here?"

"She'll let me keep Doro, as long as we're both quiet."

"That's not okay, Kenny. It's not legal. Do you want to leave? I'll help you."

"But Doro—"

"We'll take Doro too. I'll take you home. We'll call the police."

Several bottles of prescription medications cluttered the bedside table. Beatrice examined the labels. Muscle relaxers, sleeping pills, anti-depressants...even an antipsychotic drug, which Kenny had never needed. The bottles were issued from different doctors, and all contained usage warnings of confusion, grogginess, risk of falls, even death. Beatrice pocketed them and moved to the closet. She found a duffel bag, tossed the pill bottles into it, and added some clothes and shoes. She looked over her shoulder to see what Kenny wore on his feet and gasped. Beatrice had left the door open, and Melanie had slipped in as silently as

Beatrice had. She stood beside the bed. Kenny and Doro watched her with anxious expressions.

"You nosy bitch," Melanie said. "You shouldn't have come in here."

Beatrice straightened. "No, *you're* the one who shouldn't be here. You're exploiting this man, and probably overdosing him too. I'm reporting it."

"No one will believe you."

"They'll believe me." Beatrice pulled her phone from her pocket. "I'm a judge, you know."

"I wouldn't do that, if I were you." Melanie raised her hand. A syringe was tucked expertly between her fingers. She pressed the tip of it against Kenny's arm. "Give me your phone."

They stared at each other for several long moments, but it was a foregone conclusion. Beatrice had no idea what was in the syringe. It could be a harmless saline, for all she knew, but she couldn't take the chance. When Melanie pricked his skin, Beatrice tossed the phone. She aimed for Melanie's left hand, hoping it would send her off balance, but it didn't work like in the movies. Melanie leaned over, caught the phone, and slipped out the door before Beatrice could react. Beatrice rushed to the door, but she was too late. The bolt slid shut.

Beatrice turned. "Oh, Kenny, I'm sorry. I don't suppose you have a phone?"

He shook his head. "She took it a long time ago."

Beatrice went to the window and tugged, but it wouldn't budge. She looked closely to find the sill was nailed shut. "Oh, crap." If only Leigh could call the police for her...

"Kenny, we've got to get out of here." She looked around for something to pry open the window. "Do you have any tools in here? Anything sharp?"

"I already tried that," Kenny said. "There isn't anything."

It seemed he was right. She opened the dresser drawers, but found nothing except clothes and towels. Aside from the bed, the dresser was the only piece of furniture in the room. There wasn't even a chair she could throw through the window.

They were in trouble. Leigh couldn't call the police, and no one would miss Beatrice until she didn't show up for work on Monday. She had no idea what Melanie planned to do with her, but she wasn't about to sit around waiting for it.

Then she smelled smoke. Doro smelled it too. She barked again.

"Hush," Kenny said. "She'll put you in the basement."

Beatrice threw her weight at the door, but it didn't even tremble. "I don't think you have to worry about that anymore." She returned to the window in time to see the blue Prius turn the corner. "She set us on fire, Kenny."

How long would it take for one of their neighbors to notice the smoke? Too long. Already Beatrice could see the smoke trickling in from under the door. She looked helplessly at Kenny, who finally seemed to grasp how dire their situation was. His expression was grave, but not confused. He swung his feet to the floor, but was too weak and drugged to help. It was up to Beatrice.

She turned to the dresser. It was massive and too heavy for her to move. She opened a drawer and tugged, but it wouldn't come out. She rocked it and pulled again, with no success. More smoke seeped into the room. Kenny coughed. Beatrice's eyes watered. She put her hand on the door and felt how hot it had gotten in just that short amount of time. Melanie must have set the fire right outside Kenny's door.

They had no more time.

"Get back," she hollered. She wrapped one of Kenny's shirts around her hand, closed her eyes, and smashed her fist against the window. Glass shattered. Ignoring the shards, she leaned out.

"Help!"

"WILL YOU BE WARM enough?" Leigh asked.

"I wish you'd stop worrying about me," Beatrice answered, but she grabbed a sweatshirt. It was early enough in the fall that the days were still warm, but it cooled off quickly in the evening.

"There's only one way to make me stop worrying."

"Don't," Beatrice said and felt guilty when Leigh said nothing. "I wish you could come with me."

"Kenny doesn't want to see me. Tonight's about you. You're his hero."

"Me and the cute firemen who carried him out of the house. They're the real reason he's having this barbecue. I'm not stupid."

"You saved his life."

"Yeah, I did. That slimy bitch was just waiting for him to die. Luckily she didn't have the nerve to give him an overdose outright, so she gave him all those drugs to make him confused and weak and left him to fall down the stairs or maybe overdose himself."

"He didn't have that much money."

"It was a lot to her. And she'd done it before. He was the third old man she'd married, and he was the only one to survive."

"Wasn't one of the firefighters a woman? Maybe he's trying to set you up."

"Oh, come on. She was barely forty, if that."

"So? You're fifty-eight. You're not dead."

Beatrice didn't answer. She slipped her keys in her pocket and picked up the pie container to take with her to the barbecue.

"Don't forget your phone," Leigh said.

"Oh, yeah. For all the good it did last time."

"It helped them catch her. I hope the charges stick."

"She tried to kill us. They'll stick."

"It was torture waiting for you to get home that day. I was always there to protect you, but when you needed me most, I couldn't. That was hard."

"I was fine."

"You were hurt, Bea."

"Just a little." The scar on her arm was still red, but it was healing smoothly.

"It's torture worrying about you, Bea. Make it go away."

Beatrice's eyes stung, and she turned to the wall. "Don't. I can't."

"Let me go."

"No." Beatrice approached the wooden box on the sideboard. "I know it's hard for you to be stuck here like this, but at least we're together. What if it's worse where you're going?"

"We can't avoid it. None of us can."

"But we could go *together*. Don't you want to wait for me, Leigh?"

"No, love. It doesn't work like that."

"How do you know?" Beatrice's voice broke. "You haven't even made it there yet."

"I've made it farther than you. We have our own journeys over here. I need to get started on mine, and you have work to finish there. Please. Let me go."

Tears dripped down Beatrice's face. "I can't." She wrapped her arms around the box, slumped over it, and sobbed. "I can't." Soon her tears ran into the grooves that formed the words carved on top.

Leigh Scott
Beloved Wife
November 12, 1954 – January 11, 2011
Wait for Me

AN AGE OLD SOLUTION

By Lori L. Lake

MADDIE FLYNN EXITED HER car and waited. Around the corner, she saw movement and clumped along that direction in over-size tennis shoes. When she reached Sarah, her lover and reluctant co-conspirator, she said, "Your car is set for a fast getaway?"

Sarah looked a little freaked out. "Yeah, but I don't know if I can do this."

"You can. Don't worry. Just hold my arm—and act old."

"*You* act old!" Sarah whispered.

"We both have to act old, you idiot." Maddie hooked her arm with Sarah's like an old lady would and concentrated on taking slow steps. She hoped nobody noticed that her dowager's hump was a backpack she wore under an enormous scarf she'd wrapped around her ancient cardigan. She broke out into a sweat, whether from the layers of clothes or the ridiculous silver wig or nerves, she didn't know.

Sarah waved a hand. "Nobody's out tonight. Why don't we make a break for the house?"

"We can't. Just walk slow. People don't pay attention to old women. If they do remember later, they'll dismiss us. Hunch over and act like every step's painful."

"Every step *is* painful with you hanging on me."

Maddie loosened her hold and gazed about the neighborhood. She knew her nervous energy was off the chart, but she couldn't stop her mind racing or her heart thundering.

"I need a cigarette," Sarah said.

"Yeah, me too."

"You don't even smoke."

"I might after this." Tonight was do or die—or, more accurately, do or pay. And then suffer.

She'd scoped out the neighborhood extensively during the last week, which wasn't as easy as she'd thought it would be because this upscale and trendy Kenwood area in Minneapolis was a busy place by day, but slow in the evening. Few people were out and about after dark, when she most needed to check it out. She hoped she and Sarah wouldn't be noticed. Every step Maddie took increased her panic level.

A car passed and Maddie turned away, toward Sarah, as though they were chatting. A dog barked in the distance.

Sarah asked, "This asshole doesn't have a dog, does he?"

"No, that'd require him to care about something other than himself. Or at least remember to feed the pup and take him to the vet. Taddy Detwiler doesn't 'do' love and care. Okay, this is the house—the tan and brown one. Just keep on walking past it."

"Holy crap, you weren't kidding. The place is a mansion."

"Uh huh. Complete with a mini-movie theater and an actor's sound stage. Or should I call it a bed stage?"

Sarah gave her a quick searching glance. Maddie knew Sarah wasn't happy about this plan, but Maddie couldn't think of another way to solve the problem. "We'll pass by and go two doors down. That house has been dark every night. I think they're are out of town. The walkway along the side of that house is covered over with an arbor. No one will see us circle around to the back, and we can cut through to get to Taddy's house."

The backyards were dim and shadowy with only a little ambient light from nearby houses.

Sarah whispered, "You sure nobody's home?"

"Not these neighbors. Must be on vacation." Or perhaps living in their other homes in the Cayman Islands or Bermuda. The whole neighborhood screamed filthy rich.

Sarah stumbled and let out a muffled grunt. She caught Maddie's sleeve to right herself. "I hate these freakin' cobblestones."

"Calm down. Take your time." Maddie paused, listening. The night noises of cicadas hadn't stopped. She didn't hear an outcry. No lights went on. She had brought along a penlight but didn't want to use it unless they really had to. With a shove, she steered Sarah onto the back lawn.

"I better not walk through dog crap, Maddie."

"Shhh..."

Laughing nervously, Maddie led her to the big tan monstrosity where their quarry lived. The house was three stories high with a foundation at least forty feet wide and fifty feet long. And the place also had a full basement. Eight thousand square feet for one selfish, mean-spirited asswipe.

The casement windows along the side were all open as they'd been every night when Maddie surveilled the place. Taddy probably thought he was safe because the windowsills were above eye level, perhaps six feet up. Maddie unwrapped her scarf and removed the backpack. First she put on latex gloves, then took out a metal contraption and unfolded it. *Snap-snap-snap-snap* . . . a ladder, hardly a foot wide at the bottom and eight inches at the top, clicked into its six-foot height.

"Ready to be my lookout?" Maddie asked.

"What if someone comes?"

Maddie moved closer and gazed into Sarah's worried eyes. "Holler to let me know, then take off over the back fence."

"I won't leave you, sweetheart."

"We don't both need to be caught. Don't risk anything—just haul ass out of here."

"You sure you want to do this?"

"I have to."

"What if this is the wrong room?"

"It's not. I cased the place way back when. The layout's probably the same." She put a hand on Sarah's shoulder and squeezed. "Get yourself ready now. This'll all be over soon."

As Sarah adjusted her old lady slacks and sweater for better mobility, Maddie stepped into the flower bed and leaned the ladder against the wall, delighted to see that the legs wedged nicely against the edge of the sidewalk. Sarah held the ladder still, and Maddie navigated the rungs, careful of her cloddy shoes. She slid the half-open window up as far as it would go and peered into the darkened room. No one in sight, so she inched her way over the sill.

Once inside, she gave a thumbs-up to Sarah, who squatted next to the ladder looking miserable, like she was going to throw up.

While she searched the gigantic wood desk, Maddie did a slow burn about its owner. She'd met Theodore Augustus Detwiler—TAD or Taddy for short—her first term in college. He'd acted like a student, but she didn't find out until later that he'd dropped out years before and now spent his time trolling the U of M campus hunting for theater majors to suck into his whirling vortex of shame. She'd been eighteen and naïve, only recently off the bus from Rosholt, South Dakota. A farm girl with the lead roles for "Oklahoma!" and "Grease" on her résumé, she was a sucker for his slick act. He'd wined and dined her, filled her head with stories of fame and grandeur, and made assurances that she was one step away from flying to Hollywood for a screen test.

Thinking back at how stupid she'd been made her shudder.

The nude photos he'd taken early on had been one thing, but the aborted "movie" was something else. He'd worked her like a pimp slowly wears down any good girl, but when the day came to film in the soundproof movie set in his basement, she'd managed to gather enough of her wits to protest. Of course by then she'd disrobed, and some sweaty naked guy had her in a clinch on the "bed stage." She had the sense to refuse to take it any farther. Taddy started out pleading and sweet, graduated to threats, and eventually did everything but hit her. Shaking and unclothed, she made it out of the room with bruises up and down her arms from where he'd manhandled her. Behind her she heard the crew hooting and calling her name.

Fifteen years had passed, and in all that time, she'd never known that the cameras had been rolling. Not until she received a letter at work marked "personal" containing still photos from the "show." She recognized herself immediately—her red hair, pale skin, the birthmark on her right breast. She looked pretty much the same today, just not quite so innocent. On the back was written: "Thirty grand or this goes to your principal. You have 10 days to get the cash together. 50s or smaller. Instructions to come."

No signature, but she knew Taddy Detwiler's writing, even after all these years. She'd wanted to take him out but didn't want to go to jail. And she had to face it, she wasn't the killing kind. She also couldn't see how she could report the blackmail to the police without her employer finding out. It was bad enough that the pictures came to the private school where she worked with third and fourth graders. Thank God no one in the office had opened it! How quickly would they bounce her out of the job using the morals clause if someone saw these photos?

Her only choice was to steal the original photos, movie footage, and any copies—farfetched, she knew, but all she could think to do. Before it was too late and she received her "instructions," she had decided to find out more about Taddy, and breaking in was her last shot.

So here she was, going through drawers that contained very little: a dictionary, some office supplies, a couple folders of household utility bills. Clearly, the huge desk and roomy office was just for show. Taddy didn't even have a computer on it. Giving up on the near-empty drawers, she slithered out from behind the desk, around the expensive leather chairs that smelled like cigars, and paused in front of the wet bar. She was dying to slug down a few ounces of liquid courage from one of the dozens of bottles under the counter, but no. Sober and focused, she told herself.

The room was big enough to serve as both a den and a meeting place for Taddy and his sleazy porn pals. Other than some spendy-looking paintings on the wall and a newer and bigger desk, the room hadn't changed since she'd last been in it.

She wondered if Taddy could still con young girls like he used to. She'd gotten one glimpse of him getting out of his Mercedes the night before last, and all she could think was that Mr. Detwiler should change his name to Mr. Fatwiler. His suit was too small and didn't look like designer wear. His waddled toward the front door, a knuckle-dragging gorilla carrying a sack of groceries. A decade and a half had not been good to him. Besides, everybody and their sick bastard brother could film pornos these days. All you needed was a steady camera hand and a decent video camera—or even an iPhone. Technology had advanced and was nothing like in Taddy's heyday when he had an actual mini-movie studio and camera operators who knew how to do all the techie things he was so bad at. Maddie figured that Taddy's income was no longer anything like it'd been in the past, so now he'd turned to blackmail to support his extravagant tastes.

The door to the office was open. She passed through it and crept down the hall. From the other end of the house she heard a laugh track. Taddy had always been a sucker for sitcoms. He was probably hunkered down in the TV room, a giant carbuncle on the butt of humanity, drinking rum and coke. She hoped he'd fallen asleep, but she couldn't be sure, so she retraced her steps, reentered the office, and closed the door nearly all the way, not letting it click shut. She hoped what she sought was in the office, not downstairs where the filming used to occur.

She opened the sliding doors to the closet to find a surprisingly large walk-in space containing a row of six 4-drawer file cabinets and some beautifully crafted built-in shelves above and on either side of the cabinets. She clicked the penlight on and scanned the shelves. A couple hundred video cassettes labeled with dates gave way to considerably fewer DVD cases which were not labeled.

"Pssst..."

Startled, Maddie spun toward the window.

Sarah's chin rested on the sill. "You find it?"

Maddie charged past the desk and over to the window. "Shh. I'm still looking. There's a lot more to sift through than I expected."

"Well, crap," Sarah said. "Want me to come in and help?"

"No, I don't think so. Give me a minute to figure out the system." She went back to the alcove and one by one examined the tapes labeled the year she graduated from high school. Annabel, Alison Q. Alison R. Brianna. Cate. Catherine L. Catherine P. Catherine S. Cathy...and on and on all the way to Willa and Yasmine and Zoe.

Where was her name? She skimmed through the tapes for the year before and the year after, just in case something was misfiled. No luck.

Opening a cabinet drawer, she found that instead of files, it was filled with envelopes crammed with photos. Same with the next cabinet. The third cabinet contained more VHS cassettes, papers, various sized photos—everything stacked in a haphazard manner. She dropped to her knees and dug in the bottom drawer. Some tapes were labeled with numbers, some with dates, and a few with names: Stonehenge. Gooseberry Falls. Leaning Tower of Pisa. Cabot Cove. What? Did he have dirt on Jessica Fletcher? The thought almost made her smile. Were these TV and movie titles? Places they were filmed? She had no clue. The next drawers she opened were in the same shape. How the hell could she find her photos and the movie?

Maddie sat back on her heels feeling frustrated. This wasn't going to work. She wanted to cry out, to scream bloody murder—or bloody blackmail.

She heard a noise down the hall and froze. Was that someone humming?

She crawled forward into the closet and slid one door shut. Before she could reach for the other, she heard noise at the door.

He was going to find her. He would manhandle her as he had that last time she'd seen him, and he'd add to her torment by calling the police. What about her job, her life? What about Sarah? Would Sarah be able to get away? Hunched down between the wall and a file cabinet Maddie waited, hardly breathing.

The door to the office opened. A flash of light from overhead. She squinched her eyes shut and held her breath. He hummed something tuneless as he walked heavily across the carpet. She heard rustling, a drawer opened and closed. Glass tinkled. He lumbered toward her hiding place. She held her breath and squeezed into the smallest ball she could make. Thud. Something bumped against the wall, and he shuffled off, his humming gradually fading away.

Maddie opened her eyes, gasping for air. He'd shut the closet slider. Never looked inside! She slid the door open, drenched in sweat. She hadn't breathed for so long that now she panted to make up for it. The cool breeze coming in through the window raised goosebumps on her arms. The faint outline of Sarah's head popped up in the window frame. Maddie staggered across the room.

"I saw him," Sarah whispered. "He took two bottles of booze with him."

"Oh, my God. You were supposed to run!"

"And leave you here with that despicable ass? Forget it." She held up her phone. "I put 9-1-1 on speed-dial."

"We can't call the cops. He'd be the one calling. Put your phone away."

"Hurry up, will you?"

"I can't do this." Maddie shook, and her stomach hurt so bad she bent forward a little. Too much adrenalin, too many bad memories, too much fear.

Sarah said, "I'm coming in."

"No, you can't." But Maddie didn't make a move to prevent it. She stood trying to catch her breath. She felt sweaty everywhere and worried she may have peed her pants.

Sarah, not quite as lithe as Maddie, managed to navigate the window without too much noise and strode over to the closet.

Maddie mumbled, "Now we're both sitting ducks."

"Shut up and give me the flash." Sarah shone the penlight around the closet. "Holy hell."

Maddie whispered, "The shit on the shelves has some semblance of order, but the file cabinets don't."

Sarah opened a drawer, pulled out a pack of photos, and tucked the penlight under her chin. She fanned out the pictures. "Good God, these are disgusting."

Maddie had to agree. The photos she'd posed for fifteen years ago had been rather chaste compared to the spread-eagle pose of the frightened young woman in the shots Sarah held.

"He's got millions in blackmail here." Sarah tossed the photos back in the drawer, not even bothering to replace them in the envelope.

"Whoa." Maddie grabbed Sarah's arm. "You don't have gloves on."

She reached for the pictures, but Sarah held up a hand. "Forget it. I've got a better idea." She pulled out the bottom drawers of all the cabinets and rose. From the bar she grabbed a bottle of booze, opened it, and dumped the contents into the bottom drawers.

"What are you *doing?*" Maddie's panic level suddenly hit the red zone and she was sure her head was going to detonate.

Sarah opened the next drawer, allowing the entire cabinet to tip forward and rest precariously on the bottom drawer.

Maddie grabbed Sarah's shoulder and tried to pull her to her feet. "We can't do this!"

Sarah shrugged her off. "Yeah, we can." She rose and elbowed past Maddie, got two more bottles of booze, poured them into the drawers, and repeated the process again. She upended two additional bottles on the carpet inside the closet and splashed some against the shelves and wall.

Maddie stood frozen and speechless. Her heart had been pounding fast for so long that her chest hurt. She thought she might have a heart attack.

Sarah held up a bottle, a specially aged El Dorado Rum. "Go, Maddie. Time to get out."

Still rattled and trembling, Maddie clambered over the sill and nearly fell off the ladder. She caught her balance and stood on a rung halfway up, peering in. Sarah faced away from her. She bent and Maddie heard a glugging sound. The rhythm echoed in her mind. *Glug...glug...glug...glug...*

Sarah backed up to the sill, and Maddie slipped down from the ladder. Sarah came through the window and paused, her feet on the ladder rungs and upper body still inside the office.

Snick-snick... Maddie heard a quiet whooshing sound. Reddish-yellow flames bloomed inside making the dark wooden walls reflect orange.

Sarah closed the window, hopped down, and put her lighter in her pocket. Maddie stood staring. What had they done?

"Get the backpack," Sarah said. She was already disassembling the ladder. Maddie picked up the pack and held it so Sarah could stuff the ladder in it. Sarah slipped her arms through the straps and wrapped the scarf around herself.

Sarah said, "Come on—we have to go." She dragged Maddie through the neighboring yards and around to the sidewalk two doors down.

They paused in the deep shadows next to the house and peeked out toward the empty street.

Maddie stood in shock, not quite able to form a thought, before her brain finally clicked in. "What if Taddy doesn't get out?"

"Piss on him. Serves him right if you ask me. How many women like you was he blackmailing? How many lives has he ruined?"

"But he could die—"

"Nah, he'll haul his fat ass out somehow. Slugs like him always do."

Whoop-whoop-whoop...

"See," Sarah said. "His fire alarm will wake up the dead."

A door opened across the street from Taddy's house. A woman came out on the porch and pointed. She was dressed to the nines in business attire and somehow managed to tiptoe down her front stairs in the highest pair of stilettos Maddie had ever seen. Two men burst out of the house next door to Mrs. Stiletto's place. One held a cell phone to his ear. The neighborhood came to life before them, little ants emerging from their various anthills.

Maddie smelled the aroma of something rotten burning. "How the hell do we get out of here?"

Sarah straightened her tan cardigan and wrapped the scarf tighter. "We're going to wait a few minutes, 'til the fire truck arrives, and then we'll join the horde watching all the excitement. After a little while, we'll hobble off."

"Somebody will see."

"Who cares. You said it yourself. Nobody remembers elderly dames." Sarah snickered. "Keep your head down and make sure you act old."

That sounded right to Maddie. Sarah would go to her car, and Maddie would walk stiffly toward hers, and soon it'd all be over. She tugged her wig down, smoothing a lock of silver over her forehead, suddenly able to breathe a little bit.

A fire truck rounded one corner as an ambulance and police car came from the other direction.

Maddie said, "I hope they don't put it out too quickly. That whole closet needs to be completely destroyed."

"My hope," Sarah said, "is that the entire house is rubble by morning."

Maddie stepped out into the moonlight, relief flooding through her. "As far as I'm concerned, it couldn't happen to a nicer guy."

IT'S A DOG'S LIFE

By Lynn Ames

"WHAT DO YOU SAY, kids?" Mama asked. "Want to come to Starbucks with me? Want to go for a walk? Parker? Dixie? What do you say?"

"Why do you think she insists on talking to us like we're dolts? She repeats herself like we don't hear her the first time."

"Patience, Dixie. She's just trying to build enthusiasm here. She's lonely. It's been forever since her last girlfriend left. We're all she's got. Besides, we're golden retrievers, for goodness sake, surely we can act retriever-like. Go with it." To emphasize his point, Parker gave a swish of his tail and let out a woof. The sound echoed off the walls of the vestibule.

"I'll wag my tail and smile, but I swear, if she makes me sit to put that halter on—"

"You, first, Dix," Mama said. "Let's get your halter on."

Parker hid a snicker behind a golden paw.

"Okay, Park. You're next. Here you go, buddy."

Dutifully, Parker lifted his left front leg so that Mama could secure the halter around his midsection. He stuck his tongue out at Dixie as Mama gave him a big hug before opening the front door and leading them outside.

"So," Mama said, "who do you think we'll run into today? Parker, maybe we'll see your girlfriend, Elphy. And as for you little girl," Mama scratched Dixie behind the ear, "maybe we'll run into your partner-in-crime, Lucy."

"Or maybe Mama will get to order from that cute little barista—the one who looks like the hot babe on her favorite Monday night show," Dixie mumbled.

"Heh. Maybe," Parker agreed. He stumbled as Dixie pulled them off the path to sniff at a patch of grass. "Hey! Give a guy a little warning, would you? And why, oh why must you smell those same twenty blades of grass every, single time? That's just gross. Show a little dignity, will you?"

"Yeah, like the fact that you're the only male dog on the block who doesn't lift his leg makes you look so refined. Give me a break."

Dixie bumped into Parker and he grunted. "Boundaries!

You're in my space. Shove over."

"It's not my fault Mama insists on a bifurcated leash."

"Well, if you weren't always pulling in the opposite direction, maybe she wouldn't have felt a need to get one of those."

"Sure, blame me. You always do."

They turned the corner and arrived at Starbucks. Because the weather was so nice, the patio was crowded. "Yikes, guys." Mama looked perturbed. "Doesn't look like we're going to get to sit and have a leisurely latté. I'll just run in and get one to go. First, I've got to find a safe place to leave you. I don't see any of our regular pals."

"Can I pet your dogs? Please?"

Parker lifted his nose in the air. The woman standing too close to Mama smelled a lot like the can Mama took out to the curb every Wednesday night. He noticed that Mama's posture was a little stiffer than usual. He stepped between Mama and the fragrant lady.

"He's so handsome." The woman bent down and patted him on the head and Parker smiled at her. "Good boy. You're so well-behaved."

Dixie muscled in to get her share of attention and Parker stepped to his left to allow it. He watched the woman's eyes. Underneath the dirt and grime, they were kind, deep, and soulful.

"Your dogs are so sweet."

"Thank you." Mama said.

Parker noticed that Mama continued to scan the crowd, not paying much attention to this nice lady.

"I-if you're trying to figure out what to do with them while you go inside, I could watch them for you."

Mama hesitated.

"I'll stay right here." The woman continued to stroke Parker with one hand and Dixie with the other. "We won't move, will we?" She kissed Parker on top of the head and he gave her hand a lick.

That must've been the deciding factor because Mama said, "Okay. I'd really appreciate that."

When Mama was out of sight, the fragrant lady continued to pet and talk to them. "You sure are good doggies. My kids would love you. We used to have a doggie, ourselves." She sniffed.

Parker nuzzled her. She seemed so sad.

"They wouldn't let us keep the house. We ran out of money because of my husband's cancer. I had to give our dog, Maddie, to a loving family out in the country. Then, when my husband died, I had to send the kids to live with my husband's parents. It was better for them. I couldn't have them out on the street with me like this." The woman choked back a sob.

When Dixie moved in closer and nuzzled the woman, Parker nodded his approval.

"My goodness. You are the most loving doggies ever. I hope I get to see you again. Now that I found this place, I'll be here every day if I can. Maybe you'll get to come back and see me."

Parker's ears perked up as a plan started to formulate in his mind. He turned to Dixie. "We have to help her."

"What do you think we'd be able to do?"

"I don't know yet. But we have to think of something."

Just then, Mama came back. In one hand, she carried a steaming cup of something. In the other hand, she held a bag. "This is for you."

"I-it is?"

"Yes, consider it a thank you for looking after my kids."

The woman handed the leash to Mama and peered inside the bag. "Muffins, croissants, water, and orange juice. That's so thoughtful. Thank you."

"You're welcome. Thanks for keeping these guys company."

The woman bent down and wrapped her arms first around Dixie, then around Parker. "What are their names?"

"The golden big guy is Parker."

Parker gave the woman another lick.

"The little white girl is Dixie."

Dixie wagged her tail.

"Nice to meet you, Parker and Dixie. I love golden retrievers. They're so friendly."

"Well, we'd better get going. Nice to meet you..."

"Lila."

"Nice to meet you, Lila." Mama smiled at her. "Ready to go, guys? Thanks for keeping Lila company. Good job."

"WE HAVE TO HELP her."

"Who?" Dixie asked.

"Lila. Why are you so myopic?"

"So, what?"

"Myopic." Parker shook his head. "Myopic. Geez. Look at Mama's dictionary sometime while you're over sniffing the bookcase. It means single-minded, singularly focused. 'Throw the ball. Throw the ball. Throw the ball.'" Parker picked up the ball in question and dropped it again. "It's all you ever think about."

"What else is there? It's not like you're not all, 'Chew the bone. Chew the bone. Chew the bone,' you know."

Parker swatted Dixie with his paw. "Enough! We have to figure this out before Mama comes back."

"She said she was going hiking. She'll be gone for hours."

"Don't count on it." Parker put his paws up on the kitchen island and slid some pieces of paper to the side.

"What are you doing? You know we're not supposed to put our paws on the counter!"

"Lila said she ran out of money. So she must need some. Mama usually leaves some bills here." Parker grabbed an envelope that was obstructing his view and tossed it out of the way. "There! Look. Over there. Jackpot!" He extended his paw, but the bills were just out of reach. He turned his head and glared at Dixie. "Don't just stand there. Help me out."

"What do you want me to do? I'm shorter than you are."

"Get underneath my butt and give me a boost."

"I'll do it. But I'm not taking the fall when Mama figures out you stole her money."

"She helped Lila the other day. She won't be upset."

"I wouldn't count on that." Dixie wedged herself under Parker's rear end and heaved. "You need to lose some weight."

Parker mumbled under his breath, "Everybody's a critic." Out loud, he said, "One. More. Push!" He lunged forward and grabbed the neatly folded bills in his mouth, pushed off, and landed with all four paws on the floor.

"Now what?" Dixie asked.

Parker spit out the bills. "Now we have to get to that place. Lila said she's always there. Let's go bring this to her."

"Okay, but I still say it's a bad idea."

"Since when did you become a worry-wart?"

"A what?"

"Never mind. Don't you ever listen to Mama's telephone discussions?"

"No. That's prime ball-tossing time. She's so focused on the conversation, she doesn't even realize she's playing with me. It's like an automatic ball retrieval system."

"It's a wonder you get through the day. Let's go."

"No."

"What do you mean, no?"

"I mean," Dixie said, "it's an ill-conceived idea."

"Big term for you."

"Knock it off. You want me to save your butt, or not?"

Parker relented. "Okay. What's your objection?"

"Think for a minute. Did that woman strike you as someone who would accept money? I don't think she wanted charity. Did you hear how Mama worded it when she handed her the bag? She made sure it seemed like she was repaying her for watching us."

"True."

"Not only that, but if we just waltz up to her and give her the money, she's probably going to tell on us, and that means Mama will find out what we did. We're so totally going to be busted."

"True." Parker scratched his head with his back paw. "So, you're saying we need to be more subtle."

"Bingo! I knew you'd catch on."

"I TOLD YOU IT was a bad idea," Dixie said. She pushed open the latch to the back gate. Parker followed her through, then grabbed the latch and pulled the gate shut again. Dixie powered past him and through the doggie door into the kitchen.

"Why must you practically run me over to get inside every time?"

"Because it bothers you," Dixie answered.

"And it wasn't really a bad idea. I simply failed to anticipate that following Lila while remaining incognito would be so challenging. The important thing is, now we know where she goes when she leaves Starbucks."

"What are we going to do about that?"

"Help her."

"How?"

Parker considered. "We'll bring her stuff that Mama won't miss and that Lila won't be able to turn down, because she won't know where it's coming from."

"Like what, genius?"

"Like...things. We'll bring her things."

"What kind of things?" Dixie asked.

"I don't know. I don't see you making any smart suggestions." Parker's ears perked up. "Uh-oh. That's the garage door."

"Hi, guys. I'm home!"

"Quick!" Parker said. "What'd you do with the money before we left?"

"You had it."

"What? No! I gave it to you."

"Did not."

"Did too."

"Parker? Dixie? Where are you?"

"Distract her," Parker said. "Maybe she won't notice it's gone."

"Yeah, like she didn't notice when you ate the ficus bushes." Dixie picked up her ball and dropped it at Mama's feet. She looked up with her best hopeful expression.

Parker ran off as though he was looking for a toy. He scanned everywhere he could think of, but couldn't find the money. He came back with a stuffed toy. This wasn't good.

Mama put her purse down on the counter and picked up the mail that was sitting there. She moved the flower vase. "Huh. I know I put the grocery money right here. Where is it?"

Parker swallowed hard. He had to find that cash.

Dixie shot Parker a look. She picked up the ball and dropped it directly on Mama's foot.

"I'm sorry, honey. Mama's a little distracted. I know I put the money right there." She opened her purse and pulled items out. "Nope. It's not in there. Where could it have gone?" She ran up the stairs.

"Quick," Parker said. "Help me. We've got to find it and put it back. Retrace your steps."

"Let's see. I helped you get the bills off the counter. You dropped them on the floor. Then I got a drink of water. Then I dribbled water droplets everywhere when you interrupted me and ordered me to pick up the bills off the floor. Then I went out and peed..." Dixie paused. "Wait. Wait. I think I've got something."

"What?"

"I got distracted outside by a hummingbird. I might've dropped the money during the chase."

"You chased a hummingbird again? You do realize they can fly, right?"

"Leave it alone, big guy. Just because you're the world's most un-retriever-like golden retriever—"

"Stop arguing with me and go out and find the money!"

Dixie bounded through the doggie door. Parker stuck his nose out the door to keep watch.

Mama came clumping down the stairs. "Well, it's not in my shorts."

Parker called out, "Hurry up! She's coming back down."

Dixie tore through the yard and skidded to a stop on the sandstone blocks at the edge of Mama's fancy, backlit water fountain. "Uh-oh."

"Uh-oh, what?" Parker stuck his nose out farther to get a better view. "Oh, no."

He barely managed to get out of the way as Dixie flew back through the doggie door, soggy bills in her mouth.

"Maybe I'm just losing my mind," Mama said, coming down the hallway.

Dixie dropped the money on the floor and kicked it away from her. Parker shook his head, but before he could retrieve the bills, Mama walked in front of him to the refrigerator and opened it. "Nothing in here." She closed the door again. When she looked down, she spied the money.

"What in the world?" She bent down and picked up the cash. "How did you get here? And why in the world are you soggy? This makes no sense." She looked quizzically first at Parker, then at Dixie. "Nah."

Parker trotted over and sat, doing his best to look irresistibly cute.

"Did you see anything, buddy? How did the money get moved?"

Parker blinked.

"Well, now that I've got it, I can go do the shopping." She scratched him behind the ears. "Sorry to run out again so quickly, kids, but I've got to pick up a few things." She grabbed her keys and purse. "Be good kids while I'm gone."

As soon as she closed the door, Parker bounded up the stairs.

Dixie followed on his heels. "Where are you going?"

"We have to work fast."

"What are we doing?"

"Plan B."

"What's Plan B?"

"Pick items Lila and her kids might need and Mama won't miss." Parker stood on his hind legs and leaned his front paws against Mama's dresser. He pulled open a drawer.

"What's in there?"

"You really don't pay any attention, do you?" Parker pawed through the contents of the drawer. "Ah, here we go." He picked up several items in his mouth and dropped them to the floor.

Dixie counted five pairs of panties and two bras. All of the panties had the same tag in them, but were a variety of colors. "What's with those?"

"Haven't you ever noticed that when Mama wears these, her butt cheeks hang out? They're obviously too small for her, therefore she won't miss them."

"Are you sure they're not designed to fit that way?"

"Who would design something that uncomfortable? No, these are probably the perfect size for Lila's kids."

"She didn't say whether she had girls or boys. What do boys wear? We've never seen any of them get undressed. And does Mama have anything like that?"

"Do you remember? We had that one male dog sitter." Parker nosed around in the drawer some more. He dropped two more items on the floor. "I heard Mama call these boy shorts. And the others are boy's boxers. They look a little like what that guy wore. Those ought to work."

"How are we going to carry all this?" Dixie asked.

Parker shoved the drawer closed and got down. "When Mama carries bunches of stuff, she puts everything in a bag."

"You mean like the ones in the garbage cans?"

"Exactly."

"I'll grab one of those."

"Don't make a mess!"

"I won't. Mama never has guests. I'll just steal the bag out of the garbage in the guest room. There's never any garbage in that pail."

"We'd better hurry. We have to get all this stuff to the place where Lila stays before she gets back there."

Dixie dropped the bag near the pile of clothes. "And we need to be there and back before Mama comes home."

As if on cue, the garage door opened.

"Quick! Let's get this stuff in the bag," Parker said.

He and Dixie stuffed the underwear and bras in the bag.

"Where should we hide it?" Dixie asked.

"Put it in the guest bath tub. That never gets used."

Dixie grabbed the bag and ran into the guest bathroom just as the door to the house opened. As Parker turned to run downstairs and greet Mama, he caught a glimpse of red on the floor. "Oh, no. We missed a pair of panties."

"I'll take care of it. You go deal with Mama."

Parker flew down the stairs to greet Mama.

Hours later, when they were outside going potty for the last time that night, Parker asked, Dixie "What did you ever do with that pair of red underwear?"

"I put them someplace safe. Don't worry."

"Why does that make me worry more?"

"SOMETHING REALLY FREAKY IS going on," Mama said into the phone. "The other day, I noticed a bunch of my underwear and bras are missing."

Parker's ears perked up.

"No. It doesn't appear to be random. Only the Victoria's Secret thongs are gone. All of the Jockey French cuts are still there. A pair of boy shorts and my Ralph Lauren Polo boxers are missing too. I know I put them all in that drawer."

Dixie came in from the master bathroom and plopped herself down close to Parker. "I thought you said she wouldn't notice."

Parker covered his eyes with a paw.

"I swear I'm not going crazy. The drawer was partially open too. And I left a load of whites in the washing machine to wash after I got back from playing pickle ball yesterday. I ran the load as soon as I got home. When I went to transfer the clothes, everything had turned pink. The pair of red thong panties was in the load. I know I didn't do that."

Parker glared at Dixie. "*That's* the safe place you stashed those panties?"

Dixie put her head on her paws. "How was I supposed to know she had a load of whites in there?"

"No. I checked the rest of the laundry. None of the missing thongs were in there." Mama listened. "No. You don't really think it could be some crazed fan with a lingerie fetish. Do you?" Mama listened some more. "Okay. Well, I've got to go. It's movie premiere Friday, and my Facebook friends will be expecting a review from me. See you later."

Mama grabbed her purse off the counter. "Okay. Be good kids while I'm gone. It's movie day." She kissed Parker and Dixie on the top of the head. "See you soon."

When Parker heard the garage door open and close, he sprang up. "Okay. Let's get moving. We've got a lot to do."

"Now what?" Dixie asked.

"Now we bring Lila the panties and other things."

"Are you kidding me? We almost got caught just gathering up the panties. Mama is suspicious. It's too risky."

"Since when did you become risk-aversive?"

"Risk, what?"

Parker rolled his eyes. "Never mind. Stick to the ball game. Let's go." He ran up the stairs. Dixie came into the guest bedroom as he was dragging a pillow off the bed.

"Yeah, because Mama won't notice something that big has gone missing."

"Listen, it's going to start getting cool at night. You saw where Lila was sleeping. There aren't any warm blankets or pillows. It's just hard ground. Even we don't have to sleep like that."

"We could just bring her one of our beds."

Parker smacked her with a paw.

"Ouch! What was that for?"

"I know you don't read much, but you do realize that our names are on the beds? I'm sure no one would figure out where those came from!" Parker shook his head. "So hard to get good help these days."

"How are we going to carry that?"

"You're going to drag it."

"What are you going to be doing?"

Parker ignored Dixie and ran into the bathroom. He stood up on the counter and grabbed a glass bottle.

"You're going to be in so much trouble if you take that."

"Mama always smells so good after she sprays this on." He trotted back into the bedroom and shoved the bottle inside the pillowcase, then headed for the guest bedroom. Dixie followed behind him.

"Help me," he said. "This is big."

Dixie again covered her eyes with a paw. "You've lost your mind."

"We can't let Lila be cold." Parker grabbed a corner of the comforter off the bed. "Go around the other side and help me."

"This is another bad idea." But Dixie did as she was told.

Ninety minutes later they were back home and at the door to greet Mama when she arrived. "Were you good kids? Yeah?" Mama gave them each a good rubdown.

As Mama jogged up the stairs to put her flip flops away, Dixie said, "We're in for it now."

"Why must you always be such a doggie downer?"

"I'm a realist."

From upstairs came muffled hollering. "Oh, my God! What the hell happened here?"

"See, I told you so," Dixie said. She and Parker raced up the stairs.

Mama stood in the middle of the hallway with her hand over her mouth, looking from her bedroom to the guest room.

"Follow my lead." Parker rushed to Mama and brushed up against her, doing his best to act concerned.

Mama got down on her knees and wrapped her arms around him. "Are you okay, sweetheart?" Her voice quavered. "Did anyone hurt you? If anyone hurt you, I'll..."

She reached out and beckoned Dixie over with a wave of her hand. Dixie came along Mama's other side and snuggled in for a hug. When she did, Mama began to cry.

Parker's heart sank. This wasn't what he intended. He just wanted to help Lila. He licked Mama's face, drying her tears.

"Well, how do you feel now, big guy?" Dixie asked. "I told you from the start it was a bad plan. Now you've upset Mama."

"It'll be all right. She'll see we're safe, and she'll feel all better."

Mama sniffed and stood up. "Okay. We need to get to the bottom of this. It's obvious that someone's been in the house. We need to figure out who it was." She paced from one end of the hall to the other. "We need an action plan."

Dixie groaned. "This can't be good."

"Don't be such a pessimist," Parker said.

Mama strode with purpose into her office and sat down at the computer. Parker and Dixie trailed behind.

"Okay," Mama said. "The first thing we need is some security."

Parker strained to get a glimpse of the computer screen. He covered his eyes with his paws.

"What is it?" Dixie whispered.

"She's buying one of those WiFi remote pet monitoring systems."

"A what?"

"If you ever read the technology magazines Mama gets instead of trying to scratch and sniff them, you'd be up-to-date on the latest cool gadgets. It's a way for Mama to watch what we're doing when she's not home."

"Uh-oh," Dixie said.

"Exactly."

Mama said, "Okay. Step one is complete. Now for step two."

"What do you suppose that is?" Dixie asked.

"No idea."

Mama gathered some stuff together. "Let's see. Snacks, a flashlight, binoculars, those cool night vision goggles I bought last month, water, a sweatshirt in case it gets cold, a dog bed. That ought to do it."

"Is she preparing for the zombie apocalypse?" Dixie asked.

Parker whipped his head around. "You don't know what myopic means but you know about the zombie apocalypse? Amazing."

"Stick with me. I'll surprise you."

"I'm afraid of that."

"Okay, kids. Are you ready for a great adventure? We're going to get to the bottom of this. We're going to conduct a stakeout."

"I don't suppose she means we're going to get rib-eye for supper, does she?" Dixie asked.

Parker sighed. "Definitely not."

"WE'VE BEEN OUT HERE for hours," Mama said. She was sitting in the driver's seat. She stared unblinking through her binoculars, then switched to the night vision goggles.

In the backseat, Dixie lifted her sleep mask to peek at Parker. "We'd be so much more comfortable inside. If you hadn't started all this, we'd be curled up in our nice, soft beds. But no—"

"Stop your bellyaching. 'I need a sleep mask to block out the light. I need to be by the window so I don't get car-sick, even when we're standing still. I need the window open for fresh air.'" Parker gave a derisive woof. "You are so high maintenance."

"Hey. I like my creature comforts. Don't judge."

"Okay," Mama said, "we're not getting anywhere. The cameras will arrive tomorrow. We'll see what we can capture that way." Mama put the car in gear and pulled around into the garage.

DIXIE SAID, "I KNOW I sound like a broken record, but this is a really bad idea."

"It's okay. Mama's out to lunch. We just need to make one more run."

"Two words. Security cameras."

"I've got a plan for those." Parker balanced a can of spray paint between his paws. "Come here and press down on this little button here."

"What is this stuff?"

"It's to black out the camera lens so it can't record us." Parker rotated the can in his front paws until it was lined up even with the lens. "Okay, press the button now."

Dixie complied. "Where do you get this stuff?"

"Well, actually, Mama got it—"

"No. I meant, where did you come up with the idea?"

"I saw it on one of those shows Mama watches on Tuesday nights. The one with the initials."

When they had finished covering all four camera lenses, Parker stood back and admired his handiwork. "Okay. We're good to go. Let's grab the pants and shirts and get moving."

"You know Mama's going to miss these, too, right?"

"She might." Parker pulled slacks off the hangars in Mama's closet and yanked shirts out of the cubbyhole. "But we're doing her a favor."

"Uh-huh."

"We are. Every time she puts these three pairs of pants on, she looks in the mirror and says she looks like a cow in heat. And she always puts these shirts on with the pants before she says that, so if we take this stuff, we'll be sparing her from feeling bad about her body."

"You keep telling yourself that."

TWO HOURS LATER, THEY were back home and feeling well pleased with themselves when Mama arrived home.

"Hi, kids. Are you okay? Anything eventful happen?" Mama put a hand on each head and scratched Parker and Dixie behind the ears. "I tried to check in several times, but something must be wrong with the picture. I'll just have a look..." She walked over to the camera in the family room and gasped. "Somebody's tampered with this." She ran from one camera to the next, checking each one. "No. No, no, no, no, no." She sprinted up the stairs to her office. Parker and Dixie bounded along, hot on her heels.

Mama booted up the computer.

"What's she doing?"

"I don't know. I'm here just like you, aren't I?" Parker positioned himself to see the computer screen. Mama punched some keys on the keyboard, and he gasped.

"What's wrong?" Dixie asked.

"I failed to account for this eventuality."

"Speak dog, please?"

"We're screwed."

"Uh-oh."

Mama worked the mouse, clicking and pausing, clicking and pausing. "What?"

"Uh-oh," Parker sang. There, frozen on the screen, was a clear image of Dixie's nose inspecting their handiwork on the lens. Moments later and a dozen more mouse clicks, there was a barely visible glimpse of Dixie dragging Mama's pants across the bedroom floor.

Mama whirled around in her chair and looked at Parker and then Dixie. Her brow was furrowed and her jaw was set. Parker idly thought she resembled the angry Schnauzer, Max, from down the street.

"What did you do?" Mama stood and approached Dixie, wagging a finger at her. "What did you do?"

Dixie sat with her ears back. "There she goes again, repeating herself. And why do I always get the bum rap? This was your idea, genius. Take responsibility."

Parker tried not to snicker. After all, Mama did eventually figure out that the...creative...trimming of the ficus bushes was his doing and not Dixie's, even if it did take her two weeks and catching him red-pawed to discover the truth. She would probably deduce the facts in this case too.

"I am so mad at you right now. Why, Dixie? Why did you do it?"

Dixie wagged her tail and gave Mama her most ingratiating smile. It didn't work.

"Get away from me right now. I can't bear to look at you."

Dixie and Parker left the room and headed for the stairs.

Dixie said, "You'd better find a way to get me out of the dog house, mister."

"I'm sorry, I can't hear you, I've got a paw in my ear."

"Like I've never heard that one before. You better sleep with one eye open."

THREE DAYS LATER, MAMA was still steaming.

"You have to do something," Dixie said while they were on their walk.

"I have a plan."

"Fantastic. We all know how well that went last time."

"Sarcasm will get you nowhere. Follow my lead."

"If that was a pun," Dixie said, looking pointedly at the leash, "it was horrible."

Parker took off running and pulled Mama with him. Dixie followed suit.

"Where are we going?" Dixie asked.

"To Lila's place."

"What? Have you lost your mind?"

"You want to get off the hook, we have to come clean."

"Hey!" Mama shouted. "What's wrong with you two. Heel! By me! Heel!"

"You'd better hope you're right about this," Dixie said.

Several minutes later, Parker and Dixie skidded to a halt and plopped down, their tongues lolling.

"Of all the... You two are in so much trouble."

Parker got up and walked them over to Lila's makeshift tarp. He laid down and put his head on his paws. Dixie did the same.

"What the..." For the first time, Mama really looked around. "Hey! That's my pillow. And that's my comforter! And my clothes!" She bent down and got eye-to-eye with Parker and Dixie. "What's the big idea?"

Parker whimpered and gave her his best pathetic look.

"I don't want to be the one to say Mama is dense," Dixie murmured, "but I don't think she's getting it yet."

Parker sprang up. "Plan B." He pulled at them.

Again, Dixie followed his lead. "You know your Plan Bs never seem to work out."

"It will this time." With Dixie's help, he continued to yank Mama along until they reached Starbucks.

Sure enough, Lila was there, wearing one of Mama's shirts and a pair of her pants. Parker and Dixie immediately went to her and sat down. Parker sniffed her. She smelled faintly like Mama after a long day, when the spray from the glass bottle still lingered on her skin.

"If it isn't my favorite doggies. Hi, Parker and Dixie. It's so good to see you again." Lila looked up at Mama. "Do you need me to watch them while you go inside?"

Mama's mouth opened and closed, but nothing came out. She blinked.

"Is everything all right?" Lila asked.

Mama cleared her throat. Parker could see there were tears in her eyes. "Y-yes. Everything is better than all right." She bent down and hugged Parker and whispered in his ear, "Is this what you were trying to tell me? You two have been taking my stuff and giving it to Lila?"

Parker gave Mama a lick.

Mama hugged Dixie too. "I so owe you an apology. I love you and your big hearts."

"Um... Are you sure everything is okay?" Lila asked. "You seem a little emotional."

"We're fine, thanks. We just came to say hello. The kids seemed like they were missing you, so I thought we'd stop by."

Lila's face lit up. "Well, isn't that just the sweetest thing. I miss you guys, too." She kissed both dogs on the head.

"Can I get you something, Lila?"

"What? Me? Oh, no. I couldn't."

"I'd be happy to buy you a drink and something to eat."

"Really, that's not necessary. It's the darndest thing. Someone's been leaving me all sorts of stuff. Like some Secret Santa or something. I feel so cared for and loved, I couldn't ask for anything more."

"You know," Mama said, "I think I've changed my mind. I will go in and get something, after all. Can you watch the kids for me?"

"Sure."

Mama gave Lila the leash. Through the glass door, Parker saw Mama talking animatedly with someone inside. When she came out, he was with her.

"Lila, this is Calvin. He's the manager of this Starbucks."

"Oh." Lila straightened up and handed the leash back to Mama. "You probably want me to vacate the premises. I understand."

"No." As Lila turned to go, Mama put out a hand to stop her.

"Most definitely not," Calvin said. "In fact, I was coming out to ask if you'd like to work here."

"W-what?" Lila looked from Mama to Calvin.

"I'm short of good help, and you seem to have a way with folks. I thought maybe, if you were willing, I could train you to be a barista."

"For real?"

"Yes. The pay's not that great but—"

"Yes. Yes, yes, yes." Lila's smile lit up her face. "But I'm sure I'm not clean enough to work here."

"Lila?" Mama asked. "How do you feel about house sitting?"

"What do you mean?"

"I mean, I've got some friends who are relocating. They've already moved out, and they need someone to stay in their house and keep an eye on things. They would pay you for staying there. You'd be doing them a real favor."

Lila shook her head. "This can't all be real. This can't be happening to me."

"The house is within walking distance of this place, so you could walk to work. What do you say?"

Lila's grin said everything.

"Okay, then," Mama said. "It's settled. I'll go talk to my friends right now and set up a time for you to meet them."

"Okay." Lila turned to Calvin. "I accept your job offer."

"Excellent. Why don't you come inside and you can fill out the paperwork? You can start tomorrow."

Lila started to follow Calvin inside. "Wait!" She ran back over and hugged Parker and Dixie tightly. "I hope I'll keep seeing you two."

Parker wagged his tail and Dixie nuzzled Lila's neck.

"Don't worry," Mama said. "I promise, we'll be your best customers, won't we, kids?" She winked at Parker and Dixie.

"See?" Parker said to Dixie on the way home. "All's well that ends well."

"Tell that to the ficus bushes."

"Hey! They grew back." He shoved Dixie.

She purposely veered off to the left to smell her favorite twenty blades of grass.

Parker said, "That is so passive-aggressive."

"What does that even mean?"

"Passive-aggressive?"

Dixie gave him a blank look.

"Never mind," Parker said.

In a happy voice, Mama said, "I've got big treats for you both when we get home. What do you say? You want some of those? What do you say?"

Dixie sighed. "She still talks to us like we're dolts."

"Humor her. She's only human."

MOTEL NOIR
By Sandra de Helen

SUNLIGHT BOUNCED OFF EVERY bright surface in the motel parking lot. Even with sunglasses on, my throbbing migraine made me feel like something was piercing my right eye. I managed to unlock Room 202 and stumble into the dimness, grateful for relief from the light.

In an alcove next to the motel door and under a clothes pole full of bent wire hangers sat one of those fold-open luggage racks. I tossed my overnight bag toward it, flipped up the back of my trench coat like I do when I don't want to get anything on my coat. Call me cheap, but it costs more to clean my coat than it does to wash my pants. I sat heavily on the side of the six-inch deep queen-size mattress that made this room cost five dollars more than the economy rate.

I sat for a long while, waiting for my head to calm down. Now that the light wasn't my primary irritant, I noticed the smells. The room was funky—cleaning spray over an odor I couldn't identify. What did I expect? The place was a dive and always had been.

Once my head could bear movement, I stood up, removed my coat, and reached for the bifold doors of the closet. I hadn't gotten it open more than a few inches when a Hulk arm fell out and grabbed my booted ankle.

I damned near pissed my pants, if you'll pardon the expression. They call me a tough dame, but I might have leaked a drop or two. Okay, he didn't actually grab me, because he was dead. But he touched me. I jumped straight up and clear across the room. I had a gun in my hand before my feet hit the floor. I didn't scream, but I did choke out some blue words. That Hulk arm is lucky I didn't shoot it, I can tell you that.

I have a license for my Sig Sauer. I'm a private eye. Helen Black is my name. Go ahead, make the joke, I've heard it all my life. "You look like Helen Black. And not so great in white either. Har har har." So guess what color I wear every day. And guess how many kids got a black eye courtesy of Helen Black when I was in school? I told them they didn't look so good in black either. Har har har.

I didn't pull the Hulk out of the closet—that would have been tampering with evidence. I opened the bifold doors all the way, put on a pair of non-latex gloves and felt for a pulse. None. I got out my LED flashlight, got down on my knees and took a good look. The arm that had touched me was still attached. To a black man, about six foot, give or take a couple of inches, two hundred pounds or so, maybe thirty years old—hard to tell from this position—wearing jeans, hoodie, sneakers. Given the amount of blood on his shirt, it looked like he maybe died close to where he was lying. I guessed the maid had skipped the closet. Good job cleaning up the room, guys. Yuck.

Did I want to deal with this? I could just pick up my bag, go back to the front desk and say I didn't like the view. Give me a different room, or my money back, and I'd go on down the road. Let some other sucker deal with Mr. Hulk. After all, I already had a migraine. I didn't know this dude, or the motel owner, or anyone involved. I didn't owe anyone my time or energy.

Why oh why did I study ethics in college?

I picked up my bag, walked down to the front desk and told the clerk he had a problem. I let him dial the police and get me a new room on the opposite end of the building. I stashed my bag and went back to the room to see if I could be of any help to the Oceanside Police Department.

Chief Andi Whitehall herself showed up. Her only deputy was off duty, seeing as it was Christmas Eve. Yeah, that's why I was at the Oregon coast, it's what I always did. No family of my own, no partner for the past five years. I got a cheap room, watched the waves, and waited for the day to be over. This year I happened to have the added benefit of a headache, which began to lift a couple of minutes after I met Andi.

Andi reminded me of a darker-skinned, fuller-figured Halle Berry. She had short natural hair, a muscular build, a great smile, and looked like the kind of person you'd want to lie next to. Maybe. We'd have to see what she thought when she looked at me. Really looked at Helen Black, PI, not just me as a witness. I introduced myself. While we waited for the medical examiner to arrive, I told her I was a private investigator from Portland in town for the holidays, and would like to tag along on this case. I assured her I knew how to stay out of her way, and how not to trample or otherwise mess up the evidence. There was no reason in the world she had to let me get involved. I hoped she would.

After she heard my plea, she decided to let me come along, so long as I behaved professionally. I promised, and didn't even cross my fingers behind my back. This was a woman whose respect I craved from the first moment I saw her.

We made a good team collecting evidence, getting the pictures, waiting for the medical examiner. Basically she did all the work and I held stuff when she asked me to. When the medical guy got there, Andi took a few more pictures for the record, and the medical examiner did what he needed to do before moving the body.

Once the body was gone, Andi put up the yellow tape and sealed off the door. She had to leave, and she asked me to follow her back to her office to make my official statement. I jumped to do so. Once I'd written out my account, she poured us some coffee and we went over our notes as if we were partners instead of newly met colleagues. I acted as though this type of relationship happened to me all the time in the big city of Portland. She had on her professional face as well.

"I don't usually let civilians within yards of a crime scene, but you've been a big help."

"Yeah. No, I mean, I know it's a rare thing for the police to let civilians do anything more than maybe a ride-along with a uniformed officer."

"Just so we're clear."

"It's Christmas. You're being nice."

"I'm being professional and asking you to do the same."

"Of course. That's what I meant to say."

She smiled at me. I was acting like a schoolgirl, all weak in the knees, short of breath, and sweating. If I'd been having chest pain, I'd have had all the classic symptoms of a heart attack. But I recognized my behaviors for what they were. I was attracted to this woman.

No one had rented the room for more than a week, so maybe this was an inside job. Andi was going to have to call in all the motel workers for interviews. The clerk showed up to make a statement while we were talking. He'd be the first she'd talk to. I wasn't allowed to sit in, but the walls were thin, so I loitered in the hall as she did her interrogation.

"So, Jason, who was this dude in the closet up in Room 202?"

"I dunno, Chief, who?"

"Don't be a wise ass. Your records show no one checked into that room for eight days until today. This guy was shot today. Did you know him?"

"You didn't let me up there to see him and he was covered up when the people brought him out, so I don't even know what the guy looked like, okay?"

"Here, look at this picture."

"Shit, man. This guy is dead."

"Do you know him or not?"

"Never saw him before. No, wait, is he wearing an earring?"

"Yes, it's a silver cross."

"Oh."

"You know a guy with an earring?"

"Yeah, but it wasn't a silver cross."

"You saw a black dude at your motel today with an earring, but it wasn't a silver cross."

"Not at the motel. Not today, no. Just some guy I saw last night at the bar. Big guy. I couldn't see him real clear. It was dark in there. But he had an earring. I don't think it was a cross though. I thought it was a diamond."

"Could this be him?"

"I don't think so."

"Why not?"

"That guy last night was alive, and I think his earring was a diamond. I didn't know him. I never saw him before. Anyway, I'm sorry I can't be more help."

"Jason, you're a great help. Just don't leave town."

"I got to get back on the desk."

"Not so fast. I need you to write down the names and phone numbers of the other workers from the motel."

"Oh, that's easy. There's just Maria and Nelda. They're roommates. Here's their number. They take turns cleaning. Maria is on today. I guess she'll have to clean up that blood and stuff, huh?"

"We can send in professionals, but the motel owners will have to pay the bill."

"I can call the owners. I don't know if they'll pay though. On the other hand, I don't know if either Maria or Nelda will be willing to do the gore work. I wouldn't. Give me freaking nightmares."

I made myself scarce as I heard their chairs scrape back from the table. By the time Andi found me, I was in the break room, kicked back with my feet up, drinking another cup of coffee, apparently deep in thought. I put my feet down and looked as interested as if I hadn't heard the entire conversation.

"Any leads?" I asked.

"Not really. Gonna interview the maids next. Want to meet me for lunch tomorrow? Shady's makes a mean panini, and they're one of the few places in town open on Christmas Day."

"Sure. One o'clock okay?"

"Yup."

I got the feeling she didn't want or need a civilian tagging along as she worked her case, so I went back to the motel and chatted up Jason. Turned out he'd been at the Starlight the night before, which was the only gay bar in town. In fact, it was the only gay bar within forty miles on that stretch of the coast. I figured that even though it was Christmas Eve, they'd be open for all the gay singles, or for new couples celebrating in a bar instead of in front of their own tree at home. I headed over, hoping to find either the dude with the diamond earring, or someone who knew him.

The Starlight had great curbside appeal. The building was made of old growth logs, the roof of slate. The windows were large, sparkling clean, and lined with twinkling lights. The wide doors welcomed everyone, no cover charge. Inside the rooms were spacious, but comfortable and cozy. A few men and women sat at the bar, but many people were scattered throughout the main room on leather loveseats and armchairs, chatting and drinking. I could see through to a ballroom where people were dancing, and the music wasn't overwhelmingly loud. Lights were low enough for atmosphere, but not so dark I couldn't have told the difference between a diamond and a silver cross at ten feet or so. Maybe they dimmed the lights later on. Or maybe Jason would show up in the ballroom, where the lights were a bit dimmer.

High-backed stools lined a thirty foot long bar. The bar was neat, clean and well-stocked with bottles of every kind of liquor and taps of locally brewed and brand name beers. Shiny glasses were within easy reach. A smiling bartender looked up as I approached.

I sat at the bar and ordered a hot buttered rum. The bartender pulled a stick of butter out of the fridge, sliced off a hunk, put it in a mug, poured in about three ounces of dark rum, filled it with boiling water, stirred it with a glass stick, and brought it to me. The scent alone raised the score of my day from a five to a seven. The taste brought it up another point. One would be my limit as I was driving, so I was going to have to sip. I worked my nose overtime. This was some great drink. I asked the bartender for the recipe, but he would only tell me the important thing was the spices were cinnamon, nutmeg, cloves and the pinch of salt was what made them sing. I'll bet he used sea salt too, not that chemical stuff people put on their tables. I prefer pink Himalayan salt, but I'm kind of a salt snob. While I was sitting there pondering the wonders of our olfactory senses and taste buds, a young woman dressed in red and green rushed in the front door, straight up to the bar, leaned across and yelled to the bartender.

"Gordon, have you seen Nate?"

"Not since last night, Cookie."

"Did you see who he left with? Or remember what time he left?"

"I think he left alone. It got kind of crowded in here before closing. He was gone by the time I closed, I know that."

"Okay, thanks."

I had to ask.

"Uh, Cookie? You don't know me ..."

"No." She turned and gave me a look. "And you don't know me."

"Excuse me. I couldn't help over-hearing ..."

"Butt out. This is none of your business."

"I might be able to help." I said.

"How?" She gave me a scowl of doubt, which I ignored.

"Nate. What's he look like? Was he wearing an earring?"

"Maybe. Why?"

"You're missing a person. I know of a person who was found. Okay?"

"So?"

"Will you describe Nate?"

"You first."

"My person is a black dude. About six feet. Couple hundred pounds. Wearing jeans and a sweatshirt."

"And an earring, you said."

"Yes."

"Okay, that could be Nate. But it could be a thousand other men."

"In Oceanside? Last night?"

"Probably not."

"Did Nate have a diamond earring?"

"No. No, Nate's earring is a silver cross."

"Oh."

"Not him then. Right?"

"I think you're gonna want to go talk to Chief Andi Whitehall at the Oceanside Police Department."

"Nate's been arrested?"

"Nate might be involved in something. She'll need to talk to you about it."

"You going with me?"

"I'm not a law officer. Just a citizen."

"Oh hell no. You're the one got me into this. You're going with me."

I gulped down my now tepid buttered rum, and after a brief haggle, I drove Miss Cookie to the sheriff's office to see about Nate. Take my advice. Don't ever drink a tepid buttered anything. The butter had solidified, and did a terrific job of greasing my teeth and tongue. How could a drink that started out tasting so good end up more like warm root beer that had gone flat? Now I wanted to throw up. Or at least brush my teeth. Gack. In the two minutes it took to reach our destination, I searched my pockets, the glove box, the door pockets, and all the hidey holes in the car for something—anything—to get this taste out of my mouth. Finally, I found a used tissue and scrubbed my front teeth with it, just as we pulled up in front of the station.

Inside I let Cookie introduce herself to the chief while I ran my tongue over my teeth, hoping I didn't have white lint stuck to them.

In no time Andi saw that Cookie's missing person might be our found one. She arranged for Cookie to do an ID. But first she asked a couple of questions.

"What is your relationship to Nate, Cookie?"

"He's my brother."

"When did you see him last?"

"Yesterday about lunchtime. We had a late breakfast together, and we were going to have dinner together at my place last night, but he never showed up. I was sure he'd come by today, this being Christmas Eve and all."

"Okay, I'm going to take you to the morgue and see if the young man we found is your brother. Are you up for that?"

She blanched. "Like, you want me to look at a dead guy?"

The chief said, "We do have a man who was found dead who matches your description. Hey, are you feeling okay?"

"I'm all right." Suddenly Cookie's bright red and green outfit did nothing for her and she didn't look all right. Not one bit. Her skin had turned a sickly gray brown.

I volunteered to go along as support. Lucky thing I did, because Cookie wilted as soon as the morgue attendant pulled back the sheet. The earring was indeed a silver cross, although it was shinier than most. I could see how it might sparkle under the lights. Nate himself didn't look so hot. It was good to have a name to put on his toe tag. No one likes to have a John Doe lying around longer than necessary.

I took Cookie to a bench, got her a glass of water, and once she was steady, helped her back to the chief's desk for more questioning now that her skin was brightening up a bit.

Andi was back in full investigative mode now that the identification was made. "You have any idea why Nate would have been in the motel yesterday afternoon, Cookie?"

"Ask Jason. He claimed Nate wasn't at the bar last night, but I know they were fighting about something. Nate might have gone to see him at the motel."

"Do you know why they were fighting?"

"They were always fighting! Ever since they got together, they've been fighting about one thing or another. I don't know what Nate saw in Jason anyway. Jason is a prize jerkwad if you ask me."

"So Jason and Nate were together?"

"Hell yeah. Lived together since the first night they met. Acted like lesbians. Jason went and got a U-Haul that first weekend and moved his shit into my brother's place. Nate's condo is premium. You saw that dump of a motel where Jason lives. It's no wonder he was after my brother. But I don't have any idea what Nate saw in him. I told him yesterday he needed to dump that gold digger."

The chief glanced at me. Jason had just sat in her office and lied through his teeth. Surely he would have recognized his lover from the picture Andi showed him, even if Nate was dead.

Andi said, "thank you, Miss, um, Middlefield, is that right?"

"That's what it says on the page there, isn't it? You got any forms I need to fill out? Because I want to get out of here to go to the funeral home and start making arrangements. Shit, it's Christmas! Will the funeral home even be open?"

"I think they're always on call, Miss Middlefield, but we're not going to be able to release the body, your brother that is, until we've finished processing ..."

"When's that going to be?"

"The medical examiner will let us know. I'll call you. Meanwhile, if you want to go home and rest, you may. I'll call you if I have more questions."

"Rest? I need to call my family. See my friends. Who's going to take me back to my car?"

I jumped in quickly before they could lock horns again. "No worries, Cookie. I'll drive you." On the drive back I wasted no time seeing what else I could learn about Nate and Jason's relationship. Cookie was all too willing to dish.

"That Jason is a scumbag. I wish you'd known my brother." She choked back a sob. "He's the nicest guy, was, I mean." She paused and took a deep breath. "He'd give you the shirt off his back. But Jason was always nagging at him for more stuff, new this, new that, let's go to

Cancun, go on a cruise, do a three-way. Nate didn't want to do three-ways. He was kind of straight in that way, you know? He didn't do drugs, and he liked his sex one on one. I don't know what they were fighting about, but whatever it was it got Nate killed."

In between occasional bursts of tears, she told me more about Jason and Nate's love spats, all having to do with either material goods or Jason's desire for a menage á trois. Nate was only too happy to buy electronics, home furnishings, new clothes for them both, but he had a job that kept him from doing more than planning a two-week vacation that was still months away. Nate and Jason hadn't ever left Oregon together at all. Apparently, they'd been together only a couple of months.

I dropped Cookie at her car and rushed back to the Andi's office, only to find that she had left. I knew where I'd be in her shoes, so I drove to the motel. Sure enough her SUV was parked in front of the motel office. I sat in my car wondering how aggressive I dared to be. I felt pretty certain that Andi was attracted to me. I knew I had been of some help on her case. Neither of those items gave me license to butt in on her current interview with her prime suspect. I put my car in gear and drove back to her office, went inside and made a pot of coffee. I hadn't even opened the cover of the two-year-old Sheriff Magazine when she brought Jason in, his wrists handcuffed behind him. She nodded at me, and pushed him back to the cells.

Andi poured herself a cup of the fresh coffee and filled me in. Jason had claimed he was innocent, but he had made some remarks that had Andi pretty revved up. She got on the phone and called in her deputy to come babysit Jason. Once Deputy Kozak was there, she was ready to roll. She motioned for me to come along. The deputy raised an eyebrow, but said nothing as I followed Andi out the door.

In her SUV she told me Jason said he and Nate were planning a hook-up with "some dude" they'd met at the Starlight the other night, but Nate ditched Jason and left with the other guy. Nate had a passkey to the motel, so Jason figured that was how he'd ended up in my room. Jason insisted the other dude must be the killer. Andi was taking no chances. She agreed to check out Jason's story, but she wasn't ruling him out as the killer. He hadn't tested positive for gunshot residue, but he could have worn gloves or taken a shower and scrubbed it off between the time of the shooting and the time he was questioned. He certainly hadn't been wearing anything with blood spatter on it.

We went to the bar. Andi had a quiet talk with Gordon the bartender, and we headed back out. The skies were completely overcast and it was beginning to drizzle. Another gray Christmas after all.

I said, "He gave you a name and address, just like that?"

"Gordon is as eager as I am to have this issue resolved. We're a small town here, Helen. We don't like mysteries. No one wants to have to start locking their doors."

"So where're we headed?"

"About two more blocks. You stay in the car while I go inside though. I doubt Xavier is going to shoot us, but he might be feeling scared, and that makes him volatile. I'll be right back. You can keep the car running for the heat."

We were there by that time. Small beach cottage a block from the water. Lights on inside even though it wasn't quite dark yet, even with the clouds. Christmas lights were strung around the windows. A seagull screeched overhead as Andi shut the car door behind her. I watched her move quietly across the sandy lawn and up to the door, her hand on her holster, which was open and ready for business. She knocked with her left hand, and called out.

"Xavier? Xavier Mathis? It's Chief Whitehall. Open the door."

A willowy Caucasian man in his twenties opened the door dressed in pajamas and bare feet. His hair looked as if it hadn't been combed in days—whether on purpose or not I couldn't tell, but he was definitely rocking the bed head look. Andi went inside, and was back out with him in minutes. This time he was dressed in jeans, boots, sweatshirt and jacket. His hair looked the same, but his hands were in cuffs behind his back. She marched him to the car and put him in the backseat.

None of us spoke a word all the way to Andi's office. She walked him in, put him directly into the interrogation room, and cuffed him to the table. I was left outside with Deputy Kozak. He obviously didn't want to get his news from an outsider, and I desperately wanted to hear what was going on in the questioning, so we both sort of sidled up to the one-way mirror where we could see what was going on. The deputy turned on the speakers in order to hear, and gave me a look. I didn't meet his eyes, just looked around innocently, and stood my ground. He didn't kick me out because Andi had brought me in.

"Xavier, we know you killed Nate in the motel room. We just don't know why. Did you plan it? What happened?"

Xavier sat looking at the table.

"How did you get him into the closet, Xavier? Nate must have fifty or sixty pounds on you."

No answer.

"I guess he just wasn't interested in you after all. I mean he was fully dressed when we found him."

"That's all you know!" Xavier practically spat his words at Andi. The look he gave her would have made my hair fly back. She gave him a slight smile and a small nod.

"You're right, Xavier. I don't know. Why don't you tell me? Maybe I can help you get out of this mess?"

"It was an accident, okay? You have to believe me. I loved Nate. I would never have killed him."

"Loved him? How did you know him?"

"Me and Nate go way back. We met at YMCA camp. That's when we fell in love, you know? Just kids."

"Tell me everything, Xavier. What happened here?"

"Nate called me. He'd met this guy, Jason, and they had a thing. Jason moved in on him real quick, and kept after him to do stuff Nate didn't want to do. When Jason wouldn't let up on him about doing a three-way, Nate got this idea that I could get involved, Jason wouldn't know we knew each other, and somehow it would be okay. But when we got together last night, it went all wrong. Jason sussed the facts within half an hour. Sharp one, him. He started chasing us around the motel grounds with a gun, so me and Nate ran our asses off. We thought we got away when we made it to that room. We were hiding in the closet. And bam. Jason finds us. When he pulled open the door, I scrambled out from behind Nate and tried to grab the gun from Jason. But it went off and...well, you know what happened to Nate. I got the hell out of there before Jason could kill me too."

After the interview with Xavier, Andi confirmed the story with Jason, who had left Nate in the closet and rented the room to me. Hoping I would find him and what? Think I'd killed him myself? Sheesh. I guess putting the onus of having the body found by an unsuspecting guest at least got the body found before the smell did. But the cleaner should have found poor Nate. Maybe that's what Jason was counting on. If I were the owner, I'd fire everybody. I'm cranky that way.

Once Andi did her paperwork, called in the DA, and did all the essential tasks, she left the prisoners in the hands of her trusty deputy. The chief and I and repaired to the Stardust for some celebratory Chablis. No more buttered drinks for Helen Black. For the first time in years I spent my last night at the coast dancing with my new friend, and making plans for New Year's Eve.

LOST
By Jen Wright

"YOU READY?"

"Totally. Be there in fifteen."

I could tell Toni was dictating her text messages. Neither of us had adopted shorthand texting beyond LMAO or TTYL. I made one final adjustment to my pack and hauled it out to the curb.

Toni pulled up in her Outback with the canoe strapped to her roof rack. We loaded up my gear, and Candy, my partner of fifteen years, gave us both a hug and me a kiss. Candy had no desire to be out in the wilderness, but she was supportive of my need to get away.

The drive along the scenic north shore of Lake Superior never failed to inspire. The overlooks and the rock cliffs on both sides of the road were breathtaking. We'd taken the same trip to our favorite site on Keeper Lake for the past five years. Keeper Lake is two-and-a-half hours north of Duluth in the Boundary Waters Canoe Area—BWCA for short. Depending on how many campsites are unoccupied, we are usually able to put in at Keeper Lake and find a spot within an hour with no portaging.

This trip was no exception. We loaded our gear and took off, singing as we paddled, and relaxed into our BFF rhythm. We passed two open campsites in hopes that our "favorite" place would be available at the end of the lake. Sure enough, it was. The site was sheltered from the wind, had good sun exposure, and afforded incredible sunsets at the end of the day.

We angled up to a landing spot along the shore, and a small-mouth bass skittered away.

"Woo hoo," Toni called out. "The fish are already jumping."

"Can't wait to drop a line," I said with glee.

We set up our tent and the sun shower area, hung the hammocks, and arranged the rain tarp for cooking and gear protection. The bear-bagging rig went high in a tree to keep the bears from stealing our food, then we put the canoes in and started fishing.

The trip played out the same way every year. Fish, eat, nap in camp hammocks, read, and sleep.

The mid-July day was perfect, seventy-five degrees with plenty of sun. We lathered up with sun-screen and bug dope and headed off to a likely fishing spot in search of dinner.

As I steered us along a rocky ledge, Toni pulled out her well-worn copy of *Fishing in the Boundary Waters*. I knew from past history that the book didn't encourage fishing off of deep ledges, but I also knew we'd caught a lot of fish by trolling back and forth over one, so that's where we settled.

"Save the reading," I said. "You need to get your line in the water."

"Mmm-hmm," she replied, continuing to read for another minute before putting her book away and getting her pole properly rigged up. We hadn't gone more than ten feet before I got a hit on my line. I knew right away I had a bass as it hit hard and jumped out of the water.

Fishing in a canoe with light tackle is always a thrill, and this was no exception. I pulled in a nice two pounder and put it on the stringer. If we got two bigger ones, this one would go free.

"Nice job, Kim. What are you using for bait?" Toni asked, getting into the competitive spirit.

"Purple hair."

She looked at her yellow jig and decided to give it a bit more time. As we neared the end of the ledge rock, I asked, "Want to hit some shallows on the other side of the canal or head back along the cliff?"

"Let's hit the shallows." Five in the afternoon, and we had another hour or two to catch our dinner. We paddled over to the shallows, knowing that if we trolled, we risked getting snagged, so we settled in over a spot with basketball-sized rocks below. I put out an anchor, and we cast into the rocks, letting our lures sit for a full minute before reeling them in.

Toni got a hit after a few casts and landed a nice four-pound bass. With that, we called it a day and paddled over to the island where we usually clean our fish. Although regulations require you to bury your fish remains, we left ours on the rocky shore as an offering to an eagle perched on a tall tree across the channel who watched as we cleaned our fish.

We paddled to our campsite and took turns with the binoculars, watching the eagle's graceful and powerful flight over the water.

I prepped a side of instant mashed potatoes and cooked our filets with a homemade shore lunch batter made with flour and spices. All year, whenever I dreamed of the trip, I had so looked forward to this meal.

"Oh, my God, this is good," I said after the first bite.

Toni's eyes were closed as she slowly chewed. "It's heavenly."

After dinner, Toni built a fire and made hot chocolate. As we sipped, the sun dipped slowly, cascading subtle orange and yellow light among the layers of clouds.

I AWAKENED WELL AFTER dawn. The tent felt warm, even with only a sleeping bag liner covering me. Toni was up and quietly writing in a notebook. She was a prolific poet, and I didn't want to disturb her, but because we were in a tiny backpacking tent, I couldn't help but see what she was writing.

While the poem was amazing, it shocked me.

Idle

I sit with hands folded neatly in my lap
    suddenly awake
My heart held silent
    As it should be
    Cocooned but not still

    Protecting you from me
    Her from disrespect

I needn't bleed chaos into a world such as yours
I needn't bleed tainted blood anywhere
    It courses through my veins
    With a heat I scarcely remember

You will never exist at the end of my fingertips
    They yearn to dance over your warm skin as I
    with eyes shut, absorb every curve
Feel muscles tighten.

That chaos will never be mine
and so I sit with respectful
unbearably empty hands
    Idle
and fold them neatly in my lap

"What'cha working on?" I inquired.

She closed the notebook quickly. "Nothing really, I'm playing around with words. You know how I am."

"Let's hear it,"

"Not yet. Still needs a lot of work. Ready for some coffee and breakfast?"

"After I hit the latrine." I fished around in my stuff sack for some shorts and a T-shirt.

"You better get moving because I'm holding a whole night's worth of pee myself."

Getting dressed in a tiny tent is always difficult, but she hastily pulled her shirt over her head and slid her pants on while still lying down.

We both knew either one of us could go into the bushes anywhere in the vicinity of the latrine and not pose any threat to the wildlife or to the water, but our competitive natures had emerged. I got the zipper on the tent up, while she struggled into her sandals. I slipped into the water shoes I'd placed outside the tent and raced to the latrine with her close behind. Racing was a stretch, given my full bladder. Fast walking was a more accurate description. As I approached the fork where the trail to the latrine veered to the right, I no longer heard her behind me.

When I reached the outdoor "thunderbox," I couldn't believe my eyes. There she was, sitting proudly on her throne.

"What the—?"

"Shortcut," was all she said, with a wink. I did note some scratches on her legs, evidence of the length she had gone to beat me.

Back at the site, we settled into our camp seats, heating water in our fuel-efficient backpacking stove for our coffee and hot cereal mix. The word "our" hit me. I sat quietly pondering our friendship, searching my mind for any hint of a crush or un-communicated feelings. This friendship spanned ten years. In my mind, no way could Toni's poem be about me, but I still felt awkward asking her about it directly.

"You okay?" Toni asked.

"Yeah, slow to wake up."

I didn't know why I couldn't come out with it. Tell her that I had seen her poem. Ask her what it was about. The unspoken questions sat like a rock that I didn't want to come between us. I needed this friendship.

She shrugged off my answer. "What do you say the person who catches the biggest fish gets out of cleaning them?"

"You're on, but let's only count the bass. It'd be way too easy for me to catch a northern and wipe you out in the first hour."

"Whatever." She waved her hand, not giving me the satisfaction of a reaction. Therapists can be so annoying that way.

I PADDLED OVER TO an inlet on one of the adjoining lakes to cast our lines again. The fishing was incredible, and I was up three fish to two with one of mine weighing in at around four pounds. Our stringer was fat, but the competition was keeping us on the water until the fish stopped biting. Catch and release seems a little cruel, but it allowed us to keep fewer fish.

After we decided to move to a different spot, someone yelled.

"Hey, don't go! We need help!" A man and woman paddled furiously toward us, the water churning and spraying all over.

Toni and I finished reeling in our lines and waited. Their erratic approach seemed to take forever, but once they drew near, words tumbled out in a tangled mess. They came alongside, and we stabilized the boats. The only thing clear from their panic was that someone named Renee was missing.

"Slow down," I said. "My name is Kim Weiss, and I'm an off-duty police officer. I want to help, but you'll have to help me. Who is Renee?"

"Our daughter. She's missing," the woman said. She burst into tears.

"What do you mean by missing?" I asked. "Missing can mean a lot of things."

The man said, "We were portaging. Renee had to relieve herself, so she went off trail. She didn't come back."

"I thought she was just trying to get out of carrying gear," the woman said. "We tried our phones. We can't get a signal." She sounded on the edge of hysteria.

"How long has she been gone"? I asked.

"Three hours," the man said. "We've looked everywhere in the area. We called and called for her."

I looked at Toni, and she gave a nod. "Our camp is close by. Give us a few minutes to gather some gear for the search. Where shall we meet you?"

The man pointed. "We'll be at the portage. That was the last place where we were together. It's the one on the North side of the lake next to the inlet."

I grabbed my paddle. "Okay, we'll be there in a few minutes."

Both parents seemed relieved and grateful for our help as they pushed off and turned their canoe around.

Back at our camp, we stashed our day's catch in a wire basket in the lake, and I took my handgun and shoulder holster from the bottom of my pack. Toni gathered up whistles, matches, a lighter, binoculars, headlamps, and two canteens and stowed them in a small daypack. Five minutes later we were back on the water.

WE ARRIVED AT THE portage rendezvous to find both parents wired so tight they'd probably break rather than bend to deal with the reality of their missing daughter. We pulled our canoe in next to theirs. It seemed important to infuse some normalcy into this situation so Toni initiated introductions and told them a little about us. Then Ron and Kathy Rose from North Dakota told us they were newcomers to the BWCA. Their daughter Renee was thirteen, with very little experience in the wilderness.

They didn't have any GPS devices, nor did we since we were familiar with our route into Keeper Lake. I said, "How about if you two head east and then backtrack west while Toni and I go north?"

They nodded their agreement, unable to muster up the ability to speak.

"In three hours let's regroup at this portage," I said. "If for some reason we don't return, or you don't return, wait one more hour, and then paddle out to the entry point and drive the thirty-five miles to the nearest outfitter on Sawbill Lake. Most outfitters have a police radio, food, and a phone. If we get back and you're not here, we'll do the same."

"Okay," Ron choked out.

I divided maps into grids for searching and gave them my compass, and we kept Toni's.

ONCE IN THE WOODS, we hiked north, guided by Toni's compass. Whenever I found a rotted tree stump I used its position to mark our path. Occasionally we veered off our north line when we had to traverse a stream or lake edge. We both blew whistles and called out to Renee frequently.

An hour and a half into our bushwhacking, an uneasy feeling came over me. I squinted toward the sun, sure that we were heading in the wrong direction.

"How old is this compass?" I shook it and held it up for Toni to take a closer look.

"I don't know. Old."

"Have you checked it for accuracy any time in, say, the last ten years?" I asked, with more than a hint of sarcasm in my tone.

"Hmm, not so much."

"I don't think it's functioning properly, and I didn't notice until now. I have no idea which direction we've been traveling."

"Can you tell by the sun?"

"Not really. I wasn't checking along the way."

I knew my response was not the one Toni was hoping for. In our years of backcountry hiking and fishing, she had always looked to me to be navigator and guide. I counted on her for other things.

"Are we lost?" Toni's voice was therapist calm, her words quietly acknowledging the reality of our situation.

"Pretty much. We can travel back the way we came and try to find the tree stumps we set as markers for our search area. If we don't find any, our best course is to stay put until help arrives."

I studied the face of the compass again and concluded that it was acting up. At four p.m. the sun was visible to the west, yet our compass clearly pointed to the south.

Some people have little or no sense of direction, while others are gifted with an innate internal compass. Mine is usually pretty good. When I'm paying attention.

"This is pathetic," Toni said. "The search party gets lost? That's far too humbling for me."

"Let's not get ahead of ourselves here. We have some stumps to find." We walked for a solid hour and didn't see one familiar stump. Had we veered east? The question was only a hopeful feeling I wasn't sure I could trust. I thought back to where the sun was as we walked earlier, but my focus had been more on calling for Renee, and I couldn't remember.

Toni stopped to pull out a canteen, took a swig, and offered it to me.

After I downed some water, I asked, "Do *you* have any idea where we went off course?"

"I don't. I wasn't paying attention to the sun, either. Let's listen for Renee or her parents. Maybe we'll hear them calling."

We stood still. The wind was gusting at perhaps fifteen miles per hour as it usually did around this time of day. The combination of birch, poplar and other leafy trees made significant background noise. We couldn't hear a thing other than the sounds of nature.

"Damn it," I said.

"Double damn it. We can't just sit here and wait for rescue."

Much as I wanted to be rational and to follow the established protocol for our predicament, I couldn't forget that another person was lost in these woods. Potentially abducted. "True that, my friend, but we could be putting ourselves at greater risk by venturing farther away from where we started. Then a rescue will be even harder."

"Not only that, but what if Renee isn't lost? What if she was taken? We might be in the same area as the abductor."

"I have my gun. That puts things in our favor."

"Who are you trying to convince?"

At times I found Toni's profession annoying. "Both of us."

"Okay, it's not dark yet. What can we do without making the situation worse?"

"How about we walk in a large circle? That way, we won't stray too far beyond where we are right now."

"Sounds like a plan."

We walked for another hour and ended up roughly at our origination point, still with no signs of any stumps.

"What now?" Toni said.

"I guess we're going to miss the rendezvous."

At least the Roses would be going for help if we didn't show up. That is, if they followed the plan.

As a Duluth cop, I had participated in searches of hillside parks that encircle the many streams winding their way down to Lake Superior. The lake was usually visible from high points in the terrain, and we had the assistance of GPS and large search groups. Here, I was out of my league and skill set. I think Toni assumed I had more rescue experience than I did, and I didn't want to disabuse her of the notion, but I felt I should be honest. When I explained, she sank down onto a log and put her head in her hands.

Seeing my best friend in the world looking worried was hard. Although it wasn't totally my fault that we were lost, I still felt responsible. I'm sure she did, too. Her auburn curls were sprinkled with gray with a hint of sweat on the ends from our vigorous walking. She looked tired and deflated.

"It'll be dark before long. Let's find some shelter," I said, trying to busy my mind with a productive plan. "We need one in case the temperature drops. We can use a hollowed-out log or gather downed tree branches to build cover against a rock, assuming we can find one."

"It's worth a shot. We can use dry birch bark to build a fire."

We set about looking for a hollowed-out tree with little luck. No large rock outcroppings presented themselves, either. We finally found a sheltering tree to provide rain cover and built a frame structure around it out of dead logs we covered with tamarack branches. We gathered some sticks and kindling. It was starting to get dark out, so at the entrance of our shelter, we built a fire which didn't give off as much heat as I had hoped.

"You didn't happen to bring any food, did you?" I asked Toni.

"I grabbed our gorp."

"I'll never tease you again about how much stuff you bring." The addictive snack of nuts, chocolates, and raisins would at least keep us energized. "I think we could live on this for days."

"Except for the fact that we're getting low on water."

"We'll have to find a stream tomorrow while we work at getting unlost."

Wearing shorts and T-shirts and using my sweatshirt for cover, we didn't stay any too warm in our improvised shelter, but luckily the temp only dropped to around sixty-five degrees throughout the night. Rain fell lightly at times, and I pondered the beginning of our trip. It had started out so well. So like the rest of our expeditions. And it had taken such a weird turn. So unlike the rest of our trips.

All year we looked forward to our getaway, and we'd made the same pilgrimage to the BWCA for the last five summers. Even though we were both in our early fifties and portaging and paddling was hard work, returning to this pristine, million-acre network of lakes and waterways for fishing and relaxation would be our favorite destination as long as we could physically manage.

I always de-stressed from my work and public identity as Duluth Police Officer Kim Weiss, and Toni took a break from her social work clients and the emotional caretaking that exhausted her from day to day.

And now, I felt uneasy being so close to Toni. At least she'd gone to sleep right away, but my mind raced, chasing away thoughts of slumber while filling me to the brim with worry. As best friends for over ten years, our differences served in many ways to make us a great team in an emergency. I would typically spring into action, and she would talk us through the emotional situations we found ourselves in.

I wondered if Toni thought I had failed her, or if she was anxious about the missing teenager, feeling we had failed her. In our present circumstances, I empathized with what the girl was going through.

Toni and I had each other, though, which should make being lost easier. But I couldn't get the words of the poem out of my head, and that also left me feeling unsettled. Toni and I were close, but she knew I was in a committed relationship. Was she writing about me or not?

No, we were both lesbians, but I had never picked up on an attraction between us. Our friendship was something I cherished, but the poem threatened all that. Why couldn't I ask her about it?

I had always kept myself in good physical condition, and my short, dark, spiked hair and light blue eyes with long eyelashes had never been a curse to me in my younger days. I never had a difficult time finding dates. Since I'd met my partner Candy, though, I made my boundaries with other women clear. I didn't flirt anymore. If someone else flirted, I was totally oblivious to it.

I shivered, leaning into Toni a bit more than I wanted to in our strange shelter, hanging on to my faith that she and I were solid friends. Someday, we would have that discussion. When we weren't bone tired and lost in the woods. I wondered why such a terrific woman was perpetually single. She seemed complete, meaning not needing a "better half" to be happy, and she hadn't pursued any lovers for years.

She'd had some painful and bad relationships, and I suspected that was the driving force behind her single lifestyle. She was also very into her work. I knew her well, but still, I wondered if she ever got lonely.

Candy emerged into my consciousness and how much my relationship with her meant to me. Our easy day-to-day flow and level of support were as important to me as breathing. Why wouldn't Toni want the same kind of happiness?

So far, Toni's and my carefully planned getaway had been disorienting. We were both acutely aware how terrible it was to lose our way. Should I worry that our friendship had lost its way as well?

JUST AFTER MIDNIGHT, WE were awakened by the howling of wolves, a plaintive and terrifying sound that seemed far too close for our own good. We heard pups among the voices. I got up and put some sticks on the embers and stoked the fire, then uncovered some pieces of wood that I knew would burn well just in case the wolves drew near. Perhaps tomorrow we could track them. Where there were wolves, there was water.

I didn't sleep well, in the morning we awakened groggy and stiff with an acute yearning for coffee. Unfortunately there was no java to be had.

Bug bites sprinkled our arms and feet, but we were both in pretty good spirits, given the circumstances. We had a little clean water, some gorp, and each other.

We split the trail mix, then set off to look for Renee again. We blew our whistles and called out for a couple of hours before discouragement set in.

I said, "I know people step off trail to go to the bathroom and get turned around, but why wouldn't she have heard her parents calling for her? She couldn't have gone very far. Maybe her parents did her in."

"Nah," Toni said. "Those parents were genuine. She was lost. Or maybe something scared her off ? Like a skunk. Or a bear with cubs."

"Let's be sure and ask her when we're out of this mess."

Of course, my mind found other possible reasons for Renee's disappearance. Like an abduction. I had seen too much human brutality in my years as a cop to rule out foul play. But I went along with the bear scenario for the time being.

Toni said, "Let's pull out the map to see which lakes are in the immediate area. Maybe we can figure out how risky it would be to try to make it out, and how far we could go deeper into the wilderness if we missed hitting a nearby lake."

"Sounds good to me." The map covered roughly ten square miles, showing four lakes connected by a portage and a river with areas of swamp. The river was in the far north section of the map while the four lakes essentially spread out in the four directions. Keeper Lake was in the northeast section. The problem was, I didn't know where we were in relation to any of the lakes or topography.

Looking at Keeper Lake, we made a rough approximation of our northerly wandering route, placing ourselves somewhere near the river. We had hiked roughly three hours, give or take, through deep woods. Most people can hike three miles per hour on a trail and less in the woods. Theoretically, if we had traveled a straight line, we could have traveled seven and a half miles. More likely, we had traveled around five miles. I drew a 7.5-mile circle around our starting point at the portage between Keeper Lake and Perch Lake. The closest lake was likely to the northwest.

Being lost was exhausting and frustrating, and we had to find water. The sun was high in a cloudless sky, so we set off to the west in search of the closest lake or stream. Toni blew her whistle and called out as we walked.

Within an hour, we came to a small stream. We had no filter with us, but it was peak summer, and the stream felt cool. We drank our fill and topped off our water bottles. Even if the water contained bacteria or parasites, we could get treated once we were out of the woods.

I had to decide if we should follow the stream or head back to our makeshift shelter. The stream might pour into a lake, but it had the possibility of leading us farther from our origination point and would-be rescuers. The potential lake at the end of the stream likely had canoeists and campsites, but we had no idea how far we were from that lake. My thoughts and calculations leaned toward following the stream when we both froze, glancing at one another and listening intently.

I heard it again. A faint cry. It sounded like someone shouting off in the distance.

Toni pulled out her whistle and blew it, signaling with frequent shrill sounds. She stopped and we heard the sound again, this time more distinctly "Help!" My hope surged that it might be Renee. Toni blew the whistle some more.

Stopping to listen again, we heard more screaming and took off running and calling Renee's name.

A bedraggled girl with blonde hair and pale skin emerged from the trees. She looked exhausted and was dirty and covered in mosquito bites, but she was alive and present.

"Hey," I said, panting, "I'm Kim and this is Toni. We've been looking for you. You're Renee Rose, right?"

The girl nodded as tears rolled down her cheeks. Toni guided Renee to sit on a fallen tree.

I squatted down to face her. "How did you get lost?"

"I went off trail to go to the bathroom, and before I could get my pants down, a guy came up to me. Out of nowhere. He was totally psycho—he was, he was—"

Her voice rose and she sounded like she was about to have a panic attack. Toni put a hand on her arm and made soothing sounds until she was able to go on.

"He had a gun tucked into his pants. He looked totally crazy, so I took off. When I finally stopped, I didn't know where I was. I listened and listened and I didn't hear him so I called to my parents, but they didn't answer. I tried to find my way back, but I must have gotten turned around." She shrunk into herself. "The creep might be close by."

I told her she was safe now and asked what the man looked like.

"Bushy beard. Really skinny white guy in a pair of ripped jeans and brown boots. His white T-shirt was so dirty it looked gray and speckled with brown. Like poop."

Toni said, "You were smart, Renee. You got away. Good thinking on your feet."

"But I got lost. I've been wandering all around, all yesterday and all night. I was afraid to stop. I couldn't see except by the moon, but I kept moving. I can't believe I found you. How do you know my name?" Her words rushed out now. "Do you know my mom and dad? Where are they? Where are we?"

Toni put a hand on her shoulder for moral support, and I told her about meeting her parents and being recruited to help search. "We ended up lost ourselves, though." She drooped when she heard that news but still seemed happy not to be alone in the woods being chased by a psycho.

Renee said, "I heard wolves howling last night. I was so scared."

"We heard them, and we were scared, too," Toni said.

"Wolves are very afraid of us," I said. "They've never attacked humans in the BWCA."

The girl shivered. "Good."

She was tired, bit up, and dehydrated. A handful of gorp and some water helped. She sat on the log and watched as we studied the map. It provided details about the major creeks in the area. Chances were, if we followed the creek, we would run into a lake after less than a five-mile hike. Then we'd have a good chance of encountering canoeists to help us. We decided to hike out.

Toni said, "You want to get out of here and find your parents?"

"Yeah." The girl scrambled to her feet and tried to wipe her dirty hands on her pants. She looked at her palms with distaste. "I can't wait to take a bath."

"You and me both," I said, giving her a grin.

We set out. The hiking was rough. We alternated between staying in the creek bed when the rocks could be easily traversed, and hiking alongside the creek when animal trails were visible.

It felt strange doing so much hiking in an area renowned for canoeing. I tried not to think about how we could end up at a portage without a canoe to bring us to safety, and I hoped to avoid the gun-toting lunatic.

After three hours of hiking, we came to a long body of water that didn't look like any of the lakes on the map spread out before us. But a lake is a lake is a lake. We settled along the shore and waited two boring hours before a group of four canoes emerged from the south end of the lake traveling north. We yelled and waved our arms, and they paddled toward us cautiously.

Eight people—five men and three women—spilled onto dry land after beaching their canoes. A beefy, bearded guy with a sunburned face and kind eyes approached and asked our names. He told us his name was Dave, and that his group was on a church camping trip.

I explained our plight.

He said, "This is Sawtooth Lake. The nearest access road is three lakes to the south. Unfortunately, all three are pretty sizeable, and the portages are at least a mile a piece." He eyed Renee, who looked like she was about to burst into tears again. "Hang on," he said, and walked over to huddle with the rest of his group. A couple minutes later he returned. "We'd be happy to load you folks up and escort you out as far as the parking lot."

I was beyond the point of caring that we were interrupting their vacation and readily accepted the offer.

As Dave and his merry band worked to rearrange the gear in the canoes, I felt the urge to pee. Who knew how long we'd be on the water, and there was nothing worse than being stuck in a canoe when nature called. I backtracked into the woods a couple hundred feet and did my business. Halfway back, I caught sight of movement in the trees close to the lake's edge. At first I thought it might be a deer, and I quietly crept closer. About fifty feet away, I realized it wasn't a deer at all. A bedraggled man crouched in the shadow of a huge elm. He matched Renee's description, and he had a gun pointed at our little group. He stood and darted out of the tree line onto the beach.

I pulled my gun and charged after him, yelling to draw his attention. I was almost to the tree line when a bullet slammed into a tree beside me. Before the sound of the gunshot had finished echoing, I was on the ground and belly-crawling to hide behind the nearest tree.

Renee screamed. I eased toward the edge of the trees, gun in hand. Toni and the canoeists stood stiffly, hands in the air, while psycho guy pointed his weapon at them. I couldn't fire off a round because too many of the canoeists were in my line of fire.

The man grabbed Renee by her long hair. She screamed again, but the creep backed up, holding Renee in front of him as a shield. I heard the murmur of Dave's voice as he tried to talk the man into letting the girl go, but it was to no avail. The creep forced Renee up the trail.

I eased back into the woods, off the path, to try to head them off farther up the trail. Renee was resisting and shrieking, so he had his hands full, giving me a time advantage. I trotted as silently as I could, listening to the sound of her panicked voice, and emerged ahead of them on the deer path.

"Don't fight me," the man kept hollering.

"Stop it, you freak," Renee screamed. "Help!"

I ducked back into the woods. As soon as they passed me, I saw he'd stuffed his gun into the back of his jeans. He had both hands full trying to hang onto a squirming, screeching teen. I eased out of my hiding spot, came up behind him and wrapped an arm around his throat. I pressed the muzzle of my gun into the base of his skull and yelled, "Let her go or I blow your head off!"

His hands came up and grabbed my forearm.

Renee stumbled away, her terrified eyes wide.

I tightened my arm across his windpipe and shouted, "Get your ass on the ground! Now!"

He reluctantly sank to his knees, and I pushed him down onto his belly. With a knee in his back, I confiscated his gun and stuffed it in the back of my pants, then holstered my own weapon. I'd managed to get his arms behind him when I heard Toni's voice and glanced back to find her and a couple of the guys closing in on us. She had a length of rope in hand and tied his hands behind his back.

The men each grabbed an arm and dragged the abductor to his feet. He truly did look crazy. His beard and fuzzy hair were matted and full of sticks and grass, and his clothes looked like he'd lived in them for months. But it was his eyes that scared me the most. Dead, flat eyes.

"She's mine," he said in a monotone.

"Never," I said.

We all hiked back down the trail to the beach. I noticed how Renee clung to Toni and was once more grateful that my best friend was on the trip to help deal with this experience with me.

Once we got the crazy man into the center of a canoe with someone guarding him from behind, the group made preparations to paddle to the exit point of the chain of lakes.

At least when we got to their cars, there was a chance we'd have cell phone coverage to call the authorities and then reach Renee's parents to tell them she was safe.

The trip out felt like it went on forever. We'd already had a long day, but I was buoyed by the generosity of these eight paddlers who had come to our aid. I thanked Dave, who seemed to be their leader, and he said, "Wouldn't be much of a church if we looked the other way, now would we?"

I couldn't argue with that logic.

We made it to the entry point at dusk, so grateful to see the parking lot. Dave opened his car so Renee, Toni, and I could take a load off while we awaited rescue.

Dave and another man tied the kidnapper to a tree. I could tell Toni wanted to talk to the creep to see what made him tick. I discouraged her and suggested she turn her attention to Renee. They got out of the car and walked a short distance from the group to process some of what had happened.

One member of the group, Sharlene, had a cell phone. Because cell coverage was spotty, it took three 9-1-1 calls for her to relay the information about our location, and we didn't manage to connect with the Roses at all.

It turned dark, and the canoeists lit a fire and made camp. They shared some tasty stew with us and kept us laughing and not thinking too much about what had happened.

A sheriff's deputy and two men from an official search party finally arrived after ten p.m. to take custody of our criminal, but they didn't want to take Renee with them for safety reasons. Once the deputy recorded our names and got the story about what had happened, he handed me a satellite phone and asked me to call my partner. Apparently there had been news coverage regarding the missing Renee and mention of the fact that two women in one of the rescue parties had also disappeared. Candy's Spidey sense told her I was involved, and sure enough, she was right. She'd burned up the phone lines trying to get an update.

She picked up on the first ring. I brought her up to speed about what happened and assured her we were warm, well fed, and hydrated.

"Oh, my God, Kim," she said. "I can't believe all this. When will you be home?"

"In a few days?" I said hopefully.

"Don't you want to come home now where you'll be safe?"

"I think we'll be okay, Candy. How many more psychos can be left in the woods?"

"Is that supposed to make me feel better?"

"Sorry, but it's true. We'll be fine, and I bet the rest of the trip will be totally anticlimactic."

"What does Toni think?"

"Toni," I called across the fire, "you want to go home or finish our vacation?"

She gave me an "are-you-nuts look" and said, "I'm not done de-stressing yet."

That settled that. "Toni wants to stay."

We talked for several more minutes until Candy sounded less worried, then rang off. I felt lighter. I also felt ready to hit the hay. The canoeists had pitched tents for themselves, and Renee, Toni, and I slept in the back of a huge panel van. I never got cold all night.

AT FIRST LIGHT, WE breakfasted with our canoe friends, thanked them profusely, and I took down their names and contact information for the report I would be making for the local sheriff.

We hadn't even had a chance to help clear up the breakfast mess when the Roses came paddling up. The reunion with their daughter was gratifying to see, and they were extremely grateful to us for "finding" Renee. We tried to make it clear that she found us, but even Renee said we'd saved her life.

We made plans to reconnect once we were all resettled in civilization, and Toni offered to help the family and Renee fully process the trauma and aftermath following this harrowing abduction and escape. They accepted graciously.

The kindly canoeists packed up and took us on the trek to our campsite at the far end of the lake. Our bear bag remained intact, hanging high above any potential thieves, and the campsite still looked in good condition.

After bidding our new friends goodbye, we took a morning "swim," intending to clean ourselves up a little. I felt so much better to be able to rinse away the dirt and grunge I'd picked up along the way.

Later, in the canoe with our fishing lines in the water, Toni said, "Pretty surreal, huh?"

"I'm having a hard time believing that just two nights ago we didn't know where we were and had to sleep under a handmade shelter."

"Me, too."

We caught three fish and stored our catch. I looked forward to the taste of the bass, and we retired to the hammocks with books to read and a plan to nap the day away.

Over dinner, I finally worked up the courage to talk to Toni. "I saw your poem, you know. The one titled 'Idle.'"

I waited for her response. She stared at me.

"The morning when you were writing in the tent, I confess I

peeked at it. I liked it, but, um, well, I had to wonder, who's it about?" I could feel my face flaming with heat. She probably thought I was an idiot.

Toni gave me a strange look. "A client of mine. She's in love with someone who's already in a relationship. I was playing around with how to help her come out of it with some integrity. That's all that was. I'll never do anything with that poem. Never show it to her, or to anyone, for that matter." She sighed. "You probably don't realize how much poetry works as self-therapy for me. When I get struck by a concept, or a strong feeling, I have to capture it. This actually started out as a whole page of writing, and I wheedled it down to that one little poem."

"It's very good," I said.

"Thanks." She focused on her book, and I stopped blushing.

After a few moments she looked up thoughtfully and gave me a brief smile, then went back to her novel.

Clearing the air felt good, and I knew with more certainty than ever that I needed the safety of this long-term friendship. I saw by the look in her eyes that she did, too.

"Hey," I said, "when we get back home, you sure as hell better buy a new compass."

"Aye aye, Captain." She whipped off a little salute.

"I'm only an officer."

She beamed at me. "Whatever."

A FINE MESS THIS IS

By Sue Hardesty

THE TELEPHONE'S HARSH RING forced Loni to open one eye to stare at her clock. It was already 11:00 in the morning, but she'd been up late the night before chasing a crazy man who shot an ATM to smithereens. After she caught the guy, her girlfriend Lola kept Loni up the rest of the night.

As she reached for the cell phone, she knocked it off the nightstand onto her brown standard poodle. Coco jumped up and barked. Loni groaned and pulled a pillow over her head to drown out the sound, but the phone kept ringing and the dog kept barking.

Ducking from Coco's wet slurps, she reached down and, feeling along the floor, finally grabbed the phone. A shrill voice bounced against her head, making her cringe.

"Loni. You have to come. Mama needs you."

Several seconds passed before the voice registered. For a brief, glorious moment Loni thought it was Maria. "Sandi?" She had forgotten how much her dead lover sounded like her sister. "What's wrong?"

"My brother Anthony's boy. He was arrested for murder."

"You talking about Miguel? How? Why?"

"You have to come." Loni heard the desperation in Sandi's voice. "Mama's asking for you."

Loni shook the cobwebs out of her head. "Sandi? Get a lawyer and tell that kid to keep his mouth shut. Not one word. I'll text you later where to pick me up. Bye." Loni dropped the phone in the middle of the bed, groaned, and stretched.

"Who's Sandi?" Lola said in a sleepy voice as she turned over and wrapped her nude body around Loni. "Tell her you belong to me and I won't let you go."

"Sorry, sweetheart. I have to. It's family." Loni gently pried off Lola's arms and sat up in bed. As she dialed a familiar number, Loni ran her fingers through her short-cropped black hair. "Carl, it's Loni. I need a few days off."

"No."

Loni took a deep breath before she raised her voice in frustration. "Carl, listen up! I'm not asking."

After a few choice curses, Carl's low voice grunted out, "Maybe you hadn't noticed, but I'm the Sheriff around here. You work for me, and I said no. You gotta finish writing up the Thursday Truck Case before State comes asking."

Loni visualized Carl's desert-weathered face frowning at the phone. "Carl, stop pulling on your ear and listen to me. Get James to handle it. He's sitting around staring at his navel."

"That's not the way to talk about your beloved cousin."

"Bull pucky. I had to save his sorry ass before he got just a little nice, remember? Doesn't change the fact he's still a lazy shit."

"You forget we'll be short a trained forensics detective. What if there's a murder?"

"Other than Rene's plane getting sabotaged and crashing in the graveyard, when do we ever get a murder in this pissant town?"

"Let me see. There was the O'Neal family butchering the Chief. Not that he didn't deserve it. There was that kid who got knifed and crashed that Mercedes. Then how about the two cops from Tucson killed right outside of town by drug runners. Then—"

"I get it, Carl. Our town's a real hub of crime. I still have to go."

"Your grandma can't be sick again. That old Apache woman will outlive us all."

Loni had to smile. "No, no. It's Maria's family. Her twin brother's son was arrested for murder."

"Maria? Your girlfriend in L.A. that got killed?"

"Yeah. Her family took me in like I was one of them, Carl. I owe them."

"Thought you said her brother threatened to kill you if you ever came around again."

"Yeah, well. I hope he's changed his mind."

Carl's heavy sigh rebounded in Loni's ear. "I'll tell James. Is Lola going with you?"

" 'Course not. The station would fall apart without her."

"Hey!"

"Well, shit, Carl. You don't even know how to answer the phone."

"Do so."

"Picking up a phone and saying 'check's in the mail' is not what you call professional." Loni grinned at the disconnect click in her ear. Lola punched her arm. "Ouch!"

Spanglish spewed out so fast Loni couldn't follow. Loni pushed herself off the bed. "I've got to go, sweetheart," she said apologetically.

"Please, please don't go." Lola reached for Loni, as her anger changed to big tears that rolled from dark green eyes down her cheeks.

Loni hadn't seen her girlfriend this upset since her baby brother Manny got into trouble. Loni sat back down and held Lola until the sobs and the sniffles quieted. The comfort hug turned into snuggles, and Lola's hands began a new dance.

Pushing Lola's long, tangled blood-red hair off her face, Loni sighed. "I'll never figure out how to keep up with your mood changes."

"Probably not. A Mexican-Irish mix is a bit different from you stoic Indians."

Loni laughed as she uncurled, holding Lola's roaming hands so that she could sit up. "I have to go, Lola. Like I said. It's family."

"Maria's dead. I'm your lover now."

"I wish I could stay, but Maria's mama was the only mother I ever knew. She gave me her daughter to take care of, and I failed. Maybe I can help her this time."

Lola gave her the evil eye and shoved Loni away from her. She jumped out of bed and grabbed a change of clothes out of the closet and quickly dressed. "Don't bother coming back because I won't be here!"

"C'mon, Lola..." Loni watched her mercurial girlfriend in amazement as Lola grabbed a hairbrush, slammed out the door, and was gone.

Loni took time for a few deep breaths before she rose and took a quick shower. Dressed in black Levis, a gray cotton button-down shirt, and black boots, she sat on the edge of the bed and talked to Coco. Rubbing the poodle's brown muzzle, she softly cautioned her, "You have to stay, Coco. Uncle Herm will take you home, and you can play with Rinnie." Loni leaned over and hugged her, burying her face in Coco's fuzzy wool. "Gotta find Daniel and ask him to fly me to Los Angeles. Oh, God." She panicked at the thought of flying to L.A. and tightened her grip on Coco. The dog squirmed to get away, and Loni turned her loose. "Well, shit. I've got to get in one of Daniel's weenie planes."

She looked around the home she'd lived in for the past three years. Perched on the top of an airport hangar, her tiny apartment was one of her greatest joys. She loved the skylights in its rounded cathedral ceiling that let the sun warm her. The space was decorated in cheery colors and accented by throw rugs that splashed bright colors around the square, open space.

She had polished the wood floor to a high shine during those first few days home after she quit her job working in LA as a detective.

Missing Maria kept her from sleeping, and she had to have something to do, so she worked on the apartment. Loni remembered how she had ached so much for Maria's touch and the sound of her voice that she worked until she couldn't lift her arms or walk another step.

Loni called her uncle Herm to make arrangements for Coco's care. Coco recognized her name and came to sit at Loni's feet. The mournful expression on the brown, fuzzy face almost made Loni laugh. As she explained the circumstances, Loni paced, running her hand over the apartment-sized stove, icebox, and sink, which backed up to one side of the stairwell. A closet-sized room with a toilet and corner shower filled in the other side. In the center of the loft was a free-standing bed with an old quilt barely covering the mattress sides. Each bedpost sat in a tall quart jar to keep scorpions from crawling up into the bed.

Even after Herm assured Loni that he would take care of the dog, she was reluctant to leave and sorry that Lola had stormed out. Coco leaned against Loni as she stared across the tan and green speckled desert at the purple-streaked Montezuma Mountain in the distant skyline. The door banged, and she whirled around, but it wasn't Lola.

Daniel bounced over to the fridge and grabbed a can of beer. He offered it to Loni and said, "Looks like you need this more than I do."

She shook her head as he popped the top and took a swig. At least she didn't have to go looking for Daniel, Loni thought, as she again noticed how much he looked like her uncle. They were both bulky, dark Germans, strong as mules, with straight black hair that never turned grey. "Isn't it a little early for that?"

Daniel shrugged. "Forgot my lunch pail."

"Wait. I thought you took your beer out of my icebox when Lola moved in."

"Working on it." He grinned. "I saw Lola stomping out of the hangar looking pissed as hell. So what'd you do now?" Daniel sniffed. "How come it smells like sex in here?"

"It does not!" Loni said, but she knew her guilty look probably told all. "I'm not talking about it."

"The sex was that bad?"

"What? No. I got a call from Maria's sister." She was quiet for a few seconds. "Daniel? I'm glad you showed up. I need a ride to L.A."

"Oh, yeah?" Daniel snickered. "That piece of shit you call a truck break down again?"

Loni poked him in the gut. "I really need to get to L.A."

"Right now?"

"Yep." Loni went to her chest of drawers and pulled out clothes.

She shoved Levis, shirts, underwear, and socks into a purple backpack. "Right now."

"Tell you what, kid. I recommend you stick out your thumb. Or sit on it. I ain't flyin' to no goddamn L.A." Daniel chugged the beer and crunched the can flat. Looking over his shoulder he tried to hook-shot it across the room toward the recycle basket. Coco looked up as the can skittered across the floor.

Loni picked it up and handed it back to him for another try. "Come on, Daniel. Be a good cousin. It's just to the Bob Hope Airport. I really need your help. Please?"

"Godamighty. Did you really just say please?"

"Yes, dammit. Please give me a ride." Loni heard a heavy sigh behind her and grinned as she zipped her backpack.

"Good thing I only had one beer." Daniel tossed the can and this time hit the basket dead center. With a victory shout he walked out the door. Loni got out a dog biscuit for Coco before she trailed Daniel down the stairs and onto the hangar floor. She couldn't quite hear what he was saying.

"What?" she asked.

"I said I been working on this plane, and I think I found the problem. A good long run is the best way to find out."

Loni gulped. "What do you mean you *think* you found it?"

"That's what I do for a living, remember? Fix planes."

She followed him around a helicopter, two small planes, and a plane engine on a block before she jerked to a stop and stared at a white Cessna 172. "Daniel?" Loni's voice cracked. "That looks like Rene's plane! The one that crashed in the graveyard."

"Yep."

"What do you mean, yep?"

"Yep is yep. What else could it be?"

"Please don't tell me that's the same plane." Loni grabbed Daniel's shirt and got in his face. "Did you change the fuel tank selector valve?"

Daniel snorted in laughter. "That was deliberate. Epoxy squeezed in the valve does it every time."

"I know what took Rene's plane down. Is this the same plane?"

"Nope, it's not."

"Maybe someone doesn't like the owner of this plane either. Have you thought of that?" Loni ignored Daniel's chuckle. "Who does own this plane?"

"Some new rancher down Alter Valley way. His family refuses to move out of the city so he flies back and forth."

"Well, I'm not getting into that plane."

Pulling his shirttail out of Loni's hand, he walked around the Cessna 172 to make a safety check. "Fine. If you don't want me to take you to L.A., find your own way. I got a plane to fix."

He was in the plane starting the engine before Loni finally pulled herself up into the passenger seat and dragged her backpack into her lap. She buckled in, but still wanted something to hang on to.

Daniel slowly taxied out of the hangar and onto the runway. Soon in the air, he circled over the graveyard and headed west. Below them the huge tin Quonset hangar, dulled and rusted by dust and thunderstorms, squatted on the side of the runway. Beside it, a double row of single-story houses stretched along the edge of the airport runway. As the airport disappeared and the small town of Caliente became a dot behind them, the vast southern Arizona desert spread out forever in front of them.

Loni huddled down in her seat and used her backpack against the window as a pillow. She fought her fear at every air pocket that caused a sudden drop. Finally she catnapped until she felt the plane bobbing to descend. Daniel nailed a perfect landing and huge planes rolled by as he taxied into the area for small aircraft. She hugged Daniel goodbye and felt his delight in giving her cheek a whisker burn before she climbed out of the plane on wobbly knees.

Sandi waved at her from the terminal.

Loni was taken aback. She had forgotten how much Sandi looked like Maria. Long, straight black hair hung in a French braid down her back, and a big smile showed white, even teeth. Like Maria, Sandi's small-boned, slender body stood straight and confident. Loni took a big breath and gave her a hug that didn't quit right away. After she finally released Sandi, Loni wiped tears from her cheeks and let her take the backpack. Sandi grabbed her arm.

"Wait." Loni jerked Sandi to a stop. "Slow down."

"Can't." Sandi tugged Loni forward. "Mama's waiting."

"Oh, well, in that case." Loni charged on, outpacing Sandi, until the other woman got the giggles and made Loni slow down.

"I forgot how crazy you are," Sandi said. "God, I've missed you. I miss you being with my sister. I miss Maria."

Loni ignored the statements as they continued into the parking lot. "Tell me again what's going on."

"Sorry. I didn't mean to bring up Maria. Seeing you just reminded me of all the good times."

"Right. Back to why I'm here," Loni said, gritting her teeth at the continual reminders of her dead lover.

"Mama's waiting for us at Anthony and Betty's house."

Inside the car, Loni gave Sandi a sideways glance and looked down. "You do remember your brother said he'd kill me if I ever came around again."

"Anthony didn't mean it."

"You do remember Betty said I wasn't welcome in her home. Her husband wants to kill me, and Betty wants to watch."

Sandi fought her way out of the airport traffic. "I know how nasty Betty was to you. My sister-in-law just never could get past her homophobia." Sandi reached over and patted Loni's leg. "I told Mama about that, but she said not to worry and that Betty won't be a problem. Mama knew you'd want to see Miguel's room."

Loni laughed. "She's been watching too many cop shows." Loni frowned and tried to rub the worry out of her eyes. "I have no idea what she expects me to find there."

"Doesn't matter. Just make Mama happy." Sandi glanced over at Loni again. "You got another reason for not wanting to go to Betty and Anthony's house?"

"Yeah. I don't want to see all the things of Maria's and mine that Betty took from our apartment."

"Sorry?"

"Things. She took," Loni said in exasperation.

"Like what?"

"Like pictures off the walls, furniture, everything from the kitchen and living room, including antiques from my great grandparents. Clothes from our closets, linens. What she left I threw away when I moved back to Arizona."

"Oh. My. God. When did she do that?" She sounded shocked as she merged onto West Hollywood Freeway.

"Maria's funeral, remember? Mama wouldn't let me go home that night. When I got home the next day, everything was gone."

"Everything?"

Loni snorted. "Pretty much. All but one beat-up skillet, three chipped plates, a cup, two small ugly bowls in the kitchen. Some clothes she must not have liked. A few pieces of my old underwear. A wobbly chair and small end table. A few tired towels. Not much else." They were both quiet for a few moments. "It wouldn't hurt so much, but she got all the pictures of Maria except the one on my desk at work." Loni's voice turned poignant. "She even cut me out. I found the pieces scattered on the floor all over my house."

"I saw my sister's things at Anthony's house, but I thought you gave them to Betty."

"Me? Give something to Betty?"

"Why didn't you get them back? Mama would have made her return them."

Loni looked out the window for a minute. "Mama was in too much pain for me to add to it. And I couldn't go after Betty after what Maria told me."

"What?"

"About what her old man did to her. You never heard?"

Sandi turned off Hollywood Freeway onto North Highland Avenue and headed into city traffic. "Tell."

Loni hesitated. Cars and trucks swirled around them as Sandi turned onto Santa Monica Boulevard. Loni hated large cities. Nothing was sacred to the asphalt octopus with its long dark tentacles endlessly reaching to nowhere. "It was in Sacramento. Her dad was working downtown so he told Betty's mom to bring the kids and meet him in front of one of the department stores. They would buy Christmas presents for everyone and then pick up a turkey."

Sandi interrupted. "Let me guess. He never showed."

"Oh, he showed up all right. One week later and flat broke. They had to beg peanut butter and bread from a neighbor to eat." Loni looked at Sandi. "Growing up that poor damages you."

"Yes, but why did she even think she had the right to take things that were obviously yours?" Sandi eased to a stop and waited for the light to change. The people on the street were wearing costumes, and the windows all had black and orange decorations.

Loni marveled at the chaos. "I forgot about the big Halloween celebration. No wonder it feels so crowded."

"Yep." Sandi said. "Several hundred thousand people, remember?" The light changed and she pulled onto North San Vicente Boulevard. They drove by West Hollywood Park. "I think you should take the girls to the Doggy Costume Contest this Sunday."

"I would love to spend some time with your two girls again. They were always my favorites when Maria and I babysat."

"You're their favorite aunt. They ask about you."

Loni smiled, remembering the two dark-headed replicas of their mother. So full of mischief and fun. Sighing, Loni returned to the business at hand. "My favorite snitch was a drag queen named Bella who loved to show his dogs. Might be a good way to find him."

"You didn't answer my question at all. What right did Betty

have to swipe your stuff?"

"Don't you remember what families do after a death? Everything gets passed out among the living. Remember when your grandmother died? Everybody gathered to clean the house out?"

"But that only happens if no one is left living in the house."

"Somebody forgot to tell Betty that part."

"What are you going to do?"

Loni didn't answer right away. They pulled up in front of Maria's brother's house, and Loni climbed out. Over the top of the car, she said, "To be honest, hell if I know." At the door she hung back while Sandi knocked. "I don't want to hurt Betty, but that doesn't keep me from wanting to get even. I figure the best way is help her."

Sandi laughed. "Bitch!"

The door was thrown open, they stepped inside, and Mama's long, hard hug gave Loni the first touch of peace she'd felt since Maria died. "I sure have missed you, Mama."

"I know." Brow wrinkled in worry, Mama's dark eyes studied Loni. A loose braid of black hair streaked with white hung all the way down her back. Like Maria, she was short, but chubbier. Their smiles were the same. "You look softer," Mama said. "Heard you got a new girl. Is she good to you?"

"She's not Maria."

"No one ever will be. But there's always room for more love. Maybe you can visit more often now?"

"Of course." Loni let her arms fall and turned to face Betty. "So, Betty. I understand you need my help."

The skin on Betty's thin face stretched tight. "Not me. I wouldn't ask a queer half-breed to help me if she were the last person on earth."

"Betty!" Mama said. "Don't talk to her like that. She's family."

"This was your idea, Mama," Betty screeched. "I just want her the hell out of my house."

"Why?" Loni's angry voice rang out. "You afraid I'll take back the things you stole?"

"Get out!" Betty picked up a ceramic lion from the hall table and threw it.

Loni ducked, and the ceramic piece smashed against the door into brittle shards. She grabbed the doorknob and opened the door. "The only reason you threw that one was because it was mine." She stomped out, glad that Maria's brother wasn't home. Betty was about all she could take.

Once outside, she heard something else smash and break, but

kept on walking down the sidewalk and across the street to the neighborhood park where she sat on a bench. She fished her phone out of her pocket and texted Lola to tell her she had arrived safely. Switching between angry and sad, Loni closed her eyes and listened to the laughing shouts of children playing in the distance.

Someone sat and put an arm around her. "I'm sorry, Mama."

Mama hugged her. "Me, too."

Loni leaned her head on Mama's soft shoulder, glad no questions were asked, and they sat silently for a long time. Finally Mama said, "This doesn't change anything, you know. We still need your help. Time to go." She held Loni's hand all the way back to Betty's house, through the front door, and into Miguel's bedroom. Sandi followed them in and shut the door. The three women stared around the small room.

Loni asked, "What do you expect me to find, Mama?"

"I don't know. You're the one who knows how to look."

Loni sat at the desk and turned on the computer, then spent a few minutes clicking through files.

Sandi tapped her shoulder and pointed to the wall at a photo collage filled with Maria's pictures. "Those are the pictures you were talking about."

Glancing up from the computer, Loni nodded. Sandi turned to her with tears in her eyes, but Loni said, "It's okay. Forget it."

Mama asked, "What are you talking about, girls?"

Loni shot Sandi a warning look and said, "Nothing, Mama. Sandi's getting maudlin."

"Isn't that your baseball?" Sandi pointed at a baseball sitting on a shelf at the head of the single bed. "The one you caught at the Angels game? The one Maria got signed?"

Loni went over and picked it up. Rolling it around in her hand, she sighed. "The signatures are mostly gone now. I had it in a protective case."

"Kids' greasy hands do that. I'm sorry."

"Damn near broke a finger catching this ball. Hurt like a sonofabitch all night. I have no idea how Maria got these signatures, but she did. She surprised me with this on my birthday." Loni set the ball back on the shelf. "I hope Miguel's enjoying it."

Loni went back to the computer. Out of the corner of her eye, she saw Sandi pick up a jacket off the floor then make a choking sound. Sandi's legs gave way, and she sat hard on the side of the bed.

"What?" Loni asked.

"This is the jacket Maria was wearing when she was shot."

Mama gasped. "How do you know?"

"It's black leather. Look at the hole in the back. Oh, my God." Sandi dropped it. Then she picked it up again.

Loni said, "I kept it in a box in the top of my closet."

Sandi frowned. "Shouldn't it be at the precinct in an evidence box?"

Loni turned and faced Sandi and Mama. "About a year before Maria was shot, she saved a young girl from a gang rape. Her father was Pablo Perez, the clerk for the evidence locker. After that, he had a real thing for Maria. Said she was his second daughter. He used to bring her things his wife made. Mostly tamales." Loni smiled. "Which I usually ate." Loni dropped her head and struggled to continue. "He said he couldn't stand having that jacket just sitting there in the evidence box reminding him of Maria's death. One day when I was down there he shoved it at me and said, 'Please. You gotta take this.' So I did. To remember her by. I don't know how Miguel got it."

"How could Betty let her child wear this?" Sandi crumpled it to her chest, swaying in her grief and anger.

Unable to answer, Loni turned back to the student-sized faux wood desk and opened the top drawer. Shuffling through the papers, she found maps and diagrams of abandoned warehouses. "Good God," Loni exclaimed. "I think maybe Miguel's into Urbex."

"What are you talking about?" Sandi asked.

"Urban exploring. It's a thing city kids do. I don't know much about it, but it involves adventuring into old buildings and warehouses and train tunnels. Looks like whoever he played with had this game down to a science. Check this out. Somebody charged Miguel ten bucks for maps and info."

Sandi looked over her shoulder. "Wow."

"Yeah." Loni smiled. "Nice business selling information for breaking and entering." Loni searched for a cover page. "The guy even printed his name and address." Loni rolled the pages up. "I know just who to give this to."

Betty banged on the door and yelled, "Loni! My husband's on his way home, and I want you out of here now!"

Loni hugged Mama and grabbed Maria's jacket from Sandi. She made her way out of the house and back out into the sunlight with Sandi hurrying behind her.

"So what now?" Sandi asked as they drove away.

"Drop me off at the precinct. I need to talk to my old boss."

"You mean Poppy? The guy Maria and you hated so much?"

Loni grinned. "We finally got used to each other."

"Really? You mean like the time he put you both on administrative leave for pouring really, really hot sauce in his soup?"

Loni laughed. "That wasn't us. It was his secretary, but he couldn't put her on leave. He wanted to screw her."

"Did she know?" Sandi pulled up in front of the West Hollywood police precinct.

"Of course. That's why she did it." Loni's phone dinged with a text from Lola. Loni grinned and repeated the message to Sandi: "Glad you arrived safe but I'm still not talking to you."

Lola was softening.

Sandi said, "Call me when you need a lift."

Loni leaned over and hugged her before reluctantly getting out of the car. She stared at the steps leading up to familiar triple doors. She had hoped never to see this massive grey-stone building again. Baby steps, she thought. Baby step number one. That got her feet moving, and she climbed the stairs and pushed through a door where she was immediately stopped by a guard.

"Any weapons?"

"No."

Stepping back, the guard let her pass through the metal detector. Baby step two, she thought.

After she climbed more stairs and wound through narrow hallways, she shoved open the door that led into her old bullpen. She recognized no one. The two desks in the corner where she and Maria had sat facing each other were now side-by-side. She thought about how they'd stared at each other while they talked over cases. At a glass office door, she waved at a man sitting behind the desk. He beckoned her in. She'd last seen him only three years ago, but he looked much older. His belly pushed against the desk, and his receding hair had turned gray. He pulled off his glasses and rubbed the bridge of his long nose. "Why did I know you'd show up?"

"Psychic?"

He rose and came around the desk to shake her hand. "Not since you left. I don't have to watch out for somebody to fuck up any more."

Recognizing some truth in that, Loni still laughed. "You know you miss me."

"Maybe." Poppy grinned then and lowered himself into his worn leather chair. "Get some coffee before you sit."

Loni took a paper towel from the shelf and wiped out a dirty cup.

She picked up the coffee pot from a square side table and poured over-cooked coffee into the cup and added four sugars. Grinning wryly, she said, "You know, if you actually washed this pot it would hold more coffee. Maybe last you all day."

He grimaced back and gestured for her to sit.

Choosing a chair with a soft seat, Loni settled. "So, Poppy, I need help."

"No 'hello, how are you?'"

Loni grinned. "So? How are you these days, Poppy?"

"I was better until you walked in. Hope you're not looking for a job?"

"Nope. Got one."

"That's a surprise." Poppy leaned back. "Not a word from you all these years. Where the hell did you disappear to, anyway?"

"It's a long story."

Sucking on his teeth, Poppy shrugged. "I'm listening."

"Maybe another time?"

"Now's good. I really want to know what happened to my best detective who just up and deserted me. Not a word where you went. Spill. You owe me that much."

"My grandma was sick so I went home."

"Is that the Apache one?"

"How'd you know about her?"

"Heard Maria call you Apache all the time, and one day I asked her why."

Loni laughed. "Yeah. She'd do that when we were occasionally cornered by gang members, especially the young and threatening ones. She'd tell 'em I was a trained Apache warrior and loved to fight the old ways. Get them so curious to see what I'd do they'd sit down to watch and we'd run like hell. Of course they'd fall over laughing. After that most of those kids were friendly."

A nostalgic smile settled on Poppy's face. "Maria was the best I ever saw at defusing fights." Shaking out of his memories, Poppy repeated, "Still haven't told me anything. What have you been doing the last three years?"

"My grandma wasn't well, so I got a job the first year patrolling southern Arizona roads near my grandparents' ranch so I could keep an eye on her. Then I got a job as a cop working under a sheriff in a three-horse desert town called Caliente where I'd gone to school. Spent most my off time helping my granddad with his cows. Eventually got a girlfriend and that's about it."

Poppy's eyes widened, and he grinned. "Well, congratulations."

"I hope so. She was hopping mad when I left to come here."

"Sounds like the opposite of Maria."

"You could say that. I never know what to expect."

"At least you're never bored."

Nodding, Loni changed the subject, "I gotta tell you—I like the poster on your wall much better than the one the sheriff I work for has." Loni pointed at a large yellow poster and read, "I'm a cop. Be calm and hug me."

Poppy laughed. "Had a birthday last week and the guys gave me the one behind you."

Loni turned to see a big poster of Poppy sitting at his desk. Printed across the top was *World's Hottest Cop!* "Ha," she said, rolling her eyes.

"What'd your boss's poster say?"

Loni grinned. "Every day of my life forces me to add to the number of people who can kiss my ass."

"Sounds like a real charming guy."

"Was. He was a child predator and one of his victims caught up with him."

"Whoa. You're not kidding?"

"Nope."

He stared at her for a moment. "So. You got a problem."

"You could say that. Maria's mama asked me to break her grandson out of jail. Nobody says no to Mama."

Poppy sputtered a bit of his coffee onto the desk. He sopped it up with a Kleenex before he leaned back in his brown leather chair. "If you're talking about Miguel Escobar, good luck with that."

"What can you tell me?"

"I can tell you the fire department is calling it arson covering up a murder. Looks pretty cut and dried."

"Sandi said you caught Miguel running from the building as it flashed behind him. Is that all you got?"

"That and the body. We have witnesses who saw the two boys fighting three days before the fire."

"Anybody say why?"

"Looked like the boys got too serious about the Urban Explorer game they were playing. Got so competitive they turned on each other. Investigators figured they got into another fight when they found each other in the warehouse. Maybe your boy killed the kid accidentally. Maybe not. It's still arson. Since he asked for a lawyer first thing, we don't have much more."

"Tell me more about this Urban Explorer game. How come nobody was playing it when I was out on the streets?"

Poppy shrugged. "Been around awhile. It's the city equivalent of cave exploration. Instead of driving to caves, they break into old abandoned or condemned buildings. Sometimes they hunt each other. Sometimes they evade watchmen." He sat back again and linked his fingers behind his head. "This time a kid died. Already had to deal with your loud sister-in-law Betty who perjured herself trying to alibi her son."

"Why am I not surprised." Loni was silent a few seconds. "Who's the fire investigator?"

"Your old nemesis, Patrick Bunch."

"You're shittin' me."

Poppy watched Loni with a sorrowful expression.

"You are talking about the cop who shot Maria in the back, right?"

Poppy nodded.

"So after the cops washed him out, they made him a fireman? Didn't he get any jail time for Maria's killing?"

"His rich and powerful daddy eventually got him assigned as an inspector, even with no fire experience. I hear Helena Jackman has been training him. Isn't she an old friend of Maria's?"

Loni carefully sipped her coffee. "If you call someone who brought Maria out in high school a friend, then yeah. Especially after she dumped Maria and broke her heart."

"You willing to work with her?"

Loni shrugged. "I never met her but why not."

"I'll give her a call and see if she'll pick you up and take you to the scene." Poppy speed-dialed a number and waited a few seconds. "Helena? It's Poppy. I have someone here who needs your help." He was quiet for a few seconds. "No, no, I can vouch for her. It's the Escobar case." Another short silence. "Why don't you talk to her?" He handed Loni the phone.

"Hi, Helena. My name's Loni Wagner and I—"

"I know who you are. Maria's old partner, right? You want to know what happened with her nephew."

"Yes."

"I'll pick you up in twenty and take you to the scene. Several things still bother me, and I could use fresh eyes."

"You won't bring Patrick, will you?"

"No." Helena paused. "I wouldn't do that to you. It's hard enough for me to train that worthless piece of shit. See you in a few."

Loni handed the phone back to Poppy, thanked him, and hugged him goodbye.

Out on the front steps, she waited for Helena while texting Lola to ask how she was. Her reply flashed back, "WE ARE DONE!" Before Loni could reply, Helena pulled up in a pickup, rolled down the passenger window, and hollered, "Yo, Loni."

She closed her phone with a sigh and climbed in Helena's truck.

As Helena drove and sketched out a few details about the case, Loni studied Maria's old lover. Squatty butch, loud voice, purple hair in a page boy cut down to her collar, and pitch black eyes that looked right through people. She wondered what Maria had seen in Helena.

Loni said, "I don't believe Miguel would kill anyone. What kind of evidence do you have?"

"Not the best," Helena said. "Problem one. We found the dead boy in a large furnace with the door shut. He was totally protected from the fire. If the fire was supposed to cover up a murder, why would Miguel protect the body? Two. Bullet to the back of the head was more like a professional hit. And three. The fire has signs it was set by a professional arsonist."

"Not the behavior of a stupid teenager. Sounds more like somebody trying to pin it on Miguel. Maybe even hide insurance fraud with the fire."

"That's another thing. The owner never insured it so he lost everything."

"Oh. How come you think it was a professional arsonist?"

"Traces of dicy were poured in just the right places to make sure the walls would fall in."

"What did you say—dicey?"

Helena gave Loni a startled look. "Surely you've heard of dicyanoacetylene, one of the hottest burning chemicals made?"

"Yeah, I do recall it now. I once heard it called an arsonist's dream."

"We also call it dicy for short. The stuff was splashed on the outer walls. Explosives were wired in the middle of each floor so it would explode and burn from the outside. The elevator shafts made the fire burn faster. The building folded in on itself, like the towers in New York. Ashes rained down and covered everything, except the body. Evidently the arsonist—or someone—wanted to make sure the body was found fast and kept intact so it could be identified."

"What you're saying is that it was a setup and somebody is hiding the real reason." Loni was quiet for a minute. "I remember a few years back I caught an arsonist with a signature like that. I put him in jail."

"Yep. Looks like our old friend Jack Hague is back."

"I remember when Maria and I arrested him. We did a sting. He got twenty years and should still be there. Wonder if he had a student?"

"Do you know which prison he's supposed to be in?"

"He got farmed out to Huntsville in Texas."

"He still there?"

"Why don't we find out." Loni made a call on her cell phone. "Hey, Poppy. Remember Jack Hague? Can you find out if he's still incarcerated at Huntsville Prison in Texas or somewhere else? Sure. Give me a ring then. Thanks."

When they arrived at the site, Loni followed Helena around and listened to her as she pointed out burn streaks and showed her the furnace.

Once they finished the tour, Loni said, "You're right, Helena. I'm getting a real bad feeling about this one."

Poppy called back as they were getting into Helena's Ford truck. "Guess what? He escaped from prison three weeks ago. I gave them hell for not notifying us."

"Shit!"

"No shit," Poppy said.

Loni thanked him before hanging up. "What do ya know, Helena. Jack Hague is definitely back."

Neither of them spoke for the rest of the ride back. At the precinct Helena turned off the engine and put her hands on the steering wheel. Ducking her head, she said, "You took my girl, you know." She glanced at Loni. "I hated you for a long time for letting her get shot."

"Join the club." Loni frowned. "Wait, what do you mean, *your* girl. Maria said you dumped her."

"That's crap. She just said that so I didn't look so bad."

Loni smiled. "That's our Maria."

Helena snorted a laugh. "I don't have to hate you anymore, though. I have Patrick for that now. I really want to know something. Why didn't you stop her from chasing that guy? Was his crime that bad?"

"You ever stop Maria from doing what she thought was right?"

Helena thought that one over. "Why didn't you stop Patrick?"

"Oh, shit, Helena. It went down all wrong. We had the address. We requested backup and were waiting in the hall when the creep walked out of his door and spotted us. He took off for the fire escape ladder with Maria right behind him. I headed down the stairs to catch him from the other direction. Just as I got to the street I heard a shot. Patrick stood there blubbering over and over, 'I thought she was the perp.' I held her, but all I could do was watch her die. So yeah, I'm always going to blame myself for that."

Chest tight and eyes smarting with unshed tears, Loni stepped out of the pickup. Helena was silent. Loni nodded to her, carefully closed the door, and climbed the stairs back to the precinct.

In Poppy's office, she plopped into the same chair and said, "So. Jack is back."

"Could this be personal? Maybe he's trying to lure you out to get you for putting him in prison."

"Nothing else makes much sense does it? I know you can't show me the files. Can I talk to the detectives working the case?"

"Don't need to. I borrowed the file and read it while you were gone. I hadn't got around to looking at it earlier. There wasn't any insurance so nobody looked at the owner until they stumbled across a parking lot permit he filed. He wanted to charge the city for day use, but he didn't want to pay for demolishing the building. Hence the fire. He got arrested but bonded out. They don't expect him to give us Jack."

"Helena didn't seem to know this. Shouldn't somebody have told her?"

"Sure. Getting it checked twice helps make sure things are as they seem. It was a stupid mistake to overlook her."

"You doubting the evidence?"

"Always."

Loni grinned. "Could try trust."

"Don't think so. Where you staying?"

Loni pulled a card from her billfold, wrote two numbers on the back, and handed them over. "Thanks, Poppy."

"You could thank me by coming back to work. You and Maria were the best I ever had."

Loni shook her head. "It was the synergy between us that made me good. Now I've got the desert ways in me so deep I could never be successful on the city streets by myself." Loni stood and shook her old boss's hand again.

He said, "I'll hit you back when something pops."

TWO DAYS PASSED BEFORE Poppy got back to Loni. "Made a deal with the building owner and got a confession that the owner made a deal with Jack. Looks like Jack set you up to get you back here. Knew messing with one of Maria's would bring you out where he could get you."

"Why am I not surprised."

"I sent out a BOLO for him. Don't know what good it will do. Jack grew up in this town and knows where to hide. All I can say is watch your back."

"Always."

Loni picked up a message from Helena and headed across town in Sandi's car to an address where Helena requested they meet. She found the fire inspector sitting on the curb across the street from a burned-out house. From what was left, Loni could tell that it was one of those painted Victorian ladies. A couple of pale colors, two shades of blue, and some green still showed on the fallen and scattered gingerbread pieces. Loni climbed out of the car and sat on the curb beside Helena.

"What happened here?" Loni asked.

"That's my house."

Shocked, all Loni could choke out was, "Jesus, I'm so sorry."

Helena's black eyes sparked in anger. "No question about who the arsonist is."

"His message is loud and clear. I was coming to tell you the owner admitted to hiring him." Loni put an arm around Helena. "What are you going to do now?"

"I got clothes and a bunk at the fire house. I'll be all right." Helena turned to Loni with tears in her eyes. "We have to nail this son-of-a-bitch. My dog and cat were in there."

LONI ARRIVED WITH SANDI'S two girls at the doggy costume contest just as it started. She looked for her old pal Bella, the drag queen snitch, while she kept an eye on the excited girls, amazed at how much they had grown. Only ten and with long dark brown hair and dark eyes, Gracie was almost as tall as her mother. At seven, Bunny still had her baby fat, but she was quick as a rabbit. She kept leaping from one dog to another, ignoring warnings about not kissing them on the noses.

"Look!" Bunny reached up for a black brindle Great Dane strolling by with a halter on and saddle on his back. A large flopping Raggedy Ann doll was tied to the saddle. "Can I ride?"

Dressed like a cowgirl, the owner patted Bunny on the head and said, "Maybe next time."

After a quick kiss on the Great Dane's nose, the giggling Bunny found a cat wearing a tall Dr. Seuss hat, then was running after a three-legged dog and its owner, both dressed up like pirates. Catching up with the pirates, Bunny asked the owner for his eye patch but didn't get it because Loni grabbed her and carried her back to the sidewalk.

Laughing at Bunny, Loni looked up and spotted Bella proudly leading two standard poodles, one black and one white, dressed up as a bride and groom. Sprinkled over with glitter, the white poodle had a diamond collar on and the black poodle had a white bow tie. Bella was dressed as a priest and wore her Dolly Parton wig. Surrounded by curious watchers Bella would step to the side and pretend to marry the two dogs. Loni watched until the ceremony was finished before she approached.

"Hi, Bella. You should have been a priest. Love your outfit."

Bella's two poodles jumped all over Loni, spreading glitter on her face as Bella tried to give her a hug.

"My babies still remember you, Loni."

"Or they smell my dog Coco all over me."

Bella laughed, petting Loni on her head. "Hey, darlin'! You back now?"

"No." Loni wiped at her face from dog kisses and wiggled out of Bella's arms. "Just back to find someone. Hoping you can help me."

Bella's thick bottom lip pushed out in a pout. "But I miss you, girl. I want you around 'cause I'm a selfish bitch."

Loni grinned to take the bite out. "It's always all about you."

Bella pinched Loni's cheek and sighed. "Well, sweetness, much as I love to see you, I've got a contest to win. What can I help you with?"

"I'm trying to locate Jack Hague. He's escaped from prison."

"I have no idea where he is, but I know who might. Remember his cousin DannyO? His favorite hangout these days is The Tile Works. If you wait there a spell, he'll show up sooner or later."

"Can you find out where he lives?"

"No can do," Bella insisted. "He moves every day or two. And no, I don't know what he's afraid of."

ADORNED HEAD TO FOOT in black leather boots, pants, and jacket, Loni covered her nose and broad forehead with a black mask before she went hunting. Her costume fit right in with the early Halloween revelers.

At The Tile Works she found DannyO casually watching the Halloween parade outside. He hadn't changed and was skinny as ever. His pale complexion contrasted with his short-trimmed dark beard and hair. His long teeth and squat nose made him look like a laughing baboon. He was small, but he could move faster than anyone else Loni knew. She quietly slipped up behind and grabbed his arm before he could rabbit into one of his holes. Holding on, she dragged him inside, pulled a chair over with her foot, and sat him down. She had a handcuff attaching him to a chair arm before he knew what happened.

He sputtered as she yanked off her mask and grinned. "Hello, DannyO. Good to see you again."

"Loni?" DannyO slapped his free hand on his chest. "God! You scared the shit outta me!"

"Sorry ol' man. Just wanted your attention."

He leaned forward, staring at Loni. "You look different. Butch haircut? What's that about?"

"A promise I made to a friend."

"Promise? Who would promise to cut their hair like that?"

"A brother's dying request. Part of his Pima Indian tradition. I cut my hair for his burial. So. How you been?"

DannyO snorted. "As if you gave a shit. What do you want?"

"The usual. Looking for someone."

"Thought you were long gone. Alaska somewhere. You back?"

"No. Just hunting. Have a nephew to get out of jail and I need an address."

"Who you looking for?"

"Your dear cousin Jack Hague."

"Shit, Loni. Tell me he's still in that Texas prison."

"Can't. He escaped, and he's here. Already lit two fires that I know of."

She didn't think it possible, but DannyO went even more pale. "Always knew he was crazy. Especially coming back here when he could be living it up in Mexico."

"Looks like he's after me. He got my nephew accused of murder."

"How come he didn't get you in Alaska?"

"Maybe because I went to Arizona, not Alaska."

"From a frozen hell to a burning hell. What's up with that?"

"Just went home to where I was raised." Loni poked at him. "Now. About Jack."

"I haven't heard a word, but I really wouldn't mind helping you get him back in jail before he finds me."

"What'd you do to get Jack pissed at you?" she asked. "Maybe I can help."

DannyO tried to intimidate Loni with a stare. "And have you throw me in jail? Give me a day or two. Where can I reach you?" DannyO held up his free hand and rubbed two fingers against his thumb. "Anything in it for me?"

"Now that I'm back, maybe I'll let you live. Will that do?" Loni dug out a card and wrote her cell phone number on the back. "When you find him I'll pay you. Don't hang me out too long." She stuck a finger in his face. "Don't sell me out, either. You hear?" She slipped her mask back on, unlocked the handcuff, and slipped out into the crowd.

Three hours later, before midnight, Loni was relieved to get a call from DannyO.

"He's stayin' at a rental his sister owns over near the Abby Food Bar on Fairfax Ave. Heard he likes to eat there. A lot."

DannyO hung up before Loni could ask any more questions.

Fifteen minutes later Sandi dropped her off as close as she could get to the Food Bar. The streets were packed with cars and people joining the Halloween parade.

Sandi said, "I wish you'd call Poppy."

"I may not want him to see what I do, Sandi. Might have to throw me in jail."

"Well, dammit! Be careful."

"Thanks."

She opened the door with difficulty and struggled through the huge crowd toward the food court. Costumed people spilled over into parking lots and yards and mingled with those watching the parade. She bought a pair of cat ears and a cape from a corner vender to add to her black outfit and mask and then just for fun posed with a group of superheroes.

After what felt like hours, she reached the court and looked around for Jack. Leaning against a wall, he sported his usual sneer. Bib overalls, a short-sleeved red silk shirt, and a straw hat gave him a cheap scarecrow look. He was narrow shouldered, pear-shaped, heavy on the bottom, with skinny legs and a small head.

Grabbing Jack, Loni slammed him to the cement sidewalk and flipped him over, handcuffing him before he could react.

"Get off me, you fucking sonofbitch," Jack screamed. "Who do you think you are?"

She dug a gun and a knife out of his deep pockets and leaned down to speak in his ear. "That's Ms. FuckingSonofbitch to you,

Jack. Hear you been looking for me."

"Loni?"

"Yep."

"Oh, shit. How did you find me?"

Loni grunted a short laugh. "Looked in the mirror lately? You're pretty distinctive."

"I've had guys sitting at Maria's folks' house all day waiting for you to show. Where the hell did you hide?"

"Right behind you the whole time."

Jack grinned a nasty wicked smirk. "Don't matter anyway. I got a ten-thousand-dollar bounty out on you. Dead, not alive. Just a matter of time."

"Gotta find me first."

"Oh, I will. Easy to get outta worthless prisons."

"I don't think so, Jack. You're up for murder this time." She got out her cell phone. Nothing would make her happier than calling this one in.

TWO DAYS LATER, LONI rode with Mama and Sandi to Bob Hope Airport.

"Next time you come, you bring Lola, no?" Mama told her. "I need to meet her."

"If she's still speaking to me. Lola's Irish temper is as bad as her Mexican stubbornness."

"She make you happy?" Mama asked.

"Yes, Mama. She makes me happy."

Mama nodded in acceptance. "That's all that matters."

Sandi got out of the double-parked car to hug her goodbye. "Look at it this way, Loni. You might not get your stuff back from Betty, but at least her husband might not want to kill you anymore."

Loni laughed. "Nothing like warm family love to cheer me on my way." She gave Mama one last big hug and a promise to return soon. She grabbed her backpack and walked through the terminal doors. She was texting Lola just as her cell rang. A wave of relief swept through her when Lola's face popped up. She was hoping all was forgiven as she answered the call.

"All hell's breaking loose round here!" Lola's loud voice zinged through the phone, and Loni pulled it away slightly. "Where are you?" Lola asked.

"Getting on a plane. Could I have a 'hello, I missed you'?"

"After you fix this mess." Lola's voice suddenly lowered with a sultry promise. "And then anything you want."

The call disconnected and Loni was left with a huge smile on her face as she waited to board the plane. Until it occurred to her: *What mess?*

SWEET SPRING REVENGE

By Jessie Chandler

I SHIVERED AS I stood in the parking lot of Jimmy Johnson's Best Pre-Owned Vehicles. Frozen flakes floated from the heavens. The forecast called for snowfall of over an inch an hour along with winds that freeze your nostril hairs together and rip the breath from your lungs. The storm wasn't supposed to let up until sometime the next day after dumping fifteen to twenty inches of the white crap over the land of the North Star.

Welcome to spring in Minnesota.

My breath came out in foggy puffs, and I tried to use the fog to obscure the plentiful butt-crack exposed by the ill-fitting polyester pants of the man bent over in front of me. Jimmy's head was buried once again in the engine of the purple '98 Geo Metro he'd sold me.

I'd been laid off for over a year, a victim of budget cuts at a national bookstore chain, and I now worked three pizza delivery jobs to make ends meet. I was way behind on all my bills, so I needed a car that not only ran but also allowed me to make lightning-fast deliveries—deliveries which often resulted in surprisingly generous tips. Unfortunately, this deathtrap kept breaking down, and was seriously impacting my tip-earning abilities. To top it off, my girlfriend bailed when my cable TV was cancelled, and now I was on the hook for all of the apartment rent. My life had devolved into a bad country song. If I hadn't been in desperate straits for cheap but reliable wheels back in August, I'd never have coughed up the dough for the Metro. I also wouldn't have invested in the unbelievably good warranty Jimmy offered, even if I had to pay some big bucks for it.

Jimmy, the lecherous shyster he was, had to be sorry he'd suckered me into his "JJ's Best Used Vehicle Warranty." He thought he was getting over on his customers by charging a bundle for a warranty he gambled wouldn't get used often. Then I came along. Too bad I hadn't known Jimmy was a one-man freak show and official perv when I signed my name on the Xeroxed line.

The problems started with over-heating issues. Jimmy's solution: drive with the heater on in 90-degree late-summer heat. Then the tire on the passenger side sprung a leak. I told Jimmy he shouldn't have listed tires as a covered item on the warranty if he didn't want to fix it. He begrudgingly swapped the leaker for a nearly bald replacement. On the bright side, the tire didn't lose air any more. Instead, it would probably explode when I was going seventy on the interstate.

Then the alternator went out. It took him two weeks to install the new one. When I finally picked the car up, he had a black eye and an angry red welt on the back of his bald head. I had to stifle hysteria when he told me the hydraulic pistons that held the hood up gave out and the hood fell on him. I didn't feel one bit sorry for Jimmy. He deserved that and more. Last time I'd been in his office, he pinned me against the wall and mashed his filthy mouth against mine, grunting like a pig the whole time. Even if I were straight, I wouldn't want those liver lips or anything attached to them anywhere near me. I'm pretty sure good 'ol Jimmy Boy would have tried to do a whole lot more if another customer hadn't walked in. Lucky him. Much more and he would have been wearing his family jewels around his neck.

This was my fourteenth trip to the dealership. It was already dark when I arrived with the Metro sputtering mysteriously and losing power at highway speed. Bad news in this weather.

I pulled my black and red satin Mama Maria's Pizza delivery jacket tighter and stepped back, far enough, I hoped, to avoid the grope that by now I was certain was coming. I wanted to sue the asshole for sexual harassment, but working three jobs took every ounce of willpower and determination I had. I could hardly find time to sleep, much less figure out a way to pay a lawyer and sue the lecherous bastard.

Jimmy backed away from the car and removed the metal rod that now securely propped up the hood. It slammed shut with a hollow thud. "Can't find anything that might be causing the trouble, little lady. You'll be fine."

I detested when he called me "little lady," but I bit my tongue. "You said that last time."

"Honey, honey." He jittered over and threw an arm around my neck before I could sidestep away. "You can trust old Jimmy." He was a good six inches taller than I was and practically had me in a headlock. I tried to pull away, but he held tight. The smell of pot and body odor filled my nose. My eyes watered as I tried to wiggle from his grasp.

Like a heat-seeking missile his other hand shot toward me at chest level. He managed to hit his target and squeeze. I yowled and twisted, tried to knee him in the 'nads, but caught his thigh instead.

I wrenched myself from his grasp. "You're disgusting, Jimmy Johnson. Go take a goddamn cold shower."

Jimmy chuckled, the sound as sinister as his leer. "You little wildcat." He swiveled his hips Elvis-style and massaged his crotch. "It's just a matter of time. You know you want a piece of Jimmy's tonsil tickler. Big Jimmy here will make a woman out of you, and mark my words, I'll give it to you good." He chuckled with an unfocused look in his sex-crazed eyes.

I backed up, more than a little alarmed. "Get away from me, Jimmy. You're a sick puppy."

He actually reached down and unzipped his pants. "You know you want some Mr. Happy."

Over my dead body, I thought. Or yours.

I blinked at that, and, in the space of that blink, I must have completely lost my mind.

A stranger took over my brain, one that conned Jimmy into following me home. I told him I was afraid the car might break down in the now near-blizzard conditions, and he wouldn't want my frozen body on his conscience. Then I dropped a hint that I might be interested in a little Mr. Happy after all. I tried hard not to gag as the words came out.

We pulled out of the car lot, me in the Metro and Jimmy in my rearview. I squinted at Jimmy's annoying blue-white headlights as they reflected in the mirror. Snow drifted in random patterns in the headlights, and the tires sliced through at least four inches of heavy slop. Visibility was terrible.

As I drove, my new alter ego plotted. My ex-girlfriend was a *Cops* junkie. One episode featured police utilizing a PIT—Pursuit Intervention Technique—on fleeing cars to stop them by spinning them out of control, much like the bump and run in NASCAR. They made it look easy enough on TV.

I white-knuckled the steering wheel as we crossed the Mississippi River on Interstate 610. I didn't see a single other car on the road. Not too many people were stupid enough to be out in this weather except me and a rapist.

We only had to make it a quarter mile more to Jimmy's fate. The objective, the ramp connecting one interstate to another, lay ahead shrouded in swirling snow. The land the ramp circled slanted sharply down to a deep, recently thawed drainage pond. Every other time I navigated that curve in bad spring weather, I imagined how easy it would be for someone to go over the side and disappear into the frigid, muddy water below.

I slowed to a crawl and took the exit ramp. Jimmy impatiently

rode my tail with hardly room for a toothpick between my bumper and
his. You'd think he'd be a little more careful, especially in such
perilous weather.

My tires bumped along the inside edge of the lane. I cranked my
window down, praying I wouldn't lose control, and waved Jimmy
around me.

My breath whistled rapidly. As Jimmy's rear door passed, I hit the
accelerator. My tires spun wildly. The engine roared. For a second, I
didn't think I'd gain traction.

Then my tires grabbed hold, and the little Metro shot forward.

Jimmy stepped on his own gas pedal a touch too enthusiastically.
He fishtailed. What happened next occurred in slow motion. I spun
the wheel. My left front bumper kissed his right rear quarter panel
with a satisfying crunch. His car slid further out of control as the
Metro pushed it in a near circle, right toward the abyss. I kept the
accelerator mashed to the floor. The engine screamed.

I might have been screaming, too.

I met Jimmy's gaze as his car swung around. The leer was gone.
His eyes were wide, in either shock or fear. Yeah, fear sounded good. I
ripped one fist loose and flipped him off as our cars parted.

The Metro careened toward the opposite side of the ramp. I took
my foot off the accelerator. As the Metro was about to shoot off the
ramp, the tires caught and I slammed on the brakes. My car did a 180
and slid to a stop facing the wrong direction. My arms quaked and my
legs were rubber. My heart nearly pounded right through my ribs.

The snow was so thick I could hardly see ten feet ahead. I
cautiously turned the car around, and parked on the right side of the
ramp. I crawled out on wobbly legs and slogged through the snow to
the edge. Jimmy's car was gone.

"Hasta la vista, asshole," I yelled. Then I climbed back in the tin
can and drove home.

Two days later, after nearly collapsing every time the phone rang,
I saw a short article in the Twin Cities Tribune that detailed how the
police, in conjunction with the FBI, raided Jimmy's used car lot the
day after the Snowstorm of the Century dumped twenty-two inches on
the Metro area. They carried away file boxes, computers, and other
records. There were allegations against Jimmy for federal tax evasion,
trafficking stolen property, as well as swindled customers and
numerous sexual harassment complaints. The article said the police
speculated that Jimmy had been tipped off and skipped town.

I didn't know if I helped Jimmy escape or if I killed him. In my heart of hearts, I'm pretty sure it was the latter.

Not long after the night I lost my mind, I sold the Metro to a shady dealer in North Minneapolis. I quit my three jobs and moved to Tuba City, Arizona, to stay with my sister. Now I deliver hoagies on a Vespa and wait either for a settlement to come from the harassment lawsuit against Jimmy Johnson's estate, or for the cops to show up and arrest me for murder.

Whichever way it turns out, I'm damn sure it was worth those fifteen minutes of snowy springtime revenge.

THE CURIOUS CASE OF THE DISAPPEARING DILDOS

By JM Redmann

Rule Number 1 – Don't answer the phone when you're supposed to be working.

But I had.

"No, absolutely not," I said. "Mystery writer, not mystery solver. Big difference."

"I really need your help and you're the only one I can ask," Alexis pleaded.

"You're dating a cop, ask her."

There was an uncharacteristic pause before she said, "She investigates things for the FDA, not really a cop."

"She looks into bad apples?"

"And she's the last person I can tell."

"I'm not going to be party to deception."

"Emma, I'm in so much deep shit trouble and you're the only person who can help."

Oh, curiosity, you are going to kill me, aren't you?

Deep shit trouble for Alexis is on the Grand Canyon scale. She blows off things like traffic tickets, and missed payments that slay mere mortals like me. It had to be deep shit if she was asking for my help. Alexis was an ex, a long enough ago ex that we were friends. Friends, even though the last time she asked for my help it led to my finding her long lost adopted sister and said sister becoming the woman who now shares my bed, does the dishes when I cook, all that domestic happy bliss stuff. It took Alex a long time to forgive me.

I asked the fateful question; I couldn't help it. "What kind of trouble are you in?"

"I've lost the box of toys."

"Toys? Google toy store. There, I've helped."

"Not those kinds of toys."

"What kind of toys?" I shut down the game of solitaire I was staring at on the screen. I was losing anyway. A quick game is how I get the words flowing again. So far today, 20 wins, not counted losses and half a paragraph. Of which I edited twice. I was also supposed to be working on the forewords for the Croatian versions of my first nine books: *Murder in the Artistic District; After I'm Gone, Girl; The Old Lady and the Fake; Bump and Grind the Gun; Flip Off the Ice Block; Do Not Perturb; The Lucifer Inside; Exit Hounds;* and *The Goal of Time.*

"You know," Alexis said, "grown up toys."

"A Corvette? Surfboard? Chain saw?"

"Adult toys, you know, like sex things."

"Repeat that? I must be getting old. I thought you said dildos." She didn't, but I wasn't above putting words in her mouth. If she wanted my help, she was going to have to answer questions. Explicitly.

"I did. Sort of."

"Dildos? Plural?"

"That would be a yes. You see, I've been trying to expand my business, and one area with a great margin is sex toys."

Alexis runs one of the most successful restaurant chains in the area. She had started out doing the PC thing, vegan and everything (when we were together, I might add—I will never eat another green smoothie as long as I live) but then did a 180 degree turn and now does meat. Meet the Meat. Steaks, burgers, chops. Even the smoothies are now blood red. We broke up over her love of money and the multiple green, vegan experiments she insisted I try. Arugula with shaved tofu and algae aioli, I think not.

The green went away, the love of money didn't.

"I am not a dildo hunter."

She ignored that and plunged on. I had asked, after all. "So I thought for the restaurant in the Quarter, we could pick up trade on one of the slow nights by hosting a party. It's been going great, doubled our food and drink business, and I've been making a killing on the sex toys."

"Call it a tax loss."

"I can't."

"You haven't declared the income?"

"My accountant is so straight-laced. She'd die if she knew I was doing this."

I sighed and considered reopening the Solitaire game. "Then just call it a loss loss—what your sister calls stupid tax." I needed to be writing, although my deadline was only three weeks ago.

"Don't tell her!"

Duh, my ex calls me up and tells me she's lost a pile of dildos and

I'm not supposed to tell the love of my life? Yeah, right. To Alexis, I said, "She's out of town. Won't be back until next week."

"Thanks." Alex seemed so distracted by her dilemma she didn't realize she had just thanked me for telling her that my partner was out of town. I'd promised nothing beyond that. I allowed myself a smug smile since she couldn't see me. Alex continued, "I knew I could count on you. When can you start?"

My smug smile was gone, probably on her face now. Another reason I'd broken up with her was her deciding I'd agreed to do something I had no intention of doing. And thereby making me the bad guy for reneging.

"Clearly you misheard. I'm a mystery writer, not a dildo scout. I'm six months behind deadline." She knew me well enough to know three weeks behind wouldn't be enough of an excuse to actually have to write.

"This will give you material. Help you with your plot twists—"

"My plot twists are fine. It's untwisting them."

"—This could be so helpful to you, you should almost be paying me."

Gasping at the thought of paying her I left enough of a break for her to hear what I was about to say, thereby not giving me the chance to actually say it.

Alexis barreled on, "Stuff it, Emma, I said almost. It's win-win. You get real life mystery experience and do me a great favor. I bet you haven't left the house since taking Jane to the airport."

"Yes, I have." Then we both said, "To the grocery store."

She added, "That doesn't count."

"Yes, it does, it was the uptown one, not the small one in the CBD."

"Doesn't count. You need to get out."

"Okay, agreed. I'll get out but that doesn't mean—"

She cut me off. "Our special is soft-shelled crab po-boys. Get out of the house, have some lunch. Yes, on me, and check out the scene of the crime. See you in about an hour?"

The line was dead before I choked out my pathetic yes.

I had stopped at the grocery store three days ago, on my way home from taking Jane to the airport and had grabbed enough stuff for two and a half days. Peanut butter and jelly without bread is sad. Making a perfectly fried, golden brown soft-shelled crab nested in fresh-from-the-oven crusty French bread, topped with ripe-off-the-vine Creole tomatoes and spicy Cajun mayo a cruel bribe.

So I was out of the sweat pants (they needed to be washed anyway) and into my trusty all-purpose black jeans. And underwear, socks, everything needed to be presentable for the lunch crowd at MeatMeet, her French Quarter place overlooking the levee.

Lunch was free, but parking was not. Tax deduction, I thought as I put the receipt in my pocket. Not that I was going to let Alexis know, but I needed a restaurant for the next scene in my book—the body would be crawfish-boiled to death—and I could get some scene ideas from her place.

So much for the black jeans. She hustled me upstairs to the banquet room, aka the scene of the crime. "Feel the vibe and come up with a plan. I gotta go seat the mayor." And with that I was alone.

Truly alone. Just me, one set table and a big private party room.

I tried to feel stolen dildo vibes. My stomach grumbled, and not in a "come to me, baby, with that big thing," way. More a "breakfast was a long time ago and it was only one ratty overripe banana, so where is the promised po-boy?"

It seemed that dildo stealing most foul didn't do the vibe scene very well. To amuse myself while waiting, I found the chalk for the specials and put some outlines on the floor where I surmised the purloined phony penises had last been seen.

Greg, one of her long time waiters, came up with a salad, set it on the table, looked at my chalk art and left again without even the blink of an eye.

I devoured the salad. My stomach was an unforgiving creature and I needed to make up for the more brown than yellow banana of the morning.

Alexis herself came up with the po-boy. She stopped short when she saw my chalk drawings.

"I was trying to commune with the victim of the crime."

She sighed. "Great, now my cleaning crew has to deal with dead dick bodies all over the floor."

I smiled a beatific smile. She had asked me to come to the scene of the crime and be a detective.

She put the overstuffed plate on the far side of the table, then sat down, closer to me than the food. "So, Emma, other than wasting chalk, have you been thinking about how to solve this?"

I reached across the table, but she grabbed my arm. Years of hoisting pots and pans gave her good upper body strength.

The true answer, 'I haven't given it a vestige of a thought,' was not the route to the po-boy, it's bready, fried aromas wafting across the table. "Yes, I have. I need more information. Who had access?" My hand again crept across the table.

She grabbed a French fry and handed the salty morsel to me before I got there. To prove it as extra-special-fresh, the fry was so hot I dropped it. Then picked it up, blew on it a few times, and ate every potatoey-salty-fried bite.

"That's the thing, not too many people."

"You have a party where you're selling sex toys and not too many people had access?"

"Yes, look at this room. It's upstairs, one way up and one way down and you'd have to go right in front of the hostess station and bar to get in or out."

"What about staff?"

"Not a chance. I use only the A list for stuff like this, the ones who've been with me forever."

"Sex toys are expensive. Someone could be tempted."

"Plus I offered them all the wholesale price. Can't see any of them stealing to save twenty bucks." She handed me another French fry.

"Where do you keep them outside party time?"

"Here, in storage off the service area."

She stood up and I followed her to the small room tucked in the side of the room. In the back was a metal storage locker with a serious combination lock on it.

"In there," she pointed.

In true—at least as far as I fictionally knew—detective fashion, I examined the locker and even rattled the lock. The only thing out of place was a petrified mushroom peeking out from under the back leg. I didn't mention it to Alexis as I knew it would bring on a cleaning frenzy, one that might permanently separate me from my longed-for po-boy.

"Seems you have the classic locked storage locker mystery."

"Thanks, Agatha, I could have figured that out myself."

"So we have to see who had access and motive," I pontificated. Oh, where is my pipe and deerstalker cap? "Who used this room after you last saw the pilfered goods?"

"I don't know. We rent it out for private parties."

"You keep records, right?"

"Of course."

"Let me cull through them and see if anything stands out."

Alex rolled her eyes, but as she headed out she shoved the po-boy plate in my direction.

I had swallowed half of it by the time she returned.

She plopped a big notebook almost on top of my plate. The thump made the French fries jump. "Go to town." As she headed back down the stairs, she added, "Let me know if you need anything," in a tone that indicated she was looking for an excuse to tell me where I could put my anything.

I finished the food before opening the book.

Unfortunately, carefully perusing its contents did little to narrow things down. Too many conservative religious, political and football groups. Those repressed types are so much more likely to give in to temptation than us libertines. The only one I could rule out was a party for Alexis' extended family. They had only reconciled with their daughter once she opened a restaurant they wanted to go to. No way they would have stolen sex toys.

I threw the notebook down in disgust. I hadn't done much to earn the golden fried deliciousness of the po-boy. Other than let Alexis drag me into this.

However, I wasn't going to let her in on that. Not at least until I got a dinner out of this.

"So?" she demanded as she came up to clear away the plates.

"I've got some ideas, but need to cogitate on them for a while." Inspiration hit. "I'd like to talk to the staff that worked the sex toy parties and the private parties up here."

"Most of them aren't here. They won't be here until the dinner shift."

Perfect. "I can come back around then. If this room is open, I can use it. Just send one at a time for a few minutes. I promise not to disrupt things."

"You really think you can solve this?" Hope was in her voice.

"I've got a few ideas." A lie, a total lie.

"Ah, Emma, I knew I could count on you."

I smiled my most saintly smile. I let her precede me down the stairs so she couldn't see the crossed fingers behind my back.

It was a beautiful day. I'd already paid for parking, so I decided to walk around the French Quarter. Aimless wandering often helped with plot twists, so maybe it would help with solving this mystery. After around three blocks I realized the problem with real life is that it's not subject to a writer's whims. In a story I could come up with some great fictional solutions. But reality remained a blank wall. Worse, a wall covered with graffiti gibberish.

My reverie on reality was broken by a woman shouting, "My

purse! My purse is gone." It was at a decibel level that indicated the crown jewels were in said purse.

First the store security joined her, then two police officers. She had just set it down for a second, blah, blah, blah, really only a second, blah, blah.

I gawked like everyone else in the vicinity. Then I noticed something and walked up to one of the cops. "Excuse me, but that man stole her purse," I said, pointing to a fellow about half a block away, nonchalantly window shopping as if he hadn't a care in the world.

"And you know this how?" she asked.

World famous mystery writer didn't seem like the proper answer especially as the truth was closer to minor regional southern gothic crime novelist. I said, "I passed him a while back and his stomach wasn't purse sized about fifteen minutes ago." I had seen him a few blocks back and clearly something had registered in my brain. He looked like a tourist, preppy dressed, except he was wearing a sweater about two sizes too large and was not quite drunk or spacy enough to really be a tourist. Seeing him here again, with the sweater now filled out, put him at the top of the suspect list.

She headed for him, "Hey, buddy!"

Once he realized she was talking to him, he took off running. Into a tourist too drunk and oblivious to realize he was at a crime scene. The drunk tottered, and in a last ditch effort to keep from ending up in the rancid gutter, grabbed the crook by the shoulders. They both went down together. Side by side in the gutter everyone from the donkeys to anything male with a working zipper had probably peed in during the last 24 hours.

By the time they untangled themselves, the cops were slapping handcuffs on the crook, and the tourist wanted him arrested for gutter assault.

Rule Number 2 – don't hang around after you've done a good deed.

I had to loiter around to be thanked by the stolen purse woman (no reward, but she was sincere in her gratitude). So I spent most of the rest of the afternoon in the cop shop doing all the things good citizens do to help prevent crime. Every ten minutes I tried to remind myself it was material. Although it was hard to see what riveting crime thriller I could write using staring at walls that needed to be painted and thumbing through a three-month-old *Gambit* that had half the articles torn out. I didn't even get to give my statement to the cute woman cop, but to a grumpy older one who needed a lesson in proper tooth brushing and flossing. I didn't want to ask him when he'd last had spinach.

When I finally got out, it was close enough to supper to head back to Alexis' restaurant. Better to start my questioning when things were slow.

Slow enough for Rob at the bar to make me a Sazerac while Alexis was busy in the kitchen.

I took my drink upstairs to the private room and tried to think of some detective-like questions. The only thing that immediately came to mind was why the combination of rye whiskey and bitters was so good? I took another sip.

Don't concentrate on the fact that it's sex toys, but on the fact that the objects were stolen from a locked cabinet in a room with limited access.

That didn't help.

I took another sip.

That did help. Just not with any questions.

Greg entered the room and said, "Alexis said you wanted to talk to me."

Oh, yeah, that.

"Yes, I do. What have you heard about something missing from this room?"

"Oh, the lost dildos?" Bless his heart he didn't even snicker as he said it.

"Yes, those. Did you work the last party when they were seen?"

"Yep, I did. Saw Alex lock up the big chest of samples and unsold stuff right after it was done. It's one of those big plastic tubs. Hot pink, no less."

"Did you see anyone around after it was locked up?"

"Sure, lots of people. But I bet you mean around the cabinet?" I nodded yes and he continued. "Not that night. It was busy and we were tired."

"What about other parties up here? Did you work any of them and did you see anyone snooping around the cabinet?"

"No, I stay at the bar, only service staff get to climb the stairs."

"Can you think of anyone who might want to steal stuff like that?"

"Sure. But no one who works here."

"Anything else suspicious you can think of?"

"In this city?"

"Point taken."

"You want the special?" he asked.

"Sure." Then I considered, "I mean, what's the special?"

"Pecan crusted speckled trout with poached lemon-butter crabmeat on top."

"Fresh caught?"

"Yep. Don't worry, this isn't one of Alex's we-have-to-get-rid-of-this specials."

At that I said yes. All this detective work was working up an appetite.

I continued quizzing the rest of the staff who had worked the sex toy parties, but got the same answers. Everything had been locked up and only trusted staff had been in the service area.

Time for a plot twist. Oh, wait, this is real life, I have no control over them here.

Rob, bless him, brought me another Sazerac, unasked for.

"Did you work any of the parties?" I asked. If I was drinking Alex's liquor, I might as well do her bidding.

"Nope, I mostly stay behind the bar downstairs."

"See anything suspicious? That could possibly relate to the theft?"

"I saw one guy trying to go up the stairs on a night when nothing was going on up here. Claimed he was looking for the bathroom. I directed him back behind the stairs where it really is."

"Did he try again?"

"Not that I know of. Things get busy and yeah, he could have gone up there, but I'd like to think I'd notice someone coming down toting a big pink plastic tub."

"Ever seen him before?"

"No, he said he was from Milwaukee, down here for an academic conference. Society for Ethnomusicology or something like that? Is that real?"

"Sounds suspicious to me. Anything else?"

"Just Alex's stupid brother-in-law. I saw him leaving the bathroom with a rope."

"A rope? What was he doing here anyway?"

"The pork tenderloin special braised in a brandy butter sauce."

"Was that before or after the last sex toy party?"

"Hmm, I think two days after. Thursday is usually pork night."

"Was he coming from the bathroom or the stairs?"

"Bathroom, I thought. But I caught sight of him at the corner of the bar. He was stuffing a black nylon rope into his briefcase. Weird."

"That goes for most of Alex's family."

"You can say that," he said with a wink. "I can't. But I can agree with you."

Rob headed back down stairs.

I stood up and surveyed the room. Like most French Quarter buildings, the sides of this one were up against the buildings next door, so there were only windows out the front and back. This room overlooked the back alley, with offices and more storage in the front.

I examined the first window. Painted shut.

The second window. The same.

Third time is the charm. Dust does not lie. This one had been opened recently. There was a vague hand print on the glass and a space on the sill that was all too clean.

It would be hard to walk a big pink tub full of sex toys out the front door past the bar and hostess station. But what if someone had hoisted it out the window?

And could that someone possibly be Alexis' slimy brother-in-law? But why?

Greg came upstairs with my food.

I wanted to plow into it, but held my fork poised in the air with a luscious lump of crab meat on it, and continued my detective work. "Have you seen Alexis' sister and her husband here lately?"

"The outlaws, as we call them. Yes, but you can bet they weren't at the sex toy party."

"But they were here in the restaurant?"

"Yeah, it was weird. He came only once with her—the wife. Then twice without her. Three days last week and they rarely darken the door."

"Did you serve them?"

"Only once, the last time when he was here, with what he claimed was an out of town buddy of his, but I've seen the guy around."

"Around where?"

"You didn't hear this from me, but before the bathhouse closed—I only went there to work out—he occasionally came in, reeking of closet case married man. Like it was too dark to notice the ring line."

"The bro-in-law?"

"No, the guy he was with. Ted somebody."

"Pastor Ted? Say it ain't so."

"Don't know about the preaching, but he looked like the kind of man who spent time on his knees. In various positions."

"So, why would Pastor Ted and bro-in-law steal the sex toy stash?" I couldn't remember his name—the brother-in-law. He and the sister had married long after I'd broken up with Alexis, so I had no reason to remember what to call him. I only recalled Pastor Ted because of an unfortunate barbeque that Alexis talked me into going to. He introduced himself to me three times, seemingly unable to remember me because I'm no longer young and my hair is gray. All middle-aged women look alike.

The morsel and fork reached my mouth. They could not long stay asunder. OMG, lemon butter crab claw.

Greg wasn't in food ecstasy and he answered my question. "Got me. Blackmail? Extortion? They don't know where to buy them on their own?"

"Alexis might be embarrassed if her mother found out she was selling sex toys on the side, but blackmail?"

"Maybe they could be blackmailed, so they assume others could as well."

I thanked Greg for his info and asked him to send the others up for a second round of questioning. The restaurant was busy enough that I was able to eat and appreciate the trout between questioning. I even managed to work in dessert, the dark chocolate bread pudding with cognac sauce.

And another Sazerac.

No smoking guns, but I gleaned from my incisive queries that the bro-in-law was here the night of the party when the dildos were last seen. One of the women leaving the party had stopped to talk to him on her way out. No idea what the conversation was about, but she might have spilled about what was going on upstairs.

He came back the next night, with his wife. And then two nights later with Pastor Ted.

No one was able to place him going up the stairs, but the final night was a busy one, including a couple of Saints players on the scene, so as Rob put it, dead bodies could have been hidden behind the potted plants in the lobby and no one could have noticed.

While sipping my final Sazerac—I had to drive home after all—I again wandered to the window, propping a chair to stand on under it so I could get a better view outside.

Dark.

Ah, the outline of garbage cans. The garbage had to make it out to the street so there had to be access.

That was all I needed to know. The final Sazerac made it unwise to remain balanced for too long on a wobbly chair.

I had just put the chair back where it belonged and brushed off the foot print when Alexis joined me.

"So have you figured it out? Or did I just waste good food on you?"

"Food that is appreciated is never wasted. However, I have figured it out."

"Yes?" She crossed her arms, projecting skepticism.

"Your brother-in-law used a rope to lower the bin to the alley below. One of the women at the last party talked to him on her way out, which we can surmise is how he found out about the bin's contents. He was seen stuffing a rope into his briefcase. It probably happened on a real busy night."

She stared at me, open mouthed. Then she shut her mouth and said, "But how did he get into the locked storage locker."

"Because you used your birthday as the lock combo."

"I did not."

"The basketball game."

She looked away and mumbled, "It's easy to remember."

"Yeah, 69-67. Real easy to remember. How many people have you told that story to? Or rather is there anyone you haven't?"

"It's a great story. Final second. I Hail Mary a ball half-way across the court and it goes in for a three-pointer."

"That's how he got in. Loose lips sink ships. If I know you often use easy-to-remember numbers for passwords and combos, then your sister does, which means he does."

"But why?"

"Maybe he wants to blackmail you?"

"Oh, wait, I know. Grandmother Reese has been making noises about changing her will. She's not happy with Bruce and Linda because their one special child left the door open and Grandmother's cat got out. She missed bingo hunting for it."

"Did she find it?"

"It?"

"The cat? I'm worried about a lost cat."

"Yes, she did. I'm worried about what he might be planning."

"Well, good luck with that. I've done my part." I started for the stairs.

She put her hand on my arm. "Welcome home dinner for you and Jane with one of the best bottles of wine thrown in."

"One of the? Not the best?" I had just eaten; my stomach should not be ruling my thinking at the moment.

"It varies, depends on what we have in stock, what you order. It'll be good."

Sigh. It would. Alexis keeps a well stocked wine collection.

"Nice offer, but I'm not sure what I can do at this point. We can confront him, but he'll deny it. Then what?"

"You can follow him. He doesn't really know you. He'll recognize me."

"Follow him where? Like he's going to lead me to the dildos? And even if he does, then what?"

"You're smart, Emma, you'll think of something."

The only something I could think of was how crazy this was.

And how good her wine cellar was.

"Two bottles, I said."

"Done."

Damn, I was hoping she'd balk and I'd be out of this. "No promises. I'll do what I can, okay? But I'm not risking going to jail."

"I'll bail you out."

"Not risking going to jail," I emphasized.

She nodded.

Rule Number 3 – Don't agree to stupid things. Maybe this should be rule number one. No more stupid. Ever.

I needed to pee. I was sitting in my car on a boring suburban street watching a boring suburban house in hopes that I might see bro-in-law Bruce decide to move the dildos to a more secure location. I had been sitting here for over two hours. In that time, three cars had passed me by, and the screen of the TV at Bruce's place had stayed resolutely on some sports thing.

A few blocks away there was a strip of fast food places and stores. I was debating whether to drive or walk when I looked at my gas gauge. Walking it is. I quietly got out, shutting my door as softly as I could, and hoping that Bruce wouldn't pick now for the dildo break nor would there be any nosy neighbors around.

Nope, just me and my footsteps and my sloshingly overfull bladder. I pulled the hood of my black sweatshirt over my head. You know, to disguise myself like all the real detectives do. "Yes, officer, we saw a middle-aged woman in a black hoodie skulking around the neighborhood." Should I be spotted, my excuse was going to be crazy writer—I was researching a scene for the next book. That would be "crazy middle-aged woman in a black hoodie, officer."

Around a corner, one more block to relief.

A car drove past. Driver didn't even look my way.

When it stopped at the stop sign, two men jumped from behind a parked van and yanked open the driver's door.

"Get out! Leave the keys!" One of them grabbed the woman but she was still held by her seatbelt.

"I said get out!" yelled the other one. Although technically it was his friend who had said it.

"Get out of the car!" the first one bellowed again.

The woman was struggling with her seat belt. And, if my reaction was any gauge, her fear. She wasn't moving fast enough for them.

"Al, punch her!"

"No, you punch her!"

"I said for you to punch her!"

I'd like to say I was brave but the truth was my bladder could hold for at most another block, not turning around, running back to my car and driving home. Needing to pee is the key to courage.

"Hey," I yelled. "What the fuck you doing?"

"What the fuck? Who are you?"

"Al, I'm Spider's aunt," I shouted. "Don't you remember me? That's a goddamned stick shift, you can't drive it."

"Huh? What are you talking about?"

"Leave it! There's a fucking Lincoln two blocks down with the fucking keys in it. Almost fucking stole it myself but I promised my fucking kids I'd stay clean 'til Christmas. Fucking Christmas."

They let go of the woman, leaving her halfway hanging out of the car.

"Yo, thanks. Tell Spider 'lo for me." The two thugs obligingly trotted off in the direction of the fictitious Lincoln.

Wow, who knew they actually had a friend named Spider. Or maybe they were just too embarrassed to admit they couldn't remember me and were faking it. Like I often did.

I gave them a good part of a block distance then hustled to the woman, helping her right herself.

"Who are you?" she asked.

"Not who I was pretending to be. We need to get out of here before they figure out there is no car with keys in it."

"Get in," she offered. I was clearly a better option than those skinny pasty-faced boys.

I barely got the door shut when she peeled out.

"Where should I drop you?" she asked.

There was only one answer possible, "I really need to go to the bathroom."

She took me to her home another few blocks away. A nice suburban home with a powder room just inside the main entrance. So handy for guests.

While I was peeing she called the police.

They came. We described the hoodlums. The police asked us questions.

Yeah, I got to be the crazy lady mystery writer—direct quote from the more senior of the two police officers. I had to pull up some of my books on Amazon (ouch, two more bad reviews) to prove I really was a writer.

Then I had to listen to both cops tell me how writers so often got it wrong—not that they've read any of my books or even heard of me before this evening—and then about the books they planned to write when they retired. Direct quote, "You just sit at the computer and bang something out. Easy as pie."

I would not want to eat the pie he baked.

It was hours before they finally (after one last bathroom stop) dropped me off at my car.

Rule Number 4 – Really, no more stupid. I mean it this time.

In the tired wee hours of the morning, a thought came to me. Always dangerous, but at least in this case the Sazeracs were long out of my system.

Bruce was married to Alexis' younger sister. Alexis was the bright one in the family and her illumination wasn't of the high wattage. And she was a creature of routine, something she clearly got from her mother.

So it wasn't likely that Bruce had gone to great lengths to cover things up. That meant there were three likely hiding places: the trunk of his car, but I'd already scoped that out and he drove a Miata (mid-life crisis on a budget) so that was unlikely; his work, also not likely as he was a maintenance man at one of the religious colleges in the area. The third place was home, sweet, home.

It was the dregs before dawn. Even dead people were asleep by this point. What better time to do a little snooping around? It was a couple of hours before I'd need to pee again.

Halfway across the yard I realized the reason no one is out at night is because it's dark and you can't see where you're going.

Dead bodies, snakes, dirty needles. And dog shit. As my foot was hovering over disaster, my nose saved me. It gave me enough of an odiferous warning to jump-step over the suspicious dark spot. I could only hope that no self-respecting snake would be slithering near a pile of poop.

Maybe the bin was in the basement? Oh, wait, this is New Orleans (well, suburbs of, not close to the same thing). We don't do basements here unless you're really into indoor swamps.

I edged around the hedge. Despite my brilliant deduction of there being a limited number of places Bruce could hide the stolen goods in the case of the vanishing vibrators, it was still a daunting task to pinpoint in all those square feet of suburban sprawl just where the pink tub was. Assuming the goods were still in the pink tub.

For all I knew they could be in use at this very moment as Mr. & Mrs. Bro-in-law added to their sexual repertoire.

That was a scarier thought than the dead bodies and the snakes.

I could be intrepid but not trepid enough to look in their bedroom window.

I skittered around to the faint gray ribbon of the driveway and peered into the kitchen window. Busted. Dirty dishes still in the sink. (Like mine were, but I was on spouse vacation, so I had an excuse). And three boxes of marshmallow cereal on the counter. They had just one kid, so no excuse for that much of that cereal. My superiority could shine brightly there.

Alas, no pink tub. The closest thing to even a stray dildo was a banana. A rather small banana. Not that I'm a size queen, mind you. But it really wasn't the banana of my dreams.

You have a mission, I reminded myself.

Sniffing the air for lurking dog shit, I slid from the kitchen to the windows of the family room. Some boxy, square things, but given they were under the two TVs in the room (why does anyone need two TVs in one room?) didn't seem likely to be hiding the pink tub, unless Mr. Scrawny Bruce went to more trouble than he looked capable of.

The bedroom was verboten, so that left only the garage.

I had to do some dog shit dodging to get there. My eyes were getting good at spotting the dark, lumpy mounds in the grass. Did they ever clean up? Or was this their idea of organic composting? Oh, wait, dog shit meant a dog. But no barks had erupted in the night. I must be good at this, I thought, until I spied the shitting dog sleeping peacefully on the couch in the living room. He was tucked under a blanket, slobbering on it, with the TV going to keep him company. I had to hope his doggy dream—and the blaring TV—kept him dead enough to the world to not hear me outside the house.

Cars. His Miata. Red even. With custom racing stripes. Major middle-age crises with a few budget busters thrown in. She had a pink Cadillac. Menopause must be knocking at her door.

But, unless it was in that tub of a trunk, there was no hot pink dildo box inside the vehicle. It would clash with the delicate, feminine pink of her car.

That left me stumped.

And cold, hungry and feeling stupid. Time to go—

Workshop behind the garage. I was here. Might as well look.

It's so hard to be right so many times.

Two big, brightly wrapped boxes, with just enough of a megawatt, let's-play-football security light for me to see they were both addressed to Grandma with one, about the size of the pink tub, claiming to be from Alexis. I knew her well enough to know that she would never hide a present for anyone with this sister and brother-in-law.

My brilliant mind continued to dervishly deduct that this had to be his plot—make it look like Alexis was so lost to lesbian perversion that she thought a box of sex toys—and if she had a full line of display items, it would include butt plugs—were the best thing for Grandmother's 90th birthday. Or maybe the plot was glaringly obvious and clumsy and my cold feet needed to think my brain was brilliant to justify this.

My first thought was to exchange the name tags, but the packages were different enough in shape that it would probably be easy to spot—and retag them.

My next thought was to go home, call Alexis in the morning and let her deal with it.

My final thought was to just grab the box and skedaddle with it.

Rule Number 5 – Sometimes the simplest solution is the best.

I should have gone with my final thought—grab the sex toys and run. But, no, I had to be clever and show off my superior package wrapping skills. The oh-so-bright burglar light was enough illumination for me to switch the packages, wrapping them so skillfully that no one would be able to tell the different until the ultimate unwrapping.

"Emma! How fucking stupid could you be?!" Alexis was shouting at me. "My grandmother is going to unwrap a package of sex toys on her 90th birthday! I should have known better! You can only handle crime on the pages of a book!"

I thought it was brilliant at the time. Bro-in-law would be the one blamed for the trick he was trying to play on her. Of course, the time had been so early in the morning the larks hadn't started farting yet, and I'd been up more hours than were prudent at twenty, let alone my age, and caffeine, even food, was a distant memory and I was in enemy territory—the suburbs. In the sober light of the early afternoon, after a few hours of non-stop coffee drinking, I could see her point.

"That was over a thousand dollars of inventory."

That had to be retail, not wholesale, I told myself.

"One way or another, they'll know I had something to do with it!"

Yeah, because you had to make more money on top of what you were already making by selling sex toys on the side.

"I can't believe I was stupid enough to ask you to help me with this! What was I thinking?"

That makes you the first stupid one. When first stupid leads to second stupid, it's not really second stupid's fault. And furthermore—

"Did you hear what I asked you?"

I had been so lost in my internal response to Alexis that I forgot to actually listen to her.

I hastily responded, "Of course, but I assumed that you'd want to say more."

"How about this for more? What the fuck are we going to do?"

"We? What we are we talking about?"

"Us we. You got me into this!"

"No, I distinctly recall you getting me into this. I was happily writing away—"

"Never mind, that's not the point."

"Then don't make it a point if it's not the point."

"The point is what are we going to do?" she wailed.

"Calm down." She hates when I tell her to calm down, which is why I was doing it. "We know where it is and who has it. Just go back and get it."

"But it's at Bruce and Linda's house."

"So, it's stolen property. We can try sneaking in, but if they catch us, you get imperious—you do that well—tell them off and demand your stuff back."

"But then they'll know that it's my stuff."

"Alexis, they already know that. You can claim it's not yours but belongs to an unfortunate business partner. Imply it's a Mafia business partner and people—like them—will get killed if it doesn't get returned."

She considered this. And considered it some more before finally saying, "I guess that might work. Let's go."

"Go? Go where?"

"To their house."

"You want me to go with you?"

"Emma, there's not a choice. You're coming with me."

"I have to pick up Jane at the airport."

"Not until this evening."

"How do you know that?"

"She's coming in from Seattle, and there's only one nonstop flight which doesn't get in until this evening. I know because I just came back last month from the King Crab Expo there."

She was heading for her car as I was trying to come up with another excuse.

"Damn, it's material," I muttered as I followed her.

It would be easy, I told myself as we headed out there. Bro-in-law was a cheat and a coward. If he tried to confront us, he was no match for both me and Alexis. I suspected he hadn't told his wife much of what was going on. She would probably react the same as Alexis did— no sex toys for grandma. Worst case scenario was that no one was at home and some nosy neighbor would call the police. We were white, middle-aged women, and it was Alexis' sister's house. We'd get off with a bemused smile.

That pretty much covered the bases.

Except for the one we confronted when we got there.

The party had already started and Grandmother and various assorted relatives were gathered in the backyard on the swimming pool patio opening presents. I thought it was a bit nippy to be outside, but perhaps it was easier than actually cleaning up.

"What do we do now?" Alexis hissed at me.

My vote would have been to run like hell and hope they hadn't seen us.

"Alexis! I thought you weren't going to be able to make it!" Her mother—with a mother's unerring instincts—knew when her daughter was in the vicinity. "And how nice that you brought Emma. She and Emma were college roommates. So nice when people are friends for life."

I gave Alexis a sidelong glance. "Roommates, huh?"

"Smile and act nice," she muttered at me. "And get us out of here." To the assembled crowd she said, "We can't stay, but I did want to at least run by and wish you a happy birthday."

"We're still having the party at your restaurant?" Granny asked. She was as fond of meat as anyone in the family.

"Of course, but I didn't want to miss this one." Alexis was smiling through gritted teeth. So not an attractive look on her.

"We're really here because of an issue with the present Alexis left," I said. "You see . . . it's been recalled. And we need to take it away and get it replaced." Yes, that was the ticket. Except I had switched Alexis' putative package with his. "Oh, dear, it looks like the gifts have been switched. Somehow the name tag for Bruce and Linda got put on Alexis' package."

"They look fine to me," Bruce said.

"No, I'm sure they've been switched," I said, looking directly at him. The only way I could make myself clearer was to say 'I rewrapped the gifts and switched them.' He had to pick up that something was amiss.

Well, no, I often forget and underestimate idiocy. He was just smart enough to see we wanted his package and so stupid it didn't occur to him it might have been tampered with.

"They look fine to me. In fact, why don't you open ours next?" He shoved the big—perfectly wrapped, if I do say so myself—box at Granny's feet.

"No, wait, you can't," Alexis cried out as she started to elbow her way through the hovering crowd.

I couldn't decide whether to follow in her wake or edge back out and start the long (very long—we were well beyond the Orleans Parish line and I don't live close to the boundary) walk home.

For 90, Granny was spry enough to rip off half the wrapping paper in one swipe.

When dimwit Bruce saw that it revealed a hot pink tub and not his brown cardboard box containing a badminton set (I guess for Granny to watch the kids play, which means Bruce wanted it for himself and this was his generous way of giving it to her to give to him) he started his own path of elbowing through the crowd.

They reached the box at the same time, Bruce yanking one end out of Granny's hand and Alexis pulling on the other.

This was no longer material. Not unless I started writing magic realism.

It was a battle between the two of them, each pulling an end of the tub.

Then I shouted, "You're too close to the—"

Splash. Make that big, double splash.

The hot pink tub popped its lid and its contents spilled into the pool. Bruce and Alexis both grabbed for anything they could—various items were floating and in the flailing, one of them whapped a dolphin dildo and flung it right at Granny's feet.

Edging out—and walking home—seemed the far wiser decision. Until I remembered that Alexis can't swim. Dildos be damned, Jane would not be happy if I let her long lost half-sister drown only hours before I picked her up at the airport.

One of the vibrators started buzzing as the water got into the battery pack.

"Run! Save yourselves!" I yelled. "It's about to explode!"

I pushed my way to the pool through the now panicked horde. I wanted people worried about surviving, not realizing what was floating (the anal beads in their airtight plastic bag) and sinking (the pack of cock rings) in the pool.

Alexis was sputtering in the deep end. I grabbed the anal beads ever so handily floating by, ripped the bag open and flung one end to her.

She looked at me like I was crazy.

"Take it! I'll pull you out."

With the choice of being saved by a butt toy or drowning, she chose the former. Once she was close enough to the edge of the pool I took her hand and pulled her ashore.

Bruce was clambering out of the shallow end. Linda, his wife, was half-helping and half-hectoring him. "Bruce, what's going on? What are those things? Are they what I think they are? What were you thinking? How could you do this to me?"

He looked unsure of whether to get out or go under.

Everyone else was gone. Including the dolphin dildo.

Leaving Alexis gasping for breath, I got the pool net and hooked the listing pink tub, maneuvering it close enough to the edge to pull it out. I used the net to scoop up a few more things, but the cock rings were impossible to get. Maybe they would improve Bruce's marital relations.

I dumped what I could back into the pink tub, checked to make sure Alexis was still breathing—yep, she was starting to curse under her breath—and used the net to retrieve the tub's top and slapped in on.

"Let's get out of here," I said.

Still muttering curses under her breath, Alexis hoisted one end of the tub—now heavier with waterlogged toys—the plushies really suck the stuff up—and we hightailed it to her car. We paused just long enough to drain out what water we could, then shoved it in her trunk.

Even though she drives an automatic, Alexis managed to squeal the tires taking off.

I had enough sense to keep quiet and ignore her mumbled curses and how much she was dripping all over everything including my pants leg.

She jerked to a stop in front of my house.

"Emma, if I ever ask you for anything other than baking a loaf of bread for a potluck, have me committed, will you? Solving crimes is not what you should ever, ever do. Oh, and don't you dare tell Jane!"

She didn't wait for an answer, the car was already moving away as I was getting out.

I looked at my watch, I had just enough time to put on dry pants, and underwear—she'd dripped heavily enough to go through two layers—and head to the airport.

Rule Number 6 – Don't keep secrets from the love of your life.

I was right on time at the airport. Even managed to find the good chocolate bar I'd hidden for myself to eat in case I desperately needed chocolate, and instead brought it for Jane. She'd be hungry after a nonstop Seattle to New Orleans flight.

After she told me about her trip and was gobbling the chocolate (it was a good Belgian one) she asked me what I'd been up to.

"It's all true, I swear. So Alexis called me up and..."

Jane was laughing so hard by the time we exited the airport, she almost snorted chocolate up her nose.

Later, much later, Alexis told Jane—she still wasn't speaking to me—that Granny had kept the dolphin dildo. She thought the base was a great idea so that it looked like it was about to come out of the waves. She displayed in on her mantel.

Oh, and Bruce and Linda were getting a divorce.

JESSIE:
A KATE DELAFIELD STORY

By Katherine V. Forrest

"IT'S A BAD TIME for you to visit, Kate," Sheriff Jessie Graham offered in quiet apology.

"I'm glad to be here, Jess," Kate replied with equal quietness. "I know how close you are to Walt. Right now you need your friends."

Kate Delafield, sipping coffee from a Styrofoam cup, sat beside Jessie Graham's desk in one of the plain wooden chairs the county of Alta Vista provided for visitors to its Sheriff's station at Seacliff. She said to Jessie, "As I recall, he helped you get this job."

Jessie nodded. "I owe it to him."

"You say he disappeared Friday. Any theories about why—or where he might be?"

Jessie contemplated Kate Delafield, the strong face framed by fine graying hair, the intelligent, somber light blue eyes. Kate had last stopped here for a visit more than two years ago, and Anne had been with her. Anne's accident, her death, had happened two months after that, and Jessie had not learned of it until a week after the funeral...

"Woman, you're on vacation," Jessie growled, reaching to place a hand over Kate's arm, and pointedly surveying Kate's jeans and the hooded white sweatshirt adorned with a small LAPD insignia. "You're not four hours out of that smog-ridden cesspool, I'm not about to—"

"The smog's a little better in L.A. these days, Jess," Kate said with a faint smile. She slouched back into the wooden chair as if it were comfortably cushioned, and crossed an ankle over a knee. She picked up her cup of coffee. "My friend, tell me about it."

"It's a hell of a thing." For the first time in two days Jessie felt the pressure within her ease, felt a sense of comfort. She pushed herself back from her desk, rested a foot on an open desk drawer, folded her arms across her brown uniform shirt. She said in a rush of words, "There's no damn sense to it, Kate. I played cards with the man and four friends of ours Friday night. I swear he was the same as always. He left my place making jokes and waving twenty-seven dollars in winnings, and he'd taken most of those dollars from me. The next morning Walt's wife calls me, claims that in the middle of that very same night he'd taken off in pouring down rain with a bag of money under his arm, without his car, and nobody's seen hide nor hair of him since. There's no damn sense to it."

Kate shook her head sympathetically, and her eyes narrowed in scrutiny of her friend. "Any theories, Jess?"

"Theoretically," Jessie said with all the confidence she could muster, "he's a missing person. He may just turn up like a lot of them do." Then she felt a stinging behind her eyes and looked quickly away. "Kate—dammit, Kate, I know in my gut he's dead."

When she could control her voice she said almost angrily, "My gut feelings don't always turn out to be fact." She forced a semblance of a grin. "I had a gut feeling about Irene, too. That we'd be together forever."

"I know the feeling." Kate gestured at the case file on Jessie's desk. "Could I take a look?" Jessie handed it over. "Tell me everything, Jess. Everything you've got, right down to the fine hairs."

Jessie nodded gratefully. Then scowled, remembering the Saturday morning two days ago in Walt Kennon's house.

VELMA KENNON HAD BEEN seated in an armchair in the immaculate living room, her red-checked apron clashing violently with the pale lavender of the upholstery. She pulled a gray cardigan loosely around her shoulders and said in soft, reluctant tones, "He had me draw out the ten thousand from our savings Friday."

Jessie's voice was sharp with skepticism. "Why'd he have you do that? Why wouldn't he do it himself?"

"Maybe it was his way of telling me." Her voice broke. "I think he was in some kind of trouble."

If she expects me to fall for this horse manure...

"I know him," Jessie said. "You're Walt's wife—but it's only been a year for you, Velma." There was hostility in her tone that she had not intended, and she added more gently, "I grew up knowing the man, we've been close friends ever since I came back to Seacliff. I know Walt. There's no sense to this."

Velma picked up a corner of her checked apron and dabbed at a cheek. "Well, I thought Walter loved me."

Jessie asked with renewed brusqueness, "What'd Walt say he needed the ten thousand for?"

"He said I should just trust him." The voice throbbed with injury. "Said he'd explain it all later. I think he needed that money to pay someone off. I think he was in some kind of serious trouble. Maybe trouble from back when he was Sheriff here. And whoever it was took him somewhere and... Maybe the ocean."

Jessie pushed herself to her feet, shifted her hands down to rest them just above the wide belt and holster. "He'll have to be missing forty-eight hours before it's official. But I'd like to have a look around now if it's all right with you, Velma."

Velma uncrossed her thin ankles and rose to her full height, not much over five feet. Her dark eyes were reproachful. "I'd never have called you if I didn't want you looking into this any way you can. Go right ahead, look everywhere."

Jessie radioed for a car to pick up Cowan, the deputy who had accompanied her. She wanted to be alone as she sifted through the possessions of Walter Kennon. She knew she might spot something odd, some little thing Cowan could miss.

After Cowan was gone, she sat in her Sheriff's car trying to collect her thoughts and fight down an almost paralyzing foreboding. Not for a moment did she believe one detail of Velma Kennon's story.

In two days of hearings before the seven Commissioners of Alta Vista County, Jessie had learned all she needed to know about the character of Walt Kennon. Ten years a retired Sheriff, he had challenged the Commissioners not to ignore Jessie's superior record, her solid years of experience of police work in both Los Angeles and Alta Vista County, her administrative ability, her leadership qualities. Jessie knew she owed the position she had held for the past year and a half entirely to Walt Kennon.

Groping for objectivity, she reviewed the facts she readily knew about him. He was sixty-four. He'd been released from Veteran's Hospital in '46, some months after the war. Had finished his education at Cal Poly in San Luis Obispo, then come back to Seacliff and taken up police work, rising to the position of Sheriff. But the shrapnel fragments still scattered throughout both his legs and the persistent severe pain had led to his early retirement twelve years later. Of his wartime experiences she remembered him saying only, "Duty. Loyalty. A man owes it."

He had settled into the town of his birth just as Jessie had—like a thirsty plant sinking deep roots. And like Jessie, had grumbled at every evidence of the oceanside town's growth. Walt's only vacations had been to Los Angeles to visit a brother afflicted with emphysema, and he returned each time even more contemptuous of big city life. He was Jessie's kind of person: quiet and leather-tough, his friendship a hard-won prize, a man who kept to himself until some interior principle signaled him to speak—as he had for Jessie, as he had again just recently when a consortium of builders tried to force re-zoning of a section of mobile homes occupied by elderly residents.

Her mind dark with apprehension, Jessie climbed out of her car and went back into Walt Kennon's house. In the bedroom she inspected Walt's familiar plaid shirts and windbreakers, the baggy corduroys he usually wore around town and to her card games, his khaki gardening pants, the fleece-lined jacket for the few really chill days of winter, the well-worn cardigan sweaters, the one good blue suit with the white shirt protected by plastic. Like herself, Walt had few clothes; he preferred what was tried and true and comfortable. Jessie noted that the clothes Walt had worn last night—gray corduroys, a blue plaid Pendleton shirt, a black plastic raincoat—were not in the closet. Everything there seemed orderly, undisturbed.

As did Velma's closet. The contents were modest: housedresses and cotton robes, a few skirts and frilly blouses, three good woolen dresses. But inside several large zippered plastic bags were smartly styled suits and dinner dresses, high-heeled sandals and evening shoes stored in plastic compartments—all of these apparently relics from Velma's past, and all of them useless in quiet, informal Seacliff.

Jessie was glad to move her scrutiny from the bedroom to an area less evocative of Velma and Walt Kennon's marriage. In the living room, dozens of *Field and Stream* back issues on the inconspicuous bottom shelf of the small bookcase were the only concrete traces of Walt Kennon. In heterosexual marriage, Jessie mused as she browsed around the carefully appointed room, precious little of a house ever really belonged to the male; his part of the closets maybe, and the yard and garage. The living room always belonged to the woman. Yet there was no evidence of Velma in this room either, Jessie realized—or anywhere else. Odd that the house had changed so little during the entire year of Walt Kennon's second marriage.

Remembering how swiftly she'd made her own quarters austere again after the three-year disaster with Irene in Los Angeles, Jessie moved into the den adjoining the living room. She looked at a framed photo of Velma and Walt on the small, leather-topped desk, and admitted that she disliked Velma Kennon intensely.

And yet she'd accepted her at first, and willingly. Walt had been five years alone with his grief, and it was good to see him happy. And Velma was a pretty woman, and vivacious. But the buoyancy had soon left Walt's step. And Velma's prettiness and high energy seemed to fade with each succeeding month of her marriage to Walt. Only once in the past year had Walt invited the Friday night poker group to his house—when Velma was away visiting her parents in Garden Grove. Walt and Velma seemed to be two people who had leached the vitality from each other.

Jessie could easily account for Walt's faithfulness to this joyless marriage—the same reason he had never questioned his wartime obligation: Duty. Loyalty. A man owes it. As for Velma's reason, it appeared to be the classic one: she had no means of support other than Walt Kennon.

Jessie opened the top drawer of the desk. She found a twenty-five-thousand-dollar insurance policy, Velma Kennon beneficiary; a copy of a deed to property in Santa Barbara which had been signed over to Bergan Construction Company on January ninth—only two months ago; and a bank book. She opened the bank book. It showed a ten-thousand-dollar withdrawal made this past Friday and a current balance of two hundred and eighty-six thousand dollars; two hundred and fifty thousand of that amount had been deposited on January nineteenth.

Jessie gaped at the numbers for only an instant. She knew all the surface details of Walt's life—he'd willingly shared them—but never had she heard him speak specifically of his finances. No more than he had ever shared his grief and loneliness for Alice, or talked of how his legs had been shot from under him during the assault on Guadalcanal. He'd muttered about the cost of living—had grumbled at the card game about expensive repairs to his Toyota—but she knew he contributed to the support of his chronically ill brother, and he always seemed to have sufficient money. She had assumed he lived in relative comfort on a combination of military and police pensions and social security.

"Velma," Jessie called, "could you please come in here a minute?"

Velma glanced blandly at the bank book. "It's Walter's money. His savings, and proceeds from selling a house in Santa Barbara that belonged to his first wife." Her voice took on bitterness. "When my first husband died I didn't have two thin dimes left after probate."

Jessie tapped the bank book with a fingernail. "Says here it's your money as well, Velma. As joint tenant." Then she added reflectively, "I remember about that Santa Barbara house—Alice wouldn't sell it. Amazing it was worth so much money."

"The land it's on was re-zoned commercial years ago. She never did one thing with that place for years," Velma said harshly. "Never even raised the rent of the people living there. Him either, after she died."

"Alice liked the tenants," Jessie said mildly, picking up the executed deed, turning it over in her hands, her mind lighted with the image of Alice Kennon. Genial, comfortable Alice, with mink brown hair that had suddenly gone gray and then whitened over the years, and hazel eyes always radiating humor and spirit, conveying that everything about Jessie—everything—was just fine with her. She had given Walt Kennon a glow of quiet contentment for twenty-six years, until the diagnosis of pancreatic cancer. Just a scant six weeks after that, Jessie Graham had borne one of the heaviest burdens of her life— the casket of Alice Kennon to her gravesite in Rolling Hills Cemetery.

Replacing the documents, Jessie brushed a finger along the lock mechanism on the drawer. She bent down to examine it. "Walt mentioned a couple of weeks ago he'd made out a will, to make sure his brother was taken care of. One of those handwritten wills. Holographic, they call them."

Velma looked startled. "I don't know about any will." She added with belligerence, "I never saw it."

"Drawer's been forced open," Jessie stated, watching her. "You know why that'd be?"

Two thin furrows formed between the penciled brows. "The drawer's never once been locked so far as I know. I don't know what anybody'd take."

Maybe that will.

The yard was neat, well-tended, the grass wet and spongy under Jessie's feet. The pain in Walt's legs had limited how much he could do but he loved gardening, and well-cultivated flower beds bordered the front of the house and the side hedge. Last night's heavy rain had separated and caked the dirt around the bushes.

Jessie walked up the driveway past the house and opened the garage. The gray Toyota was parked against one wall. Garden utensils lined the opposite wall. A few wood-working tools lay on a scarred bench. She picked up a plastic hood and covered the circular saw that Walt used to cut his firewood. A movement caught her eyes. She glanced over to catch the flutter of curtain at the kitchen window.

So Velma was watching her. With heightened senses she examined the garage minutely, donning a pair of Walt's work gloves to pick up and study each tool. She found nothing unusual until she came to a well-used but very clean shovel. At the kitchen window, Velma Kennon watched openly as Jessie studied it. She replaced the shovel and went into the house.

Velma stood at the kitchen counter slicing a tomato; its rich earthy odor reached Jessie. It occurred to her that she had always seen Velma Kennon in a colorless dress covered by a red-checked apron with big pockets.

Jessie said evenly, "That's a mighty clean shovel out there in the garage."

"Walter left it out in the rain last week," Velma said, her eyes on the knife slicing through the ripe red tomato.

"Didn't rain last week," Jessie informed her.

"Well, whenever it last did," Velma said in exasperation.

Jessie said, not bothering to soften her skepticism, "Being careless with one of his tools isn't something Walt would do."

Velma's knife stilled. She stared at Jessie, then said with asperity, "It doesn't sound like Walter to just go off and disappear without a trace, either."

"Don't think that's what he did."

She locked eyes with Velma Kennon. Velma's unreadable dark stare did not waver. Finally Jessie said, "Could I trouble you for the keys to the Toyota?"

She followed Velma into the living room. Velma picked up her purse from the desk.

"Could I trouble you to look at the purse," Jessie said. "Just routine."

"Of course," Velma said with distinct sarcasm and thrust the leather bag at Jessie, her fingers rigid. "As I recall, I think I've got thirty-two dollars in bills, and a little change."

Jessie did not reply. Of course Velma wouldn't be stupid enough to carry any of that ten thousand dollars in her purse. Removing one object at a time, she carefully placed on the desk a comb, wallet, lipstick, compact, metal nail file, package of tissues, ballpoint pen, checkbook. The checkbook register showed ordinary transactions.

"The ten thousand," Jessie said. "What denominations did the bank give you?" She examined the zippered pocket and lining of the black leather purse.

"Five hundred in twenties," Velma muttered, her lips in a thin tight line, "the rest in fifties and hundreds."

Jessie nodded. "That's quite a wad of cash." She handed the purse back to Velma. "I'll let you put everything back the way you want. We have to look at everything, Velma. Just routine," she added absently, thinking that Walt had bought chips at the poker game with two tens.

Jessie unlocked the car. The Toyota Celica showed the usual signs of five-year wear, and smelled of Walt's pipe tobacco. She added the powerful beam of her flashlight to the morning sunlight, and examined the interior. She'd impound the car. Elbert and Ron over at Martinsville would go over it thoroughly. But there were no visible stains. Of any kind.

Deep in thought, she walked slowly to her own car and replaced the flashlight in its sprocket. Money and property were the reasons for many marriages—and the motive for the vast majority of crime. Most people would say Velma was not the type to kill, but she knew anybody was the type. Knew it from those years of police work down in Los Angeles and fifty-two years of plain hard living. Only their Maker knew why people did the things they did.

Something had happened to Walt—and Velma had done it. Of that Jessie was certain. She shifted her gun belt, adjusting the heavy holster, wishing she could do the same for her leaden heart. Velma had done something to him, and taken him somewhere to dispose of him.

But where? And how? It just wasn't physically possible for a hundred-and-ten-pound woman of nearly fifty to do much with a man Walt's size, certainly not against his will, and not if he was dead weight, either. Walt had become heavier recently. He was a good hundred and seventy pounds, maybe more. He'd joked ruefully about it just last night as he helped himself to potato chips and dip at the poker game.

Another memory of the poker game leaped into Jessie's mind. She whirled and trotted back to the Toyota. Walt's complaint about expensive repairs to the Toyota—he'd picked up the car on the way to the poker game, he'd had it in for a brake relining and carburetor work, plus routine maintenance.

Jessie yanked open the car door, knelt to scan the Union Oil sticker on the door frame, then compared the mileage figure written there by the service station to the mileage on the speedometer, jotting the numbers in her notepad. Velma Kennon watched from the kitchen window.

From the time Walt had picked up the car it had been driven two miles and whatever number of tenths that were unaccounted for. Gil's Union Oil Station was around the corner from the Kennon house. Walt had driven from there to Jessie's house for poker. Based on the time Velma had given as Walt's arrival home, he'd come directly here from the poker game. By marking off those distances in her own car she could tell if Walt's car had been driven after he'd arrived at his house. One thing she knew for sure: If this car had been driven, it hadn't been driven far.

Concealing her excitement, Jessie clumped back into the house. "Velma," she asked, "you drive that car after Walt got home last night?"

"Why...no. Of course not."

"I'm sealing it off, impounding it for the time being. I'll say goodbye to you for now."

Velma wiped her hands on her checked apron. "Something bad's happened to him," she said. "I know it."

I'll bet you do.

"I guarantee," Jessie said, her tone heavy and ominous, "I'll find out. One way or the other, I'll find out."

She had turned then and stalked out to her police car.

JESSIE HAD TAKEN KATE to an early dinner at the Sandpiper, a weathered clapboard restaurant on a steep hillside overlooking Seacliff and the Pacific. She restrained herself from supplying more details of Walt Kennon's disappearance while Kate gazed at a bank of fog drifting its way in over the horizon, over white-capped swells of gray-blue ocean.

"As good a career as you had in L.A.," Kate said musingly, "I can see what compelled you to come back here."

Jessie smiled and realized she had not smiled in the past three days. "Much as I don't understand it, Kate, I see that you belong where you are, too. They need the best cops they can find down there in that nether side of hell."

Smiling, Kate picked up her scotch. "You don't get lonely up here, Jess, away from any sort of...activity?"

"Gay women, you mean." Jessie refrained from pointing out that Kate herself was on vacation alone. "We do have gay people here—hell, we're everywhere. Seacliff has fourteen thousand population now. It's a fair-sized place. A few folks know about me. Some of them have long memories. I was chasing after girls in this town from the time I was six."

She chuckled along with Kate. "I'm private about myself just naturally. But I can't say I'm all that careful, even though some people here would jump at any reason to see me gone. They can't abide the idea of a woman Sheriff, let alone—"

Jessie broke off to Kate's raised hand. Their first course, clam chowder, had arrived. Intoxicated by the aroma, Jessie dipped her spoon eagerly into the rich meaty creaminess, realizing she had scarcely eaten since Saturday. As the waitress moved away, Jesse continued, wolfing down the chowder as she spoke, "I'll tell you the truth. My time with Irene told me one thing plain as day—I'm cut out to be a bachelor. I'm still your perfectly normal queer." She added with an embarrassed grin, "I do love women. I drive up to San Francisco now and again and get in some girl chasing. But this town is my family, I've got roots here, and responsibility, good friends—" She broke off and put down her soup spoon. Walt's disappearance was again like an iron weight in her stomach, displacing further desire for food.

"Tell me about the Kennon car." Kate's voice was dry, business-like. "I assume it checked out clean?"

Jessie's smile was inward. Kate had not changed much; when her mind was locked into the details of a case, she spared limited attention for even such distractions as spectacular views of the Pacific or general conversation.

"No traces of blood," Jessie answered, "not in the car or on any of the tools. And Velma was made joint tenant on the savings account the week after Walt married her. Walt's the kind to do something like that."

Kate finished the last spoonful of her chowder, pushed the bowl away. She steepled her fingers and contemplated Jessie over them. "That's a point, Jess. If you're right about your gut feeling, then the motive here figures to be money, pure and simple. Since she's joint tenant, why would she do anything to Walt? Why wouldn't she just clean out that account and take off?"

Jessie nodded. "It's a good point. But I've figured out a couple of reasons. Velma doesn't seem the type to run even if she knew how to cover her tracks, and that's a lot harder to do in these days of computers. She'd have to cover her tracks awfully well with Walt after her, him being an ex-cop. I think she'd figure he'd track her down, so she wouldn't feel safe for a minute."

"And if she simply divorced him," Kate mused, "she probably wouldn't come out with much of a settlement, considering the length of their marriage."

Jessie moved her soup bowl aside and pulled a folded sheet from the Kennon case file, a real estate map of Seacliff. "I've measured mileage to the exact tenth, Kate. Drove from Gil's Union Station to my house, then back to Walt's. I've got to think he came as direct as he could to my place—Gil at the station said Walt picked the car up at six fifty-five, five minutes before the station closed. Walt arrived just after seven, like he usually did, and I've got four other witnesses to prove it."

"And afterward," Kate contributed, "aside from Velma's statement about when he arrived home, he wouldn't have reason to go anywhere. It was pouring rain—"

"And everything in town was closed, anyway," Jessie concluded. "So I got one and eight-tenths miles clicked off what Walt drove. That leaves an extra two tenths to account for, plus whatever other tenths were on there because the gas station only wrote down the whole number. Meaning Walt or Velma drove the car half of that distance, and Velma drove it back the other half."

Jessie extracted a pen from her uniform shirt pocket with the ease of habit. "Here's the Kennon house." She indicated a point on the map in the center of a circle inscribed in pencil. "I took a protractor and measured and drew this circle around the Kennon house—"

Kate reached for the map, studied it closely. Jessie said, "Most of it's residential."

"True," Kate said, "but there's some vacant land in here, Jess, and part of a cemetery."

"Rolling Hills Cemetery," Jessie said with a nod. "Alice Kennon's buried just on the other side of my circle. The cemetery's all grass, kept perfect, just like a lawn. I checked it out Sunday. And all that vacant land, I walked every bit of it, Kate. I looked at every damn square inch."

"You said it rained hard Friday night," Kate pointed out. "Heavy rain could cover up traces of a grave."

Jessie looked at her soberly. "I'll tell you the truth. I don't expect to find a grave. I mean, how could a little thing like Velma Kennon dig a grave? Anybody who's ever put a shovel into the ground can tell you uncultivated earth is like digging into cement. Earth wet from rain is like lifting a pile of rocks."

Their food arrived. Jessie looked at her swordfish with indifference. Kate sprinkled lemon on her lobster, then cut off a piece and munched it as she continued her study of the real estate map.

Jessie said, "Let me fill you in about the other leads I checked out."

"SHERIFF GRAHAM," THE YOUNG teller had said nervously, "I gave Mrs. Kennon just what she asked for—"

"I know you did, Sarah. Now just relax," Jessie said in her most reassuring tones. "There's no problem about it at all. Were any of the bills in series?"

Sarah nodded. "But that much money in cash, I had to take it from the PG&E payroll, and that's close onto a hundred fifty thousand dollars, so there's no telling which of those bills I gave her."

Disappointed, Jessie said, "Thank you, Sarah. You call me now if you see any transaction Mrs. Kennon makes that's unusual, all right? Confidential, you have my word."

Jessie interviewed Ms. Neville, the librarian, who had telephoned Saturday afternoon as word of Walter Kennon's disappearance spread around town.

"It was six weeks ago, Sheriff." Ms. Neville peered at Jessie over the narrow rectangles of her reading glasses. "She never did check anything out. Every day for a week she came in here. And hasn't been back since." Her words were a sibilant, penetrating whisper in the single-room cavern that was Seacliff's public library, crowded and murmurous at this mid-afternoon hour on the weekend. "Can't say what she was reading, either. And that's what seemed so suspicious. She'd just put her book right back up on the shelf and move off if I came anywhere near."

The librarian's reproachful frown deepened. "Why would anybody care if another person saw what she was reading?"

Maybe she just flat resented your nosiness, Jessie thought. But she said gently, "Ms. Neville, can you tell me what general section she spent her time in?"

"The sciences. Anatomy. Medicine."

JESSIE CUT SEVERAL PIECES from her swordfish, moved them around on her plate. "I'll tell you what else I did. I talked to everybody in the Kennon neighborhood—nothing. I ran a check on Velma Kennon's background—nothing. I sent urgent inquiries to every doctor and pharmacy in Alta Vista County, all I've turned up so far is a Darvon prescription when Walt had dental surgery."

Jessie took a forkful of baked potato. "I tell you, Kate, I'm baffled. I can't figure what Velma did or how she did it. Right now my theory..." She thrust the forkful of potato down in recoil from the images. "I think maybe she's chopped him up and got a piece tucked here and there." She braced, expecting incredulous laughter.

But Kate said firmly, "Jess, put that nightmare out of your head. I'm not claiming this woman doesn't have the alligator mentality it takes to do such a thing. We both know better. But look at your own body, think about all those quarts of blood. Imagine anybody trying to cut through bone and muscle. Imagine the kidneys, the intestines. With all respect, Jess—"

Jessie nodded hurriedly, feeling both foolish and immensely relieved. "Got to be an answer to this, Kate. Got to be."

Kate said, "Why don't I take a few bites of that swordfish you don't want?"

Jessie cut a large section from her fish. "The rest of this'll be a nice treat for Damon, my cat."

Kate nodded absently, her eyes once more on the Pacific. "Before we go to your place, I'd like to you to drive me around the circle on this map. While it's still light."

VELMA KENNON SAT IN her living room sipping tea, the day's *Courier* in her lap. But she was watching the patrol car, a black menace drifting along her street. Having passed the house twice, it would circle the block and come back once more. And a half hour from now, repeat the process. Velma knew the habits of Seacliff's Sheriff's Department well; she had been under its close surveillance for the past three days.

With an irritated shrug she unfolded the *Courier*. Her eyes were instantly drawn by a name in a small headline down the page:

Former D.A.R. Chapter Pres.
Margaret Paxton Dies Here

She shook the paper open and scanned the short article extolling the accomplishments of Margaret Paxton, sister to the recently deceased Grant Paxton, then turned to the obituary page. The notice was almost identical to the one six days ago which had branded itself into her memory. Chilled, she dropped the paper back into her lap, stared out at the black police car cruising back past the house.

Not much longer, she reassured herself, sipping the hot, bracing tea. Only a matter of days before Sheriff Jessie Graham could no longer justify detaining her in Seacliff, before the Sheriff would have to pursue her all the way to the coast of Florida if she wanted to continue her useless surveillance. A few years from now, Velma Gardiner Kennon would be the stuff of memory and legend in this town, the suspected murderess who had somehow conjured away the body of her husband.

Soon...it would all happen soon, and exactly as she'd planned. She had a nice solid nest egg now, and the day would come when she'd have even more—when Walter was declared dead and his life insurance paid off, and the title to the house would clear as well. A few more days and she'd have her freedom. After two years of pure misery, she'd earned it.

Never again would she suffer the humiliation of facing the future without resources. She would be able to forget those months of paralysis after Johnny's heart attack and the stunning news of his insolvency, when all the security she'd taken for granted for nearly thirty years had been wiped out. And the bitter months afterward when she'd been forced to live on the proceeds from her few good pieces of jewelry, when she'd learned how friendships just melted away once you were in trouble. And the job she'd been forced to accept as cashier in the dining room of The Duquesne, a hotel frequented by traveling salesmen and the women who found its dining room and bar convenient for assignations with those salesmen.

Walter Kennon had been an anomaly in such surroundings, pure chance bringing him there for the ten days of his visit with his ill brother. His interest in her had been tentative, shy and awkward; and she, having by this time taken cold-eyed stock of her situation, knew that marrying a man like the colorless, uninteresting Walter Kennon was probably about as well as she could do.

When he said she resembled his deeply mourned Alice, she had laid siege to Walter Kennon's affections by asking myriad questions about Alice, then pretending to be like her in every way she could devise. To her despair, Walter had returned to Seacliff after those ten days—but a month later reappeared to sheepishly propose marriage. That very same day she resigned her detested job and, in triumph, traveled back with him to Seacliff.

But the town was slow-paced and quiet beyond all imagining. The spring and summer months of cloudy, foggy weather were depressing, unmitigated by the presence of the ocean, and the modest stucco or frame houses and their ordinary inhabitants were equally depressing. Her first husband had loved to socialize, to dance and drink. Walter Kennon sternly disapproved of alcohol and looked forward only to his weekly poker game. Of all her pretense before their marriage, he was most unforgiving of the lie that she, like Alice, knew the game of poker and loved to play it.

But, deadly dull as Walter Kennon might be, he was, she conceded, kind and decent, and a good provider. She lived comfortably, if not agreeably.

In the first days of their marriage he had shown her the contents of the locked desk drawer. "So you can rest easy about everything," he told her. "There'll be plenty enough for you, but I've written out this will making it a condition my brother Ralph's taken care of, too. I've made Jessie Graham executor. I'm depending on you both."

She had agreed, of course. She seldom disagreed, argued even more rarely. As the waif taken under his wing, any wishes of hers were subordinate to his decisions, and in his house she could not so much as move a pillow from sofa to chair without him moving it back. The ghost of Alice Kennon pervaded every room including the bedroom: Walter was indifferent to her physically.

Every aspect of their marriage was a sham, and her status in the life of this man, her distinct inferior, added a fresh layer of gall to all her other humiliations. Walter Kennon had married her only to keep his memories alive, to serve as a reflection of his enshrined Alice.

Smothered by her life, without any acceptable alternative, she daydreamed of moving back to Los Angeles to flaunt economic independence under the noses of the "friends" who had deserted her. She yearned to live independently amid the bright lights and energy of a major city. She longed for freedom unencumbered by Walter Kennon.

Then the letter from Bergan Construction Company had arrived. The company was interested in the property in Santa Barbara, prepared to make an offer. There was a toll-free eight-hundred number to call.

Walter had crumpled the letter, thrown it into the trash. "Alice's parents left her that house. The Herreras, they've lived there for years, Alice promised they could stay so long as they pay the taxes and upkeep on the place. I'm bound to keep that promise."

She had fished out the letter and called the toll-free number the following day. And learned that the land was now re-zoned, and Bergan Construction would offer a quarter of a million dollars clear cash, the buyer paying all expenses of the sale. Stunned by the magnitude of the offer, she explained the situation. Perhaps, Jack Bergan suggested, with Mrs. Kennon's approval—and provided he had her cooperation in the matter of selling the property to him—he himself might talk to the tenants. Perhaps they could be persuaded to move out on their own.

Two weeks later a terse communication had arrived from Mr. and Mrs. Raul Herrera. At the end of the month they would be vacating the home they had lived in for nearly thirty years. The brevity of the note, its coldness, had bewildered, then hurt, then infuriated Walter.

At the height of his railing over the Herreras' lack of gratitude, Velma detailed the problems involved in refurbishing the house and finding suitable new tenants. When another letter from Jack Bergan fortuitously arrived in the next day's mail, Walter picked up the phone and called the eight-hundred number. Velma did not know how Jack Bergan had managed the Herreras' eviction, nor did she ever inquire.

She was now joint tenant on a bank account amounting to over two hundred and ninety thousand dollars and heir to the house and Walter's life insurance and pensions besides. She could not simply take the money from the bank account—even if Walter's friends at the bank did not notify him moments after such a withdrawal. Where could she run to that Walter would not find her? No, it would all be hers only when Walter died, and never mind that blood-sucking brother of his.

If only Walter would die.

The phrase echoing in her mind, she immediately told herself she meant nothing by it. Over the following days, as the thought further implanted itself, she argued that she was not truly contemplating murder, merely examining the possibility out of pure curiosity. And she continued to repeat this to herself during the months she spent seeking a method, a foolproof plan: she was merely searching out the solution to a difficult and fascinating puzzle, the only interesting thing she'd found to do since coming to this dreary town.

It was no easy matter, she learned, to safely rid oneself of a   person. Modern crime detection techniques were too highly sophisticated. And when the person was an ex-Sheriff who knew how to protect himself, who had strong ties to current law enforcement, the problem was immeasurably more thorny.

She dismissed the idea of a handgun. How did one go about finding an unregistered weapon and disposing of it properly afterward? Walter of course had a gun—his old service revolver—but the possibility of arranging an accident with that weapon seemed hopeless.

And how did one go about obtaining undetectable or untraceable poison? Stabbing was out of the question, requiring expertise as well as a high degree of luck, and making a dreadful mess besides. Other methods—gassing, bludgeoning, pushing Walter from a height, arranging an accident with the car—presented their own problems. What if the result was not death but permanent injury? What could be worse than being condemned to caring for Walter Kennon, invalid, for the rest of her life or his? And if she was caught and convicted of murder, she would undoubtedly go to jail for the rest of her life, if not face a hideous death inhaling cyanide in California's gas chamber.

Given the fact that any method had to be absolutely foolproof, arranging Walter's death by other than natural causes seemed an impossibility. Yet there had to be some way...

AS JESSIE TRAVERSED THE circle she had drawn on the real estate map, Kate asked several times to stop. Once she got out of the car to look over a low bluff into a grassy ravine; then to tramp a weed-choked lot; then to scuff a jogging shoe in the dirt of another lot recently cleared of its brush. As daylight faded to gray, she had Jessie stop at Rolling Hills Cemetery.

Jessie stood with Kate on the tar-surfaced road alongside the graveyard, its long green hillside extending all the way down to the fog-shrouded sea perhaps a quarter of a mile away. A hand extended over her eyes as if she were shading them from the sun, Kate looked out over the perfectly sodded graves with their imbedded granite markers.

Realizing the memories undoubtedly triggered by this scene, Jessie offered gruffly, "My folks are buried here, you know." She gestured toward a distant green hill. "On the old side where Alice Kennon is. It doesn't have these flat headstones that all look alike." As Kate nodded in reply, Jessie reflected that she herself was getting just as cantankerous as Walt Kennon about every change in the world she knew and loved.

Kate lowered herself to a knee and ran a hand over the bent Bermuda grass of the hillside. "Tell me again what Walt was wearing Friday night."

"Gray corduroys, a blue plaid Pendleton shirt."

"A plastic raincoat, you said."

"That too. He arrived in it, left in it. A black one."

Kate stood, brushed her hands together to remove the dust of the grass. She walked slowly and for some distance along the hillside, stopping just beyond a white stake to examine a single tire track beside the paved road, any distinguishing features of the track obliterated by the recent rain.

"I have to tell you," Jessie muttered, staring down the smooth, steep hillside, "I considered the notion Velma might've rolled him down this hill and all the way to the ocean, I really did. I even walked it. But the land flattens out down there—" she gestured, "—a good hundred yards at the bottom of the hill. No way she could push or drag him to where the hill drops again. No way in hell."

Kate said, "I'd have considered the exact same idea, Jess."

Her hand once more across her eyes, Kate again surveyed the cemetery, which was deepening into gray shadows as nightfall approached. Jessie felt a renewed comfort that Kate was here and reviewing every detail of this investigation with her.

"Jess."

Alerted by the tone, Jessie looked sharply at Kate, but she was turned away from her.

"Anne told me once she wanted cremation." The tone was low, distant. "But I buried her, you know. Cremation was what her family wanted too, but they were good enough to leave me alone about it. The thing was, she burned to death. I couldn't bear to burn her again. Can you understand that?"

Jessie managed to find her voice. "I do understand. I do."

"But I think about her all the time there in the ground. And her not wanting to be where she is."

Jessie took Kate's arm. "I think she'd want exactly what you wanted," she said quietly, firmly. "I think she'd understand. I think she wouldn't mind."

Kate turned to Jessie, slid an arm around her waist, walked with Jessie toward the police car.

VELMA COULD NOT REMEMBER the precise moment when she made the clear and irrevocable decision to kill Walter, but it was soon after that morning when she waited in the car as Walter paid his weekly visit to Alice's grave. She observed the cemetery custodians rolling a freshly sodded grave, completing the interment process for a funeral held the day before, and she realized then that the true key lay not in foolproof method but in foolproof disposal of the body.

In the days afterward she deduced a method for ending Walter's life that would leave no evidence behind, deduced the exact circumstances that would allow her to handle more than a hundred and seventy pounds of dead weight. She decided that she would roil the waters of an investigation by withdrawing ten thousand dollars— any lesser amount seeming insufficient to confuse the issue of Walter's disappearance—and stash the money under the flower beds where it could remain until safe to remove; and if it was discovered in the meantime, what did that prove?

To validate her choice of weapon she made several trips to the library. Then she carefully fashioned her disposable, untraceable bludgeon from sand mixed with heavy steel bolts she found in Walter's tool chest, packing the material into one of Walter's thick wool socks until she was satisfied with the weight and heft. Knowing the act itself would take every ounce of strength, her every fiber of nerve, she waited in a state of feverish dread for ideal conditions.

Each morning she wrenched open the *Courier* to the obituary page. Over a period of the next five weeks there were seven burials at Rolling Hills—but either they were in the old section of the cemetery, or the weather was clear. Twelve times it rained—but there was no funeral.

Each morning as Walter ate his breakfast and prepared for a new day of golf or fishing or gardening, her anxiety grew. It was now March, and the prime rainy season along the Pacific coast was waning. She might very well have to wait until late in the year before the rains returned—six more months at least of living with Walter in this dismal town before she had a likely opportunity.

Then she rose on a Friday morning to gathering black clouds over the ocean and a forecast of rain, occasionally heavy, throughout the day and night. She pulled from her apron pocket a two day old obituary:

GRANT R. PAXTON, 68, beloved husband
of Margaret Paxton; loving father of John
and Edward Paxton; devoted grandfather
of Christopher and Julie Paxton.
Services Friday, Mar. 7, 11:00am at
First Presbyterian Church; interment
at Rolling Hills Cemetery.

She had already checked out the Paxton plot. It was located near the cemetery road and held two Paxtons already, with room for four more. Best of all, tonight was poker night. She would not need a pretext to lure Walter to the car at a late hour. Fearful as she was, just as well he would not be home until that late hour.

Pacing the living room, she heard his car pull into the detached garage just before midnight. She flung a raincoat over her shoulders and dashed from the house, her heart thudding, a hand clutching the crude truncheon weighting down her apron pocket.

Walter, his black plastic raincoat shiny with rain, emerged from the car and blinked at her in surprise.

Her voice raspy with strain, she gasped, "I just noticed I lost the diamond in my ring. I'm positive it's in the back of the car."

With a muffled exclamation he turned and yanked open the rear door. Her heart hammering against her ribs, she pushed the raincoat from her shoulders and stepped swiftly up beside him. Gripping the weapon in both hands she swung it behind her to give it the widest possible arc.

He bent down to climb into the car, then started to rise. "The car's been at Phil's station. How—"

She hit him squarely and with all of her strength just along the side and toward the back of the head, exactly where the medical and anatomy books said it was most dangerous to sustain a heavy blow.

There was a single sound from him, a grunted expulsion, then he pitched forward onto the back seat.

She stared, appalled at the concavity in his head, the gray matted hair welling with blood. What had she done wrong? There shouldn't be any blood—there couldn't be any stains on the car's upholstery. Panic-stricken, she stuffed the weapon into her apron pocket, hastily untied the apron and climbed over Walter's back to roughly, tightly bind his head.

She felt for the pulse in his wrist, his neck, as the books had said, as she'd practiced on herself. A second blow would not be necessary; there was no pulse. And she could see that the apron had stanched any flow of blood. Calmer now, she climbed out of the car and went around to the other door. Gripping his shoulders, she pulled and tugged at him, sliding him across the seat on his slick plastic raincoat until he was fully in the car. She closed both doors and retrieved her raincoat, and prepared for the rest of what needed to be done.

HANDS IN THE BACK pockets of her jeans, Kate stared out the huge windows of Jessie's living room, across the redwood deck at the fog-shrouded lights strung out along the ocean shoreline. As Barbra Streisand sang from Jessie's tape player, Kate prowled the room, looking over the record and tape collection, the bookshelves, poking at the fire, looking at the books again.

"Woman, what's bugging you," Jessie growled. "Sit down and relax, you're making Damon nervous." The marmalade-colored cat in her lap was stirring, its ears pricked.

Kate obediently lowered herself into the armchair beside the fire, picked up her scotch. "You sure I can't get you something, Jess?" She gestured to the wicker wine rack against the dining room wall. "You've got some nice reds over there."

Jessie shook her head. "Haven't had a thing to drink since this all began. It's enough trouble as it is to keep my head clear. I'm so tired, a glass of wine would put me out like a light."

"How about some coffee?" Kate's tone was solicitous. "Be glad to make it for you."

"Nope, that'll keep me wide awake and I hope to sleep a few hours tonight." She looked sharply at Kate, who was fidgeting with her scotch. She reiterated, "What's bugging you, woman?"

"Jess..." Kate put the scotch down on her coaster.

It was the same quiet use of her name as at the cemetery, and Jessie watched her uneasily.

"There was a funeral last week at Rolling Hills Cemetery," Kate said. It was a statement, not a question.

"Probably," Jessie answered, a prickling sensation along the back of her neck. "There's usually about one a week. I know for sure they buried Grant Paxton there. He ran Seacliff Realty. I knew him to say hello to."

"He was buried last Friday."

Jessie stared at her. "I don't know about that, but I can check it in a second."

She pulled herself out of her leather recliner and moved to the stack of papers on the brick hearth. "I haven't looked at a newspaper in days." She sorted through the stack until she found last Friday's *Courier*, opened it to the obituary page.

Jessie dropped the paper back onto the stack, sat down on the hearth and looked up at Kate. Her hands, all of her flesh was cold. "Like you said, Paxton was buried Friday. What are you telling me, Kate?"

Kate closed her eyes. "I'm sorry, Jess. Your gut feeling about Walter...is right."

Jessie rubbed her arms, edged closer to the fire. "I knew it." But still she had hoped.

"I'm sorry, Jess," Kate repeated.

"It's better that I know. Just tell me how this was done."

DRIVING SLOWLY THROUGH THE sheeting windblown rain, Velma pulled onto the road above Rolling Hills Cemetery and extinguished the car lights. The night was opaque in its blackness, and she drifted the car along until the fourth white roadside marker loomed by her side window. She pulled over carefully onto the grassy side of the road just beyond the marker and turned off the engine. She stripped off her raincoat. It would be useless in this downpour, and encumbering. She got out, opened the rear door of the Toyota.

Pulling, tugging Walter by his shoulders, her foot braced against the side of the car, she inched him across the seat until his head emerged from the car and struck the grass. Quickly she climbed into the car behind him and pushed his legs until he pitched fully out.

She closed the car doors, got the shovel out of the trunk. Again she pulled and tugged at Walter until he lay sideways on the hill. Bracing herself once more, she gave his body a mighty shove. He tumbled down the slope, his head flopping. She lost sight of him in the rain-filled blackness.

Carrying the shovel, wiping the pelting rain from her eyes, she staggered down the steep hill and nearly stumbled over his body. She slid the shovel down the hill knowing she could find it later, then pushed Walter, rolling him over and over in the spongy Bermuda grass, the apron coming off his head.

Standing between his legs as if she were pulling a plow, she dragged him farther, the wet slippery grass and Walter's slick plastic raincoat enabling her to maneuver him, as she had judged they would. She and her mother had once used a similar method—a quilt under a huge heavy chest to move it down into the basement. But she had been so much younger then.

Rain streaming from her hair into her blind eyes, she moaned with her straining effort. Would she ever get there? Then she tripped over the edge of the tarpaulin and pitched headlong onto the mound of the newly dug Paxton grave.

She sat on the tarpaulin and rested a few moments, her chest heaving. Then she climbed to her feet and used her tiny flashlight to locate the shovel as well as the apron which had come off Walter's head. She removed the rock-weighted tarpaulin, then the freshly laid strips of sod over Grant Paxton's grave, placing the strips with care on the tarpaulin to keep them intact.

Frenziedly, she began to dig, throwing shovel after shovel of the loose dirt onto the tarpaulin. The earth was becoming heavier as the teeming rain soaked it. When she reached a depth of several feet, she turned quickly to Walter.

Gritting her teeth, her arms quivering with the effort, she tugged and maneuvered him to the edge of the grave. Then gave him one final push. He thudded into the grave, face down. She threw in the apron, the weapon still in its pocket, and Walter's car keys.

She shoveled the earth back, grunting with the heaviness of each shovelful, her entire body trembling with this final exertion, and reshaped the mass of it into a mound, the surface a rapidly smoothing mud. Then she laid the strips of sod back. And reset the tarpaulin. And the rocks weighting the corners of the tarpaulin. Then she shook the muddy earth from the shovel, wiped it on the grass.

Her legs giving way, her limbs jerking, she collapsed on the hillside in an agony of exhaustion, thinking she might die here herself. The rain picked up in fury, pelting her mercilessly, and she lay unmoving, allowing it to slash the mud from her hands, her feet and legs, her clothes, her face.

As strength seeped back into her, she reviewed her next steps—no time now to make the slightest mistake. She would drive home, change into dry clothes. Destroy Walter's handwritten will in the fireplace and pulverize the ashes—

Abruptly she sat up. She had already made a mistake. The key to the desk was on Walter's key chain. She had buried it along with Walter. She lay back down again. It wasn't that much of a mistake. A sturdy kitchen knife would be sufficient to spring the desk drawer. After taking this much risk she definitely would not share any of her gains with anyone. It was now nearly one o'clock. At two she would call the Sheriff's office and report Walter missing, and then it would all be finished.

When her limbs finally ceased their trembling, she struggled to her feet and switched on the small flashlight to inspect her handiwork. The Paxton grave looked untouched, the thundering rain continuing to wash away all traces of her presence. Even the shovel had been scoured clean of its evidence. Finally she summoned strength for the climb up the hill to the car, and to freedom. She had done it. And no one could possibly guess how.

JESSIE MOVED AWAY FROM the fire. She was warm, heated by anger, her mind seething with the image of the false grief on Velma Kennon's face that Saturday morning, scant hours after Velma had ruthlessly killed her own husband and Jessie's irreplaceable friend.

"I'm sorry," Kate said softly. "There was no good or gentle way to tell you any of this."

No one, Jessie thought, could have been more gentle than Kate. Not even Irene would be as good with her as this woman with whom she shared an alien profession whose daily stock in trade was violence, who had herself been touched by the annihilating hand of death.

Kate said, "Of course you won't know if I'm right until—"

"I know it now." Jessie took a deep breath. "Everything you've theorized makes perfect sense. It does. To do what she did and then put him in someone else's grave—" She hissed, "It's obscene."

Kate murmured, "Maybe I can get you some of that wine now?"

Jessie shook her head. She walked over to Kate, sat down on the ottoman in front of her armchair. "I can't imagine how you figured this out."

"Anne told me," Kate said.

Jessie gaped at her.

"And then you told me the rest. The answers all came at Rolling Hills." Kate's eyes were fixed unseeingly on the fire. Her voice was remote. "Looking over that place, I was remembering the day after Anne was buried. I drove out to the cemetery very early that next morning. I wanted to be with her. I wanted to dig with my bare hands till I could be in there with her."

Jessie, her eyes stinging, kept her silence. Kate's renewed anguish over Anne was her fault. In sharing Jessie's sorrow, Kate had ripped the scar tissue from her own grief.

Kate's voice strengthened. "But you're the one who's responsible for solving this crime. How many investigating officers would have thought to check that Union Oil sticker? Velma Kennon would have gotten away with murder except for you. And your notion about Velma rolling him down the hill and all the way to the ocean—when I realized she wouldn't have to roll him far at all, it came together then, how a new grave as soon as it's rolled and sodded looks just like any other grave. And how Velma could use the rain, the slope of the cemetery and its bent Bermuda grass, Walt's slippery raincoat—" Fixing her somber eyes on Jessie, Kate shrugged. "And aside from all that, it seems after thirteen years in the cop business I'm beginning to think right along with the criminals."

Jessie sighed. She said softly, "You'd best get on to bed, Kate. Much as I want to, I can't lock Velma up tonight—not a thing to be done 'til morning and I get the search warrant to go in and get Walt. You've got only these few days of vacation, I want you out of here bright and early—"

"I'll stay up with you," Kate said firmly.

Jessie shook her head. "It's all on my shoulders now, Kate. I'd like to be alone with my thoughts."

Kate said quietly, "I do understand that, Jess."

With Kate settled in the guest bedroom, Jessie sat in her armchair and stared into the fire. But she did not yet think of Walt Kennon, or begin to mourn him. There was time enough for that. Instead she thought about Kate Delafield on vacation, making her solitary, lonely way up the California coast.

THE NEXT MORNING, VELMA again looked at the *Courier's* obituary page. Margaret Paxton would be buried today next to her dead husband—and Velma's. Velma swallowed the last of her tea and dismissed a brief impulse to attend. That would be foolish, would only arouse comment, if not suspicion. She had not realized that the bond of friendship between Walter Kennon and Jessie Graham ran as deep as it did—and she could not be too careful in these final days of the Sheriff's investigation.

Velma looked up, to see a patrol car coming up the block toward her house. Odd. This was out of pattern—another patrol car had already performed its half-hourly surveillance routine only fifteen minutes ago.

Then the patrol car was joined by Jessie Graham's car with its gold Sheriff's insignia. With a surge of alarm Velma watched both cars turn into her driveway as yet another police car came from the opposite direction to join them, screeching to a stop in front of the house.

Feeling the blood drain from her face, Velma watched Jessie Graham climb out of her car and adjust the gun belt over her dark brown trousers. The Sheriff reached into her car to retrieve some sort of plastic sack, then marched toward the house at a purposeful pace, flanked by three deputies who drew their weapons as they approached the door.

What could this be? What had gone wrong? She had made no mistakes, nothing had gone wrong, there was no way on earth Jessie Graham could know anything.

Harassment, she decided. A last-ditch, desperation attempt to panic her, stampede her into making a mistake. Seeing the neighbors gather on their lawns and sidewalks to observe, Velma angrily threw open her front door. "What's the meaning of this...circus?"

"You're under arrest, Velma." The words were said with barely controlled rage; the dark eyes were implacably cold.

Holding the plastic sack by a corner, Sheriff Jessie Graham held it up to Velma's eyes.

A hand at her throat as if cyanide fumes were already choking her, Velma stared at her dirty, blood-stained apron.

CONTRIBUTOR BIOGRAPHIES AND SELECT BIBLIOGRAPHIES

Lynn Ames

In addition to crime fiction, Lynn is a versatile author who has written best-selling romances including *Heartsong, Eyes on the Stars, One~Love, The Flip Side of Desire, All That Lies Within,* and *Bright Lights of Summer.* She is also one of five authors of the award-winning novella collection, *Outsiders.* Lynn's fiction has garnered three Goldie awards, the Arizona Book Award for Best Gay/Lesbian book, and the coveted Ann Bannon Popular Fiction Award for *All That Lies Within,* which was also a Lambda Literary Award Finalist, winner of a Rainbow Award for Lesbian Romance, and was honored as one of the top ten lesbian books of 2013. Lynn is the founder of Phoenix Rising Press. She was the press secretary to the New York state senate minority leader and spokesperson for the nation's third-largest prison system and has worked as an award-winning broadcast journalist, an editor of a critically acclaimed national magazine, and is a nationally recognized speaker and public relations professional. Her website: www.LynnAmes.com.

Mission: Classified Series
Beyond Instinct (2011)
Above Reproach (2012)

The Kate and Jay Series
The Price of Fame (2004)
The Cost of Commitment (2004)
The Value of Valor (2005)

Jessie Chandler

Jessie is the award-winning author of the Shay O'Hanlon Caper series. Her debut novel, *Bingo Barge Murder,* was a finalist for a Goldie and won the Golden Crown Ann Bannon Popular Choice Award. *Hide and Snake Murder,* the second novel in the series, won a Golden Crown Goldie Award, and an Independent Publisher Book Award (IPPY) for LGBT fiction. *Hide and Snake Murder* and the third in the series, *Pickle in the Middle Murder,* were both USA Book Award finalists. *Chip Off the Ice Block Murder* won the LGBT fiction category of the 2014 USA Book Awards and was also a finalist in the mystery category of the 2014 Rainbow Book Awards. The first book in Chandler's new Operation Series, *Operation Stop Hate*, was published in early 2015. *Blood Money Murder*, the fifth book in the Shay O'Hanlon Caper series, will be released mid-2015. Chandler is working on the first book in her new Art Thief Series, with tentative release for 2016. Chandler lives in Minneapolis, Minnesota, with her wife and two mutts, Fozzy Bear and Ollie. In the fall and winter, Jessie writes. She spends spring and summer selling T-shirts and other assorted trinkets at conferences, fairs, and festivals.

Her website: www.JessieChandler.com.

The Operation Series
Operation Stop Hate (2015)

The Shay O'Hanlon Caper Series
Bingo Barge Murder (2011)
Hide and Snake Murder (2012)
Pickle in the Middle Murder (2013)
Chip Off the Ice Block Murder (2014)
Blood Money Murder (forthcoming)

Sandra de Helen

Sandra writes the Shirley Combs/Dr. Mary Watson mystery series. *The Hounding* and *The Illustrious Client* are widely available, and she is working on the third installment in the series. Sandra is a poet, essayist, short story writer, and has been a produced playwright for many years. Her one-act play *Singer Clashes with Cougar* was produced in New York in 2014 by {Your Name Here} A Queer Theatre Company. Sandra is a proud member of GCLS, Sisters in Crime, and the Dramatists Guild. She lives and writes in Portland, Oregon.

Her website: www.Redcrested.com.

The Shirley Combs/ Dr. Mary Watson Series
The Hounding (2012)
The Illustrious Client (2013)
The Valley of Fear (forthcoming)

Katherine V. Forrest

Katherine V. Forrest's sixteen works of fiction include the lesbian classics *Curious Wine* and *Daughters of a Coral Dawn* and nine novels in the celebrated Kate Delafield mystery series. Honors and awards include five Lambda Literary Awards, the Publishing Triangle's Bill Whitehead Lifetime Achievement Award, the Golden Crown Literary Society's Trailblazer Award, Lambda Literary Foundation's Pioneer Award. She has edited numerous anthologies and authored reviews and articles which have appeared in numerous books, periodicals, and publications. Profiled in *USA Today*, *The San Francisco Chronicle*, *The Bloomsbury Review*, and in most major national and international LGBT publications, she is also a teacher of the craft of writing, most recently at Stanford University. She is president emeritus of the Lambda Literary Foundation and was supervising editor at the legendary Naiad Press from 1983 to 1994. Currently she is supervising editor at Spinsters Ink and editor at large at Bella Books. Katherine and her partner of 24 years and their two feline companions live in the beautiful Southern California desert.

Her website: www.KatherineVForrest.com.

The Kate Delafield Mystery Series
Amateur City (1984)
Murder at the Nightwood Bar (1987)
The Beverly Malibu (1989)
Murder by Tradition (1991)
Liberty Square (1996)
Apparition Alley (1997)
Sleeping Bones (1999)
Hancock Park (2004)
High Desert (2013)

Sue Hardesty

Sue was born in southern Arizona where desert dwelling was her childhood life. Her mother followed her father into prospecting, and the family went from one claim to the next. She trailed her father from one water-hole to another as they worked half-Brahma steers. Her beloved horse, a white desert-sure and wise broom-tail, always managed to get her home. Sue lost this idyllic way of life when she was sent off for book learning. She became a school teacher, later morphing into teaching in the communications field. She met Nel, the love of her life, at Arizona State University. Once she retired, the desert heat lost its appeal, so Sue and Nel moved to a Northwest coastal town as close to water as possible and over the years opened a bookstore and two bed and breakfasts, worked on renovating and building houses, started a publishing company, took up photography, and edited *The Butch Cook Book*. Sue has written three novels, two about Loni Wagner and another called PANIC about three teens stranded in the desert. For the future? She may write other novels. Or take more photos. What she does know is that she's looking forward to what's behind the next door she opens. Her website: www.SueHardestyBooks.com.

The Loni Wagner Series
The Truck Comes on Thursday (2011)
Bus Stop at the Last Chance (2014)
Book Three in the Loni Wagner Series (forthcoming)

Lori L. Lake

In her youth, Lori became a fan of the crime fiction genre after watching reruns of "Perry Mason" and reading Agatha Christie mysteries. In addition to editing anthologies and writing short story collections, romances, historical fiction, and writing advice books, she writes two crime fiction series: The Gun Series and The Public Eye Series. The first Eye mystery, *Buyer's Remorse,* won a 2012 Golden Crown Goldie, and the second, *A Very Public Eye*, won a 2014 Rainbow Award. She has received the prestigious Ann Bannon Award and was honored with the Alice B. Award for her body of work. Her editing skills have yielded a Lambda Literary Finalist in the anthology category. Lori lives in Portland, Oregon, which she returned to in 2009 after 26 years in snowy Minnesota. Her next mystery release is the fifth book in The Gun Series, *Gunpoint*.
Her website: www.LoriLLake.com.

The Gun Series
Gun Shy (2001)
Under The Gun (2002)
Have Gun We'll Travel (2005)
Jump The Gun (2013)
Gunpoint (forthcoming)

The Public Eye Series
Buyer's Remorse (2011)
A Very Public Eye (2012)

Andi Marquette

Andi is a native of New Mexico and Colorado and an award-winning mystery, speculative fiction, and romance writer. She also has the dubious

good fortune to be an editor who spent 15 years working in publishing, a career track that sucked her in while she was completing a doctorate in history. She is co-editor of *Skulls and Crossbones: Tales of Women Pirates* and the Rainbow runner-up *All You Can Eat: A Buffet of Lesbian Erotica and Romance*. Her most recent novels are *Day of the Dead*, the Goldie-nominated finalist *The Edge of Rebellion*, and the romance *From the Hat Down*, a follow-up to the novella *From the Boots Up*, a Rainbow Award runner-up. When Andi's not co-editing anthologies or writing novels, novellas, and stories, she serves as both an editor for *Luna Station Quarterly*, an ezine that features speculative fiction written by women, and as co-admin of the popular blogsite Women and Words. When she's not doing that, well, hopefully she's managing to get a bit of sleep.
Her website: www.AndiMarquette.com.

New Mexico Mystery Series
Land of Entrapment: A K.C. Fontero Mystery (2008)
State of Denial: A Chris Gutierrez Mystery (2008)
The Ties that Bind: A K.C. Fontero Mystery (2009)
Day of the Dead: A Chris Gutierrez Mystery (2013)

Kate McLachlan

An award-winning author, Kate writes lesbian novels in all genres, including historicals, mysteries, romances, and three books in the popular RIP time-travel series. Her books have received awards from the Golden Crown Literary Society and have been finalists for Lambda Literary Awards and the Rainbow Awards. Kate lives in Washington State—the dry side—with her writer wife, Tonie Chacon, and their dogs and cats.
Her website: www.KateMclachlan.com.

Standalones
Murder and the Hurdy Gurdy Girl (2013)
Ten Little Lesbians – featuring sleuth Beatrice Scott (Summer, 2015)

VK Powell

A thirty-year veteran of a mid-sized police department, VK's career spanned numerous positions including beat officer, homicide detective, field sergeant, vice/narcotics lieutenant, district captain, and assistant chief of police. Now retired, she devotes her time to writing, traveling, and volunteering. VK is the author of three erotic short stories, one romantic short story, and eight novels of romantic intrigue set in the world of law

enforcement, all published by Bold Strokes Books.
Her website: www.VKPowellauthor.com.

Standalones
To Protect and Serve (2008)
Suspect Passions (2009)
Fever (2010)
Justifiable Risk (2011)
Haunting Whispers (2012)
Exit Wounds (2013)
About Face (2014)
Deception (August 2015)

J.M. Redmann

JM has published eight novels featuring New Orleans PI Micky Knight. Her books have won First Place in the ForeWord mystery category, several Lambda Literary Awards, been on the American Library Association GLBT Roundtable's Over the Rainbow list, and won a Golden Crown Award. Her book *The Intersection of Law and Desire* was an Editor's Choice of the San Francisco Chronicle and a recommended book by Maureen Corrigan of NPR's Fresh Air. She is also the co-editor with Greg Herren of *Night Shadows: Queer Horror* and *Women of the Mean Streets: Lesbian Noir*. JM currently lives, works and frolics in New Orleans.
Her website: www.JMRedmann.com.

The Micky Knight Series
Death by the Riverside (1990)
Death of Jocasta (1992)
The Intersection of Law and Desire (1995)
Lost Daughters (1999)
Death of a Dying Man (2009)
Water Mark (2010)
Ill Will (2012)
The Shoal of Time (2013)

Elizabeth Sims

Elizabeth is the author of the Lambda Award-winning Lillian Byrd Crime Series as well as the Rita Farmer Mysteries. She writes frequently for *Writer's Digest* magazine, where she is a contributing editor. Her popular instructional title, *You've Got a Book in You: A Stress-Free Guide to*

Writing the Book of Your Dreams (Writer's Digest Books) has helped thousands of writers overcome anxiety and unleash their best author selves. Elizabeth earned degrees in English from Michigan State University and Wayne State University, where she won the Tompkins Award for Graduate Fiction. She belongs to several literary societies as well as American Mensa.

Her website: www.ElizabethSims.com.

The Lillian Byrd Crime Series
Holy Hell (2002)
Damn Straight (2003)
Lucky Stiff (2004)
Easy Street (2005)
Left Field (2015)

The Rita Farmer Mysteries
The Actress (2008)
The Extra (2009)
On Location (2010)

Carsen Taite

Carsen's goal as an author is to spin tales with plot lines as interesting as the cases she encountered in her career as a criminal defense lawyer. A Lambda Literary Award finalist and two-time Goldie winner, Carsen has authored numerous novels and short stories including the Luca Bennett Mystery series, the newly minted Lone Star Law Series, and many novels and stories of romantic suspense and intrigue set in the world of law enforcement. She is currently working on her thirteenth novel, *Reasonable Doubt*, a tale of romantic intrigue.

Her website: www.CarsenTaite.com.

Standalones
Truelesbianlove.com (2008)
It Should be a Crime (2009)
Do Not Disturb (2010)
Nothing but the Truth (2011)
The Best Defense (2011)
Beyond Innocence (2012)
Rush (2013)

Courtship (2014)

The Luca Bennett Mystery Series
Slingshot (2012)
Battle Axe (2013)
Switchblade (2014)

Lone Star Law Series
Lay Down the Law (2015)

S.Y. Thompson

At the age of seventeen, Susan joined the Marine Corps and spent ten years serving her country. After two tours in Lebanon and participation in the invasion of Grenada, she returned to the States and decided it was time to lay down roots. Instead she joined the San Diego Sheriff's Department and spent another seven years in California law enforcement before an on-the-job injury forced retirement. Susan returned to Texas and wrote fan fiction for ten years before deciding to publish. In addition to writing suspense and romantic intrigue set in the world of law enforcement, she has also dabbled with science fiction in *Destination Alara* and romance in *Beyond the Garden*. Her days are filled with writing and playing with her dog and five cats (plus the strays that drop by for dinner on a daily basis). Her website: www.SYThompson.com.

The Under Series
Under the Midnight Cloak (2013)
Under Devil's Snare (2014)

Standalones
Now You See Me (2013)
Fractured Futures (2013)
Woeful Pines (2015)
Norwood Manor: A Novella (2015)
Illusive Witness (2015)

Linda M. Vogt

A retired college journalism instructor and freelance writer, Linda has written many feature stories for The Oregonian. Her short story, "Roar," is based on an actual event. Her first mystery novel, *No Thru Road*, was

published in 2015, and she is working on the second book in the series. Linda is a musician and produces concerts and an annual women's music weekend with her friends in a four-woman band, Motherlode. She lives just outside Portland, Oregon, and enjoys camping, fishing and road trips with her pals and her terrier-mix companion, Scout.
Her website: www.LindaMVogt.com

The Riley Logan Series
No Thru Road (2015)

Jen Wright

Jen Wright is the author of the popular Jo Spence Series. Her books offer an excellent mix of the whodunit and of inside knowledge from a professional lifetime working in the field of law enforcement administration. She is Superintendent of the Arrowhead Juvenile Center where she has worked for the past three decades. She has trained on behalf of the National Drug Court Institute, American Probation and Parole Association, Bureau of Justice Assistance, Praxis International, Minnesota Program Development, Battered Women's Justice Program, Minnesota Department of Corrections, and Arrowhead Regional Corrections in the areas of domestic violence, gender responsive services, drug courts, and juvenile probation issues. Jen has a BA degree in Sociology with a concentration in Criminology and is working toward a Masters degree in Public Administration. She lives in Clover Valley, a small community located northeast of Duluth near the north shore of Lake Superior, where she shares life with her partner, Carol, and their loving canine companions in a tight-knit community of friends.
Her website: www.CloverValleyPress.com/Wright.html

The Jo Spence Series
Killer Storm (2007)
Big Noise (2009)
Dead Ahead (2011)

PERMISSIONS

ABOUT THE EDITORS

JESSIE CHANDLER's short stories have appeared in Why Did Santa Leave a Body; Women in Uniform; and Writes of Spring. Her popular Shay O'Hanlon Caper Series has received many awards including the 2014 USA Book Award for LGBT Fiction, Golden Crown "Goldies," the Ann Bannon Popular Choice Award, and an IPPY for Best LGBT Fiction from the Independent Publisher Book Awards. This is Jessie's first foray into editing an anthology. She lives in a suburb of Minneapolis, Minnesota.

LORI L. LAKE's mystery stories have appeared in many anthologies including *Women of the Mean Streets: Lesbian Noir; The Silence of the Loons; Fifteen Tales of Murder, Mayhem, and Malice; Once Upon a Crime*; and *Writes of Spring*. She has edited three other anthologies including the Lambda Literary Award Finalist, *The Milk of Human Kindness: Lesbian Authors Write about Mothers and Daughters*. Her novel-length fiction has received Golden Crown Literary "Goldies," Rainbow Awards, the Ann Bannon Popular Choice Award, and multiple StoneWall Society Awards. Her body of work has also received the prestigious Alice B Medal. Lori lives in Portland, Oregon.

www.ingramcontent.com/pod-product-compliance
Lightning Source LLC
Chambersburg PA
CBHW020403120726
47904CB00002B/683